Keegan's Chronicles

Julia Crane

Valknut Press

Keegan's Chronicles: Coexist, Conflicted, Consumed
Copyright © 2011-2012 by Julia Crane

Published by Valknut Press, LLC
Clarksville, TN

ISBN-10: 1624110223
ISBN-13: 978-1-62411-022-1
First print edition, Createspace, August 2012

All rights reserved.
This book is protected under the copyright laws of the United States of America. Any reproduction or other unauthorized use of the material or artwork herein is prohibited. No part of this book may be used or reproduced in any manner whatsoever without prior written permission of the author.

This novel is a work of fiction. Any references to historical events; to real people, living or dead; or to real locales are intended only to give the fiction a sense of reality and authenticity. Names, characters, places, and incidents either are the product of the author's imagination or are used fictitiously, and their resemblance, if any, to real-life counterparts is entirely coincidental.

Edited by Rosanne Catalano and Claire Teter
Cover art by Stephanie Mooney | Mooney Designs
Formatting by CyberWitch Press, LLC

Table of Contents

Coexist 1

Conflicted 131

Consumed 279

Coexist

Book One

For my mother.
Thank you for sharing your love of books,
and teaching your children to use their imaginations.

Prophecy:

An elfin child on the side of light,
Born with the gift of sight,
Tells when light and dark shall meet,
But not who will face defeat.
Eldest son of a warrior great,
The child will determine elfin fate.

The Book of Elfin Prophecy
Compiled 112 BCE

Chapter 1

Keegan's call echoed in Rourk's mind as he finished his last rep. She always came to him when he least expected her; her call always made it hard to focus on anything else. His hands gripped the bar tightly as he tried to ignore the pull of her thoughts. He started a new set, focusing on training, on the cold steel, on the smell of sweat in the room—anything to clear his mind of the girl who possessed him.

Taking a deep breath, he shook his head and unclenched his jaw. He finished up the set quickly, then painfully forced his hands to uncurl from the bar. The tips of his fingers were bloodless—a fine metaphor for how she usually made him feel. He wiped his face and tossed the towel in the bin. The rest of the workout would have to wait.

Using one of his secondary gifts, he closed his eyes and visualized her face. It took no effort for him to picture her. Rourk zoomed in like a high-powered lens, bringing her into focus. He smiled. She was at her favorite spot, a private corner of paradise on her parents' land.

Her beautiful auburn hair blended in with the fall leaves that surrounded her. Her pale green, ankle-length dress flowed ethereally around her body, making her an oasis in the rust-colored woods.

A smile spread across her face as she inspected a rock from the creek; Rourk laughed when she slipped it into her camera bag.

The first time she had thought his name—several years ago—it had taken him *hours* to sense her location. When the pull came now, it took just twenty minute for him to hike through some familiar woods. Time had strengthened their bond.

Grabbing his bag, he jumped in his old, beat-up truck and headed towards his chosen, probably driving a little faster than necessary. When he heard her call, he could never get there fast enough.

He drove as close as he could, then hastily climbed the rugged terrain. The dirt had the loose feel of earth unpacked by human feet; with every step, he sank a little, hindering his progress. Even when he wasn't training, Rourk spent a lot of his time in the woods. The forest was like a second home to him.

The sun sparkled through the canopy above him, illuminating the path he forged through the trees, though it didn't offer any warmth in the cool afternoon. It was a great day for photos, so Rourk wasn't surprised that she had brought her camera out. A branch scraped him across the face and he impatiently pushed it to the side, hardly caring whether it had left a mark. He just wanted to reach her.

Finally, he reached the top, bursting through the tree line and into pure daylight. His heart pounded. He could sense that she was near.

Rourk stood rigid, his lean body tensed as he looked over the edge of the jagged cliff. *Why do I do this to myself? I shouldn't even be here. She's killing me. I have no self-control.*

Elfin elders used complicated methods to arrange ideal marriages between young elves. They kept the formula on a need-to-know basis, so he would never know how they chose the auburn-haired beauty for him. Of all the many non-humans in this world, his kind held their secrets closest. But no matter how or why, Rourk felt grateful just to have her.

The elders chose an elf's lifemate at birth, but lifemates could not meet until they both turned eighteen. Ordinarily, neither knew their other half until they came of age. The elders of long ago had decided it was better that way, since the bond could be all-consuming. They wanted their children to have a normal childhood. Rourk had always felt comforted by knowing that his other half waited out there.

So how did he find her?

Someone had told her his name, so now his chosen pulled him closer to her each time she thought of him, as involuntarily as breathing. At first he resisted with ease, but as he got closer to eighteen, curiosity got the better of him. Sometimes he wished he'd never answered her call, so he wouldn't have to endure the agony of waiting now.

He loved seeing her—even if it made waiting painful.

Rourk focused attention back on his chosen. The water washed around her feet as she stood on the rocks, camera in hand as usual. One minute, she skipped across the rocks like a child and the next, she stopped, a look of total concentration on her face. Then she started snapping photos.

Staring at her, Rourk squatted and rested his hands on his knees, wondering what she saw through her lens. He watched as she jumped from a rock and slipped, landing on another. Her arms flailed as she almost fell into the water.

His heart lurched. He needed to protect her; he tensed to jump in after her. Then her laugh echoed up to him like music and her face broke into a huge grin. She steadied herself, taking more photos. Rourk relaxed, content to stand and watch her for hours.

Rourk didn't even know her name, but he knew he'd never seen anyone so magnificent in his life. Her wavy hair glistened in the sunlight. She had a delicate, round face with large, blue-green eyes and full lips. With her cheeks flushed from the cold fall air, she reminded him of a porcelain doll. He knew that her looks deceived; her bold, daring eyes gave her away. She constantly observed her surroundings. Rourk smiled to himself; soon they would be together.

It took a lot of self-control not to approach her, but Rourk would not break the rules. Many decades before, the elders implemented a punishment of an added year apart lifemates met early.

Rourk didn't know if he could take an extra year without his chosen. In any case, his military upbringing had given Rourk a healthy respect for rules. He had long ago accepted that they were in place for a reason, and he had to be patient. Their time would come, even though she was over a year younger than he, which meant he would have to wait longer than he would like.

He pondered all this as he watched her pack up, lovingly storing her camera away in its bag while her hair fell softly over her face. When she disappeared down the path to her house, Rourk sighed, turned and left.

Keegan sat at her small, black desk looking through the photos she'd taken that morning. Her hair had been driving her crazy for the last hour, falling over her face with nearly every movement, so she pulled it into a bun. Securing it with a pencil, she continued to study the shots. She noticed a few decent ones she could add to her Tumblr page; she had a small circle of followers there who seemed to enjoy her pictures as much as she loved taking them. She loved photography. Life was nothing more than a series of moments and a picture could capture that moment.

Her moments often felt empty. Sighing, she turned her head to gaze out the window, her chin resting in her hand as she let her mind wander. If she had Rourk, maybe she would feel...more fulfilled. She knew nothing about her partner but his name. A couple of years ago, her brother Thaddeus, a seer, had told her that she should think of Rourk's name if she ever felt she was in danger.

Of course, she thought his name all the time, even when she wasn't in danger. She loved the sound of it: Rourk. She pictured him as a powerful warrior like her father, but she wouldn't know for sure until they met. He could turn out to be a seer like her brother or a healer like her mother. He might have any of the various elfin powers. She didn't care what kind of gift he had; she just didn't want to wait any longer.

Keegan smiled, leaning back in her seat to prop one bare foot on the edge of her chair. Most humans automatically imagined elves as Santa Claus's little helpers with enormous ears and fuzzy green tights. That couldn't be further from the truth.

Seriously, she had never met an elf that worked for Santa.

Evolution allowed them to blend in with the humans, though females tended to be smaller than average—mostly a couple of inches taller or shorter than five feet. They did have the pointed ears, but in a cute way, and not overly large like those in most mythology projects. Most of their ancestors came from Ireland, so the elves tended to have reddish hair.

She certainly didn't think her room looked like a storybook elf's room. Two pale grey walls complemented the vivid turquoise of the other two. She had artistically arranged framed posters of her favorite bands and several of her favorite snapshots all around the room. A fluffy purple comforter and four fat pillows decorated the bed, where she also kept a few of her childhood stuffed animals.

Most of all, she loved the light—lots of daylight from her windows. Her room felt her safe haven, almost as much as her spot in the woods.

The sound of the door opening downstairs startled her out of her thoughts. Her parents wouldn't be home this early and her pesky brother had gone to Sam's house. She closed her eyes and pictured the front door. What she saw brought a smile to her face. It was Anna, one of her best friends.

Anna had been trying to sneak up on Keegan since they first met in the fourth grade. Keegan made it a point of pride—and stubbornness—never to let her; it was a game and Keegan liked to win. It drove Anna crazy, but luckily she was too laid-back to do anything about it. Keegan debated with herself whether or not to let Anna succeed just this one time. *I don't think so.* She smiled to herself.

She focused her mind and felt the familiar tingling throughout her body. Now she was in no hurry—Anna couldn't see her. She had to be careful not to be caught, but invisibility tended not to attract attention. Personally, she thought her invisibility was the coolest ability in the family, but her mom just thought it was ironic, since Keegan always wanted to be the center of attention.

Down in the kitchen, Anna wistfully looked around. She loved coming to Keegan's house. It always felt so inviting; their home radiated a certain calm. The soothing sound of the rushing water from the massive wall fountain and the energy from the crystals collected by Keegan's mother soothed her the moment Anna stepped through the door. A sense of serenity washed over her.

The house felt empty of inhabitants. Only the chirping of birds outside the open window broke the steady hum of the refrigerator. Six placemats perfectly spaced around a lovely centerpiece of wildflowers Keegan's mom must have picked decorated the large, clean wooden table. Anna put a hand to the tabletop and closed her eyes, allowing the peace of the home to overtake her. She needed it.

Trying not to laugh, Keegan crept up behind Anna, who seemed oblivious. Her best friend looked completely off in space. Keegan focused her mind again and, amid the tingling, she materialized before tapping her friend's shoulder. "Gotcha!"

Anna turned and laughed, feigning surprise.

Oh Keegan, I always know when you're there. If you only knew that I have secrets of my own. Anna had known for years about Keegan's family. One of her friends had the ability to spot other creatures of the light or dark. But they all knew how elves liked to keep their secrets, so Anna never let on that she knew. She figured someday Keegan would tell her on her own.

As usual, Anna had outlined her green eyes in heavy eyeliner—blue today—to highlight her long, thick lashes. With shimmery pink lip gloss on her pencil-lined lips, she looked like a rock star.

Keegan glanced over her eccentric friend's outfit to see what style she'd adopted for the day. Her bangs, which she habitually pushed to the side, were purple today beneath a black top hat that only Anna could pull off. The rest of the day's ensemble consisted of a grey tank top, a blue cardigan, and a pink skirt with bright yellow flowers that came just above her knees. To pull the look together, she wore sparkly silver Converse shoes.

"You know I hate you," Keegan said with a grin, bumping her best friend's shoulder playfully with her own.

Anna stared at Keegan indignantly, her skinny arms crossed. "Why would you hate me?"

"Who else could pull off that outfit and make it look natural?" Keegan said.

Anna gave a little curtsy and giggled. "Thank you."

"You're not going to believe what happened today!" Anna continued, grinning from ear to ear and jumping up and down so that her skirt flounced. Her shoes caught the sunlight shining through the window, sending sparkles across the walls of the kitchen like a disco ball.

Playing along, Keegan bounced up and down, too. "Let me guess. Xavier finally asked you out?"

"I wish!" For a brief moment, sadness replaced the excited look on Anna's face. Xavier had been her friend since childhood. Anna had recently realized her feelings for him were more than friendship, but, sadly, he didn't return her feelings.

"All right, just tell me what's got you so excited," Keegan said.

"Well, when I was walking to the bus, I saw a sign for a New Age fair tomorrow!" Anna jumped up and down. "It's a sign. We must go!"

Keegan grinned. "Anna, you seriously believe in all that nonsense?"

Looking shocked Anna replied, "Certainly! There has to be something more to this world than meets the eye."

If you only knew Anna, there is so much more to this world than humans know, Keegan thought. However, she was not about to reveal that knowledge.

"Don't forget to call Lauren and fill her in," Keegan told her.

"But, of course," Anna said, pressing a hand to her chest innocently. "If there were only the two of us we couldn't be called the three amigos."

Keegan rolled her eyes, laughing.

The girls popped some popcorn and chatted in front of the television for a while, muting the commercials and blaring the reality show they both loved. When she had to leave, Anna gave Keegan a hug and headed out.

While the girls watched TV, Keegan's mom, Emerald, had come home from taking Warrick to the park. Now she worked on her laptop while Warrick pushed a toy truck around under the table.

"Don't stay up too late," she warned as Keegan passed the kitchen.

"I won't." Keegan rolled her eyes. "Where's Dad?"

"Camp. He'll be home late." She flicked her blue eyes up to her daughter. "I mean it. Go to bed at a decent time. What did you have for dinner?"

"I had mac and cheese earlier."

"Any leftovers?" Her mom raised an eyebrow.

"Nope." Keegan made her way to the staircase.

With a little time to kill before she got tired, Keegan decided to look through her photos again. Her favorite, a photo of a leaf blowing by itself in the wind, reminded her of herself. She often felt all alone, just floating along. As much as she loved hanging out with her human friends, like hanging with Anna earlier, she wished she could tell them what she truly was.

Staring at her photos, she realized that she loved photographing the beauty of nature best of all. Something about the outdoors fascinated her. It amazed her that she could document the seasons as they changed. Elves loved nature, and she hoped evolution never changed that.

She put the camera and computer away; Keegan knew she should go to bed. Time always seemed to get away from her when she found herself caught up in the editing and uploading of her photos. She had a hard enough time waking up normally, let alone when she stayed up all hours of the night.

Keegan put on her favorite plaid pajamas and crawled into bed, pulling her purple blanket under her chin. A faint smile played on her lips as she thought of Anna's eagerness for the fair tomorrow. It would probably be fun.

Chapter 2

Keegan woke up late, as usual, after hitting the snooze button too many times. The blaring alarm had finally gotten on her nerves. Rolling out of bed and into the bathroom, she stared at her reflection in the mirror. Faced with tangled, messy hair and smudged mascara, she just wanted to crawl back in bed. But she could hear her family downstairs having breakfast, so she decided to join them.

Her mom stood at the counter pouring hot water over a mug of tea leaves. She looked comfortable in a pair of pale blue jeans and a fitted white button-down shirt, her feet bare on the stones of the kitchen floor. Emerald glanced over her shoulder as Keegan trudged sleepily into the kitchen, surprised to see her daughter. "What gets you out of bed before noon on a weekend?"

Keegan plopped down on the stool across from her father. "I have plans with Anna." She reached over and grabbed a slice of toast off her dad's plate.

"You're lucky your mother burnt the toast or you'd be in trouble." Dad grinned through a mouth full of eggs, his hazel eyes sparkling merrily at her. He had the local daily newspaper spread on the table before him and half a glass of her mom's freshly squeezed orange juice in one hand.

"The toast isn't burnt," Mom said, laughing as she took a seat next to him and tugged playfully at his full, orange beard. As usual, she had put a plate of food in front of her husband and her son, but hadn't made one of her own. Keegan's mom stared at her over the teacup. "I'm sure you guys will have fun. Don't stay out too long." She took a sip of her tea. "Do you need any money?"

"Sure," Keegan answered, snagging her dad's remaining piece of toast and making a funny face at her baby brother, Warrick. She loved the sound of his laugh. "I can always use a little more for Starbucks."

While her mother ventured across the kitchen to rifle through her purse,

Keegan looked over at her brother Thaddeus. No more silent than usual, he seemed lost in his own thoughts as he slowly ate his Cocoa Pebbles. "Hey, Thaddeus, any plans today or are you going to do your recluse act and stay in your room?"

"For your information, Sam is coming over." He gave her a dirty look across the table. "We're going to play paintball."

"You guys are lame. Get out and around people instead of hiding in the woods or locked in your room."

"Whatever, Keegan. Just because I don't want to go shopping all day and act like a fool with my friends...."

Keegan hopped to her feet and plucked Warrick from his highchair. She sang loudly as she spun around the room, the baby babbling happily in her arms.

"Mom, make her shut up—she sucks," Thaddeus complained.

"She does not." Her mother managed to tuck a folded bill in the pocket of Keegan's sweatpants as she twirled by.

"She only does that to get on my nerves." Thaddeus slouched in his seat, crossing his arms angrily over his chest.

"Somebody is grumpy this morning!" Keegan sang brightly to Warrick, who laughed maniacally in return.

"That's not true; she sings even when you aren't home," her mother said, sipping her tea. Her sparkling eyes followed her daughter around the room. She smiled. "Be careful, Keegan. That's a baby full of eggs and bacon."

Once Keegan finished the song, she swept dramatically across the room and, with one last spin, she handed Warrick to her dad. Running up the stairs, she headed for the bathroom to shower.

Wrapped in a towel after her shower, she looked through her closet. *What does one wear when about to find out the future?* Finally, Keegan decided on a pair of dark skinny jeans and grey shirt. At the last minute, she grabbed a teal scarf to bring out her eyes. One last twirl in front of the mirror and she was satisfied with her choice. She ran down the stairs.

"See you later," she called as she rushed out the door.

Keegan jumped on her bike and rode to her favorite Starbucks. The day was shaping up to be a lot nicer than the day before. The sun beat its warmth down on her pale skin. Slightly annoyed with herself, she realized she forgot to put on sunscreen. *Great*, she thought, *now my freckles will come out more.*

She loved the ride, as always. The heavily forested main road leading from her parents' property to the Starbucks in the strip mall smelled of pine and always seemed to rustle like a living body in the breeze. Keegan loved being on her bike.

When she walked in to the café, she took a deep breath. She loved the smell of Starbucks, the soothing noises of the barista's machines, and the chattering people who always filled the café.

Keegan delighted in the coffee shop atmosphere. She loved to sit for hours and take in the wide variety of people. She amused herself by trying to identify human or supernatural customers, and she made up full scenarios for strangers in her mind. Today, she had the tall, shapely brunette behind her in line pegged as a secret agent. She suspected the short, pudgy guy with the horrible comb-over was an electrician who dreaded going home to his annoying family. Last but not least, something about the emo girl in the corner with her face in a book reminded Keegan of a fairy.

Looking around one last time before she gave her order, she noticed a sexy guy with dark, shaggy hair and piercing blue eyes watching her. Smirking to herself, she thought, *Vampire or werewolf.*

With her usual white chocolate mocha in hand, Keegan glanced at her friends. Anna and Lauren had already gotten drinks and claimed their usual table. They knew better than to expect Keegan to be on time. *I can't really blame them.* She chuckled as she made her way across the room.

Tilting her head, she gave a sly smile to the dark-haired stranger as she passed him.

Keegan took in the sight of her two best friends as they laughed together. It still amazed her that, even with their different personalities, they could be such incredible friends after so much time had passed. She thought for sure when they moved onto high school they would drift apart, but their relationship proved too strong for that.

Lauren looked gorgeous as usual with her long, dark curly hair, pale skin, and her caramel eyes. She jumped up and hugged Keegan, making Keegan to spill her drink.

"I'm so excited to go to the fair! I've never had a psychic reading before!" Lauren squealed.

"Slow down," Keegan said. "You just spilled the coffee all over me."

"Whatever. You know you can't make it through a cup of coffee without spilling it on yourself. You're worse than a toddler."

Keegan laughed. "Good point."

Lauren's positive attitude charmed everyone. Always quick to smile and the first to compliment someone, she purposely came across as not particularly bright. With her SAT scores, she could get into any college she wanted. Keegan had no idea why she downplayed her intelligence. She had asked once, and Lauren had said she didn't want people to expect too much, and then be let down. Keegan thought that was a ridiculous reason.

Lauren looked like a typical cheerleader with long legs and an athletic build, and her wardrobe made other girls jealous. For the fair, she had worn a knee-length, pink floral dress that oozed the runway look, and she had belted the gauzy material with a large, brown belt that matched her ankle boots. She belonged in a Hollister ad.

As Keegan slid into her chair, Lauren looked at them expectantly. "Josh sent me this long love letter. He actually wrote it by hand. Do you guys think he's getting too clingy?"

"Well, you have been dating over a year. It's obviously pretty serious." Anna rolled her eyes and took a sip of her drink. She had topped her long-sleeved black t-shirt with a pink vest and added matching pink leggings under her black skirt. Today, her purple bangs hung from a lacy black beret.

Keegan secretly envied Lauren her steady boyfriend. "I think you should dump him," she said. "There are so many hot guys you could date. You'll be old and married before you know it. You might as well enjoy it now."

"Keegan, just because you have dated half the school doesn't mean everyone else has to," Lauren retorted, poking her friend on the arm.

Keegan gave them a wicked grin. "There are just so many boys and so little time."

Anna laughed so hard she started hiccupping, which caused Lauren to spit her drink out.

Keegan glanced at Lauren to make sure she wasn't choking, then laughed, handing her a napkin to wipe her chin. "You guys need serious help."

Keegan could joke with the girls, but they didn't know that she had less than two years left to date. She knew Rourk, her chosen, would be perfect for her—when she turned eighteen and met him. If only the rest of the world believed as elves did, Keegan felt sure the divorce rate would be much lower.

A kick under the table brought Keegan back to the present. "Ow!"

"Shh! You're such an idiot sometimes." Anna jerked her head towards the door. Keegan glanced casually around to see what the kick had been for. It didn't take a genius to figure out what Anna wanted her to see. *Wow.*

The guy they ogled was beyond hot, even though he was older. He stood over six feet tall, with dark black hair that looked like he had just got caught in a windstorm. She swore he could see into her soul as his striking blue eyes caught hers.

Way too hot to be a human. Sorcerer? Everyone seemed to be under his spell the moment he walked through the door. They all tried not to stare. Lauren fanned herself, and they all laughed.

From outside the coffee shop Rourk stood hidden, watching Keegan through the window as she sat laughing with her friends. Her fleeting thoughts had summoned him again, and his pulse quickened as he fought the urge to go inside.

Pushing a hand agitatedly through his shaggy hair, Rourk tried to focus on breathing. He leaned against the brick wall of the store behind him, rubbing his temples with both hands. The urge to speak to her made his heart ache. It took everything he had to remain rooted to the sidewalk, hidden in the shadows, when she was so close. He had to watch from a distance as usual. She laughed at something one of her friends said and he wished he could hear her laugh.

Suddenly, they gathered their things and left the coffee shop.

Rourk made a snap decision to follow them.

The girls decided to walk to the fair instead of taking Lauren's car. The weather was perfect, pleasantly cool with not a rain cloud in sight. The fresh air felt incredible against Keegan's skin. She closed her eyes, tilted her head towards the sun, and spun in a circle. "Fall is my favorite time of year," she said wistfully.

Lauren shook her head, smiling. "Earth to Keegan, we're talking about the fair."

"Do you think they will tell me something about Xavier?" Anna wondered aloud, completely ignoring her friends' ramblings.

"Maybe, but I think you have to ask about him. At least that's how it goes on the TV shows." Lauren glanced over at Keegan, swinging her small purse at her side as they walked. "What do you think?"

"I'm not sure. You would think if they were real psychics they would see it without being asked," Keegan answered.

"Makes sense," Anna said. "I don't think I'll mention him. Besides, it's bad enough when he makes it obvious he only thinks of me as a friend. I don't think I could handle psychic rejection as well."

Lauren clapped her hands and jumped around. "Eek! We're almost there! This is so exciting!"

Lauren's enthusiasm surprised Keegan. The fair didn't quite sound like her thing. She probably hoped someone would predict that she and Josh would be married, have three kids, and live happily ever after.

At first glance, the fair disappointed Keegan. She had been expecting...well, she wasn't sure exactly what. This looked like some boring craft fair in a church basement. A bunch of old people sat at few tables and stands arranged around the room. The few attendees milling around the place didn't seem to be buying anything. Still, she could hear her mother in her head, *Don't judge a book by its cover, Keegan.* She decided she might as well relax and try to have fun with her friends.

Keegan noticed a large red sign at the entrance of the fair that said, "NO PHOTOGRAPHY." Mumbling under her breath, she put her camera back in the bag.

They visited each stand, admiring the jewelry, crystals, tarot cards, and other items. There were certainly some fascinating things. Keegan picked up a moonstone necklace for her mother. A small sign said it would bring considerable fortune. Keegan also knew it enhanced healing. It was one of her favorites. She loved to hold it up to the light and look through it to see the colors.

Lauren stopped in front of a stand with a woman dressed like a stereotypical fortune teller. The brilliant red of her long, curly hair reminded Keegan of a clown's nose. Despite being slightly overweight, fortyish, and wearing a multi-colored dress that gave her an outrageous gypsy appearance, she had a kind face. Gesturing to a pile of rocks on her table, she told Lauren, "Pick one and hand it to me. I can tell your future."

Lauren did so. When the woman had the rock, she closed her eyes and ran her small hands around it for a few moments before looking up at Lauren with a warm smile.

"You will do great things and succeed in whatever you put your mind to. I also see that you should put your focus into law."

Lauren's mouth gaped open; her dream was to be a lawyer. The girls all looked at each other in disbelief.

Anna jumped up and down, yelling, "Me next!" She grabbed a rock and handed it across the table.

The woman did the same thing again, closing her eyes and feeling the rock. "Child, you have a beautiful soul but you will struggle in life if you do not let go of the sadness inside of you."

Keegan and Lauren glanced over at Anna, surprised to see her brush away a tear. "Thank you," she said quietly, putting the rock in her pocket.

Finally, Keegan's turn came. Placing her hands over the pile of rocks, she grasped the one that called to her and handed it to the woman. The woman kept her eyes closed for an extremely long time. When she finally opened them, she looked at Keegan warily. Keegan's heart raced. What if the woman knew she wasn't human? What if she said so?

The woman sighed, handing the rock back to her. "I'm sorry; I feel nothing."

"What do you mean you feel nothing?" Keegan protested.

"That's just how it works sometimes. I'm sorry." She shrugged.

Keegan wanted to ask the psychic some questions, but Anna and Lauren dragged her to the next stand. She turned to look back and the woman returned her stare, her face expressionless. Keegan thought for sure something wasn't quite right. *Could she possibly know?* Maybe the woman looked at her strangely because she really couldn't read Keegan. It seemed odd, not to mention disappointing. Keegan wanted to hear what the psychic had to say about her.

The three girls spent hours browsing, which turned out to be a lot of fun.

The crowd steadily built in the room so that it no longer looked sad and unused. With the dim light and the noise of guests, it felt like a fair now. After enough time had passed, Keegan's feet started to hurt. She yawned and stretched dramatically.

"Are you guys ready to go?" she asked, tugging at Anna's sleeve.

Lauren nodded vehemently. "I shouldn't have worn these boots. I'm exhausted."

Though she had done well hiding it for most of the day, Anna had obviously been shaken by the psychic's words. Her eyes looked haunted as she just shrugged and said, "Sure, let's go get dinner."

As they walked towards the door, Keegan sensed someone watching her. She glanced around the room, searching for the source of the feeling. Startled, she came face-to-face with another elf.

Elves could recognize each other if they crossed paths. Except, of course, for future lifemates. The Elders cloaked them from each other by magic. But Keegan had never seen anything quite like this elf. Her stunning beauty didn't surprise Keegan; all elves tend to be overly attractive. This one had short black hair, pale skin, rosy cheeks, and the greenest eyes Keegan had ever seen on a person, like the eyes of a cat.

The darkness around the stranger surprised Keegan—and alarmed her. She had heard of dark elves. Wherever there was light there had to be dark, but actually seeing it felt very different from knowing it in her mind. She'd never seen a dark elf with her own eyes. She had heard they mainly lived up north and rarely made efforts to be a part of the human world. Since her childhood, she'd thought of them almost like specters—bogeymen from folk stories.

Keegan's body went cold. She tensed up, and all her senses heightened as the stranger caught her eyes.

"Do you know her?" Anna asked, looking from Keegan to the other girl.

Keegan couldn't talk. The dark elf held her eyes; Keegan could not move unless the girl allowed it.

Finally, the dark elf averted her gaze. Keegan's body relaxed. A distracted look crossed her face. "She looks familiar, but let's get out of here." At that moment, Keegan only wanted to rush home and talk to her mother.

From a distance, Rourk watched with a grim expression on his handsome face.

What was that exchange all about and who was the dark elf?

He had to make a choice. He could follow the girls or go inside and talk to the dark elf. As much as it pained him to watch Keegan walk away, he hurried into the building. He needed to know if she was in danger.

Rourk scanned the room, but he didn't see the dark elf anywhere. *Where could she have gone?* Closing his eyes, he breathed deeply. He felt the coldness wash over him. He saw her with his mind's eye. The dark elf had taken the back door and was walking casually down the alley. At times like this, he felt grateful to be the descendent of a great warrior. He'd trained his whole life for his calling—from the time he got out of bed in the morning until the time he went to sleep at night. Hell, he even dreamed about the techniques he'd learned. He needed to put them to good use.

    Silently he advanced. He was the hunter and she, his prey.

Chapter 3

Keegan planted a smile on her face, trying not to think about what had just happened. "I'm starving! Isn't it Lauren's turn to pick?" She turned to Anna and at the same time they yelled, "Wendy's!"

"Funny guys. I don't always choose Wendy's." Lauren pouted.

Keegan and Anna exchanged glances. Anna asked, "Name one time you didn't pick Wendy's?"

Lauren paused and thought about it for a moment. "Fine, you're right. I love Wendy's. If I had to choose my last supper, it would be a Junior Bacon Cheeseburger, fries, and a frosty."

Shaking her head, Keegan put her arms through theirs and dragged them down the street. She was grateful for the distraction, but in the back of her mind, she still worried about the dark elf and what seeing her could have meant.

Once they got to Wendy's, Keegan went with a frosty and a baked potato.

"I still don't get this whole vegetarian thing you are going through," Lauren told her, wrinkling her nose at Keegan's baked potato.

Keegan reached across and grabbed one of Lauren's fries to dip in her frosty. "I just suddenly got creeped out by eating animals. I want to help animals, not eat them."

Anna and Lauren both rolled their eyes. Keegan was always crusading for something.

Keegan genuinely wanted to ask Anna about what the psychic had said about her sadness, but figured if that her friend wanted to talk about it, she would.

Lauren, on the other hand, was not quite as tactful. She blurted out, "Anna, you have to tell us what is going on with you. Are you really sad?"

Anna tilted her face down so that her purple bangs hung over her eyes.

She didn't say anything.

Seeing Anna's hesitation, Keegan reached over to touch Anna's hand and said, "If you don't want to talk about it, it's okay."

Lauren butted in. "No, it's not okay. She's our best friend. If we can help, we need to know."

"I've wanted to talk to you guys," Anna said softly, looking down at her hands clasped in her lap. "I just didn't know how to bring it up. My parents are getting a divorce."

"What?" gasped Lauren, shocked.

"They've been fighting for years," Anna told them, finally looking up. "I'm kinda relieved. I know they'll be happier apart. My dad has a drinking problem. He's such a jerk to everyone. I hate the way he talks to my mom. She's even on medication for depression."

Lauren jumped up, running around the table, pulling Anna out of her seat, and wrapping her arms around her. "It will be okay. I just wish you had told us sooner."

Keegan got to her feet, joining in the group hug. "Don't keep secrets from us anymore, okay?"

Anna smiled. "I'll try not to."

As if I have room to talk, Keegan thought as they all returned to their seats.

Keegan played with her iPhone, moving it around the table as she spoke. "I really had no clue. Your family always seems so happy when they're out in public."

Anna met her eyes across the table. "I guess you never really know what goes on behind closed doors."

Keegan grimaced. *Ain't that the truth.*

"I'm worried about my sister," Anna said. "I don't know how she's going to handle it. She's always been daddy's girl."

The three were silent a moment; Keegan had no idea what to say to make Anna feel better.

A mischievous grin crossed Lauren's face. "Okay, enough negative thoughts for one day. We are going to Patrick's party tomorrow night, right?"

Anna smiled. "Yeah, why not? At least I'll be able to see Xavier."

Keegan laughed. "Patrick is super cute."

Lauren looked at Keegan in disbelief. "He's also obnoxious as hell. You have the strangest taste."

"Blah, blah, blah…who cares? I didn't say I wanted to marry the guy," Keegan responded, waving off Lauren's comment.

"Good point. What are you guys wearing?" Anna asked.

"We'll figure out later what to wear," Lauren said. "What's the theme this time?"

"Dress to the nines." Anna sounded slightly annoyed.

"Oh, that will be fun. We can all dress up. I needed an excuse to buy a new dress." Lauren glanced over at Keegan. "You know what that means?"

"Shopping!" they replied in unison. Anna looked at them as if they were crazy.

After they finished eating, they walked back to Starbucks where Lauren had parked her car. Keegan unchained her bike from the bike rack in front of the cafe and the three of them managed to shove it in Lauren's trunk, though the back tire jutted out. They took Anna home first, and then Lauren dropped Keegan off at her place, helping her unload her bicycle and roll it in the garage.

Keegan pushed the heavy door open and walked into the house with her shoulders slumped, letting out a big sigh as she found her mother in the kitchen.

Mom looked up from her cup of tea, her blue eyes big under her ginger pixie cut hair. She had a hardback book open on the table, one small hand holding her place. She frowned and asked, "What's bothering you?"

Keegan pulled out the stool next to her mom and sat down, letting her head rest in her hands. "My day was weird. I wanted to talk to you about it."

She filled her mother in on all the details, from what had happened at the fair to learning about Anna's parents' divorce. She ended her story by asking her mom to give Anna's mother a healing soon.

Her mother's response took her by surprise. "Keegan, how could you have gone to a place with psychics without telling me?"

"Mom, it was just for fun. I didn't think anything of it. Anna was so excited."

Her mother sighed, a worried look crossing her face. "You have no idea the trouble this could bring us."

Confused, Keegan asked, "Do you mean because of the dark elf?"

Still worried, her mother said, "This is much bigger than you can understand. Once your father gets home, we'll have your grandmother come over and then decide what to do."

Her mother jumped up to make phone calls.

It wasn't like her mom to be so cryptic. Keegan shivered, brushing the feeling away. She didn't understand, but she hoped that her mom was just overreacting. Grabbing her iPad, she went up to her room.

She decided to research dark elves. Google had a surprising amount of information, though most of it was obviously incorrect. The dark elf didn't seem bothered by being out during the day, and, far from ugly, she blended in well. Most humans would be shocked if they knew how many supernatural beings they passed each day.

Before the front door had even opened, Keegan knew her father was home. After her mom's reaction, she worried about what her dad would say.

A few minutes later, she heard her grandmother arrive, the soft mumble of her voice drifting to Keegan's room. Her father's voice boomed up the stairs, "Family meeting!"

Keegan dragged herself from her desk chair and headed down the hall. Thaddeus glared at her as she passed his open doorway. Sitting on the floor in front of his television, game controller in hand, he rolled his eyes. "Are you kidding me, Keegan? What have you done this time? I'm in the middle of a game."

Keegan stopped, leaning on the doorjamb with a sigh. "Just get downstairs. You know how dad gets if he thinks we're not listening to him."

Thaddeus reached over, grumbling under his breath, and turned off the Xbox. "This better be good."

"I thought you knew everything," Keegan teased as they started down the hall. She messed up her brother's soft auburn hair. Though he was four years younger than she, he was quickly catching up to her in height.

"Shut up. You know that's not how it works," he responded, ducking away from her grasp.

They headed down the stairs as if marching to their deaths. Unplanned family meetings generally did not mean anything good.

Warrick sat in the corner building towers out of his brightly colored blocks, too young for the family meeting. Keegan envied him. No one knew yet what his power would be. Warrick had not even turned two, but his inquisitive eyes revealed that he understood more than most kids his age. He babbled happily at her as she passed, so she gave him a quick kiss on the top of head.

Her mother and father sat on one side of the table. Her grandmother, Mary, sat quietly on the other side in her pressed khaki slacks and blue cardigan sweater.

Grandmother, a tiny woman with bright red hair and clear blue eyes, always said her healing abilities kept her looking young. Her round, rosy face, always kind and usually smiling, looked more somber than Keegan had ever seen.

Keegan's father liked things organized and official. His stocky body seemed to take up the entire kitchen as he sat in his favorite chair and gazed sternly across the table at Keegan. "We have called this family meeting to deal with the consequences of Keegan's actions."

Keegan flushed with anger. "Excuse me? Consequences of my actions? All I did was go out with my friends. Why are you all making such a big deal out of this?"

Her grandmother placed a warm hand over hers, shooting Richard a look. "There are things that you don't know, and we hoped we had more time to teach you. We wanted to let you all be kids and not worry about the challenges we elves face."

As if on cue, Warrick toppled his blocks and filled the house with laughter. Turning her wise eyes back to Keegan, Mary continued, "Do you know what your father does?"

Keegan glanced at her father. Richard's stern eyes watched her silently, his large, muscular arms crossed over his chest. The scars that marked his skin had been there as long as she could remember. "Um, yeah. He's the leader of the elfin army of light. He keeps us safe, even though he never tells us where he goes or why."

"Yes, that is true, but he serves a greater purpose than that," her grandmother explained, giving Keegan's father a soothing smile.

Still confused, Keegan asked, "That doesn't even make any sense."

Her grandmother closed her eyes. When she reopened them, she said, "The war between dark and light has been waged since the beginning of time. Great care has been taken to shield it from the eyes of humans. Prophecies foretell that your father will lead the elves in the great battle, the final battle." She paused. "No prophecy tells who will win in the end."

"Why are we even fighting? And why is this the first I've heard of it?"

Emerald and Richard exchanged glances with Mary. Emerald sat forward, reaching across the table for her daughter's hand. Feeling a little weird, Keegan took her mom's hand with her free one, her grandmother still holding the other. They were acting like someone had died.

Her mother spoke. "Keegan, the fight began thousands of years ago. Light and dark elves didn't always hate each other. Once, we lived together in peace. At the time, one family ruled the elves. Two sons fought over land; other elves chose sides. As strong emotions often do, the hatred has only built in the years since." Her mother smiled sadly. "This battle has been coming for a long time. We cannot stop it. We should have told you, but we just wanted to protect you."

"Protect me from what?" demanded Keegan, frustrated. None of this made any sense. How could she have been kept in the dark about something as huge as this?

"Growing up too fast," her father said.

"I'm not a piece of glass. I can handle it." Keegan narrowed her eyes and glared across the table at her father. "Something more is going on," she mumbled.

She looked over at Thaddeus. "Shouldn't he be able to tell us something?"

Thaddeus shook his head.

Although only twelve, he was one of the most powerful seers their kind had ever known—and he was only just beginning to come into his powers. Keegan always had a hard time believing that her brother, who drove her crazy and lived on his Xbox, could see the future. As he'd begun seeing the future, he'd become antisocial, preferring digital friends to real ones—except for Samual, another elf he'd been best friends with forever.

Thaddeus felt overwhelmed around people. He couldn't block his gift yet, so he foresaw all the good—and all the terrible—things that would happen.

Her grandmother picked up the conversation. "He cannot see it because it has not been determined yet."

"Well, then we still have a chance. What does my visit to the fair have to do with this?"

"Keegan, most of the people at those fairs are fakes, just in it for the money. On rare occasions, however, they possess true gifts. As you know, people do not always use their gifts for positive reasons. Going to a place like that could have given the dark elves an opportunity to find out more about us."

Grandmother leaned back in her chair and ran her hand across the green linen tablecloth on the table. Without saying a word, Emerald stood to get her some more tea.

"You said that you couldn't move when the girl made eye contact with you. Do you know why you couldn't move?" Grandmother paused as Keegan shook her head, then continued. "She was going through your mind and you didn't even know it. Thankfully, you didn't know anything of use to her."

Still feeling defensive, Keegan asked, "Why are you telling me about this *now*?"

With a soothing voice, her grandmother replied, "Because the time of the battle grows near, and we need our family to be prepared." She thanked Emerald with her eyes as her daughter placed a steaming mug in front of her.

Keegan's parents sat close together, holding hands. Her mother looked worried and her father looked determined.

Keegan didn't see what had everyone so worked up. So the elves had fought a war forever. Many elves fought for the light, and they had powers. Not to mention all the other supernatural beings on the side of light. She honestly didn't think they had anything to worry about.

"Has everyone said all you have to say? Because if so, I'd like to go to my room," Keegan said.

Her father slammed his fist on the table, startling Warrick, who started crying. Emerald rushed to his side as her father snarled, "Damn it, Keegan! You need to take this seriously. We are talking about the end of the elves as a race. Do you want that?"

That threw her for a loop. "What do you mean?"

"I mean that if we do not win this, the elves of the light will be gone and evil will take over. Is that what you want?" He looked like an avenging god, as if he should be holding a lightning bolt, preparing to smite his enemies.

They had her attention. She hadn't even met Rourk yet, and she really looked forward to her future with him. "I'm sorry."

"There is something else you need to know, my love," Mary went on.

Keegan looked contritely away from her dad, giving her attention to her grandmother.

"The Book of Elfin prophecy specifically mentions a child of the light who will be born with the gift of sight, a child whose father will lead the elves in battle."

Keegan glanced back to her father. He nodded, taking a deep breath and letting it out before he spoke. "A child who could save our people."

She turned to her brother and scoffed, "You? You're going to save us?"

"Me," Thaddeus agreed, so softly Keegan almost didn't hear him.

Keegan let go of her grandmother's hand, falling back in her seat, stunned. "Oh."

Her family waited in silence for a long moment, letting the information sink in.

Keegan pulled herself together, even though her heart beat like a hummingbird's wings. She had no idea what to say. "Okay. Tell me what you would like me to do."

Looking over at his daughter thankfully, Richard drew a deep breath. "For starters, we need to work on your fighting skills. Your brother can protect himself admirably well. You, on the other hand, need some work."

Keegan glared at her brother across the table.

He smirked back at her.

Their father caught the exchange. "Not so fast, son," he said. "You are going to be the one to train her."

Her brother's reaction was priceless. A look of disbelief came over his face, quickly replaced by the same look her father wore whenever he accepted a task. Keegan knew she was in trouble.

Elves rarely had two main powers, like Thaddeus did. Keegan's father came from a long line of warriors; he passed that on to his son. Along with his seer's gift, Thaddeus also had a warrior's gift of strength, physical and mental. Only one other elf in known history had that combination of gifts. Usually other elves needed to protect seers, but not Thaddeus. His two gifts made for a deadly combination.

Training with Thaddeus would be grueling. He'd take no pity on her.

As if her father had thought the same thing, he continued, "Thaddeus, you need to practice on different ways protecting yourself. I will have your mother work with you."

Her mother spoke up, "We don't expect you to give up your lives. We just want you to take your spare time to sharpen your skills. You also need to be more aware. Creatures of the dark will start showing up more often the closer we get."

After the meeting ended, Keegan hugged her grandmother, said goodnight to everyone else, and went up to her room. Mentally exhausted, she grabbed her phone and fell back on the bed. Five texts waited for her. Anna asked what she planned to wear to the party. Lauren wondered if Josh could come with her to the party, and Donald wanted to know if she wanted to go to the movies with him, Spencer, Sam and Calvron. That text brought a smile to her face. She really liked Donald; too bad he didn't feel the same. *Oh well.* There was always Patrick—who had sent her two texts. Apparently, he had heard she was coming to the party. News traveled fast.

She didn't bother to reply to any of the messages; she had too much running through her head.

Her parents had to be overreacting with all their talk of a great battle. She lay in bed and thought about that for a while. What if all elves—or even most of them—really did die and she never got to meet Rourk? She had their whole life planned out! She'd been dreaming of meeting her chosen since she was a little girl.

With all her thoughts muddled and swirling through her mind, Keegan eventually drifted off to sleep.

Chapter 4

Rourk tensed as Keegan thought his name, but quickly pushed it away. He had other things to deal with at the moment. This dark elf, clearly well trained, had evaded him so far. He sensed movement to the right of him, but he looked straight ahead. If he looked to the right, she would be gone. He did his best to appear baffled, like he couldn't figure out where she might be.

The dark elf moved forward, thinking he'd lost sight of her.

Rourk pounced. She might have been well trained, but she didn't stand a chance he was gifted. For good measure, he shielded his mind as he threw her against the wall.

She looked annoyed—probably because she couldn't use her own gift on him.

"What do you want with the girl?" Rourk asked.

The dark elf glared back at him. "I want nothing from her. I just happened to notice another elf and wanted to read her mind."

He pushed his forearm deep into her throat, "What were you doing at the fair?" he growled as the dark elf struggled under his grasp.

She flinched at the strength in his hold, then looked into his grey eyes. "I was just having fun. I was bored, and I enjoy messing with humans."

Rourk searched her face and decided she was telling the truth. Relaxing his grip, he stared into her eyes. "Make no mistake. If you go near the girl again—"

She shrugged her shoulders. "Whatever. I have no interest in the girl."

Rourk sensed her struggle to look calm; he could tell she was shaken.

"She's your chosen?"

Startled, Rourk clenched his jaw, angry at himself for letting so much emotion show. Chosen or not, he should control how Keegan affected him.

When he didn't answer, the girl eyed him. "She's lucky."

"What?" Rourk narrowed his eyes.

"Lucky to have someone who cares so much for her." Looking down at her black leather Converse, the girl scuffed her foot against the concrete. "I still have a year to meet my mate."

That simple sentence struck something inside him. He had another year to wait, too.

"Just get out of here," Rourk sighed.

"Why are you letting me go?" she asked curiously.

"You're a mind reader. Dark elves may kill innocents, but light elves live by a code."

She stared at him, clearly surprised, then turned and hurried down the alley.

He watched the dark elf depart. She turned once to look at him. As he watched the girl disappear around the corner, he hoped his chosen had made it home safely.

Someone knocked on the door, waking Keegan. Sitting up, she rubbed her eyes and called, "Come in."

Her mom stuck her head in and smiled. "Hey."

Keegan grinned back, smoothing her hands back through her hair. "Hey, Mom."

Emerald walked in, pulling the door shut behind her, and sat on the edge of the bed. She pushed a strand of hair from Keegan's face, her blue eyes searching. "What are you thinking about?"

Keegan glanced up at her mother sheepishly. "My chosen."

A smile crossed her mom's face as she recalled the days when she dreamt about her own chosen. "You'll meet him soon enough."

Sighing, Keegan said, "It seems to be taking forever. Why do I have to wait until I'm eighteen?"

"You know why. For now, just focus on enjoying your high school years. Have fun with your friends. Be a teenager."

Keegan knew she couldn't win that argument. So she snuggled against her mom's side and asked, "Will you tell me the story of how you met Dad?"

Her mother's blue eyes lit up. She climbed into bed and put her arm around her daughter. "As you know, we're forbidden to meet our partners before we're both of age. Your father was much older than me, so he had to wait longer than most."

Keegan watched her mother's face as she spoke. She loved hearing this story; it took away any doubt or fear she had about meeting Rourk.

Her mother continued, "I needed a new book, so I went to the bookstore. But first I stopped at the café© in the back for a coffee. I looked around as I added cream, and I made eye contact with a man. My physical reaction to him shocked me so much that I almost spilled my coffee. I left, forgetting all about my book."

Keegan asked the same question she always asked, "Why did you leave?"

A slight smile appeared on her mother's lips. "I felt guilty. I knew I would marry my chosen, the man I'd meet in three months. I shouldn't have been so instantly drawn to another."

Keegan sat up a little on the bed, as if to hear the rest of the story a little better.

"I walked as fast as I could, knowing someone was behind me. I willed myself not to look back. I never thought it could be him. He followed me the whole way down the mall. Once I reached the end, I had to turn around. He planted himself in front of me, his legs spread wide and his hands in his pockets. I thought, *Who does this man think he is, following me, and why is he acting so arrogantly?*

After a brief pause, her mother said, "He asked me if I would like to go out with him. I said no. He was so confident, though, that he gave me his number and told me to call when I changed my mind."

Keegan loved that part of the story because she could imagine it clearly. Emerald's face was luminous, her eyes in the past.

"I looked at the number often, but wouldn't let myself call him. I was really upset—why I couldn't get this stranger out of my thoughts? I felt so nervous when the time came to meet your father. I was worried I wouldn't be attracted to him, or that we would have nothing in common. You can imagine my surprise when I came face-to-face with the arrogant stranger."

"And neither of you had any idea that the stranger you had met at the mall was your chosen?" Keegan asked, though she already knew.

Emerald laughed. "Nope, we didn't know at all!"

Looking up, her cheek resting against her mother's shoulder, Keegan said, "I hope I will be as happy as you and dad."

Her mom slid from the bed, her warmth leaving Keegan's side. She reached over and pulled the blanket up as she had done so many times when Keegan was a child. "That's the beauty of our kind. You will be. He's meant for you."

Keegan grabbed her pillow and tucked her arm under it, then rolled to her side. "Do you think he'll get me a ruby engagement ring?"

Emerald laughed. "I guess we will have to wait and see."

Her mother had an unusual name, even for an elf—Emerald. The day they had met, Keegan's father gave Emerald a box holding a stunning antique emerald engagement ring. He said that he knew it was meant for her, even though he didn't know her name when he found it.

Ever since Keegan was a little girl, she had dreamed of her wedding day. The details changed, but she knew for sure that she wanted her engagement ring to be a ruby set in diamonds, in an antique setting. She hoped Rourk wouldn't mind. He probably planned to give her a diamond like everyone else.

Maybe not. Maybe he would know exactly what she wanted. She imagined ways Rourk might propose to her until she drifted off to sleep.

Keegan woke the next morning, feeling that she had slept like a rock. Just thinking that brought a smile to her face. She loved metaphors. Rocks didn't sleep; energy always filled them.

Remembering the party that night at Patrick's, she jumped out of bed and into the shower. Her brother banged on the door and told her to stop singing. She sang even louder.

To pass time, Keegan walked through the woods, taking some more pictures and enjoying the sunshine. She knew fall would end soon. When winter crept in, it would be too cold take photographs outside.

She loved their land. Before Keegan was born, her parents had purchased the seventy acres of untamed wild, mostly wooded and surrounded by farmland, so the seclusion was absolute. Her father's security measures made it safe for her to wander freely. Even though she made fun of Thaddeus and Sam for spending so much time in the woods, she was guilty of it herself.

Keegan spent much of the afternoon lounging around her room with the television on while she chatted on Facebook with friends. All everybody could talk about was the party.

For dinner, Emerald made stir-fry, cooking a wok of vegetables for Keegan, then piling a second wok with beef for Thaddeus and Richard. Her family's idle chitchat made Keegan antsy; the day had seemed to drag on eternally.

Lauren and Anna showed up around seven to help her get ready for the party, bringing their makeup bags. She had to admit they both looked hot. Lauren wore a strapless dress with black and white polka dots with a fuchsia sash at the waist. The short dress accented her long legs, and the dark color made a stark contrast to her pale skin. Anna wore black skinny jeans with a gorgeous floral tunic that showed off her long neck. She refused to conform to the "dress to the nines" theme.

Keegan took a bunch of photos of them to post later. With Anna's wildly colored makeup and Lauren's smoky eyes, they were made to be photographed.

Keegan decided on a green, one-shoulder, chiffon dress with black heels.

She let Anna do her makeup after she promised not to get too wild. Lauren put Keegan's hair up with loose curls falling down around her face.

"Your lips and eyes stand out even more than usual with your hair up," Lauren said, fluffing the curls around Keegan's face.

"Aw, thank you, but I think all the credit goes to you and your magical skills," Keegan responded, happy with the girl who stared back at her in the mirror.

Lauren laughed, gesturing to herself dramatically. "I am quite magical."

Standing up, Keegan paused so Anna could run a blusher brush over Keegan's cheeks one last time.

"Anna, you should change into flats," Keegan said, frowning up at her friend. "You already tower over me as it is."

"Sure, blame me for your diminutive stature. If I didn't know any better, I would think you were secretly a pixie."

"As if!" Keegan laughed loudly.

Once they were all satisfied with their looks, it was time to go.

Chapter 5

Initially they planned to take Lauren's car, but Keegan's father offered to drive them. Keegan didn't know if he was worried they would drink or he just really wanted to do something for his daughter. Whatever his reason, Keegan didn't mind; she didn't get to see enough of him. He dropped them off—fashionably late, of course. By the time they arrived, the party was in full swing.

Patrick lived in a big suburban neighborhood, in a nice, two-story brick Colonial house with lovely landscaping and enough space between the houses to justify a party. All the windows were lit up and the solid *thump-thump* of the bass could be heard from the sidewalk.

They walked through the door, giggling. Patrick, obviously drunk and with his arm around some blonde chick, sauntered over to them. The blonde pouted.

"You guys are going to catch this house on fire," he said loudly, throwing his arms around Keegan and Lauren. The blonde girl did not appear to be thrilled by the statement; her glare spoke volumes.

Lauren and Anna looked at Keegan, who just rolled her eyes, grabbed their arms, and pushed past Patrick. He was officially off her list.

Lauren found Josh with astonishing speed. They had barely entered the mass of the party dancing in the living room, when the two of them were off making out in a corner.

The music blared, too loud for conversation. The room smelled like liquor and sweat as partygoers rubbed against one another in the dimly lit room. One of Keegan's favorite songs came on, so she grabbed Anna. They lost themselves on the dance floor.

Halfway through the song, Patrick danced his way onto the floor and screamed over the music, "Hey, I thought you were coming here to see me?"

Shooting him a disgusted look, Keegan turned away and pulled Anna further across the room. *Guys are such jerks.* She couldn't wait until she turned eighteen and didn't have to deal with them any longer. She wondered what Rourk was doing at that very moment. Was he at a party with a girl?

Why is she doing this to me? Rourk moaned inwardly. She seemed to think of him a lot these days. It drove him crazy.

Not even playing *Left for Dead* on his Xbox 360 helped. He felt a mindless urge to throw his controller at the wall. Realizing he couldn't focus on slaying zombies, he tossed down the controller and got to his feet, just like a puppy dog obeying its master. At least, that's what he felt like.

He closed his eyes to locate her. He liked the hunt and tried to figure out her location from her surroundings. Grabbing his keys of his desk, he headed for the truck and set off in search of her.

He heard the music from a block away. He parked, then walked to the house, where he closed his eyes. He didn't like what he saw. *What is she doing here?* he thought. *There are so many drunk kids acting like fools, and she's dancing like she doesn't have a care in the world.*

Rourk watched as a blond kid approached his chosen. The kid, obviously drunk, appeared to want her to dance with him, but she turned away. The guy grabbed her by the shoulder and turned her around, causing anger to surge up inside Rourk. When she pushed the kid away again, none too gently, Rourk didn't bother to suppress the smirk on his face.

When an orange-haired, lanky boy approached her, she looked excited to see him. He started dancing with her and her friends, but Rourk couldn't tell if the kid was really dancing or just playing around. He looked like an imbecile. Unfortunately, he could tell she liked the guy just from the look on her face.

His heart slammed in his chest and adrenaline raced through him. He couldn't stand the thought of his mate having a crush on someone. He could not get over the effect the girl had on him. Even all his training did not prepare him for the feelings she evoked in him.

Turn and leave, he kept telling himself, but his legs wouldn't cooperate. He was captivated by her, and not just by her beauty. There was something more.

Keegan felt relieved to see Donald approach them. She was getting sick of Patrick constantly annoying her with his disgusting beer breath and too-friendly hands. She smiled as Donald danced up to her and Anna.

"Where did you learn to dance, Donald?" she said, trying to suppress the giggles his gyrating instilled in her.

He grinned broadly, his chest puffing out like a rooster as his hips shook. "On TV—I practice at home in front of the mirror."

Keegan laughed. She never quite knew if he was serious or just trying to make them laugh, but he danced like a crazy person. She seriously hoped he was messing around.

Keegan noticed Anna with Xavier, deep in conversation in the corner of the room. In the meantime, Spencer and Sam came up to her and Donald and they all danced together.

Keegan yelled in Spencer's ear. "Does Donald know he dances like a crazy person?"

Spencer laughed, "The insane thing is that he really thinks he's a good dancer."

They glanced over at Donald. He danced away, sweat pouring down his face, not paying attention to anyone. They all shook their heads and laughed.

The guys eventually moved on to try to flirt with other girls.

Keegan felt left out. Lauren and Josh were still in the same spot, lips locked, while Anna flirted relentlessly with Xavier on the couch. Keegan wanted to leave, but knew she couldn't go without the others. Gazing around at everyone having fun, Keegan decided to go outside and get some fresh air.

Keegan stepped into the still night, wrapping her arms around herself for warmth. The single light illuminated the empty porch, the white railing, and the mismatched furniture. She leaned her elbows on the railing, taking a deep breath. Someone in the neighborhood had a fireplace going; the smell of burning wood filled the air.

Keegan squinted out into the street and noticed someone standing on the other side. She couldn't see very far with the light at her back and the glare from the street lights, but it was obviously a man. Instead of being chilled by a stranger watching her, she had an odd urge to walk over and talk to him. She wouldn't—her father would kill her if she talked to a stranger in the middle of the night. But she wondered. *Why is he just standing there?*

Rourk couldn't believe it when she walked out the door. The light of the porch gave her a kind of halo as she gazed out across the street. Her auburn hair burned like fire when lit from behind. She looked amazing in that dress, her bare shoulder delicate and pale. When she looked in his direction, his heartbeat accelerated. He'd never been this close to her and he wondered why she'd come outside all alone at night. Didn't she know it wasn't safe?

As if she could read his mind, Keegan turned around and went back inside the house.

Thinking of the blond boy, Rourk thought maybe she would have been safer outside. *This is getting ridiculous*, he told himself. He needed to stay away from her. He couldn't keep stalking her for another two years. Rourk found some relief in knowing he would be eighteen in less than a year. Then he could follow in his father's footsteps and join the military. He needed to be away from her until they could meet

Seeing her like this can't be healthy.

The girls called Keegan's Aunt Katrina to pick them up. They had each had a couple of drinks, and Keegan didn't feel like listening to her parents' lectures. Plus, Aunt Kat was cool. She had an open call policy. If they ever got in trouble or just needed a ride home, they could call anytime day or night. As long as they were not in danger, she wouldn't tell anyone's parents. But Katrina was a terrible liar, so Keegan figured her mom knew every time.

Kat could read minds, so she always knew if the girls had done anything majorly bad. She pulled up in her dark green Subaru Outback with *Cash Cash* blaring. The girls piled in the car, talking a mile a minute.

"I love picking you guys up," Aunt Kat said. "It reminds me of all my crazy times as a teen. Of course, you guys are mild compared to me and Keegan's mother."

The girls laughed, stumbling over each other as they piled into the backseat together. Anna slammed the door shut.

"I doubt my mom was all that crazy," Keegan said.

Kat smirked as she pulled away from the curb. "Oh, you'd be surprised."

"Tell us some stories."

"No way; I keep your secrets and I'll keep hers as well," Kat said sternly, her eyes twinkling at them in the rearview mirror.

Kat pulled into the driveway at Keegan's. "Hey, Anna, maybe you should get it over with and put the moves on Xavier. See what happens."

Anna's mouth gaped. "There is something funny about you, Kat. I was just thinking the same thing."

Kat just gave her a mysterious smile. "Get out of here. Have a good sleepover, and I'm glad you called. It makes my day when I can help you guys."

The girls blew kisses to her as they ran up the doorstep.

Keegan definitely needed some sleep. Everyone would be headed home at lunchtime and she already dreaded the afternoon.

Tomorrow she would start training with her brother. She was not looking forward to getting her butt kicked by a twelve-year-old.

Chapter 6

Her family had trained together for as long as Keegan could remember. She just never took to it, which seemed to disappoint her parents. Unfortunately, she had to focus now—and practice for real.

Since she was rusty, Thaddeus decided to start with swords, her least favorite. Keegan knew it was useless to protest that being left-handed, not to mention uncoordinated, left her at a disadvantage. Grabbing the training swords, they went over the same *kata* what seemed like a thousand times. They drew their swords, made a single strike and re-sheathed it. At first, bored, she just wanted it over with, but soon the movement became almost relaxing. Finally, the motion felt fluid as her mind cleared.

"Keegan, we're done," Thaddeus said, packing away their equipment.

"Huh? We just started," Keegan protested, the tip of her sword resting on the ground.

Thaddeus looked at her funny. "Check out the clock."

The time surprised Keegan; it hadn't felt like any at all.

Weeks passed between school, training, taking pictures, and hanging out with her friends. The time seemed to fly by. Her father left again. She had no idea where he went—just that he was gone for weeks, and sometimes months, at a time. Eventually he returned, often with a new scar.

Keegan walked through the door one day and saw her father sitting at the table in front of his MacBook.

"How was school?" he said, giving her a big smile through his beard.

Keegan tossed her backpack on the floor, crossing the kitchen to search for a drink in the fridge. "Same as usual, nothing too exciting."

"Come have a chat with your old man." He patted the chair next to him.

"Dad, what do we have to talk about? I know you're not going to tell me where you've been." Keegan grinned, looking back at him over her shoulder with her face in the refrigerator.

"You would just think it was boring if I did." Richard shrugged.

"Uh-huh. I'm sure a secret mission to save us from destruction would be boring. Do you want a drink?" She grabbed a couple of sodas and sat across from her dad.

"Your brother told me you are making great progress."

Trying to hide her surprise, Keegan shrugged. "I don't really care what he thinks."

"Then why are you trying not to smile?"

The sheer pleasure she felt from those simple words amused her.

Keegan's mother came through the door, arms full of groceries. "Richard, would you mind getting the rest of the bags from the car?"

She looked frazzled. Keegan grabbed a slipping bag before it hit the floor. "What's wrong?"

Her mother stared at her, raising an eyebrow as she put her bags on the kitchen table. "I still have so much to do and everyone is going to be here in two hours."

Taken aback, Keegan said, "Umm, everyone is going to be here for what?"

Keegan's mom looked at her like she was an alien. "How could you forget? Today is your cousin Merrick's birthday and the party is here."

Richard came back through the door carrying several bags just in time to hear her mom's declaration. By the look on his face, Keegan felt sure her father wished he'd stayed gone one more day. Her family could be called a *handful*. Soon they would host a house full of elves and all the mischief that came along with them.

Keegan's mother busied herself in the kitchen making one of the few dishes everyone liked: meatball subs. Emerald liked making the dish because she just had to throw the meat in the slow cooker, add some sauce, and heat up the bread.

Of course, since Keegan had converted to vegetarianism, her mom would make her an alternative meal, usually a veggie sub or just a salad. Keegan had to admit, the thought of meatball subs almost made her want to cave. All she had to do was think of the animal that gave up their life for the meal, and the temptation would pass.

Keegan often wondered why her mother was a stay-at-home mom. She didn't seem to enjoy any of the cooking, the cleaning, the volunteering, or the homework. She could have easily gotten a job if she wanted, but for whatever reason she chose not to.

It used to bother Keegan that her mother didn't use her healing power for good like her grandmother. Mary, a nurse, worked around sick people all the time. She had to be careful not to draw attention to herself, so she rarely gave a full healing. She told Keegan that just removing some discomfort from her patients was often enough. Her family thought the patients sensed something different about her. She also received more thank you cards than any other nurse. Even the doctors asked for her when severe cases arrived.

Years before, Keegan had followed her mother around with her mind's eye one day, just to see what she did with herself. Keegan's memory drifted back to that day. No one in her family would follow someone that way, with the mind's eye, unless they feared danger. They respected each other's privacy. But Keegan had always been too curious for her own good.

She watched as her mother went to the gym, the bookstore, and then did some shopping. Keegan gave up for a while. When she focused on her mom one last time, what she saw made her proud to be her mother's daughter. Somewhere dark and dingy, Emerald bent over a woman with her three kids gathered around her. The woman had been severely beaten. Blood trickled from her mouth and she had a hunched over, on-the-brink-of-death feel. The kids looked terrified.

Emerald closed her eyes. A look of peace came over her face. She held her hands over the woman's body and, as Keegan watched with her mind, healed the woman. It was amazing to witness. After some time, the children calmed down. The woman grabbed her mother's hands and said thank you. Emerald told them to collect their things and say goodbye because they were not coming back to this life. She gave them money, a car, and the keys to a new place, far away from their current surroundings.

Emerald could help these women because, luckily, their family never really had to worry about money. Keegan's Uncle John had an analytical gift. He saw patterns in numbers, which gave him an edge with stocks and business ventures. Because of his gift, their family had always been well taken care of.

That night, after Keegan had watched the healing, her mother had walked through the door, looked Keegan in the eye, and said, "Now you know."

Keegan had trouble reading her mother at times. She thought Emerald was annoyed that her privacy had been invaded. But her mom also seemed glad that Keegan witnessed the healing.

Keegan had followed her mother to the kitchen to make tea, which her mom always did, whenever she walked through the door.

After a brief hesitation, Keegan asked, "Do you do that often?"

Her mom glanced over with a slight smile on her face. "Only when they are ready," she said. "I used to work at a women's shelter."

This surprised Keegan. She had no idea.

"It was before you were born. I spent days and nights healing many poor women like the one today."

Keegan raised an eyebrow. "Well, why did you stop?"

Her mom grabbed the tea bags, and then turned to face Keegan. "I worked there for years, until eventually I realized I wasn't helping them. They usually went back to the abuser. I would give them a full healing, and they would feel wonderful. Somehow, almost all of them managed to convince themselves that the abuser would change. Of course they never did, and the women would return to the shelter. I would heal them and the process would repeat itself. Using my gift made me miserable. I could not understand how these women would take a fresh start and go back to their former lives. Then your father helped me see what I needed to do."

When her mother paused, Keegan nodded for her to continue.

"He told me to walk away. I was appalled, at first. How could I walk away from those in need? He explained that my gift was mine to use as I wanted. If working at the shelter made me unhappy, then it wasn't worth it.

"Those women weren't willing to start over. He asked me to think back and find the common thread in the small percentage of women who took the opportunity to make a new life. I realized something. Almost all of them had children who had witnessed the abuse and almost all were a breath away from death."

Keegan had sat back, cup in hand, digesting what her mother had said. "So how do you find out when they are ready now?"

Her mother smiled sadly. "A network of elves on the side of the light, elves who want to help the humans, track these cases. Some of them work in shelters or hospitals. Some are school teachers who see signs of abuse in their students. And once in a while I get a call that someone needs my gift."

Keegan's mom tapped her on the shoulder, bringing her back from her memory.

"Keegan, I told you to make sure the bathrooms were clean."

Her mom always seemed so stressed out when they were having company; she wanted everything to be perfect. Like anyone noticed or cared.

Keegan looked forward to having her family over. For one thing, she'd have excellent opportunities to use her camera. And the kids got to use their gifts around others. That was probably the hardest part of being an elfin child. It sucked to have these awesome powers, and not be able to share them with your friends.

The family almost always gathered at her house, which had been built like a fortress as well as a house. On seventy acres surrounded by farms, everyone could be themselves and not worry about neighbors. A gate guarded the long and winding driveway, and a massive stone fence, with security cameras on it, surrounded the property. The cameras just deterred trespassers, as elfin abilities would let the family know about an attack well in advance.

The house itself was not that large, a two-story, wooden house made mostly of glass. The military grade glass made it possible for them to see out, but no one could see in. Her father said he chose the glass in case of severe storms, but they all knew better.

Keegan loved the ceiling-to-floor fountain that separated the living room from the dining room. Like a wall of rushing water, it made the whole house relaxing.

The property was pretty amazing. Her mother loved rocks of all kinds, and her brother liked to use them for free running, so they had large rocks landscaped around the place. Running trails with sporadic workout stations for training wove seamlessly with the land. They had a huge shooting range that would make any soldier envious. To top it all off, they had a stunning natural swimming pool and an underground shelter that could hold everyone, even the extended family. They kept the shelter stocked with enough supplies to last a year if they needed it, although they hoped they would never have to.

Aunt Brigid arrived first with Keegan's cousins, Keara and Jonathan. Of the three sisters, Brigid was the extravagant one. She had on designer jeans that had to cost over two hundred dollars and a bright red, low-plunging wrap shirt that Keegan knew had to be a high-end label. An outrageously expensive purse pulled the outfit together. Brigid's husband worked hard to keep her in the lap of luxury. Keegan loved tagging along with her Aunt Brigid, who liked any excuse to shop until she dropped. Plus, always the life of the party, Brigid could make anyone laugh.

Shortly after Brigid arrived, Katrina showed up with her two children, Merrick and Mackena.

The first thing Katrina said was, "Nice shirt, Brigid."

With a knowing glance down at her chest, Brigid retorted, "Hey, these are bought and paid for. I need to flaunt them every chance I get."

Keegan could hear her mother laughing in the kitchen. *Let the chaos begin.*

Once all the kids arrived, they wanted to play hide-and-seek. Of course, this wasn't a fair game. Keegan always won. Even though they could all visualize the others in their mind, no one else could disappear at will. What could she say? They liked to play and she liked to win.

Warrick ran around giggling as he followed his cousins. He loved having other kids to play with.

Keegan enjoyed watching the kids use their gifts. Looking for his sister, Jonathan used telekinesis to move things around. Merrick turned into a bunny and hopped around with Mackena chasing after him.

No one knew what Mack's gift would be; gifts didn't usually develop until the elves turned five.

Keegan always thought Keara felt out of place. Her cousin knew she wasn't quite like the other elves. Everyone else had pale skin and flushed cheeks. Not Keara. She had beautiful light mocha skin with rosy cheeks and pointy ears. They always tried to convince her how lucky she was, but she had yet to see it.

Her coloring came from her father. Usually elves only partnered with other elves. But Brigid had fallen in love with a warlock before she met her destined partner, and Keara was conceived.

Keara could change the weather, or turn on and off anything electrical—and that was just for now. As she grew, she would find out more about her abilities. Unfortunately, her warlock father took off; they never heard from again. Eventually, Brigid agreed to meet her chosen mate and she had been with him ever since.

Keegan's mom sounded off from the kitchen. "Kids, come in to eat."

"Mom, we're not finished," Keegan groaned.

"Now!"

The kids mumbled as they headed to the dining room, where the delicious food quickly ended the complaining.

Keegan noticed her uncle had arrived. Nicknamed Paul Bunyan for his incredible height and weight—over 200 pounds, quite large for an elf—he was deep in conversation with Keegan's dad.

Keegan's grandmother finished icing the cake. It looked delicious. They sang *Happy Birthday*, and then Merrick tore through his presents, most of which he liked. He opened one and started to say, "Hey, I didn't ask—" Then he stopped mid-sentence. "This is awesome! I've always wanted one."

They all looked over at Brigid, who could manipulate thoughts. She just shrugged her shoulders and smiled. Always the black sheep of the family, she had no issue using her power to have a little fun.

After the party ended, Keegan said goodnight, heading up to her room to get ready for school the next day. She had a big test in physics. Math and science came easy to her, so she didn't need to study—although she was not even in the same ballpark as her Uncle John when it came to numbers.

Still, something about science drew her in, and it was like her mind worked differently than other kids'. When teachers asked her to explain a problem, she would get the correct answer, but often in a way they had never thought of doing it. Sometimes they even thought Keegan had cheated because she finished so much faster than the others—and she didn't have to write out all the work to get the correct answer.

She planned to sleep well tonight. She knew she'd ace the test, easy.

Chapter 7

Keegan smiled as she walked down the hall and saw her friends waiting for her. She attended a Catholic school and—other than the uniforms—she thought it was fantastic. Oddly enough for a teenager, she loved going to school. There, she felt normal around her human friends.

Like the other girls, she managed to add some individuality to the uniforms with jewelry, makeup, and hair accessories. Lately, she'd taken to adding a scarf to her uniform, and so far no one had told her to take it off. She'd picked up that fashion trend on her trip to Dubai with her family. They traveled a lot, at least twice a year, and always took trips out of the country. Her parents wanted them to see that there was more to the world than the United States.

Keegan saw Katie timidly walking up to her. Katie had a hard time making friends and, even though the two of them had gotten close, Keegan sensed that Katie still didn't feel like part of the gang.

"Did you finish your math homework?" Katie asked.

"Of course, this morning on the ride over here." Keegan shifted her backpack to the other shoulder. The thing weighed a ton.

"I have no idea how you can do that," Katie said. "It takes me hours to do math work."

"Do you need any help?"

"Yeah, but just on a couple of questions."

"No problem, I'll help you at the end of English class."

Katie smiled gratefully. "You're a life saver. I don't think I would pass without your help."

Keegan wondered what Katie and her other human friends would think if they found out what she was, but he couldn't reveal her secret anyway. She imagined what would happen if she told them; they would look at her like some kind of freak. Humans seemed to fear magic— and anything unfamiliar.

Anna and Lauren had Keegan's locker open and were applying their makeup when she walked up.

"You guys really need to get your own mirrors," Keegan said, rolling her eyes.

"There's no fun in that. Besides, your mirror is magical or something. It makes us look amazing," Lauren said over her shoulder.

"Uh-huh, I'm sure the $5.99 Target mirror has magical properties."

Keegan pushed them aside to stow her backpack and check her own makeup.

In the mirror, Keegan saw Donald behind he; he was so cute with his orange hair. He happened to look up at the same time, and she met his blue eyes in the mirror. She smiled at him, but he couldn't see.

Donald turned away from Keegan. *Why does she have to be an elf?* Not that he had an issue with the fact that she wasn't human. He wasn't human either. But elves took the secrecy thing way more seriously than any creatures he knew. He never got why they kept their powers to themselves. And sheltering Keegan like that bordered on ridiculous. Everyone knew about her family, but she had no clue about them.

His feelings for her drove him crazy. He knew that she could never share them, not in the way he needed. Being an elf meant she could only really love her chosen mate. He could date her, but it would never lead anywhere. Last year, she had chased him for a while, and he had told her he only liked her as a friend—one of the hardest things he ever had to do. But he'd rather be her friend than a passing fancy so he'd settled for that. He had to settle for that.

Taking another quick glance at Keegan, he banged his head back against the front of his locker. He loved everything about her. She was funny, smart, friendly, confident, considerate, and adorably clumsy, not to mention insanely beautiful. The room felt brighter the moment Keegan walked in. *Ugh.* He felt so corny just thinking about his feelings for her.

Sam, who happened to be one of the hottest guys in school, threw a piece of paper across the hallway at her. Keegan tried to look cool by catching it, but of course she failed miserably. Anna picked up the crumbled paper and hit Spencer in the head, which made them all laugh.

Donald, Sam, Spencer, and Calvron were inseparable. On the rare occasion that one of them would wander off by himself, he usually complained about the others. Everyone said they were worse than women in a beauty shop.

The bell rang and students scattered to their classrooms.

Keegan aced her test, and the rest of the day went by in a blur. Her least favorite part of the day was gym class. Everyone made fun of her lack of coordination.

Today, things felt different, though. Even the coach noticed. They played soccer and not once did she trip and fall or miss the ball. For the first time ever, Keegan scored a goal and she even had some decent blocks. She felt strong and confident.

Obviously, her training with Thaddeus was paying off. Maybe her father had something when he said time and practice could change anything. They had certainly worked for Thaddeus.

While Keegan enjoyed high school, her brother was homeschooled. All elf children destined to be warriors started homeschooling in the sixth grade. It allowed them to focus on their training, which included absorbing vast amounts of knowledge and honing their analytical skills. Most of their training took place at a camp where they spent hours in the field learning the ways of a warrior, then they completed their studies at home on their own. They spent countless hours reading and had a strong grasp of history. Her brother could recite whole books, which she found kind of creepy.

As Keegan walked out of school, her phone went off in her pocket. She grabbed it and looked at the caller ID; it was her Aunt Kat.

"Hey, what's up?" Keegan said.

"Can you babysit tonight? Drew and I need a date night."

"How could I say no to my favorite aunt?"

"Uh-huh. I thought Brigid was your favorite since she spoils you."

"Fine, then. It's a tie."

"Well, hopefully I'll be your favorite after you see the present I got for you."

Later that evening, Katrina walked through the door with the biggest grin on her face, obviously rather proud of herself for something. "Guess which of your favorite aunts has four tickets to *30 Seconds to Mars?*"

Keegan squealed with delight. The concert had been sold out for weeks.

"Just make sure to tell those girls that there will be no making out with their boyfriends on my watch." Kat took them to many concerts, and the last time she got mad at Lauren for meeting up with Josh and making out during the whole show. She'd said they could do plenty of that on their own time.

Keegan called Anna and Lauren right away and put them on a three-way call. "Kat just hooked us up with *30 Seconds to Mars* tickets!" Keegan squealed.

She had to move the phone away from her ear when the other two girls started screaming. "I know—she's the best. I have to go; I'm watching Merrick and Mackenna tonight. We'll go over what we'll wear at school."

The girls said their goodbyes, and Keegan turned to face Katrina.

"They say they love you and that you are the most amazing person in the world."

Kat smiled, her face glowing.

Chapter 8

Rourk ran swiftly through the woods as his attacker closed in on him. He could hear his own heartbeat pounding in his head. Sweat poured down his face and he felt pure joy. He lived for this kind of stuff. He was born to do it. He was leading his victim…

It would all be over soon.

He loved the sound of branches cracking under his pursuer's feet. That kind of sloppy footwork deserved a reprimand, which he would deliver after the chase ended.

Slowing down, Rourk took cover behind a large tree. He listened, and heard only the familiar sounds of nature: birds chirping, squirrels running, even the sound of a deer in the distance. He did not hear the sound of footsteps. This brought a grin to his face. Perhaps he had found a worthy opponent after all. He could take the easy way and close his eyes—but that would be cheating. He scanned quickly and saw nothing.

Think, Rourk.

Even in the vast woods, the cat-and-mouse game meant his pursuer wouldn't be far. The quiet surprised him; he expected sounds of heavy breathing, since they'd been running for hours.

Then, like a lightbulb going on, Rourk knew. He looked *up*. "You are a sly little devil," he said. Taking aim with his paintball gun, he fired. "Show yourself."

The boy dropped nimbly from the tree and eyed Rourk. After a brief moment, he crossed the space between them, removing his paintball mask.

Rourk froze, shocked. The kid couldn't have been more than twelve. The boy's eyes perplexed him even more. They were the same clear blue-green as his chosen's, but this kid's eyes looked older—wiser.

Rourk kept his face still; even caught off guard, a warrior never showed his thoughts on his face.

"What is your name?" Rourk asked.

"My name is Thaddeus, and you are Rourk."

Stunned, Rourk demanded, "How do you know my name?"

"Someday you'll be my brother-in-law," he said, as if it were obvious.

Rourk took a moment to process the information. "Why did you stop running and climb the tree?"

Thaddeus smiled, "I knew you were done playing. You'd have captured me after you faked a fall."

Speechless, Rourk just stared at him. Finally, he said, "So you're Richard's son. I have heard a lot about you. I'll tell your father that he should be proud to have such a remarkable son. No student has ever come close to catching me."

"I'll get you next time." After a slight pause, Thaddeus grinned impishly. "Probably."

Rourk laughed, unable to help himself. He shouldn't form friendships with his students, but he liked Thaddeus.

All at once, it dawned on him. Richard, the man who he looked up to the most, was his chosen's father. How could that be? Richard had never treated him any differently than the others. Rourk shook his head, grateful he hadn't learned this when he was younger. Over the years, he'd proven himself to Richard—without the added stress of trying to impress his future father-in-law.

"Have you told her anything about me?" Rourk asked softly.

He replied, "Only your name."

"Why would you do that?"

"Someday she will be in danger, and you will need to save her. She has to be able to call you."

This rattled Rourk to the core. He knew better than to ask for more details, even though he wanted to grab the boy and shake it out of him. He couldn't ask a seer for details. He could barely believe that Thaddeus had told him as much as he did—and given his sister the ability to call Rourk when she needed help.

Rourk looked him in the eyes. "Thank you. You have my word that I will do everything in my power to keep your sister safe. Can I ask you one thing?"

Thaddeus shrugged, eyeing Rourk with interest. "That depends."

Meeting his eyes, Rourk asked, "What's her name?"

Thaddeus laughed. "Her name is Keegan."

Rourk said the name in his head a few times, getting used to the sound of it.

"The name suits her," Thaddeus said. "It means 'little fiery one'."

"Why am I pulled to her, but not her to me?"

"Magic, of course. You know the cloak hiding lifemates from each other until they turn eighteen? I had yours removed."

"How did you manage that?"

"That's two questions, Rourk. You know I can't disclose that information. But I will tell you this. Once it was known that I was the child in the prophecy, my reach became pretty much unlimited. I have at my disposal anything that could allow our race to live on."

Rourk nodded his head at the boy in understanding, his chosen's name echoing in his mind.

Rourk sat in his office staring at the wall. His mind raced. *How had Thaddeus even been assigned to him?* As Keegan's father, Richard should want to keep them separated. The only logical explanation was that they wanted him to know. Maybe they had faith that he could change the future. So there had to be some deadly threat to Keegan that they wanted to neutralize.

Attempting to change the natural course of destiny was not done lightly. It had to be happening soon, before Keegan turned eighteen and they met. Could it be something to do with the great battle? Why else would they intervene?

Rourk didn't want to overstep his boundaries, but he had to talk to Richard. He made his way across camp, heading directly into Richard's office.

When Richard saw Rourk, he broke into his easy smile. "I've been waiting for you."

Rourk was always surprised by Richard's ability to put people at ease. One of the traits that made him an exceptional leader, it explained why men were so devoted to him.

"I wasn't sure if I should come talk to you or not. However, after going over it repeatedly, I had to. There is a flaw in this plan."

"Every plan has a flaw, but we must make do with what we have." Richard gave Rourk a placid smile and crossed his hands over the desk to lean forward.

Rourk paused and considered his words. "Can I war game this out with you?"

Richard sighed. "Very well. I will hear you out."

War gaming meant thinking through the outcome of a mission beforehand. That way they could make sure they anticipated the variables that could affect the outcome.

"I don't think this will work without Keegan being aware of the plan. How can we be certain that she will even think of me if she is in danger?"

This brought a loud laugh from Richard. "Son, you have a lot to learn about women. There are many flaws to our plan, but *that* is not one of them."

His reaction surprised Rourk. "How can you be so certain?"

Richard smiled. "As warriors, we do not fear death. We couldn't possibly do our job if we did. That's what makes us different from the others. We simply hope to die bravely. However, on every occasion that I have come close to death, I have always thought of my wife. So you can imagine a sixteen-year-old would think of her chosen."

Rourk stared at the man, trying to hide his astonishment. "Will I meet her—before she even turns seventeen?"

Richard put his hand on Rourk's shoulder. "This is why you're good enough for my daughter, and the reason that I am relieving you of your training duties. Now your job is to protect Keegan."

Chapter 9

Thaddeus banged on her door and Keegan groaned. Why did he have to bother her so early? She tried to convince him to let her train in the evening, but Thaddeus wouldn't hear of it. She couldn't believe her little brother bossed her around like that. Wasn't there some unspoken rule putting the eldest sibling in charge?

"I'm coming." She yelled, flinging off the covers. She stomped into the bathroom stared at herself in the mirror. She looked exhausted. Her eyes had dark circles, and her skin looked paler than usual. *Lovely.*

Quickly, she flung her hair into a ponytail and pulled on a pair of black workout pants, sports bra, and a Powerpuff Girls t-shirt for inspiration.

Keegan made her way down the stairs and into the workout room where Thaddeus waited, his face all business.

"Let the torture begin." Keegan mumbled.

Their father walked in to observe the training.

In the middle of their sprints, Richard's voice boomed, "Vanish, Keegan!"

She hesitated, which, of course, was a mistake. She hated to disappoint him.

He called them over and told Thaddeus to work on her reaction skills. "She needs to be able to use her gift without hesitation, no matter what," he said.

Keegan hated when they talked about her like she wasn't there.

Richard turned to her. "Keegan, you have a skill that any soldier would kill for, but it does you no good if you're not able to use it when needed. Before a knife comes down on you, a bullet is fired, or someone gets a hold on you, you should be gone. Of course, it's only to be used in a life or death situation, and until then you fight. We cannot give away our secret, and if you went invisible in front of a human, it might draw some attention. Nonetheless, do not hesitate if your life is at stake."

Keegan started to say something about those scenarios being ridiculous, but her father's expression stopped her. She just nodded.

Thaddeus drilled her for another hour after her dad left, but she didn't feel as if she'd improved at all. Keegan had only used her gift for fun before, and it had always been at a leisurely pace. She wasn't sure if she could do what her father wanted.

When they took a water break, Keegan asked Thaddeus something that had been weighing on her mind a lot lately. "Thad, why don't I ever see dark elves? Or, I mean, very rarely, anyway."

Thaddeus wiped his face with a towel. "It's not a big mystery. They just don't come down south very often. They prefer the cold up north."

She crinkled up her nose. "I guess I just don't get why we're fighting. I mean, yeah, yeah, history and ancient rules, but it just seems like we should be past that by now."

"Yeah, well, talk to the dark elves about that." Thaddeus threw the towel down and walked back towards the center of the room.

"Are they really that bad?" Keegan raised an eyebrow.

Thaddeus's jaw clenched and he looked away. "You have no idea."

"What's the worst thing you've seen them do?" Keegan challenged him.

"You know I can't talk about that stuff, but let's just say that elves in the army of light do not always return from missions."

Keegan's eyes widened. "You mean they're killed by dark elves?"

"That's exactly what I mean. Let's finish up this training so I can get back to my studies."

She'd known that her father got his scars somehow, but she never wanted to think about where they came from. Just hearing that dark elves had taken the lives of elfin soldiers made her blood boil.

Keegan had a date tonight, a first date with a new boy in school. She had been surprised when Tom asked her out. He seemed really shy. With so much on her mind, she wanted to say no, but her mother insisted she act like she normally would. *Elf parents are way too concerned about their kids being normal,* Keegan thought with a sigh.

Looking through her closet, she tried to find an outfit that wouldn't look like she had tried too hard. She settled on a pair of skinny jeans and turquoise v-neck shirt. They were only going bowling after all.

The doorbell rang, so she grabbed her sweater and hurried down the stairs. Her legs burned with every step. These days she always felt sore.

"I'll see you guys later," Keegan yelled into the living room.

Her father yelled back, "Remember the number one rule of dating."

Keegan rolled her eyes. "I'm not going to walk out if he sits with his back to the door, Dad. Not everyone believes they need to be on high alert at all times."

Richard appeared from the living room and walking towards his daughter. "If he's not able or willing to protect you, he is not worth your time." He kissed her on the head. "Have fun and don't stay out too late."

He stared at the door after it closed. It was hard to believe that she was so grown up. In his mind, he still pictured her as a little girl with pigtails begging for a ride on his shoulders. The memories brought a smile to his face.

Rourk no longer had to wait for Keegan to think his name. She was his responsibility now. He watched as a truck pulled up. A tall guy with dark hair got out and went to the door. Keegan came out looking happy and beautiful, as usual. The guy opened the door for her, and she grabbed his shoulder to pull herself up into the cab.

Rourk felt a pang of jealousy.

Once they pulled out, he followed them at a distance. *Where are they going, and who is this guy?*

Eventually they pulled into the bowling alley. Rourk groaned. *You have to be kidding me.* He decided not to go in. He watched her from the outside, using his mind's eye.

As he watched her bowl, he laughed to himself. *She is a terrible bowler.* She barely hit any pins. She seemed to be enjoying herself though, perhaps a little too much. He saw her touch her date's arm a couple of times. The kid got a strike, and she hugged him.

Rourk clenched his jaw, then forced himself relax.

A black pickup pulled into the parking spot beside him. A guy hopped out and hurried around the passenger side.

Rourk's body went into hyper-alert mode.

It was a creature of the dark.

Rourk closed his eyes and pulled the guy into focus—pointed ears and dark hair. Definitely a dark elf.

What were they doing here?

His thoughts jumped to Keegan, inside and unaware, as the man helped a woman from the cab of the truck. Rourk didn't bother to verify it—her long, thick black hair and even inkier eyes proved she was dark, too.

Opening his door as quietly as possible, Rourk jumped out of his truck. The couple walked closer to the door, so he had to think fast. He crept up behind them.

"Hey," Rourk said evenly.

The elf turned and smirked, twisting the jagged scar down the left side of his face. The pupil of his left eye was paler than the right. "Well, what do we have here? An elf of the light wants to play?" In one smooth motion, the dark elf pulled a blade out of his belt.

The woman leered at Rourk and backed away to watch.

An eerie calm overtook Rourk at the sight of the elf's knife.

After a moment's hesitation while both men played the scene out in their heads, the dark elf swiped, the blade slicing through the air with deadly efficiency. Rourk moved forward and grabbed the man's wrist before the knife could make contact, turning into the man's momentum and trapping his knife arm between his own.

Rourk slammed his elbow into the elf's bicep. The dark elf grunted, but somehow held onto the knife. He jerked it back, the tip slicing into Rourk's arm at an awkward angle. Furious, Rourk slammed his knee into the elf's stomach, causing him to double over, but the knife remained firmly in his grip.

The dark elf lashed out desperately, launching his body into Rourk. They fell into a heap on the ground, and the knife slashed into Rourk's shoulder, the cold steel sending pain shooting down his arm. Rourk used his own body weight to level the dark elf, rolling the man beneath him. Rourk reared back and loosed a violent punch to the elf's temple.

The dark elf fell limp, out cold—for now.

Barely winded by the scuffle, Rourk pushed up to his feet, whipping around to stare at the woman. She stood wide-eyed on the sidewalk, glancing from her boyfriend to Rourk and back.

Rourk took a single step towards her, and she started running.

Chuckling, Rourk let her go. She was a tiny wisp of a thing, anyway, and he had to deal with the male dark elf's body.

He looked around to make sure no one had seen the fight. Rourk dragged the elf over to his truck, making sure his keys were in his pocket before he pushed the elf onto the bench seat. If anyone noticed, they would think it was just some drunk.

Rourk pulled out his phone and called Richard. When the older man's gruff voice crossed the line, Rourk quickly filled him in on what had occurred.

"Bring the dark elf to the camp," Richard said with an edge to his voice.

"I can't leave Keegan," Rourk replied.

Richard swore under his breath. "Where are you?"

Rourk gave him directions. After he hung up, he dug around in the bed of his truck until he found some old, fraying rope. He opened the cab and tied the dark elf's hands behind his back.

Keegan's father arrived shortly after. Richard offered his hand and they shook. "Rourk."

"Sir." Rourk nodded. He pulled open the door and motioned to the unconscious elf. "Be careful. He won't be out much longer."

Richard nodded. As always, the man's immensity struck Rourk. The leader of the light picked up the dark elf as if he weighed nothing and threw him over his shoulder, striding off to his truck.

A couple of hours later, the kid drove Keegan straight back to her house. Rourk watched him walk her to the door. *Don't do it.*

The kid stood there awkwardly, then turned and waved goodbye as he went back to his truck.

Rourk needed to pull himself together. If they'd kissed, he didn't know if he could have controlled himself. He wondered briefly if the assignment might be too much for him. Richard wouldn't have asked him to do it if it weren't important. He needed to think of her as an assignment and nothing more.

Easier said than done.

Chapter 10

Keegan walked outside and found her mother on the porch swing. She sat down next to her.

The day was another of sunshine, but the air held a chilly breeze. Emerald, wrapped in a brightly colored shawl, had her feet planted firmly on the wooden boards of the porch as she swung.

After a moment's pause, Keegan said, "Mom, I keep thinking about Anna's mother. I really think you should give her a healing."

Emerald glanced at her daughter. Keegan had never before asked her to give a healing. "I guess I could call her. I think she'd be surprised, though. It not like we talk on a regular basis."

Keegan smiled. "Thanks. Try not to let on that Anna told me about it?"

"Well, that will be almost impossible, Keegan. I'll figure something out so Anna doesn't get in trouble for confiding in you."

After Keegan walked away, Emerald could not stop thinking about their conversation. She felt the need to help Anna's mother. Anna was one of Keegan's best friends. Whatever Anna's mother went through would affect Anna. She hesitated and then headed inside to the phone.

It rang several times before a sleepy voice answered, "Hello?"

"Hello, Jennifer, it's Emerald. Keegan's mother," she added.

"Hi, there. What's up?"

"I know this is unusual, but would you mind if I came over to visit?"

There was a brief silence; she'd probably surprised Jennifer. "Ah...sure. Of course, you can come over."

Anna's parents lived modestly in a small stone ranch house not too far from

Keegan's own home. Jennifer, a tall, thin woman with dark circles under her brown eyes, had pulled her long brown hair into a messy ponytail. Dressed casually in jeans and a plain white t-shirt, with pink flip-flops on her long feet, she met Emerald at the door with a tentative smile.

Emerald decided not to beat around the bush.

"I overheard the girls talking, and I understand you're having problems with depression."

Clearly uncomfortable, Jennifer looked down at her feet. "Why would Anna tell them that?"

Emerald reached out and put her hand on her shoulder. "There is nothing to be embarrassed about. I think I might be able to help you."

"How so?"

"I'm a second degree reiki healer," Emerald explained. "It's a type of healing that can help remove blockages, like the ones that cause depression."

Jennifer seemed interested. For a split second, she almost looked hopeful. "It's worth a shot at this point. What's the saying—it can only go up from here?"

Emerald smiled. "We'll need a quiet place where you can lie down."

"You're in luck—everyone's out for the day. I don't need to kick the cat out, do I?"

"The cat should be fine." Emerald liked that Jennifer tried to have a sense of humor despite the sadness that obviously filled her.

Jennifer led her into the spare bedroom, a quiet room in the back of the house with soft blue walls and minimal furniture—a twin bed with no headboard but a pretty floral quilt and a white chest of drawers holding a single vase of fresh roses. It was cool and dim.

"All you have to do is close your eyes and relax," Emerald told her as Jennifer slid onto the bed. "You may or may not feel heat coming from my hands, but even if you don't, it will still work."

With a serious nod, Jennifer settled against the pillow and closed her eyes.

"I'm going to turn on some relaxing music, and then we will start." Emerald pulled her iPod from her back pocket and connected it to the small radio sitting on the bedside table. The light sound of flutes and chimes filled the room.

Moving her hands over Jennifer's body, Emerald quickly realized something was not right. Humans had a certain type of energy and Jennifer's was not human. *What in the world was she?* How could she not have known? All those years Anna had been coming to their house. Still, Emerald kept her thoughts to herself. She gave Jennifer a complete healing.

Jennifer seemed amazed by how happy she felt afterwards. "I don't recall feeling this normal in a long time. It's like a cloud has been lifted from my soul.

I'd kiss ya, but you don't seem like the type," Jennifer joked.

"No kissing required. I'm glad I could help." Emerald knew exactly what the other woman felt, because she could feel it, too. Humans believed that healing drained healers, but that couldn't be further from the truth. Every time Emerald gave a healing, she felt as renewed as the person who received it. She almost felt selfish for using her gift on others when she received so much in return.

As she walked out the door, Emerald handed Jennifer a St. Dymphna medallion. "Keep this with you always."

Grasping it in her hand, Jennifer said, "What is it for?"

Emerald thought for a moment, then said, "She is the saint of emotional and mental disorders, and the medallion will help ward off the depression."

Jennifer's eyes teared up. Already, the dark circles under them were fading. She sniffed, brushing away a tear before it could fall. "Thank you. I can never repay you for this."

Emerald smiled. "There is nothing to repay. Please call me if you feel it coming back."

Emerald might not have known what kind of creature Jennifer was, but she knew Jennifer was on the side of the light. She also knew that there would be no call. During the healing, she had removed all the blockages. Jennifer would be the healthiest she had ever been in her life. Plus, the medallion had been energized with healing properties.

Jennifer shut the door and thought, *Reiki, my ass! That woman is gifted.*

All these years and she had been clueless that Keegan's family wasn't human. Whatever Emerald was, Jennifer now was in her debt.

Jennifer had lost her will to live and had been walking around like a shell of a person. Now she felt energized and more alive than ever. Her husband would come home to a different woman. She wondered if it would be enough to save their marriage.

But, even if it wasn't, she would be fine. She was strong enough to be on her own. She should have known marrying a human would be bad for her soul. Jennifer debated asking Anna if she knew anything about Keegan's secret, but she decided against it.

Ultimately, it was Keegan's secret to keep.

Chapter 11

Thaddeus was beyond frustrated. He had been working with his mother for weeks, trying to shield his gift. It seemed impossible. They had finally admitted either he needed to be older or his sight was too strong to block.

He had been getting flashes of visions more often. With the battle rapidly approaching, he worried about whether they would be ready. Sometimes he wondered what it would be like to have a normal mind without constant visions.

Thaddeus pushed his thoughts aside. He knew better than to let his mind wander during a fight. He needed to focus on Keegan; she had gotten stronger and faster. The training had made a tremendous difference in her skills.

Thaddeus pressed forward with his attack, forcing Keegan backwards. He immediately lunged forward again, but Keegan swiftly blocked his sword. In a quick burst, she pushed him back several steps. With little effort, Thaddeus parried her strikes and then went after her.

They'd been sparring for over an hour. He decided to end it now. He drove forward and lifted his sword for the final blow. Just before his sword made contact, she vanished. Thaddeus sheathed his sword with slight smile on his lips.

"Way to go, Keegan—just disappear when I'm about to win!"

Keegan reappeared two steps to the left, grinning.

His voice quieter, Thaddeus said, "I mean it, though. That's what Dad wanted you to do."

A goofy grin spread across her face. Her brother rarely admitted that she impressed him. "Thanks." And she vanished again.

Wiping the sweat off his face, he grabbed a drink and headed for the shower. He needed to talk to his father. After changing into a pair of jeans and his favorite Metallica t-shirt, he headed in his father's direction.

Thaddeus stood outside of Richard's study, which looked more like a library than an office. He knocked sharply on the door before entering. One of his favorite rooms in the house, it had teak bookshelves covering all the walls. Taking a deep breath, he enjoyed the faint scent of wood. This room gave credence to one of his father's favorite sayings: *Knowledge is power not only in warfare, but in life.* He had books on every topic imaginable.

His father looked up from his book and leaned back in his chair, giving his son his undivided attention.

"I believe she is ready," Thaddeus said.

Richard sighed, putting down his book to rub his face with both hands. He looked back up, his relief apparent on his face. "I was worried that you would not have enough time to prepare her."

Thad's first visions as a child had shown Keegan dying. He must have been about six at the time. His visions did not always show the whole picture, usually just snapshots, and he could still picture this one as clear as day.

She lay on the ground, an arrow through her heart. Blood sprayed everywhere. People screamed. Swords clashed. Blackness. As quickly as that vision ended, another one started. In this one, he saw a fork in the road. Keegan, laughing, ran to the right. Behind her came a tall boy with reddish hair, also laughing. He grabbed her by the waist and swung her around.

Keegan was a pain, but she was still his sister, and he couldn't stand the thought of her dying. Especially if he had a chance to prevent it. Thaddeus should never have told his father about the vision, but, at the time, he did know the code for seers—he had been just a boy. His father had been hesitant about intervening at first, but for his own flesh and blood…

At the time, Thaddeus hadn't known about the prophecy or the Great Battle, either. As a child, he'd been sure that the vision meant that if Keegan was with the boy with rusty hair, she would live and, if not, she would die.

It had taken him a while to find the boy. Once he recognized Rourk, Thaddeus's father seemed okay with the whole idea. Rourk was a warrior, and not just any warrior—he was a great warrior. The Army of the Light had already noticed Rourk's natural talent.

With no good plans available, Thaddeus asked the elders to remove the cloak so Rourk could see Keegan. Rourk would know her, but she would not know him.

Unbeknownst to his father, Thaddeus also decided to give Keegan Rourk's name. She always begged him to tell her about her chosen, so he just finally told her Rourk's name. Thaddeus also told her if she ever felt like she was in danger, she should think his name.

After Thaddeus left the room, Richard relaxed against the back of his chair. He had always seen something special in his son. Although only a boy, Thaddeus had never been a regular child. Learning that the prophecy referred to his son hadn't surprised him.

His mind drifted to Rourk, another extraordinary young man. As commander of the specialized unit, Richard oversaw the preparation of the young warriors. The ones who showed promise received special training at a young age, preparing them to join their specialized unit. Rourk had stood out, even earlier than most. Everyone saw his potential. Richard had never come across a better warrior.

When the young warriors finished training and came of age, they spent time in the human military. They could choose their branch as long as they ended up in the special operations community. Then they could choose to stay in the human military or return to the elfin army of the light. Almost all elves return to the elfin military after their stint with the humans. Richard had decided to stay in the U.S. Army Special Forces until he reached retirement age. He could not walk away from the many wars being waged, and he could make a valuable contribution there.

Now retired, he felt glad to be back amongst his people. He belonged here.

Chapter 12

Keegan tossed piles of clothes on the floor, searching for the perfect outfit to wear to the concert.

Why is it always so hard to find something to wear? She looked around her room. She'd flung clothes all over the place. *So many outfits and still nothing to wear.*

Picking up her phone, she texted Lauren to meet her at the mall. If she couldn't find anything to wear in her room, then she needed to buy something.

Keegan's mom dropped her off at Target, and she walked from there. It wasn't that far, but she still felt annoyed that her mom didn't take her the whole way—because the walk would be good for her. As much as Keegan hated to admit it, she did feel better with the sun shining down on her and the fresh air on her skin.

Rourk followed, not far behind, and wondered where she lead him this time. Following her, he'd noticed patterns in her behavior. For instance, she couldn't pass a Starbucks without getting a white chocolate mocha—which she bought almost daily. And, of course, she went shopping. *What could she possibly want or need all the clothing for?*

Keegan's phone bothered Rourk the most. She texted constantly, oblivious to everything around her. This left her so vulnerable that he wished he could grab her phone and smash it. Taking a deep breath, he reminded himself that he would protect her. He would be her eyes and ears.

Since Rourk could detect other non-humans, he had noticed more creatures of the dark lately. They were coming out of the woodwork. He had always known they were there, but his new assignment had heightened his awareness. He wondered if Keegan knew how many of the kids at her school weren't human. Rourk couldn't always tell what kind of creature they were, but he always knew if they were with the light or dark. So far, he had only seen her interact with others from the light.

They weren't elves, though, that much he knew.

Rourk found it interesting that Keegan got so much pleasure from shopping. He didn't have any sisters, and his mother had died when he was young, so Rourk had not spent much time around the opposite sex. He had never even had a girlfriend. Rourk had left school younger than most, because he showed promise.

Keegan decided on a white tank top and skinny jeans. Now, on to accessories. She wished she could have all the many beautiful things in the world.

She'd been shopping with Lauren for hours. They went in store after store, trying on hats, sunglasses, shoes, and jewelry. They spent most of the time they laughing at each other, like when Keegan put on a floppy hat and oversized glasses, then walked the aisle like a catwalk. She made a quick spin and turned to Lauren, lowering her glasses, which inspired Lauren to join in. They put on their own fashion show, and people stared at them, but they didn't notice or care.

When the girls finally finished shopping, Lauren's mother picked them up and dropped Keegan off at home. Rourk felt relieved, as always, when he knew she arrived home safely. Now, he could go home and get some sleep.

Keegan's mother was folding laundry when she walked in. Emerald leaned her head out of the laundry room door and asked, "What did you get to wear for the concert?"

Keegan smiled. "White tank top and skinny jeans."

Her mother's face changed so quickly it made Keegan's head spin.

Uh-oh. Her mother had a quick temper.

Calmly, Emerald said, "Keegan, go up to your room and pick out your favorite pair of jeans and top."

Puzzled, she went upstairs and did as she was told.

When she returned, her mother glared. "Now throw them in the trash."

A look of shock crossed Keegan's face. "What?"

Her mom went back to folding the clothes. "You have at least a half dozen white tank tops and pairs of skinny jeans upstairs. You are so spoiled, Keegan. You don't even appreciate all you have."

Keegan looked down at the outfit in her hand and back at her mother. "Mom, these are my favorite jeans!"

"Throw them away now, before I change my mind and ground you."

"Can't I at least donate them? They are way too nice to be tossed in the garbage."

Her mother's face softened slightly. "That's a good idea. We'll go through our stuff this weekend and clear out our closets."

Keegan hadn't exactly had that mind. She left the clothes on the counter, stomped up the stairs, and slammed her door. She was so mad at her mother. This was ridiculous—if she had said she got a blue shirt none of this would have happened. Now, she had lost her favorite pair of jeans. Her mom got so mad over the stupidest things. At least she got to keep the outfit for the concert. But she had to give away an outfit that cost twice as much as the new one. It made no sense!

Rourk walked into the house where his father, Greg, sat in the living room with the lights off. Rourk sank into the oversized leather chair across from his father, putting his feet on the coffee table. They sat in silence for several minutes.

"So, how was your day, Dad? Anything interesting going on?"

"Not really, just the usual."

They lapsed back into silence. His father never had much to say. Ever since Rourk's mother died, his dad had closed himself off from everyone, and Rourk missed the days when the man had been filled with life. They used to spend so much time together.

Staring at his father, he thought, *We look nothing alike.* Rourk took after his mother's side of the family. His dad looked like he could be a movie star. He had dark hair graying at the temples, intense blue eyes, and a strong jaw line. The guys at work called him Fisher, kidding him that he looked like the live version of Sam Fisher from *Splinter Cell.* Even with age, the lines just seem to give him more character. Women practically threw themselves at his dad, which just amused Rourk. No one stood a chance though; he was altogether indifferent toward women. Rourk's mother had been the only one for him.

His father didn't bother asking about his day, even though Rourk knew he must have heard about the new assignment. Retired military like Richard, Greg worked with Keegan's dad. Rourk wouldn't exactly call them friends, but they unquestionably had a mutual respect for one another.

Rourk stretched and yawned, "I'm headed to bed. I'll see you tomorrow."

"Goodnight."

Keegan was going to the concert tomorrow. It was going to be a long day, and Rourk needed his sleep.

Chapter 13

Keegan woke up to the sound of a little hand knocking on the door yelling, "Kee-kee-kee!"

Ugh. She pulled the blankets over her head. Why had she taught Warrick how to knock on doors? It was funny when he did it to Thaddeus. He sounded so cute, though, that she couldn't resist. Before long, she gave in and opened the door.

Her little brother ran in and crawled in bed with her. She couldn't possibly stay mad when he always woke up so happy. Reaching over, she grabbed her iPad and selected *30 Seconds to Mars* to play. She was already excited about the concert even though it was still ten hours away.

Keegan finally stumbled downstairs a couple hours later. Both her aunts had come over for a visit. It was strange to see the three sisters sitting together; they looked a lot alike, and yet each was so different from the other. They all had round faces and the same blue eyes, with subtle differences in their noses and lips. Of course, they all had different hair—Brigid's, long, dark, and wavy; Kat's, long, curly, and auburn; and her mother's ginger locks, recently chopped into a short pixie cut.

Keegan felt glad she only had brothers. She wouldn't want to deal with sisters. They seemed to be getting along now, but usually drama lurked around the corner when they got together. Too tired to pay attention to what they were talking about, she and Warrick went to lie on the couch.

From outside, Keegan heard lead hitting steel. Obviously her dad and Thaddeus were down at the range. She would have joined them if she weren't so tired.

Her family sure enjoyed shooting guns. They constantly had competitions, but, to make things fair, her dad had to shoot with only one hand and from twice the distance as everyone else. Of course, he still managed to win most of the time.

Ironically, tradition prohibited elves from using guns in any battles between light and dark—and forbade any other modern high tech gadgets. They honored their ancestors by keeping the traditions. Her father claimed that their honor demanded it. He always added that true warriors preferred to meet their enemy face to face. She'd been learning a lot of these things from Thaddeus lately, things that she'd been clueless about before.

The day passed more quickly than Keegan expected. She read some of her new book and edited more photos. Then it was time to get ready for the concert. Katrina would be there soon, and then they would pick up the rest of girls on the way. Yet, for some reason, Keegan couldn't shake the feeling that something terrible was going to happen.

Keegan knocked on her brother's door.

"Come in," he yelled.

When she walked in, he had his nose to the television screen and the game controller in his hands, as always.

She walked up to him and said, "Do you think I look good enough to go to the concert?"

He looked up from his game, pursing his lips as he eyed her. "You look even uglier than usual."

Relief washed over her. "Are you sure?" She knew he never lied to her about such things; he just always said the opposite of what he meant. It was kind of their inside joke.

She'd really gone into his room to see if he would warn her about the concert. But he said nothing and went right back to his game, effectively shutting her out. Keegan watched him for a while, then left.

After she shut the door, Thaddeus grimaced. At times, he felt like he couldn't handle his gift. Anyone with his gift soon learned that they must not interfere with fate. But why have this so-called gift if he couldn't help others? He wanted to tell his sister to stay home from the stupid concert. Instead, he took his father's advice and worked on his breathing to control the fear racing through him. Taking a deep breath, he held it for the count of three, exhaled for the count of three, and repeated that until he felt his heartbeat return to normal.

Thaddeus couldn't help feeling restless. He glanced over at his sneakers, but decided he do better without them. He walked through the house and yelled, "Going for a run."

Thaddeus passed through the kitchen where his dad was working on his MacBook. Richard glanced down at his son's feet. "Would you like some company?"

It was impossible to tell his father no, so Thaddeus grumbled, "Sure."

His father shut the laptop and got to his feet. "Give me a second."

Thaddeus waited on one of the large rocks outside the door until his father came out of the house wearing nothing but running shorts. Thaddeus tried not to stare at the scars that covered his body. He'd always been in awe of his father. In the boy's eyes, he looked more like a Viking than an elf. He looked so powerful most people feared him.

His father stroked his red beard, a sure sign that he was thinking.

Thaddeus grinned. "Sure you don't want to grab your shoes, old man?" He knew his father should not run without shoes. His left foot had severe nerve damage, so Thaddeus knew the run would be painful for him. He also knew and appreciated the reasoning behind it. A born leader, his father had a leader's instinct. He could inspire admiration and give others a sense of equality at the same time.

"Lead the way, son."

Thaddeus took off in a sprint, his father close behind him. The wind felt great against his face. He loved feeling the ground beneath his feet. He always felt so free when he was running. Even with his father beside him, it felt like he was alone.

They ran for miles, jumping and dodging fallen trees, mostly staying on the winding trails. Richard knew better than to say anything to his son. He would talk when he felt ready. Right now, the boy just needed his dad to be there for him. Richard loved his family more than anything. He could never truly understand what Thaddeus faced because of his gift. He could only give his son the tools he needed to deal with it. Physical activity was one of those mechanisms.

Eventually, Thaddeus collapsed on the ground, exhausted. Looking over at his father, he mumbled, "Thank you."

Rourk arrived hours before the concert started. From a security standpoint, the situation was not ideal by any means. It would be almost impossible to keep an eye on her from a distance. Tonight he would have to get closer to her than ever before. Just the thought made his pulse race. To his advantage, the place would be packed, and she had no idea what he looked like.

This had turned into more of a nightmare than he had imagined. He needed help to protect her in this chaos, but in reality he had no support. He took some comfort in knowing that Richard knew his daughter's plans and didn't feel the need to send reinforcements.

A staggering number of people came to the concert. Not to mention the numerous creatures of light and dark slipping in among the humans packing the place. Rourk hoped that they'd all come for the same reason—to enjoy the concert.

Rourk pushed his way through the crowd, searching for Keegan. He closed his eyes to find her location in relation to the stage, then headed in that direction. The lights went out and everyone screamed. He felt his chest tighten up. Then what sounded like explosions went off and the stage lit up. The opening act had started.

Rourk's head pounded; the music blared. All around him people danced, sang at the top of their lungs, and crushed up against each other. Every time he advanced, he got pushed back by the crowd. He needed to get close enough to protect her.

The people drinking and smoking pot made him sick. He could never understand how people considered getting drunk and losing control fun. A drunk driver had killed his mother, and not even his father could save her.

With more urgency, he pushed his way through, finally getting Keegan in his sights. Rourk studied her. He noticed she looked back with concern on her face. Did she sense danger? Could she possibly recognize him? Eventually she seemed to relax and enjoy the music. Rourk never even glanced at the stage; he kept his eyes only on her.

He thought it was over, but he forgot about the encores. His whole body tensed. Squealing and giggling, Keegan even took a turn crowd surfing. *What the hell are they doing?* No one seemed bothered—if anything, they seemed excited. Lauren and Anna laughed and screamed. Even her aunt seemed to find it funny. Where were they taking her?

Rourk forced his way through the crowd, but every time he came close, they sent her in a different direction. He closed his eyes and pictured her face. She smiled and yelled with excitement. He scanned the crowd, noting the others being passed around. He had never been to a concert before and hadn't realized how often this happened. Obviously, he should get out more.

He frantically tried to get to her. *Where did she go?* He closed his eyes again; she looked okay, but he could not get her exact location. There were too many people, and it was too dark.

Abruptly, he stopped. She came closer to the wall. Rourk moved across the arena, making it easier for him to push his way through the crowd. He closed his eyes again and did not like what he saw. A look of alarm had replaced Keegan's excitement. Rourk realized the crowd no longer had her. Four guys carried her toward the side of the arena.

Time stood still. Rourk felt the rage building in his chest. He no longer heard the music; people seemed to part, making a path for him. He pushed through as the four men who held Keegan wrestled her out of the crowd. They set her on her feet, and the biggest of the men pushed Keegan toward the wall.

Keegan was terrified.

Her eyes darted frantically around as she tried to think a way out of this situation. *How could this be happening, even with all my training?* She knew she could not defend herself against four guys. A drop of sweat fell from her face, and her heart raced.

The biggest one pushed her up against the wall. She could smell the alcohol on his breath.

"Well, aren't you a fine piece of meat?"

Glaring at him, she said, "Get your hands off me."

"A feisty one, eh?" he laughed.

Without thinking, she drove her knee into his groin. He groaned and doubled over. The others advanced, but the big one yelled, "She's mine."

She wanted to throw up when he groped her chest. *Please don't do this*, she thought. *I belong to Rourk.*

His name pierced Rourk's heart. Nothing mattered to him except keeping her safe. *How dare they put their hands on her?* He wanted to make them pay.

Out of nowhere, Keegan felt her attacker pulled off of her. She looked up just as a flash of light went off. Her heart dropped; she felt like she was in a free fall as she stared into the most beautiful face she'd ever seen. His grey eyes met hers, then he nodded slightly.

After a split second that felt like a lifetime, Keegan whispered, "Rourk?"

He yelled over the crowd, "Go to the exit and text your friends to meet you." His voice sounded like music to her ears—deep, but not too deep, and filled with authority.

As much as she hated to leave, she didn't dare ignore him. She ran away, pushing her way through the people.

Rourk's hand yanked back the guy's head; he covered his mouth so no one would hear him scream. He leaned down and whispered in his ear, "She is mine." Without hesitation he violently wrenched the man's head to the right, then left, snapping his neck. He let the body fall to the ground.

Rourk didn't worry about being noticed. All the noise and darkness made it the perfect kill spot. As he expected, the other three had split. Once they realized they faced more than just a girl, they scattered.

Cowards. What kind of man attacks an innocent girl?

Keegan's heart pounded. She couldn't wrap her mind around what happened. *Was that actually Rourk who saved me? Why was he here?* She looked all over for him, but he was gone.

She felt dirty. She wanted to go home and take a shower. The concert, the mass of bodies and the noise, frightened her now.

Katrina and the girls found her. As they headed out, Anna and Lauren went on and on about how awesome it was that she got to crowd surf. Keegan turned and said, "It wasn't as much fun as you think. I'm probably going to be bruised tomorrow." She wanted to tell them what had happened, but then she would have to explain Rourk. Humans would never understand.

Katrina stayed unusually quiet on the drive home. After they dropped off Keegan's friends, she pulled into a gas station parking lot.

A look of concern on her face, she turned to Keegan and asked, "Are you okay?"

Knowing better than to lie to a mind reader, Keegan shook her head. "I have never been that scared in my life."

Katrina looked about to cry. "I am so sorry—I should never have let that to happen. Your parents are going to kill me."

"You know that's ridiculous. You couldn't have done anything. It ended well, thanks to the mysterious guy who saved me. Katrina, I really think it was my chosen."

Katrina looked at Keegan, but said nothing.

Chapter 14

On his way home, Rourk called Richard to fill him in. He didn't go into details. Rourk told him that a couple of guys had tried to attack Keegan, and he took care of it. Richard asked if the attackers had been a creatures of the dark. Rourk paused for a second. "No, they were human."

Once Rourk knew Keegan got safely home, he headed for home himself. He walked in, finding his father sitting in the same spot as he had the day before.

"I killed a man today," Rourk said.

His father stood up. "Come into the kitchen and we'll talk."

His dad turned on the coffee, his movements methodical. The darkness outside the small kitchen window was absolute. Rourk sat at the table, resting his head in his hands.

"The first kill is always the hardest, but it gets easier," Greg said quietly, turning to face his son.

Rourk met his father's troubled eyes. "Father, the only thing that bothers me is that I felt nothing. No remorse. I always thought it'd be hard to take a life, that it would haunt me. I snapped his neck and walked away as if nothing happened. I felt calm. How could I feel calm about killing?"

Taking his time before he spoke, his father turned away to pour coffee in the mugs. "We know life's sacred—probably better than most because of the loss of your mother. However, since birth you've been trained to be a warrior. It's who you are. It's in your blood. Taking life is part of it. Your training has prepared you. There's no shame in that. If anything, you are lucky. Nothing would make me happier than knowing you're able to escape the nightmares that haunt some soldiers."

They lapsed back into silence as his father placed Rourk's coffee in front of him and sat across the table. It was the longest conversation they'd had in a very long time.

When his sister walked through the door, Thaddeus sighed, relieved. He looked at her closely; she seemed to be alright.

Noticing his look, she said wryly, "You could have warned me."

"Keegan, you know I couldn't. Believe me, it's much harder for me than you can imagine."

She surprised him by saying, "Rourk saved me."

"How do you know it was him?"

With a dreamy look on her face, Keegan replied, "I just know."

He was curious. "Did he talk to you?"

Thaddeus knew his father had ordered Rourk to guard his sister, so he knew it been Rourk. He just wondered how she recognized him. Would his father allow them to meet now? If they knew each other, it would make it much easier for Rourk to protect her.

"Only to tell me to leave," Keegan responded, shaking off her reverie. "I'm really tired and need to get some sleep."

Keegan took a long hot shower and then got in bed. She pictured his grey eyes and felt her pulse quicken. It had to have been Rourk. Sure, she had found guys attractive, but never in her life had anyone else had that kind of effect on her. She would have followed him to the end of the world if he asked. One year and five months, and she would be with him for the rest of her life. She hoped she didn't have to wait that long to see him again. Eventually, she drifted off to sleep, hoping to see him in her dreams.

Thaddeus loved going to bed. He always had vision-free, dreamless nights. Like a reset switch for his brain, that sleep kept him from going crazy. He closed his eyes and surrendered to it.

Looking frantically around, he tried to figure out where he was. His body felt strange, as if he looked through someone else's eyes. Fear raced through his veins. Never had he felt this scared. Lots of blood everywhere, body parts, screams. Dear God, where was he? Green, the land was so green, even stained with blood. He looked up and saw a beautiful orange moon. It looked out of place with all the destruction.

Thaddeus woke, drenched in sweat. He looked at his clock; it felt as if the dream only lasted a few seconds, but two hours had passed. He removed the blanket with trembling fingers and got out of bed, his feet unsteady. He didn't know what to do, but he had to talk to his father. Thaddeus knew he would be sleeping, but it couldn't wait.

He knocked on the door lightly. Richard heard the knock and slowly slid from beneath the covers, trying not to wake his wife. He glanced over at her, his heart full. Even after all these years, she still had the same effect on him as she did the first day they met.

Richard opened the door. His son stood on the other side, fear etched on his face. Richard knew better than to coddle him now.

He strode out past his son, nodding for him to follow. Richard led him down the steps and out onto the porch.

"Have a seat, son."

Taking a deep shaky breath, Thaddeus sat on the porch swing and said, "I had a dream. Well, since I don't dream, it had to be a vision."

Waiting patiently, his father nodded.

"Father, it was horrible."

Richard leaned forward. "Tell me exactly what you saw, and don't leave anything out. Close your eyes and picture the scene."

Closing his eyes, Thaddeus saw the dream, just like he had the first time. "There's so much blood, body parts everywhere, and the noise." Unconsciously, he covered his ears.

"Thaddeus, I need the details, not your feelings. Use your breathing exercises."

As usual, his father was right. After a few deep breaths, he felt better and could concentrate more.

"The land is green with rolling hills. So many dead bodies, even women and children."

Richard gripped the arm of his chair. "I need more. What else do you see?"

Thaddeus glanced left, then right, scanning over the bodies. The light from the moon—somehow he knew that mattered. "The moon is large and orange." Opening his eyes, he said, "That is all I see—I'm sorry."

His father looked up at the sky and said, "Thank you, gods, for this gift." He reached over and grasped his son by the shoulders. "I could kiss you."

Thaddeus said nothing.

His father got up and paced the porch. "This is brilliant. We know the time and place of the battle; we have the upper hand."

His breathing had returned to normal, and he was no longer afraid. Thaddeus raised an eyebrow, "Care to fill me in?"

"I believe this is a good omen. Fate always has its way. The battle will take place in Ireland during the harvest moon." He smiled slightly, his eyes tired. "Ironic, isn't it? Your mother was named after Ireland, the Emerald Isle. Your mother and I got engaged on the night of a harvest moon. And this year it falls on Keegan's birthday. Now those things mark the time and place of battle." He paused. "We have five months to prepare. Thaddeus, tomorrow we'll hold a meeting, and you will have to speak. You are the most respected seer of our time. I need you to think like a warrior and only give out as much information as necessary. There's no need to tell anything other than the time and place. Do you understand?"

Thaddeus grinned. "Law Four from *The 48 Laws of Power* by Robert Green. Always say less than necessary."

They had many preparations to make. Richard looked down at his watch—0300. He picked up his iPhone and texted his brother-in-laws a simple message: CAMP NOW. He hesitated, then sent a text to Rourk: CAMP NOW, BRING YOUR FATHER.

Rourk heard his phone go off. Groggy with sleep, he flipped it open, saw the text, and was instantly awake. He threw on his clothes from yesterday, not caring if they were clean or not. Fully alert, he walked into his father's room without bothering to knock. "Richard needs us," he called into the dark.

His father bolted out of bed. With haste, he got ready, and they made the drive to camp, arriving just as the other men did.

Richard looked at Rourk. "You've been relieved of your duty."

Rourk's face did not change, but his mind raced. *Did he find out I killed that guy?* He could think of nothing else he'd done that would cause his dismissal. He felt a dull ache in his heart at the thought of not seeing Keegan again.

"Thaddeus has had a vision," Richard said.

All eyes turned to Thaddeus. He sat with his hands clasped in his lap and his face serene.

"I have seen the place and date of the Great Battle," Thaddeus said, his voice strong and sure. The men all looked slightly surprised, glancing around at each other in shock, yet eager to learn more. "We have five months to prepare. On September twelfth, during the harvest moon, our battle will be raging."

They all had questions, but knew Thaddeus could not answer.

Richard stepped forward, commanding the room. "This obviously gives us the upper hand. We must prepare our men. With this knowledge, I feel we will prevail."

Thaddeus's uncle, Drew, smiled and replied, "Save your pep talks for the soldiers."

Richard grinned, "You're right; force of habit."

They all relaxed and sat down as equals to discuss the preparations. They were all powerful men, but the one who held the most power was the youngest—Thaddeus. Rourk was glad he was on their side.

Relieved to know Richard wasn't angry with him, Rourk felt honored to be part of the small group making preparations for the battle. Rourk also knew he had to push Keegan out of his thoughts for now. He needed to be one hundred percent focused on what lay ahead. Of course, keeping Keegan off his mind had proven to be extremely difficult. She'd been thinking about him almost constantly since the concert. Rourk knew that, if they didn't win this battle, he would never have the pleasure of getting to know her.

They had to win.

Chapter 15

Keegan woke up after a dreamless night's sleep. Usually she looked forward to it, but today she didn't want to go to school. Everyone paled in comparison to Rourk. She had to figure out a way to find him. He obviously lived nearby if he came to the concert. She still couldn't figure out why he had been there. Her mother would say that it was fate. Keegan thought it made a bit too much of a coincidence.

Keegan and her mother still hadn't talked since the jeans incident. Both stubborn, they could stay angry for days sometimes. But Keegan really wanted to tell her mom about Rourk. She came down the stairs to find her mother sitting at the kitchen table, reading the newspaper and sipping a mug of tea.

"Mom, I'm sorry." She really didn't know what she was apologizing for, but she knew the quickest way back into her mom's good graces.

Her mother was silent a moment. "Perhaps I overreacted. I just don't want you to take things for granted."

Keegan smiled and gave her a hug, then slid into the seat next to her. "You won't believe what happened at the concert."

"What happened?" Looking at her daughter, Emerald felt a rush of warmth mixed with relief. Of course, Katrina had already filled her in on what happened, and she just felt grateful to have her daughter home, unharmed. Katrina did not believe Rourk could possibly have been the boy who came to the rescue. When Keegan got to that part of the story, she described Rourk in detail, shocking her mother.

"Mom, I know it was him, it had to be."

Her mom looked thoughtful, then answered slowly. "I hope it was him. Then you'll have a wonderful story to tell your children at bedtime."

After she dropped Keegan off at school, Emerald had a phone call to make.

Richard's phone rang as he sat over some paperwork at his desk, with an intense headache. Surprised, he saw it was his wife. She never called.

"Will you be coming home for lunch?"

He sighed, "You know I would love to, but I am very busy today."

In a calm tone, she said, "I think it would be a good idea if you made time to see me. If you would like I can come to camp or we can meet somewhere."

This tone meant trouble. His wife had the quickest temper of anyone he had ever met, so he worried when she seemed eerily calm. "On second thought, of course I have time to come home and have lunch with my beautiful wife. I will be there before noon."

She hung up the phone without saying goodbye.

Richard didn't have time to dissect whatever had upset his wife. He would deal with it when he got there. He knew he would never understand the way her mind worked; she had always been a mystery to him.

In one of his favorite books, a character named Francisco d'Anconia said, "*Contradictions do not exist. Whenever you think you are facing a contradiction, check your premises. You will find that one of them is wrong*"

Smiling, Richard thought, *Francisco, you have not met my wife.*

At school, Keegan could not stop thinking of Rourk. Usually loud and bubbly, she didn't even have the patience for Donald and his crew today. They seemed so childish. She knew Rourk would never act like them. They ran around the halls, trying to catch and attack one another. Normally, she would join them, but now it just seemed lame. She felt like yelling at them to grow up.

Keegan sent a text to her mom. *Can I come home early?*

Of course, her mom wanted to know why. How could she explain she just suddenly felt like she didn't belong there anymore?

I have a headache.

The response came quickly. *Motrin.*

Ugh! Keegan thought.

Please, Mom, I just don't want to be here. Everyone's getting on my nerves, they seem so childish.

After a long break Keegan received a response. *No, I will pick you up at the normal time.*

Emerald slammed her phone on the counter. What was Richard thinking? She decided to go to the gym. She needed to burn off some frustration. It would be hard enough to control herself when she talked to her husband. He once told her that if he could change one thing about her it would be her temper. She tried to control it, but it didn't always work. She had her father to thank for passing down the trait.

Emerald met up with Richard when he arrived home and shared her frustrations with him.

"Believe it or not, I also went through hell during the three months after we met," he said. "Thankfully, I threw myself into my job. My friends thought I had gone crazy. I no longer chased women and didn't want to drink or go out." Richard frowned. "I'm sorry I didn't think that far ahead. I was selfish. My only concern was keeping our daughter safe, and I knew Rourk would protect her with his life."

Emerald sighed. She accepted that he knew things he couldn't tell her.

"So what do you think we should do?" he asked.

Taking a deep breath, she said, "I think we should allow them to be together."

He had not expected her to say that. He raised a brow. "Are you sure that is a good idea?"

"I think it is our only option. I will not allow our daughter to be miserable because you made a mistake in judgment."

He'd been expecting that sharp tongue. She always knew just what to say to get under his skin. "What about the elders?"

"Richard, obviously fate has taken ahold of this situation. Even the elders would have to accept what has been put into play cannot be stopped."

"Let's compromise," he said. "We will allow them to meet on her seventeenth birthday."

She looked at him suspiciously. "That is five months away."

He closed his eyes, thinking. He could only tell her the truth. "Rourk will be busy until then. The great battle will take place on Keegan's birthday."

Emerald walked towards the couch and sat down, stunned. "So soon? I thought we would have more time."

He could see her quickly going over scenarios. He found her sharp mind appealing—it made her just as dangerous as the most experienced soldiers. He wished he could take credit for that, but her father had trained her. He never got the son he wanted, so he passed his skills on to the next best thing, his tomboy daughter. She had all the training that Thaddeus had and then some. Emerald's father had been fearless—the worst kind of solider. Without fear, a soldier won't use the most valuable weapon, which, of course, is the mind. As a result, he was killed in battle.

"Em, do you remember the first time we sparred?" Richard asked fondly.

She smiled. "Of course. You underestimated me."

He laughed. "You looked so innocent and tiny. In the end, I never respected anyone more, and I still feel that way. Whatever you think we should do, we'll do it."

He knew he had said the right thing when he saw her shoulders relax.

"What does a man have to do to get fed around here?" he said. "I don't have much time left."

Once Richard left, Emerald sat down to think. She knew he was correct. She smiled. He usually got things right, but she didn't like to let him know. She also knew he only had Keegan's best interests at heart and she shouldn't be angry at him for that. Keegan and Rourk could wait until after the battle. With so much on Rourk's mind, throwing Keegan into the mix would almost be cruel. Emerald would to have to work hard to keep Keegan occupied in the meantime.

Emerald picked Keegan up from school that day, giving her a big smile as she climbed in the car. She couldn't help thinking how beautiful her daughter was, even in her school uniform. "So I was thinking. You know how your birthday is in five months?"

Keegan tucked her backpack on the floorboard between her legs and turned wide eyes to her mother. She loved her birthday almost as much as she loved the presents.

"We promised you when you turned seventeen that we would get you a car." Emerald saw the spark come back to Keegan's eyes.

"I know exactly what I want—a navy blue, four-door Jeep. Of course, it will have to be lifted and have big tires. Dad said I could only get a two-door jeep, but do you think you can convince him a four-door would be better?"

Emerald smiled. "Well, they are safer."

Keegan started bouncing up and down like a five-year-old again. Her daughter could drive her crazy at times, but she loved her more than life itself.

"Would you like to test drive some?" Emerald asked.

Keegan looked over in disbelief. "Seriously?"

They spent the rest of the day driving from one dealership to the next looking at Jeeps, and then headed for home.

They came home to a dark, empty house. Emerald knew Richard would not be home for dinner. As she draped her purse over a chair at the table, she reminded herself that he would probably miss many meals over the next few months. She glanced over at the shoes that lined the doorway; she didn't see Thaddeus's. He'd have another late night at the camp as well.

A rush of hot despair filled her. Her baby had been born for the great battle, and she couldn't save him from his destiny.

Emerald ran hand through her hair. *He's just a boy. How can he handle what is to come?*

She sat in silence for several moments before she could compose herself enough to pick up the phone and invite her sisters over for dinner. They gladly accepted, and she wondered how much they knew about all the training. But having them there would also help keep Keegan's mind off things. Distraction was the game plan.

Keara walked through the door first, wearing a long, flowing skirt with pink flowers and a fitted, long sleeved t-shirt that looked great on her tall frame. She'd done her hair wild and standing up all over the place.

"Nice 'fro, Keara," Keegan said. She patted the top of her cousin's wiry, dark hair; it went down like a sponge.

Keara did a little dance, bopped her hair around, and snapped her fingers. She looked like someone from the seventies.

"I love your hair, Keara. If I had your hair, I'd wear it wild all the time—it looks awesome," Keegan said.

"Yeah, yeah, that's easy for you to say. It takes hours to get it relaxed or braided. I'd trade with you in a second. Mom won't let me wear it like this very often."

"Brigid, you need to let Keara wear her hair like this; it's incredible. I'm so jealous."

"Sure, Keegan. As long as you come over and deal with it, she can wear it any way she wants."

Keara sighed and slumped down on to the couch.

"So what's been going on with you? How's school? You like any boys?" Keegan asked Keara as she sat down next to her on the cushions.

"School sucks, nothing has been going on with me, and you know I don't like boys. I'm going to be a nun."

"Wait until you meet your chosen; your thoughts of becoming a nun will be out the window."

Keara turned her eyes to her cousin, sadness filling them. "Keegan, we don't even know if I'll *have* a chosen. I'm not full blooded like you guys."

"You'll have a chosen, you're too awesome not to."

Keegan had never really thought of that issue. She knew that being different made it hard for Keara, but she never really thought of the consequences that came with her being half-elf.

"Let's go play with the rest of the kids," Keegan said. "I think we should take them outside and you can start a rainstorm. That way we can play in the puddles."

Keara smiled wickedly as they headed out the door.

Emerald and her sisters stayed in the living room, chatting away.

Kat broke the ice, bringing up what they were all thinking about. "It's hard to believe that The Great Battle will take place in our lifetime, and we are all so deeply involved. Life as we know it could be over soon. Do you think we will be able to win?"

Brigid looked away. "John says the numbers are against us."

They all lapsed into silence. Everyone knew John could calculate the probabilities.

Emerald leaned back in her chair. "Fate has been set in motion. We need to wait and see."

Katrina looked annoyed. "How can you just sit back all relaxed and say fate will decide? Your husband leads the army of the light."

This was the wrong thing to say. Glaring at her sister, Emerald snapped, "You should talk, both of you. Neither of you could protect yourself if you needed. If I see anyone sitting back and relaxing, it's you."

Her comment struck a nerve. Both women envied the time their father had spent training her. Although, at the time, neither of them had any interest.

Katrina knew enough to diffuse the situation. "You have a valid point."

Emerald had tried several times to get Katrina interested in training. Katrina would humor her for a little while. She'd even seemed to enjoy *Krav Maga*. But she always lost interest after a short time and stopped going.

Emerald had an idea. "What do you say you guys start coming over in the evenings, and we will train together? Keegan has been training, and now that Thaddeus is busy, she's lost her training partner."

Brigid and Katrina glanced at each other. Finally, Brigid shrugged. "Sure, why not? We have nothing better to do."

Keegan came into the room with Warrick and Mackenna clinging to her legs and giggling.

Katrina said, "You've got three new training partners."

Keegan stared at them. "What are you talking about?"

"Your mother pointed out that we can't really protect ourselves. We decided to join your training sessions," Brigid said with a grin. "Aren't you lucky?"

Keegan smiled. "That sounds like fun."

Chapter 16

The weeks blurred together for Keegan. Usually she loved summer vacation, her favorite time of the year. This year she just wanted to mope around. She didn't feel like going out, but her mother made sure she spent time with her friends. Her mom bought them all movie tickets, bowling passes, and even tickets for miniature golf once.

Her mother didn't seem too worried about spoiling her now. Her friends thought she had the coolest mom ever, but sometimes Keegan thought her mother was testing her. Why else would she be so unnecessarily generous?

Keegan had to admit that she'd remembered to say thank you more often lately. Seeing how excited her friends got over the gifts from her mom made her realize she probably didn't genuinely appreciate all the things she had.

The progress her sisters had made in three months impressed Emerald tremendously. Keegan really blew her away. Her daughter didn't realize how much she'd advanced, or that she made an excellent instructor. Katrina and Brigid learned quickly because Keegan had a knack for making things seem easy.

Keegan held the pad up as Katrina worked on her foot strikes.

Katrina glanced slyly at Emerald. "So, sis, I think I'm ready to take you."

Emerald grinned. "It's about time."

Katrina said, "I'll grab the headgear."

"Don't bother," Emerald said. "I'm a healer, remember?"

Brigid smirked and settled against the wall. "This I gotta see."

Katrina walked towards the middle of the room, thinking, *Come on, Kat, you can do this. You have the advantage of knowing her next move.*

Emerald started singing *Three Blind Mice* in her mind. She knew it would distract Katrina, who could hear her thoughts.

Katrina turned around and Emerald yanked her shoulder down, delivering an intensely painful knee strike to her solar plexus. Doubling over, Katrina took an elbow to the side of her face. Her blood splashed across the floor.

"Really, sis, you didn't think I would forget that you read minds, did you?" Emerald said. She stepped back several paces to let her sister get back up.

That little wench, Katrina thought as she ran towards her sister. Emerald ran towards her at the same time; one hand slammed her chest as the other arm drove an elbow into Kat's throat. It happened so quickly that Katrina, knocked off balance, landed on her ass.

"Are we done here?" Emerald asked.

Katrina looked up. "Yes, we're done."

Emerald reached down to help her sister up. Katrina delivered a heel kick to the inside of her thigh. Emerald dropped to her knee, keeping her grip on Katrina's hand. "Very nice," she grunted, slamming her forehead into her sister's head.

Kat saw stars. "Okay, okay. I'm really done this time."

"I have to say, Katrina, I'm impressed."

Wiping the blood off her face, Katrina said, "Whatever! You kicked my ass."

"Yes, but you took the lesson and used it. The element of surprise." Emerald smiled. "Another lesson. You couldn't have read my mind if you tried. I have been doing this for so long that I just react, without thought."

Katrina looked puzzled. "Well. Why did you sing?"

Emerald took a swig of water, wiped her mouth, and replied, "It was actually two lessons in one. You can't rely on your gift, and it also distracted you. Anytime you can distract your opponent, do it."

Emerald looked over at Brigid. "You want a go at it?"

Brigid glanced down at the blood on Katarina. "I think I'll pass today. Maybe next time."

Emerald asked, "Would you like me to heal you, Katrina?"

Katrina paused briefly. "No, that's okay. Drew will think it's sexy."

They all laughed.

After her aunts left, the silence started to press in on Keegan. She went into her mother's bedroom and perched on the end of the bed. "Mom, my heart hurts."

Emerald's own heart beat a little faster. She sat down and reached out to brush Keegan's auburn hair away from her face. "What do you mean?"

"I've never felt so empty before. I feel like I'm just going through the days and they mean nothing." Keegan's eyes filled with tears. "Can you fix me?"

After a moment's pause, Emerald nodded slowly. "I might be able to help you, but not with a healing. Perhaps you need the truth. You did see Rourk at the concert."

"I knew it was him." To her surprise, Keegan felt tears running down her face. She frowned. "How do you know it was him? Why was he there?"

Emerald looked at her daughter and felt a rush of sympathy. "It's a long story, but I'll try to tell it quickly. So many things had been set in motion long before we were born. Your brother and your father have roles foretold in prophecy—you know that. You do not know that Thaddeus had a vision about you, that you will be key in deciding the outcome of the battle."

Keegan crinkled her nose. "How could I be involved?"

Looking sternly at her daughter, Emerald said, "It doesn't matter how or why, it just is." She fell silent for a minute, then continued. "Your father assigned Rourk to watch over you, to keep you safe."

A look of alarm crossed Keegan's face. "He's been watching me? For how long? Why didn't anyone tell me?"

Emerald stood up, laying her hand on her daughter's shoulder. "Your father and I have agreed to let you meet Rourk after your birthday, a year earlier than planned."

"We'll be together?" Keegan gasped. "Why do I have to wait until my birthday? What difference can two months make?"

Getting impatient now, Keegan could only think of running to find Rourk. She had never wanted anything so badly in her life. She leapt to her feet and started pacing the room. "Please, Mom, tell me where he is. I will do anything, I swear."

Grabbing her daughter by the shoulders, Emerald said sternly, "Look at me. You need to focus. You cannot meet him until after your birthday. You need to accept that."

"Why? None of this makes any sense." Keegan verged on hysteria, mindless with her desire to find Rourk right that minute.

Emerald paused. "I am going to tell you something that you cannot repeat to anyone. Do you understand?"

Keegan took a deep breath, trying to calm herself down. "Yes, I understand."

Her mother seemed to relax. "The great battle will take place on your birthday."

"What? Are you serious?" A surge of panic raced through Keegan. "What if he dies in battle? What if we're defeated? We will never meet. Mom, this is so unfair—I feel like I can't breathe."

Sharply, her mother responded, "Pull yourself together, Keegan. Like it or not, this family bears a great deal of responsibility for the survival of our kind. And Rourk needs to focus on preparing for the battle. You would only distract him. I'm not joking, Keegan; this is a matter of life and death. You will train, spend time with your friends, and just be happy knowing that you will be with Rourk soon. You've waited this long; a couple more months will not matter."

Keegan tried to collect herself. She knew her mother was right—it just really sucked.

"Oh, and we'll be spending your birthday in Ireland."

Glaring at her mother, Keegan said, "You want to keep us apart so much that you'd send me to another country?"

"On the contrary, daughter, Rourk will also be in Ireland. Our whole family will be there. Soldiers will need healing and some of our other gifts might come in handy."

Keegan was speechless.

The next day, Keegan lost herself in her thoughts as she sat by the pool. Her friends yelled and screamed, splashing around in the water.

Donald came up to her, his hair all wet and sticking up. His electric orange board shorts looked funny with his orange hair. He sat down in the chair next to her and kicked up his long legs on the table.

They sat in silence for a few moments, then Donald cleared his throat. "I was wondering if you wanted to catch a movie or something this weekend?"

Keegan jerked as she realized he was talking to her. "Um, yeah, maybe."

She went back to her thoughts without even looking at him. *We are going to Ireland for the great battle. It's going to start on my freaking birthday! How could this have happened? Do we actually stand a chance of winning against the dark elves?*

Donald scooted back his chair and jumped up, the heavy metal chair almost falling over.

Keegan glanced up, catching the shocked look that crossed Donald's face right before he bolted. Surprised, she watched him skirt the pool and make a beeline for Spencer and Calvron. Knowing them, they probably needed to plan their next water gun fight, or what kind of pizza to order.

She realized she should have spent more time talking to him. He was probably mad because she had been ignoring him lately. Whatever. She had more important things going on. She closed her eyes and tried to forget the great battle.

Chapter 17

Richard took his time walking around camp. After only a few minutes, he could see the deep fatigue in his men, etched in the lines on their faces and the dirt on their hands. They had been training night and day, and everyone missed their families.

He had yet to tell them that the great battle was upon them. Of course, they all expected as much since the training schedule had been increased so drastically. The last few months had been grueling.

They knew they were going to Ireland for a training mission, but nothing more. He would tell them the truth before they headed out. He trusted his men with his life, but their relatives had gifts, and many could read minds. Richard just couldn't risk the information getting into the wrong hands before it was time to leave. If a relative knew, and a dark elf happened by them, the light would lose their upper hand. He wouldn't take that risk.

Sighing, Richard knew they all needed a break to keep morale up.

Richard glanced at his watch. Almost lunch time. "Rourk," he called.

Rourk sat on a bench nearby, sharpening his weapon. The boy looked up, brow furrowed, then shot to his feet and saluted. "Sir?"

"Pass the word that there will be a meeting in front of the mess hall in thirty minutes."

"Yes, sir," Rourk answered with a brisk nod. He put his weapon away and marched off.

It would cause a lot of grumbling from the men. They all hated last minute meetings, and to cut into their lunch made it even worse.

Richard stood in front of his tent and waited for them to gather around. Once they were all present, Richard spoke. "I want you all to know that I appreciate the hard work you have put in. I know you miss your families. I miss mine, as well. Tomorrow, I would like you all to bring your family members here for a cookout. Everything will be supplied; you just have to show up." He gazed at the crowd, relieved to see smiles on the faces of many of his men.

"After that, I don't want to see any of you for three days. As for today, you are all done. Go home and relax. You've earned it."

With a few honest words, he took the spirit of his men from weary and fatigued to excited.

Richard gathered his gear and threw it in the truck, then waited for Thaddeus to jump in so they could make their way home. He looked forward to taking a break himself. Even though he had lived through many battles, no one was guaranteed tomorrow. He missed his wife and children and, if he died in the Great Battle, he didn't want to regret not spending time with his loved ones.

"The men seem happy." Thaddeus leaned his head back on the seat and closed his eyes as they pulled onto the highway.

Richard looked over at his pale, weary son. "You should ask your mother for a healing to restore your body."

Thaddeus kept his eyes closed. "Hardly seems fair to the others. Are you going to get a healing?"

"You know I won't allow your mother to heal me unless I'm on the brink of death." Richard smiled—his stance on healings provided an ongoing source of amusement for his wife.

"Like father, like son, I guess." In the silence that followed, Thaddeus's head rolled to the side and his breathing became deep and even. Richard let him sleep for the entire forty-five minute drive home.

After he parked in the driveway, Richard shook Thad awake. The two grabbed their gear and tossed it into the garage before making their way to the front door.

Emerald sat on the couch with her feet kicked up on the coffee table, a book open on her lap. She looked up, surprised to see her husband and son walk through the door so early.

She raised an eyebrow. "Should I be alarmed?"

Thaddeus threw his jacket over the back of the armchair and walked towards the stairs without answering.

"Thaddeus!" Emerald barked.

"What?" His tone oozed irritation.

"How many times do I have to tell you to hang up your jacket? That chair isn't a coat rack."

Thaddeus rolled his eyes and strode back through the room to yank his jacket from the chair. Instead of hanging it up, he made his way upstairs.

Emerald turned a wry smile towards her husband and slammed her book shut, gently placing it on the table before standing. "I'm not ready for his teen years."

Richard crossed to her and pulled her into his arms, breathing deeply of her familiar smell. "I noticed the men looked worn out, so I sent them home."

"I'm happy you're here," she murmured against his shoulder.

"We're also going to have a cookout at the camp tomorrow. I told them to bring their families, and I've given them three days off after that." He leaned back, a look of mischief in his eyes. "So you know what that means?"

Her face went from smooth and happy to annoyed in one fluid instant. "That Keegan and Rourk will be in the same place at the same time?"

Richard groaned. He could have kicked himself. How had he not thought of that?

Emerald pushed away from him, holding her hands up in supplication. "Richard, I'm too tired to fight. What's done is done; we will let it take its course. I'm glad you have some time off. I've missed you."

Richard stared at his wife, gauging her mood. He hadn't expected to get off the hook that quickly. When she stood on tiptoe to press a warm kiss to his lips, he grinned and swept her into his arms again. "I was thinking we should take the kids to your mother's and go away for the weekend. It's been too long since we've been alone."

Smiling, she said, "That sounds like a wonderful idea. Let's not go too far, though. How does a cabin in the woods sound?"

"You read my mind."

Chapter 18

The next day the camp bustled with excitement, with music playing, people dancing, and food cooking. Elfin children ran amok all over the place.

Rourk wasn't a fan chaos and crowds, but he understood it came with being in a unit. Richard knew that events like this helped build cohesion among the soldiers. Rourk had to admit he was enjoying himself, standing back and taking it all in. He loved watching the children play.

Keegan had dreaded going to the stupid cookout. Only the prospect of taking a lot of pictures made it bearable. She liked to capture people unaware, acting naturally.

Her dad had left early to make sure everything was prepared. Her mother put off their departure as long as possible, but soon they had to go. Keegan knew they needed to be there for her father. Keegan wished she could bring her friends, but outsiders were not allowed at the camp.

Much to her surprise, the excitement infected Keegan before long. Hundreds, if not thousands, had come. Something hard to describe, but very special happened around elfin families; she could feel the love and admiration all around. Couples danced. Laughter echoed everywhere. Kids squealed in delight.

Keegan smiled, the happiest she had felt in months. She snapped pictures as she made her way through the crowd. She thought she probably got some of her best shots ever. Everywhere she looked, she saw joyful faces.

Keegan looked through her lens and froze. Quickly recovering, she snapped a picture. He looked as perfect as she remembered from the night of the concert. He watched the kids play, contentment written on his face. Her heart pounded.

Rourk is here.

When she thought his name, he turned and made eye contact with her.

They stood staring at each other, neither sure what to do.

Emerald spotted the interaction and nudged Richard. They both looked over, knowing they could change nothing at this point. They watched as Rourk strode through the crowd. Their daughter stood, still as a photograph, with a look of awe on her face.

Richard and Emerald looked away, allowing their daughter to have the moment to herself. They knew there was a real possibility that Rourk would die in Ireland. She deserved this time.

Keegan felt nervous as Rourk walked toward her. What should she say? In an instant, he stood in front of her. She felt his fingers trace the side of her face. She looked up into his grey eyes as he leaned down and kissed her.

Keegan had kissed boys before, but she'd never felt anything like this. It was the weirdest sensation, as if she had an electrical current running through her body. His arms felt so powerful where they encircled her. The noise around them sounded muffled and distant. She had never imagined a kiss could feel so intoxicating. She had no idea how long it lasted—probably not long—but it felt like an eternity.

When they broke away, Keegan looked up at him. "Wow, did you feel that?"

Speechless, Rourk stared at her with a look of adoration.

Suddenly, Keegan heard everyone clapping and cheering for them. Her face flushed a deep shade of red.

Rourk, on the other hand, looked proud. His hand found hers and it felt as natural as if they had been together for years. They connected with no awkwardness, as if they'd fused into one.

Keegan pulled him toward the games. She smiled up at him. "I bet I could beat you at darts."

"You're on," he replied with a grin, "but don't cry when I beat you."

He actually beat her twice. After the second time, Rourk smiled and shrugged.

Keegan put her hands on her hips. "Best out of five."

"Forget it, you'll never beat me. Let's go grab something to eat."

Keegan took off running towards the woods and Rourk followed. He laughed as he grabbed her by the waist and spun her around. They fell to the ground, and Rourk rolled to absorb the impact as Keegan sprawled across his chest.

Breathless at his closeness and his warmth, Keegan stared down at him. "I have waited for you my whole life."

"Sure you have. I've seen you enjoying yourself with a few guys," Rourk teased.

"Whatever. I'm sure you've had your share of girlfriends." Keegan rolled off of him.

"Nope, none. You are my first and only." Rourk reached for her, pulled her near, and kissed her.

"I wish we could stay here forever. I think this is the best day of my life," Keegan said as she leaned back against him.

Someone yelled their names. Rourk gave her a quick kiss and pulled her up. As they walked, elves kept coming up and congratulating them, talking about how they all thought it was so sweet Keegan and Rourk were able to meet before their time.

The rest of the day went by in a blur.

When it came time to leave, her parents approached them. "Your father and I have plans to go away for the weekend. Your brothers are going to your grandmother's. Would you two like to join us?"

Keegan gaped at her mother. Was she serious? Her heart leapt with hope.

Rourk replied, "Of course, we would love to join you—as long as it's okay with Keegan."

Keegan looked at him like he'd lost his mind. "I want to spend as much time as possible with you."

Richard seemed kind of surprised as he looked at his wife. "We will have to call and change the reservations to a cabin with three bedrooms."

Looking at them both, Emerald said, "There is a condition to this. You guys can have this weekend together, but you will not see each other again until you get to Ireland, is that clear?"

The idea of being separated brought pain to Keegan's chest, but she nodded agreement. Rourk had to focus on the preparations for the battle. Rourk also agreed. They both felt grateful for any time they could spend together.

"We will be leaving in two hours," Emerald said, "so I suggest you part ways and gather up whatever you will need for the weekend."

Back at home, Keegan felt like she was floating on clouds—she didn't know such feelings existed. Glancing around her room, she threw clothing into her bag. Her mother had said a cabin. Knowing her mom, she'd better dress for the occasion. They would probably end up on a long trek. She threw on a pair of hiking pants, shirt, and boots. She grabbed her necessities out of the bathroom and yelled to her parents that she was ready.

Her parents, both folding clothes into duffel bags, looked at each other in amazement over their bed and laughed. Usually Keegan, always the last to be ready, took forever making sure she packed the perfect outfits and got her hair just right.

"I could get used to this," Emerald said with a chuckle.

"Let's hope Rourk continues to have this effect on her," Richard replied.

They piled into her mother's Land Rover Defender. Keegan had to admit it was a seriously cool vehicle, painted matte black with rugged tires and a rack on top. Her mother rode in one on their last safari in Africa and said she loved it. Her father, seeing an opportunity to surprise his wife, had one delivered to the house before they got back. Keegan ran her hand over the soft leather seat. She couldn't wait to have Rourk by her side.

Her father pulled into Rourk's driveway. Keegan skipped up the drive and knocked on the door, which Rourk's father answered. Keegan smiled, finding him very good-looking for an older man.

"Hello, Mr. Kavanagh. I've been looking forward to meeting you." She peeked around him to get a glance of the house.

Rourk's father opened the door wider, inviting her in. "You have made Rourk happier than I have seen him in a long time. He'll be out in just a second."

She glanced around the house, surprised to see signs of a female touch. She had expected a dirty bachelor pad, but dainty curtains hung in the kitchen and the living room looked warm and inviting.

"You have a lovely home," Keegan said.

His father nodded. "Thank you. I haven't changed a thing since my wife passed away."

Ah, that made sense. "Well, she had great taste."

"She would have loved to have met you." He smiled warmly at her.

Keegan's face flushed. "Thank you, that means a lot."

Rourk appeared from the hallway, and her heart skipped a beat. Would she ever get used to his overwhelming beauty? Not good-looking in the conventional way, his face looked rugged, angled, with confident eyes. He looked exactly like what he was—a warrior. She could not believe he was all hers.

He met her eyes, and a smile spread across his face. He quickly glanced at his dad. "I'll see you in a couple of days."

Rourk reached down to grab Keegan's hand and squeeze it. He was much taller than she expected—not that she intended to complain about his perfection.

They ran down the front steps and to where the car waited in the driveway. She felt like jumping up and down in excitement for the weekend. They had no idea where they were headed, or how long it would take. And none of that mattered, as long as they went together.

During the drive, Keegan asked Rourk questions, talking a mile a minute. She wanted to know everything about him.

"What's your favorite color?"

"Green."

"Really? Green is my favorite color, too."

Her father turned in his seat to grin at her. "Keegan, I think green is a very common favorite color for elves."

She stuck her tongue out at him and continued drilling Rourk.

"Glass half empty or half full?"

"That would depend on how thirsty I am." He smiled.

She considered his answer. "Very clever. I've never heard that reply before."

She leaned her head on his shoulder, and they lapsed into a comfortable silence. Keegan gazed out the window, wishing they could stop. She wanted to take some photos of the breathtaking scenery. In the end, though, she would rather get to their destination.

The drive took a couple of hours. Finally, her father turned down a narrow, winding road. Rourk laughed when Keegan tightened her grip on his arm as her father made a swift turn. Richard drove like crazy man. She would be glad when they could get out and walk. Twenty minutes later, they turned into a hidden driveway.

Keegan loved going to new places. It felt like a grand adventure. As long as she could remember, her family had traveled all over the world, and seeing new sights always excited her. Even though they hadn't traveled far from their home this time, they seemed to be driving into a hidden oasis.

"Have you guys been here before?" she asked. She noticed the look that passed between her parents. Both had secret smiles on their faces.

"Yes, we've been here," her mom answered. "We usually come to a small cabin with one room. Out of all the places we have been, we love this one best. We had planned to keep it a secret from everyone."

They stopped, and her father said, "We walk from here, so grab your things."

They hiked up the rugged terrain, and Keegan felt like she'd stepped into a magical wonderland. The stunning scenery featured rolling green hills and sparkling sunshine that stole through the canopy to illuminate the flora on the ground. Keegan grabbed her camera out of the bag and started snapping pictures. Even though elves had adapted to living among human civilization, they still felt most at home in nature. She stopped and inhaled the fragrance of the wildflowers scattered around her.

"Mom, do you know the name of this flower?" Keegan asked, bending down to train the lens of her camera on a beautiful lavender flower.

"No, sorry. I always forget the names," Emerald answered, coming to a stop to wait for her daughter.

"Well, this is a dwarf iris. It's named after the goddess of the rainbow. It's also the Tennessee state flower."

"Why did you ask if you already knew the answer?" her mother asked, exchanging an amused look with her husband.

"Well, you're always right, so I wanted to throw something out there that I knew you didn't know." Keegan looked up from her camera and gave her a devious smile. Rourk chuckled.

"That sounds like something your father would do." Emerald sighed, rolling her eyes. She gave Rourk a sympathetic look. "Rourk, you have to watch this girl."

"I'll be sure to put her in her place when it's needed," he said, amused.

Richard laughed and placed a hand on Rourk's shoulder. "Good luck with that."

They walked deeper into the woods. What appeared to be snow covering the forest floor was actually a lovely spring beauty flower that blanketed the ground. Keegan couldn't help herself; she stooped once more to the ground, lifting her camera to catch the sea of white.

Richard glanced over at Rourk, who kept his gray eyes trained on Keegan with a look that bordered on adoration. "You better get used to this, son. It takes two to three times longer to get anywhere with her when she has the camera in hand."

Looking amused, Rourk said, "I would wait forever for her."

Lost in photography, Keegan missed their exchange.

Emerald nudged Keegan. "We need to pick up our pace if we're to get there before nightfall. You'll have plenty of time to explore the forest tomorrow."

Reluctantly, Keegan put her camera away and wondered how much further they had to go. They kept ascending the trails, if one could call them that. She hoped her father hadn't gone off the path and gotten them lost. Her muscles ached. They'd been trekking a long time.

Unexpectedly she heard the tranquil sound of water splashing against rocks. A waterfall must be close by. She squeezed Rourk's hand.

"Dad, can we please find the waterfall?"

Glancing behind him, he threw over his shoulder, "You're in luck. We're headed in that direction. We are almost to the cabin."

They hiked another four hundred meters or so, then her father abruptly turned off the path and into the woods. Rourk held branch after branch for her, preventing them from smacking her in the face. She saw her father pushing his way through a huge stand of bushes. *This is ridiculous.* She could feel herself getting annoyed. It was no longer fun—she was sore and tired. The sun began to set, and she started to worry.

Keegan glanced around. *Oh great, we're lost.* She glanced at Rourk, who looked completely at ease but focused. He had complete confidence in her father.

Just when she decided to say something to her father, the view stunned her into silence. They came around the shrubbery only to see a wooden swing bridge. She grasped the rope and tentatively stepped onto the wooden slats. It swayed and, when she looked down, she felt a rush of adrenaline run through her. She hadn't realized how high they had climbed. She felt like running across the bridge, but her parents walked calmly in front of them.

Reaching back, she grabbed her camera out of the bag. They had to walk single file on the narrow bridge. She got some great shots of Rourk and her parents. She wished she'd brought a larger lens. With the ground so far away, she would not be able to do it justice. It was definitely worth the time it took to get there.

Once they made it across, her father promised they wouldn't have to walk much further. Thankfully, he told the truth.

They came across a rustic cabin nestled in the woods like something out of a fairy tale. Made of gray weathered boards, it looked old and run-down. Brilliantly colored flowers overflowed their beds in the front yard while the leaves of the forest behind the cabin shone in the sunshine. A single gravel pathway led to the front door, where her mom retrieved the key hidden under a flower pot.

Speechless, Keegan walked through the door. The outside might look decrepit, but the inside looked like a page from a magazine, modern yet simple.

The front door opened into a central great room, with a ceiling that peaked overhead and a wall dominated by a large fireplace built of river stones. A brown leather couch and armchairs rested on the dark hardwood floors, made with unusually wide planks.

"What kind of wood is this?" she asked her dad.

He replied with a look of admiration, "Hand-scraped oak."

Grabbing Rourk's hand, Keegan pulled him to the couch and sank into the leather. She wanted to explore the rest of the cabin, but her feet were killing her. A small sigh escaped her lips as she leaned her head against Rourk's shoulder. "This is what I want our home to look like."

Chapter 19

Keegan woke up with a blanket on her. It took her a moment to realize where she was; she always felt a little disoriented waking up in a strange place. Smiling, she remembered that she was at the cabin with Rourk. She needed to find him. They only had a short time together, and she had wasted some of it on a nap. What was she thinking?

The house smelled wonderful. Keegan walked into the kitchen, wiping the sleep from her eyes. Again, the simple beauty struck her. She would not have guessed a modern kitchen waited behind the door of the weathered cabin. Keegan had never seen anything like the floor in the kitchen. Made of flat stone in a variety of sizes and colors, the texture felt wonderful on her bare feet, like walking on a large, flat rock. The ceiling, made of the same wood as the floor in the living room, soared above professional grade stainless steel appliances. Surprising her, Rourk stood over the stove, something she would have never imagined, and yet he made it look completely natural.

"Is there anything you can't do?" Keegan asked.

Rourk turned to her with a wide grin. "I see someone finally decided to wake up."

Giving him a sleepy smile, she threw her arms around his waist and leaned her head against his chest. She could feel his powerful muscles beneath his shirt. "What are you making?"

He ran his hands through her hair, sending chills down her spine. "Well, I planned to make some rare steaks, but Emerald informed me that you are a vegetarian." He had a perplexed look on his face. "So I went with spaghetti, homemade sauce, and garlic bread. The cabinets and refrigerator are stocked with everything you could think of."

She inhaled the incredible aroma of garlic, tomatoes, and other spices.

Rourk turned back to the stove to stir the sauce. "To answer the question you asked earlier, after my mother died, either I learned to cook, or we lived on frozen pizza and canned ravioli."

Keegan could not imagine growing up without her mom, and she felt a pang of empathy for him. "I'm sure your mother would be proud of the way you turned out," she said.

Rourk gave her a look of gratitude. "She would have loved you. Anyway, let's change the subject."

At that moment, her parents came through the door. Keegan couldn't help smiling. Her parents complemented each other so well. Just one look at them together made it obvious they were meant to be. She wondered if she and Rourk looked like that.

Her dad said, "Is the food ready yet? I'm so hungry I could eat a horse. Although my daughter might object to that."

Everyone except Keegan found his remark funny.

They enjoyed the incredible food, and her parents didn't hang out long after they all cleared the table. Her mom gave them a warning look as she pointed out their rooms. She paused, then reminded them to stay in separate rooms.

Rourk looked insulted. "I would never do anything to harm your daughter's honor."

Emerald gave him a knowing look. "I'm not worried about you."

Horrified, Keegan groaned. "Mom, get out of here."

They stayed up most of the night talking, wanting to learn everything about the other. They shared condensed stories of their lives along with their likes and dislikes and found they had a lot in common.

At some point late in the night, Keegan glanced into Rourk's steady grey eyes. "Aren't you worried that this feels too easy? I was expecting lots of awkward moments when we met."

Rourk smiled at her, his strong hands wrapped around hers. "I expected it to be exactly like this. My father once described meeting your chosen partner. He said your chosen feels like an extension of yourself. That, without your partner, you're only half of the person you are meant to be. When you connect with them, you finally feel complete."

After a slight pause he continued. "Until that moment, elves always feel that they're missing something, but something undefinable. Even though we're individuals, it's as if we are one. Of course, we won't always agree. We'll have different views on things. I mean, you're a vegetarian. That makes no sense to me. But that's what you want, and I'd go out of my way to make sure you get it. Each chosen sees the best in the other and helps to bring it out. Although…everything always has a price."

Keegan crinkled up her nose. "What do you mean, a price?"

"Honestly, I don't know. I've asked my father, but he never really answered. He told me it should be obvious from looking at him. He hasn't been the same man since my mother died. I've always thought the grief of losing her changed him, but maybe there is something more—the pain of the bond breaking or something. He did tell me that even a day with your chosen was worth it, no matter what the price."

Keegan looked over, a little uncertain. "I find it...unsettling to know I would do anything for you. I would give up everything to make you happy."

He crossed the distance between them, placing a slow kiss on her lips. Pulling away, he told her, "Keegan, I'd never ask you or even allow you to give up anything for me. I feel the same about you. If you told me you didn't want me to be a soldier, I would do as you wished."

The suggestion startled her. "I would never ask that of you! That's who you are, and I would never take your identity away."

He smiled. "That's exactly my point. Elves don't divorce—for that very reason. It's natural for us to encourage our partners. One partner's happiness brings the other happiness. There's nothing more I want for you than to live up to your full potential."

After hours of talking, they unenthusiastically agreed they should go to bed. Keegan's bedroom, as beautiful as the rest of the house, included a bath with an amazing bathtub. She couldn't resist the humungous wooden bowl with pebbles around the edge. She made the water as hot as she could stand and then slowly lowered herself into the hot water until she felt her body relax. Her muscles needed it after the trek. Leaning her head against the back of the tub, she closed her eyes and played the day over in her mind.

She still couldn't believe Rourk was there with her, like a dream come true. Then her thoughts turned towards the battle, and she felt sick to her stomach. She couldn't stand the thought of her loved ones putting their lives at risk. *Please, gods, let them make it through this alive.*

Chapter 20

Keegan woke to the smell of bacon, which brought a smile to her face. Rolling out of bed, she reached her arms in the air for a good stretch. She still felt tired, but she looked over at the clock—nine o'clock already. She'd gotten about six hours of sleep.

She rubbed her eyes and debated taking a shower and changing, then decided against it. Instead, she went downstairs with her hair a mess and wearing her fuzzy dolphin PJ's.

Rourk stood at the stove again, this time with a spatula in one hand and the handle of the skillet in the other. He appeared to be completely at home. He looked up when she entered the room. "You are the most beautiful creature I have ever laid eyes on."

A quick glance told her that he was not joking, and suddenly her face felt hot. She'd been called beautiful her whole life, but at that moment, for the first time, she believed it to be true.

Her face flushed. "Where are Mom and Dad?"

"They headed out a while ago. They told me to tell you they won't be back till much later."

A mischievous grin crossed her face.

Rourk laughed. "Now I see why your mother warned me. Go sit down, and I'll bring your breakfast. How does an omelet with cheese sound?"

"Amazing as long as there is some toast to go with it."

A few minutes later he brought her a plate with an omelet and two pieces of buttered toast. Keegan smiled up at him. "Thank you, you're so sweet."

They ate in silence and savored each other's company, stealing glances across the table at each other and smiling when they got caught. When they finished eating, Rourk said, "Why don't you get ready and we'll go off in search of the waterfall?"

She ran over to kiss him and then skipped up the stairs. She came back down about forty-five minutes later ready to head out, and noticed Rourk had packed a lunch for them. His thoughtfulness made her glow.

Rourk hefted the basket onto his forearm and draped the blanket over it. Keegan took hold of his other hand as they walked out the door and down the pathway. She hadn't known she could possibly feel so alive. Her heart felt like it could burst at any moment.

The sun shone brightly despite the slight chill in the air, but Keegan felt only the warmth of Rourk's hand in hers.

It took about an hour to reach the waterfall. It must have been over two hundred feet high. Water cascaded at a rapid pace down the rocks, stairstepping into a rolling, whirling pool that flowed into a small stream. Lush green foliage surrounded the falls, making them stand out in a vista worthy of a painting.

Keegan felt like they'd found their own slice of paradise. It had a magical feel to it, and she understood why her parents had not wanted to share their special place with anyone. She quickly got lost in her camera. She loved capturing Rourk in a natural setting. He looked so peaceful, at one with nature.

Rourk spread the blanket out in a grassy clearing. Keegan grabbed the basket and placed it in the middle of the blanket. She sank to her knees and peeked inside, smiling when she saw the peanut butter and jelly sandwiches, fruit, cookies, and iced tea.

Keegan pulled out a sandwich and handed it to Rourk. Her hand brushed his, and she gasped when the electricity coursed through her body. His slate grey eyes met hers and she could only think what an incredible man Rourk was.

"I hope I brought enough food." Rourk gave her a lopsided grin. "I know you like to eat."

Keegan scooted over next to him and leaned her head against his shoulder. She took a bite of the sandwich. "I'm sure it will do for now."

Rourk leaned down and kissed the top of her head.

They stayed out until the sun started to set. "We better get back to the cabin before your parents get worried."

The weekend went by in a blur, the happiest time in her life. Keegan felt so grateful to her parents for allowing them to be together, despite the prohibitions.

The journey home did not feel as joyful. Keegan couldn't imagine being without Rourk again. She knew it wasn't for long, but even a little time away would seem like a lifetime to her.

As if he could read her thoughts, Rourk leaned over and whispered, "This will all be over soon, and we will be able to be together." He squeezed her hand. "Instead of focusing on the negative, be thankful for the time we shared. When you feel lonely, just remember this weekend."

She smiled, knowing he was right, but that didn't mean it would be easy.

They arrived at his house, but she didn't skip up the path this time. They walked slowly, and each dreaded reaching the door.

Keegan willed herself not to cry. She had to be strong.

Rourk tenderly moved a strand of hair from Keegan's face. He pulled her close to him. Placing his hand under her chin, he tilted her head towards his, and softly kissed her on the lips. Releasing her, he smiled. "See you in Ireland." He opened the door and closed it behind him.

Rourk didn't dare allow himself to look out the window when she left, he just felt relieved that his father wasn't there. He didn't feel like talking to anyone. He went to his room and lay on his bed. Staring at the ceiling, he recalled the weekend as if watching a movie, and eventually the deep sadness cleared. He needed to compartmentalize and focus on the battle. The sooner they got this over with, the sooner he could get her back. That had to be his primary goal now.

Rourk slept for a while, then woke up and went about his normal routine. He walked to the kitchen and made himself a protein shake. Grabbing a book and dictionary, he sat at the table. Scanning through random pages of the book, he found a word he wasn't sure of. Reading the surrounding sentences, he came up with a definition, then checked the dictionary and moved on to another. He didn't find many words that stumped him, but old habits die hard.

Rourk went into his garage, tossed his shirt off, and jumped on the rower. He rowed five kilometers, did a hundred push-ups, a hundred sit-ups, and then a hundred pull-ups—and went back for another five kilometer row. Once he hit about thirty-five hundred meters, he smiled. Keegan was awake and thinking of him. He loved knowing he had crossed her mind.

Rourk finished up his workout, showered, and headed into work.

When he got there, he noticed the men seemed to be rejuvenated after the long weekend. It was just what they had needed. Richard knew his men well. They still had some intense training ahead of them in preparation for the battle. Rourk could feel the energy in the air even though no one said anything. They all knew the time was rapidly approaching.

The next morning Keegan walked through the school doors with a smile on her face. She laughed when she saw Spencer run up behind Donald and smack the back of his head. Donald took off chasing him down the hall. It was nice to see things were back to normal.

Lauren walked up beside her and tossed an arm around her shoulder in a hug. She had her curly hair pulled into a sleek ponytail. "You are glowing, Keegan. What has you in such a good mood?"

Keegan flushed, thinking of Rourk. She wished she could tell Lauren about him and the weekend. On the other hand, it felt like a magnificent secret she didn't want to share. "I'm not sure, I just feel happy to be alive. I know that sounds stupid."

"No, it doesn't. I'm just glad to see you're out of your funk. It's not as much fun when you mope."

"Sorry about that," Keegan said as they drew near to her locker. "I'm not sure what got into me."

"It doesn't matter as long as you're happy now."

The days before the battle passed quickly. Before she knew it, Keegan's birthday was only a few days away. The family started preparing for their trip to Ireland.

Something occurred to Keegan, and asked her mother how all the soldiers would get to Ireland with all their gear. Her mother had just laughed. "Keegan, what good is our magic if we can't use it once in a while? You know how you can watch someone with your mind's eye? Well, some elves can do that with their bodies, which is called teleportation. The really strong ones can bring others with them. We have enough with the gift that getting the soldiers anywhere unseen is not an issue."

Keegan crinkled her nose. "Then why do we have to take the long overseas flight?"

Her mom grinned. "Your father likes to get frequent flyer points."

Chapter 21

Thaddeus lounged against the brick wall of the building, listening to the camp come alive with chatter as the men waited for his father to arrive. They all sensed they were not going on a training mission, that the time had come for the great battle of the prophecy. Many of them had dreamed of this since childhood. Thaddeus tried not to think of all the men around him who would not make it home. His gift weighed heavy on his heart.

A hush settled over the crowd as Richard approached the podium, dressed like the rest of them in faded green camouflage fatigues and a worn, tan baseball cap imprinted with a skull on his head. Nothing at all pinpointed him as the commander; it wasn't needed. The respect for him went beyond that. Confidence radiated from the man.

"You've all worked hard to get ready for this moment. Hell, you've been training for this your whole life." He paused, his face stern. "The battle is upon us. We go to Ireland, not for a training mission, but to fight the enemy. The dark elves want to remove us from existence. We will not allow that to happen." Cheers filled the field, and he gave them a moment to die down. "I will lead you during the battle—it's my honor to do so. I want you all to remember, that even though you follow me into battle, you fight for yourself, for your family, for our very existence. Honor above all!"

When he finished, the ground shook from the roars of the men.

Preparations continued, they planned to leave at nightfall. Magic obviously had its perks. Before long, they would all be in place, arriving a week early to get the lay of the land and have everything set up before the harvest moon. Advance scout parties had been in place for weeks. Richard had sent his best men, minus Rourk. So far everything had gone as planned. Of course, plans seldom went off without a hitch.

When the time came, Thaddeus teleported alongside his father and a couple other men. The elf gifted with teleportation held out his arm so they could all take hold. Thaddeus' stomach fell as the ground disappeared with a dizzying sensation. Streaks of color blurred in his vision and he felt as if he were on a rollercoaster, hanging on to the other elf's arm tightly. In less than a few seconds, it ended.

He looked around, trying to gain his bearings with his stomach still rolling. It was daytime in Ireland, so he took in the majestic scenery that would become such a beautiful spot for the horrors of war. The battle would be cloaked with magic, and they would not be visible to the human eye. Magic was as much a curse as it was a blessing.

As far as he could see, the hills and valleys swept across the land in shades of green. In a clear, brilliant blue sky, clouds like picture-perfect pillows seemed to hang lower in the sky than they did back home. In the distance, he saw the smoke from several farmhouses and the telltale specks of white on the ground that could only be grazing sheep.

He watched as his father went around, barking out orders, a constant presence for the soldiers. Thaddeus noticed he'd occasionally offer to help with erecting tents or building fires. The men, already in awe of him, respected him even more for his compassion.

They could have used magic to set up the tents and get everything in order, but his father knew that setting up their own camp gave them something to keep their hands and minds busy.

Thaddeus walked up to stand beside his father, and together they took in the scene before them. Men, scattered all over the camp, each did something to make the camp functional. Soldiers set up tents, sharpened weapons, set fires, and distributed equipment. Some of the units sang as they worked. To an outsider, it would look like complete chaos, but that couldn't be further from the truth. These elves made organized and efficient soldiers.

"What do you think, son?"

"I think it's an impressive sight." Thaddeus paused, and then said, "I'm slightly nervous, to tell you the truth."

"I'd worry about you if you weren't." His father's eyes never left the rows and rows of tents.

"How long do you think it will take to prepare the camp?"

Richard smiled as he scanned the fields of men. "We'll be done in two days."

"Any new reports from the scout party?" Thaddeus asked.

"Yes. Some dark elves have arrived, just a small reconnaissance team. They will be arriving shortly." Patting his son on the shoulder, he said, "Thanks to you, we got here first."

"Should we worry about an ambush?"

His father looked grim. "No, elves are too honorable to break the code of battle, even dark elves. Of course, we'll have gifted in place to alert us, just in case." His father looked at him, searching his face. "Have you seen an ambush I should be aware of?"

Thaddeus met his father's eyes. "I have not."

Richard watched his son walk away. He could feel his blood pumping through his veins. As a secondary gift, he had a heightened awareness of his body. It affected all of his senses, and gave him a significant advantage in battle. His mind processed at an accelerated rate, increasing his reaction time. Only his wife knew of this gift; she'd figured it out on her own.

Thinking of his wife, he closed his eyes to check on her. She was reading a book to Warrick. He couldn't conceal his smile when he saw the title. Not even two years old and his bedtime story was *The Illiad.*

Emerald glanced up and smiled. She knew he was there. Their bond had grown stronger over the years, and each of them could tell when the other checked in. They could even talk to each other, but that took a lot of energy, so they rarely did. Just being able to see each other made their long separations bearable. Fortunately, each also had the ability to block the other if needed.

Richard had been involved in numerous battles in his lifetime, but none of this magnitude. During his time in the Special Forces he worked in small man teams. Even in the Army of the Light, he mostly took solo missions.

Now, with thousands of soldiers at the camp, more gifted arrived daily, women and children among them. Some of the children had gifts too powerful to leave behind. They would not engage in the battle, but healers and weather manipulators would be vital to the war.

Emerald and the rest of his family would arrive tomorrow, the day before the battle. Though eager to see them, he also worried. Having to put Thaddeus in danger felt bad enough.

The vision of Keegan dying haunted the back of his mind.

Meanwhile, Thaddeus and Rourk rested in their small tent, barely big enough for their sleeping bags and belongings. Luckily, they'd come during the least rainy of the seasons in Ireland, but, if they hadn't, the canvas tent would keep them warm and dry, despite its age.

Thaddeus glanced at Rourk, who calmly focused on cleaning his sword with an oil cloth. Soon, they would both experience their first real battle.

"Are you nervous?" Thaddeus asked.

Without looking up, Rourk replied, "No, just excited. I know I'm not supposed to be excited, but I can't help it. We were born to do this. Are you nervous? You have a lot of pressure on you. Not to mention that you're just a kid."

The older boy sounded like he might be joking with that last part, but Thad couldn't tell. When Rourk's gray eyes met his own, he felt the urge to be honest. "I'm nervous; I really have no idea how I'm supposed to pull this off. I have to keep reminding myself the burden falls not on me, but on my gift and I have no control over it."

"You are very wise for your age."

Thaddeus shrugged his shoulders. "I've never felt my age."

"What do you think of the rules of war?"

"Let's go over them again. It might calm my nerves," Thaddeus replied.

Rourk nodded. He sat up straighter, cleared his throat, and spoke, "Our ancestors set down the rules thousands of years ago. The fighting commences only during the daylight hours—by nightfall, both sides disband and return to the camp. It keeps up morale, as well as rejuvenates the soldiers for the next day's battle."

"It seems like that would unnecessarily lengthen the war," Thaddeus remarked.

Inclining his head in agreement, Rourk said, "Yes, it does. But the elders believe you should face your enemy and give them a chance to defend themselves while both sides are at their strongest. In the human world, this sort of code seems old-fashioned, but I have 'death before dishonor' so ingrained in my mind that I can't imagine any other way."

Thaddeus nodded thoughtfully.

Rourk paused, then continued in a formal tone. "Magic can be used in elfin battles, but an amendment to the rules, made nearly a hundred years ago, forbids using guns."

"I've always thought that was kinda stupid," Thaddeus said with a short laugh.

Rourk's, his voice stern and his eyes hard, said, "'Friendly fire isn't.' All the magical energy on the battle field could affect the accuracy of such weapons." Rourk's steady eyes met his young comrade's. "Your thoughts?"

Thaddeus stared at Rourk, thinking before he replied. "Well, it sucks we can't use guns."

Rourk didn't say anything.

"But I can see that magic might affect the weapons and cause more harm than good. I can't imagine accidentally shooting someone I know. And, I have to admit," Thaddeus went on with a shrug, "I'm glad that fighting stops at nightfall. A chance to recuperate."

Rourk nodded. "Most elves do appreciate the fresh start."

"I'm really surprised, though, that the dark elves follow the laws. I would think they would cheat."

"Even though their morals may be a bit…looser than our own, the dark elves do honor many of the same laws. Your father says they would see breaking the code as a dishonor. They do not consider a winning by cheating a real victory."

"And I am happy with the fact that we can use magic." Thaddeus grinned. "Gives us something to work with. However, that also means they can use magic. What about you? What do you think?"

"I think it's important that we honor our ancestors and keep with tradition. Honor above all," Rourk said evenly.

"I agree with you, that is the most important element in all of this." Rourk took a deep breath. "Okay, well. I need to get some sleep. Keegan arrives tomorrow."

"Yes, I know. Goodnight."

The flight was long and uncomfortable. Keegan hadn't been feeling so great the last couple of days. Hopefully she wasn't coming down with something. She could have asked her mother for a healing, but she didn't want to bother her. Eleven hours in such a small space had left Keegan feeling deeply unsettled, particularly knowing where the plane was taking her. She was glad when they finally stepped off the plane and into the bustle of the Shannon airport.

She had always wanted to visit Ireland, but thought it would be under better circumstances. She barely had time to notice anything as Emerald pushed the family toward the rental car place, her face tight and distressed. Brigid and Katrina kept unusually quiet.

The drive to the battlefield couldn't have taken an hour, but it felt like forever to Keegan. She wanted to catch a glimpse of Rourk at the camp, but she also knew that, once they arrived, it would all be real.

"What am I supposed to do?" Keegan asked quietly. She had no idea what was expected of her.

"You will help take care of the wounded," Katrina said from the back.

"I'm not a healer." Keegan's eyes widened.

"Of course you're not, but you can still help. You can help with cooking for the soldiers, giving out supplies, and cleaning up the wounds until a healer is available."

Keegan leaned back in her seat. The reality of the situation had still not hit her. The wounded wouldn't be strangers, but possibly her father, brother, and chosen. Her mind couldn't seem to accept that.

Emerald steered the car far away from civilization and deep into the countryside of Ireland. Keegan kept her forehead pressed to the cold glass, watching the small towns and farmsteads pass outside. The sun, high in the sky, illuminated mothers pushing their babies in strollers down cobblestone streets and laughing people enjoying late lunches at outdoor pubs. As they moved further in the country, certain sights struck Keegan especially, like an abandoned castle only a few feet from the road, or an old, crumbling church sitting on a farm where a young girl in big boots followed behind her father into the sheep pen. Lives moved forward all around her, while hers came to a standstill.

The scene waiting for them at the camp left them all speechless.

The tents seemed to go on forever. Thousands of soldiers walked around in full gear, laughing and joking. Some gathered around campfires, deep in conversation, while others wiled away time by kicking a dirty soccer ball around. The voices and clanking metal filled the air with sound and an electric tension. It was amazing that magic cloaked the scene from human eyes.

Emerald closed her eyes to let her husband know they had arrived.

Keegan watched as her father made his way through the crowd, stopping to talk to some of the soldiers. She smiled when he picked up a gifted child and tossed him in the air until the child broke into a giggling fit. Elves made way for him to pass until eventually he reached them.

"You guys are a sight for sore eyes. Follow me, and I'll show you to your tents."

Keegan glanced frantically around, hoping to catch a glimpse of Rourk, though she knew she didn't have a chance of spotting him among so many people. Her heart ached, knowing they were so close, but not together.

After they had settled into their own tents, Keegan decided to take a walk around the camp; she wasn't ashamed to admit to herself she hoped to find Rourk. She was surprised to see so many different types of creatures. A tiger, followed closely by a lion and a panther almost knocked her down as they ran around her.

The tiger walked up and rubbed his head on her leg. She looked down, startled to see human eyes peering back at her. She couldn't shake the feeling she had seen them before. The three big cats ran off, playfully swatting at each other and rolling around, but they generally circling her.

The lion nudged her leg. She looked down into another pair of human eyes. She looked over at the panther and thought, *This can't be possible.* Looking into the tiger's blue eyes, she said, "Donald? Is that you?"

Right before her eyes, he morphed into his human form. She had been around magic her whole life, so the transformation didn't surprise her, but she had never expected it from him.

"How did this happen? What are you guys? I know you're not elves. Have you known about me all along?"

"Keegan, everyone knows you're an elf. Calvron can spot a creature of the light miles away. No offense, but you elves are kinda snobbish, keeping to yourselves and not hanging out with other creatures."

She let that information sink in for a moment, but had to admit he had a point. She had never known of elves to reach out and be friends with other creatures. If elves lived everywhere, it made sense that other creatures of the light and dark did, too.

Were they really snobs? Secrecy had been drilled into her since a young age, not because they were better than others, just to make sure their race stayed out of the eyes of humans. Obviously, things would have to change now that she knew the truth about her friends.

"Sorry—I really didn't know. I wish you guys had said something." Keegan flushed, embarrassed.

"It was more fun letting you think we didn't know." Donald grinned.

"So how did you find out about this? Is there, like, a creature of the light newsletter I've missed out on?"

Donald shrugged sheepishly. "I overheard your thoughts about the battle the other day. I didn't mean to, but you broadcast so loud I couldn't help it. So, I called a few friends who passed the word. Creatures of the light from all walks of life will be showing up."

She threw her arms around him. "Thank you, thank you, thank you."

His face turned bright red.

When she glanced back, Sam and Spencer stood there, grinning. "So, what are you guys?"

Spencer laughed. "Nothing as fancy as an elf—just your everyday, run-of-the-mill shape shifters. You might be surprised to know how many creatures of the light go to our school. Not to mention the principal."

Keegan, indeed shocked, felt more than a little frustrated. They all knew about her and she was clueless. "What about Calvron?"

"Wizard," Donald said. Keegan shook her head. All this time she thought she was the only non-human at school.

"Lauren?"

"Fairy."

No, this could not be true. "Anna?"

"She's an unusual case. Her mom is a spirit walker, and her father's human. So we're really not sure about her."

This fascinated Keegan; she'd been wrong on nearly everything she had thought she'd known about her world. She started to get a little miffed that they had kept their secrets from her, but realized she couldn't really talk—she'd kept her own secrets. "What about Katie?"

"Human."

Keegan sighed. At least one friend was the way she imagined.

The guys said their goodbyes and wished her luck before morphing into their animal forms once more. Keegan watched them race away, her chest tight.

What if something happened to them?

She couldn't think that way, it would drive her crazy. Keegan trudged back to her tent. Her mother sat rocking Warrick in the corner, while both of her aunts lay wide-eyed and sleepless in their sleeping bags.

The battle would commence at sunrise.

Chapter 22

Keegan had never realized how absolute silence could be in the minutes before dawn. Maybe because the expectation of battle filled the air, not even birds sang.

Her heart pounded as she stood silent with the other women and children. They watched as the soldiers crested the hill and disappeared to the battlefield.

As the sun lightened the sky, a thunderous battle roar echoed through the valley, followed by the unmistakable sound of swords clashing.

The battle had begun.

The camp fell to chaos. Too far from the battle to see the actual fighting, Keegan could hear it. The noises and smells overwhelmed her senses. The coppery smell of blood filled the air. The clanging of steel against steel, the screams, and an overall eerie feeling filled her body.

Before long, the wounded began to stumble back to camp. The first soldier her mother healed was so young that Keegan immediately thought of Rourk. She pushed her negative thoughts away. He would be fine. He had to be.

"Katrina, what can I do?" Keegan asked as Katrina hurried up to Emerald, a dark bottle in her hands.

Falling to her knees next to her sister, Katrina opened the bottle to pour into the man's wounds. "Grab some towels and bring them over here. After that, help tend to the wounded. I know you can't heal them, but you can do basic first aid while they wait for a healing."

Keegan rushed off to help, the reality of war starting to hit her.

A thick fog blanketed the green rolling hills, reducing visibility to only two or three feet. The battle between the gifted had gotten to the point where Richard didn't know if one of his weather manipulators had caused the fog, or the dark elves.

Either way, Richard was in his element. His fingers tingled as he touched his weapon of choice, a *Kusarigama* this time. The sickle and chain combination originated in Japan as early as the twelfth century.

Many of the dark elves had chosen larger, heavier weapons, which needed to be swung with considerable force to be effective. In the fog, they risked hitting their own kind as often as the enemy. In contrast, Richard's *Kusarigama* felt alive. It blocked, entangled, and then killed each opponent brought into its path as if it led a dance, with Richard following, exerting just enough energy to avoid tiring too soon. He killed many dark elves that day.

Thaddeus was grateful for the fog. No one could see more than the enemy they engaged. It seemed one-on-one worked better for him; he could concentrate that way. When he could see all the fighting around him, he saw distracting flashes of the others' deaths. Facing one enemy meant he only had visions of that individual, which actually helped him fight.

A flash of his opponent's unguarded neck caused Thaddeus to reverse his sword, swinging for the opening. He severed the elf's head, and moved on to the next. He felt slightly exhilarated.

Rourk felt nothing. His goal filled his head, to kill as many of the bastards as he could. He had never felt so relaxed in his life. It almost felt as if his body floated through combat, although he saw his feet firmly planted on the ground.

He wished the fog would lift so he could take on more than one at a time.

The battle raged on all day, the noise deafening. Eventually the fog lifted; it didn't last too long. Scores died on both sides.

Healing consumed Emerald, along with all the other healers. They saved countless lives, but some were beyond help. It tore her apart to see those young soldiers die. At least the older soldiers she knew died doing what they loved. They would be remembered as heroes, as all great warriors hoped. Those who died during the great battle would always be remembered with honor.

Night descended upon them and relief spread throughout the camp. Exhausted, everyone needed a hot meal and sleep, yet energy coursed through the camp. Keegan helped serve food to the soldiers. The men looked both exhilarated and exhausted. In every face she looked into, she longed to see Rourk's grey eyes, but it was not to be.

Keegan ran into the three cats as she carried another platter of food to the soldiers. Once they saw her, they morphed into their human forms. They talked excitedly among themselves about the battle.

"Hey, Keegan," Sam said.

"You guys look like you enjoyed yourselves," she told them quietly, still in shock herself.

"Keegan, it is amazing out there! I feel like a different person. I'm so focused, and so hyperaware. I can't really explain it, but it's amazing." Sam looked down at the ground when he finally stopped talking.

"Well, glad you guys are enjoying yourselves. Be careful out there tomorrow. I have to finish passing out food, so I'll let you guys get back to your war stories." They said goodnight, barely stopping their excited chatter.

Looking up at the huge orange moon, Keegan realized it was her birthday. Usually she made a big ordeal of it, reminding everyone not to forget to get her a gift. This year she thought she would give up all her birthdays if they could just survive the battle.

After helping clean up, she headed to her tent ready to fall into a deep sleep. As she bent down to crawl in the tent, an exuberant, "Happy birthday!" and a homemade cake greeted her.

Her mother came over and gave her a hug. "Your Jeep is waiting in the driveway."

Keegan smiled slightly, but knew she'd give up everything she owned for this madness to end.

After having a slice of cake, she climbed into her sleeping bag. She felt something scratch her, so she reached down and pulled out a piece of paper.

Keegan, I am sorry I could not spend your special day with you. I will make it up to you. Forever Yours, Rourk.

Pressing the letter to her chest, she felt a tear drop down her face as she drifted off to sleep.

Chapter 23

Four days came and went, each day the same as the last. Keegan carried her sword everywhere she went—all the women and children did. Each morning seemed colder and more filled with death.

The loss of life was staggering. Keegan saw one of her father's best friends carried off the battleground and it shook her to the core.

Keegan wrapped a bandage around a young soldier's arm, and when she glanced up her heart stilled. Rourk threw his sword—blade broken—in a pile and grabbed a new one.

Rourk.

He looked up, and his grey eyes met hers. Without a word, he turned and headed back into battle.

She finished dressing the wound and jumped up to follow Rourk.

Keegan crossed the dew-covered valley and mounted the hill that separated the camp from the battle. She drew her sword as she approached. She didn't plan to get close enough to need it, but better to be safe than sorry.

The destruction horrified her. Following the sharp sound of blades singing through the air, she saw body parts flying. She heard screams of rage, as well as screams of agony.

Her eyes darted around as she tried to catch a glimpse of Rourk, but he had faded into the soldiers, and she couldn't pick him out. She knew she should go back to the tents, but she couldn't stop looking at the destruction before her.

Surprised, she spotted the three large cats. They looked majestic out there—she saw Spencer pounce and swipe his claws across someone's neck, severing his artery. Sam clamped his jaw on an elf's neck, and he thrashed the dark elf like a rag doll. Donald looked massive tearing through the soldiers. He took three out in the blink of an eye. They looked so fierce; she saw them in a whole new light. She couldn't tear her eyes away from them.

A loud roar echoed, and Donald fell to the ground. Keegan didn't think, she just ran, slashing her way through the crowd. Her sword connected with a couple of dark elves and part of her watched, horrified, as their bodies fell, but she pushed on anyway. Her need to reach her friend outweighed anything else.

Donald was still breathing, but blood poured out of the deep wound in his chest. She didn't think he was going to make it. Sam and Spencer's moans filled the air, but they fought on.

Relief flooded her when her mother pushed her aside.

"We'll talk about your brash decision to leave the camp and walk into the middle of a battle later," Emerald snapped. "Cover me, Keegan, and I can save him."

Terrified, Keegan grasped her sword firmly and prayed she wouldn't need to use it again.

Her mom knelt down and placed her hands above the tiger's chest. She closed her eyes and lifted her face. Then she looked back at Keegan, her face relieved. "The wound would have been fatal, but we reached him in time, Keegan."

Relief filled Keegan. When Emerald finished the healing, the tiger lifted his head and licked her face, and Keegan smiled tensely. She patted the gigantic cat. The tiger got to his feet and, with one last glance at Keegan, took off back into battle.

Her mother stood up. "Follow me, Keegan. We need to get out of here as quick as possible."

She couldn't agree more. Her mother slashed through elves, and Keegan kept as close as she could.

Something made Keegan look to the side. A dark elf drew his bow, aiming for her. She disappeared, dodging to the side.

"Keegan!" her mother screamed. Emerald watched in horror as the arrow sped toward her daughter. Then she went numb as the arrow stopped midair.

Keegan searched the sky in the split second she had before it hit. Time seemed to slow. She could feel the pounding of the battle in the ground beneath her feet and the cool air brushing across her skin. The battle silenced around her as the sharp sting of the arrow shattered her awareness. Starbursts exploded in her eyes, an array of colors that faded to black.

Emerald heard the body drop. Keegan could only be dead. Even wounded, she would have appeared, standing, wherever she stepped to dodge the arrow.

When she looked back at her daughter, Keegan sprawled on the ground, an arrow through her heart.

"NO!" Emerald screamed in agony, dropping to her knees even as she knew it was too late.

Frantically, Emerald tried to save her, but her gift could not bring back the dead.

A coldness entered Rourk's body. He closed his eyes and saw Keegan on the ground, her mother sobbing, clutching her daughter. Everyone engaged in the battle literally froze in place, swords stopping in mid-swing, bodies balanced as if in a strange painting. Time stood still.

Only Rourk and Keegan's family could move. They all raced towards her body, crying and kneeling on the ground next to her.

Thaddeus, frozen in disbelief, stared at his vision in the flesh. It was over. They would lose. Sure, the battle would go on, but in the end there would be blackness. He had failed. Richard cried silent tears as he knelt on the ground, holding his daughter's hand, his other arm supporting his wife.

Rourk felt a fury he had never known. In a quiet, dangerous voice, he said, "They will all die."

Emerald looked into his steel grey eyes and felt his rage seep into her. She stumbled to her feet, wiping the tears from her face, and grabbed the hilt of her sword. The heaviness in her hands felt real. She stood up beside Rourk. "They took my daughter; I will take their lives. No mercy for the dark. They will die."

Together, the two raced forward, killing dark elves who stood frozen, unable to fight back.

Rourk had no intention of leaving the battle alive. He didn't want to live in a world without Keegan. He would join her on the other side, but not before he avenged her death.

Thaddeus didn't know what to do. The prophecy said he could save them from annihilation, yet his visions kept coming true. He couldn't see a way out of this. He couldn't push his grief for his sister aside.

He needed to think, he needed to be alone—like at home when he could go for a run and just let go. His sister had just been killed and now his mother had gone over the edge. Had the time of the light elves really ended? He couldn't accept that. There had to be something he could do.

Richard silently picked Keegan up, cradling her against his chest. Grief seeped through him as he looked down at his only daughter. It was useless to go after his wife; nothing could stop the rage that coursed through her veins. He felt her agony inside him.

She and Rourk were no longer thinking as soldiers. They were hellbent on revenge.

Flashes of his daughter's childhood went through his mind.

She was five and he followed behind her on the driveway, his hand gripping the seat of her bicycle without its training wheels. He still remembered the way she had fallen, scraped her knees, and stood up, brushing her hands off to do it again.

She was nine, dancing around the kitchen like a ballerina with her skinny arms in the air and socks on her feet. Richard recalled how she slid after one particularly hard twirl and knocked Emerald's favorite blue vase from the table. They had cleaned it up, the two of them, and hidden the shards at the bottom of the trash can. Emerald found out anyway.

Just a few weeks before, she had stood in the living room, rolling her eyes at his bad jokes. Richard had wondered when she had become such a beautiful young woman.

As he carried his daughter away, the battle fell into motion once more around them. The spell had been lifted. The singing metal clangs that had sounded for five days straight barely reached his ears. The movement of the men fighting around him, the scent of death—none of it mattered. He didn't care about the war or their inevitable fate, he only cared about getting his daughter away from the scene of her death.

Suddenly, chanting overwhelmed the sound of the battle. Richard could not understand the words; it sounded like gibberish. He looked around, searching for the source, and saw a woman walking towards them.

Her long, white robe flowed behind her. Her brown hair fell down the side of her shoulders, framing her pure face with soft brown eyes. She was almost translucent. Richard could tell that only he and Thaddeus could see her because no one else gave her a second glance. And he knew she must be a spirit walker. He had heard of them, but had never laid eyes on one.

Thaddeus whispered, "It's Anna's mother."

Chapter 24

Gently, the luminous woman took Keegan from his arms, her chant turning into what sounded like a spell. Keegan's body took on the same translucent sheen as the woman's. The colors started to come back, but paler, faded at first and then brighter. They watched, shocked, as Keegan's eyes fluttered open.

Looking up at his father in shock, Thaddeus whispered, "Dark magic."

Keegan's eyes slowly focused. She tried to look around, but her vision blurred. The earsplitting noise overwhelmed her. Her mind raced as she tried to figure out what the noises were. Who was holding her? She was being cradled in someone's arms. Panic rose in her throat.

"Keegan, can you hear me?" His voice sounded desperate. She recognized it, but she couldn't place it. She blinked her eyes a few times and her vision finally cleared a bit. She tried to speak, but nothing would come out. A wave of dizziness washed over her, then darkness.

"What have you done to our daughter?" Richard asked, stepping forward.

"I gave her life back. Your wife gave me my life back, and this is my repayment." The woman spoke matter-of-factly.

"Yes, but at what cost? Only black magic can bring someone back from the dead."

"There will be consequences, but she is alive. Isn't that enough? I would do anything to protect my own daughters, even if it meant using black magic. If you and your wife do not approve of my actions, they can be reversed within twenty-four hours."

Richard took his daughter back, holding her gently against him. He knew that would be impossible. He would not give back this gift. Whatever the consequences, they would work through them.

"Why is she not responding?" Richard said.

"Her body has undergone a major transformation, which causes sensory overload. She will be out for at least a day, if not more. Her body needs time to recover. I will stay with her while she recovers in case anything goes wrong. Your wife should be here; a healing might help speed up the process."

Richard closed his eyes and mentally screamed, *Emerald, she is alive.*

Emerald's sword was raised. Without pause she slashed, and another body dropped to the ground. She couldn't close her eyes to see what Richard saw, she would die in the thick of the battle if she looked away for a second. Scanning quickly, she searched for Rourk. She heard his animalistic scream as he drove a dagger through a dark elf. She had to get to him. As much as she wanted to run to her daughter, she had to let him know. She fought her way close enough to get his attention.

"Keegan is alive!"

She couldn't possibly have said what he thought she did. Rourk's opponent advanced, and he countered swiftly. Frozen, uncomprehending, he glanced over at Emerald. "Alive?" The word made no sense.

Trying to process the information, he let his guard down. In that moment, a dark elf drove a blade through his stomach.

Rourk looked down at the blood. Stomach wounds were the worst; he would bleed out slowly. His hand drifted to the wound and his vision swam.

Emerald let out a pained yell and rushed the dark elf, her own sword high above her head. The elf parried the blow and sent the blade spinning away. He swiped at Emerald. She leapt back, arms flailing as she lost her balance and landed hard on her back. The dark elf charged, murder written on his face.

Rourk could already feel the results of the blood loss. His arms moved too slowly as he heaved his sword across the space between them. The effort knocked him off his feet; he landed on his knees, staring wide-eyed at the sword as it slid into place next to Emerald.

Her hand closed over the hilt just as the dark elf's sword fell. Emerald flipped to the left, away from the impact, and brought Rourk's sword up in a swift, deadly arc. The dark elf fell, and Emerald clambered to her feet, breathless.

"Come on," she said, her voice high. "We have to get you out of here."

Rourk couldn't feel his legs, but he slid an arm around her fragile, surprisingly strong shoulders and allowed her to heave him up. They darted through the crowd, Emerald grunting as she supported a half-conscious Rourk and evaded fighting elves. She prayed that no one noticed them; she couldn't battle and help Rourk at the same time.

With the edge of the battlefield in sight, she was blindsided. The force of the dark elf's blow knocked her off her feet. She landed on her elbows, crying out as pain shot through her arms.

Rourk's battle yell rang out louder than any of the other sounds around them. Emerald rolled, lashing out as she stumbled to her feet. Her blade hit nothing—Rourk stood over the fallen elf, hands clenched at his sides. The dark elf's neck bent at an odd angle.

Emerald wanted to thank him, but she knew there would be time for that later. She gripped his waist and rushed him forward, his feet stumbling. They made it safely off the battlefield.

Laying him down on the ground, Emerald went to work. She smiled down at him, her hair sticking up wildly and a stripe of blood across her dirty cheek. "I don't know how or why, but Keegan is alive."

Rourk wanted to jump up, but couldn't. He had to wait until she finished. He would be no good to Keegan dead. He closed his eyes but saw nothing when he sought her.

"I don't understand," he said. "I can't see her."

Emerald closed her eyes. She couldn't see her daughter, either. Had she heard Richard wrong? Closing her eyes, she focused on her husband. He sat beside their daughter's body. Her eyes were closed, and she was not moving.

Sensing her, Richard thought, *She is alive, but she'll be out for a while.*

Emerald responded, *I'm hurrying. Rourk needed a healing. We'll be there shortly.*

Some healings took longer than others, and Rourk's was one of the longer ones. When she finished up, she helped the young man to his feet and they set off at a rapid pace for Richard's tent. Emerald flung the tent flap open and ran to her daughter.

Kneeling beside her daughter, Emerald felt for a pulse. It was shallow, but she had one. Emerald focused every ounce of energy she had, and called forth her ancestors. She knew it could be done because her own mother had told her so, but she herself had never before asked for the ancestors.

Now she felt them surround her, and begged for their help in healing Keegan. She smiled when she felt her grandmother's hands touch hers. She closed her eyes; they began their work.

Emerald instantly felt something off. She knew her daughter's energy field, and it had been altered. Keegan usually had a particularly warm energy that felt like the sun shining directly on her. Now, her energy felt as cool as the air from a nighttime stroll in the fall. Emerald pushed aside her fears and focused on the healing; maybe when healed Keegan, she would feel normal. Three generations of healers worked on Keegan, she would be fine.

Emerald sat over her daughter's prone form. The healing continued for well over two hours, the longest healing she had ever given. Eventually, Keegan's breathing returned to normal and her pulse grew stronger, though slightly lower than it should be. She was still unconscious. But she lived; she would pull through.

Then Emerald realized that Anna's mother was there. Jennifer had sat silently through the healing, staying at Keegan's side as she had promised. "I don't understand. How can she be alive? You're a spirit walker?"

Jennifer gazed almost lovingly at her. "Yes, I am a spirit walker."

Her voice uncertain, Emerald asked, "I thought spirit walkers just helped people to the other side?" She had a sinking feeling in her chest, and she almost didn't want her to continue.

"I used black magic to bring her back." Jennifer stated flatly, as if she were worried about the other woman's reaction. Her tall, thin body slumped against the side of the tent, her unwavering brown eyes patient.

"How could you have used black magic when you are on the side of the light? I have felt your soul; you are a creature of the light."

Jennifer took a deep breath, her chest rising and falling slowly. "My parents died when I was young, and my grandmother, a witch, raised me. She worked for the dark; how she went from light to dark is a long story. She taught me black magic, and I didn't know there was anything wrong with it. As I got older, I realized that my grandmother was evil and turned from her teachings. This is the first time I have ever used black magic to bring someone back from the dead. When I saw Keegan passing, my heart ached for you. I did the same thing I would have done for my own daughters."

Emerald looked up with tears in her eyes. "Thank you for saving my daughter. Can you…do you know how this will affect her? Rourk and I could not see her with our mind's eye when we tried."

"I'm sorry," Jennifer murmured, shaking her head. "I don't know exactly how her body will react. There will be changes like the one you mentioned. We have to wait till she wakes up to see. She has a strong soul. The best way that I can think to explain it is that she will have a spark of dark in her. Her light will be strong enough to keep it at bay."

Thaddeus paced the tent like a caged animal, avoiding looking at his sister as his mind whirled. His voice broke the uncomfortable silence that followed Jennifer's declaration. "I need to be alone to think."

Richard looked up and nodded at his son. Glancing at Jennifer, he asked, "She will be out for at least twenty-four hours?"

Jennifer nodded.

Richard leaned down and kissed his daughter on the forehead. "Rourk, we need to get back out there."

As much as it pained him, Rourk knew he was right. He simply nodded, unable to speak.

Richard looked over at Jennifer, "We will be forever in your debt." He shared a look with his wife and marched out back to the battlefield with Rourk following.

Thaddeus felt like he was missing something right in front of his face. He went back over the events—his visions had come true. Keegan had died, masses of elves—including women and children—had died and yet, the light still fought on. They still had a chance, so why couldn't he see it? Why him? Why was he the one who determined the outcome of the battle? What made him different from other seers? He was a warrior, too, that was the only difference.

Time just moved too quickly. He needed it to slow down, so he could figure things out before it was too late. Soon night would fall, stopping the fighting until sunrise. He had to think of something before then. Though not sure why, he had a feeling his window of opportunity would close if he didn't figure it out before tomorrow.

Thaddeus felt a brief pang of guilt. He should be out there fighting with his unit, but he knew he needed to be a seer now and let the others fight.

Suddenly, a light bulb went off in his head.

He began to form a plan.

Chapter 25

Keegan dreamed. She stood in a field of wildflowers, the most beautiful thing she'd ever laid eyes on, and it seemed to stretch on forever. As far as she could see, the bold colors of the flowers waved beneath a bright, sunny sky. She ran and laughed with the wind on her face. Stopping, she twirled around and around until everything became blurry. She heard a loud roar, and she fell to the ground, startled.

Frightened, Keegan frantically looked around. When her vision stopped spinning, she saw a massive tiger in the distance slowly stalking towards her. Too afraid to run, she froze in place. The tiger approached and walked around her in a circle. Coming to a halt, he laid down and stretched out. She reached for him, petting the beautiful animal.

In the heat of battle, Rourk felt he wasn't all there. He knew that kind of distraction could get him killed. He needed to focus and be in the moment, but his mind wanted to wander to Keegan.

He was scared. Hell, he was terrified. He could not sense her. *What did that mean? Had their connection been broken by the black magic?* He focused, screaming within himself as he channeled the energy into a swipe of his sword that took off his opponent's head. He knew he could do nothing for her now; he had to wait for her to wake up tomorrow.

For now, Rourk could take out his frustration on the enemy. He felt the calm surge through his body. Once again, he fought as if floating on air. The strikes came so naturally that he felt at one with his blade. Countless died by his hand before the day ended.

Night descended upon them and relief spread throughout the camp. The soldiers shoved food down their throats and exchanged war stories. The fight for their existence still energized them. The weariness had not settled in yet. Richard knew that, if this kept up much longer, that's exactly what would happen.

Richard heard his son approach and turned to greet him. Earlier, Thaddeus had been tired and drawn, with dark circles under his eyes, but now he stood tall, his eyes shining.

"Father, I've had a vision. I need to be brought to the leader of the dark."

Richard physically took a step back. "Have you lost your mind, son? I cannot allow you to go over to the side of the dark."

Thaddeus spoke firmly, not as a son to his father, but as a gifted seer to the leader of the light. "This is not a request—either you take me or I will go by myself."

Richard could think of nothing that could change his son's mind. He resigned himself to the idea. "Let me grab something to eat and we will go."

Thaddeus held his father's gaze. "We will go now."

Nodding, Richard grabbed his gear and they headed out. He hoped his son knew what he was doing. Just the thought of coming face to face with his nemesis, Creed, made his blood boil. It would take all of his willpower to follow the rules of war.

It took them over an hour by foot to reach the camp of the dark elves. The army of the dark had chosen a spot set deep in a small valley between hills; their sea of illuminated tents lit the valley. The camp was set up essentially like their own. Richard could see no real differences, but he could feel it.

Entering the area felt like they'd stepped into an air conditioned room. A guard in full gear challenged them, his sword tip pointing at Richard's face. Richard glared at him. "We are here to see your leader, Creed. Tell him my son has had a vision and needs to see him at once."

Even creatures of the dark offered profound respect to those gifted with sight. The guard glanced at Thaddeus and almost bowed, but stopped himself. "I will be right back. Wait here." He gestured, calling over his relief.

Thaddeus and Richard pointedly remained silent. Upset about entering the enemy's territory with his son, Richard had no idea what to say. Thaddeus was terrified.

The guard quickly returned. "Follow me."

Conversations stopped as the man led them through the camp. Every dark soldier turned in their direction, following the three men with wary eyes as they passed.

Creed's tent looked no different from any other. He even looked like a normal person, though Richard knew he could not be underestimated. Despite his average appearance, he was dangerous. One did not get to be the leader of the dark without merit.

Creed glanced up when they walked in. He nodded slightly at them both, his blue eyes hard. "I've heard you've had a vision and need to see me?"

Thaddeus stepped forward, "Sir, my vision has shown that if we continue with this war, we will all die. Both armies are equally matched. If you added up the numbers of the dead right now, you would see they are the same. This battle will effectively eliminate our kind, both light and dark. My vision showed me the only way to stop this is to call a truce.

He paused, looking thoughtfully at Creed. "I have also made some connections on my own, if you care to hear them."

Creed waved his hand for Thaddeus to continue, one eyebrow raised sardonically.

"Who is to say that light is just and dark is evil? What if light is just light and dark is just dark? What if we have been brainwashed to believe we should hate each other? Today, I saw my mother and future brother-in-law cross over to the side of the dark. They were no longer fighting for good or to save their kind. They were fueled by pure revenge. I also witnessed with my own eyes my sister being brought back to life by black magic. Does that mean she is evil now? I cannot believe that to be the case."

"I look around your camp and your soldiers look the same as our soldiers. We all fight for something we believe in. What if what we believe in has been false all along? I do not suggest that we become friends. I do suggest that we show each other the respect we both deserve. Why kill off our own race? We are all elves, aren't we?"

Creed stood up and paced the room quietly for a moment, his hands clasped behind his back. Then he looked up, his emotions clear on his face. "My son died today. He did not even believe in war—he thought we should sit down and discuss our differences and work it out amicably.

The leader of the dark drew a ragged breath. "I laughed at him and called him foolish. When I heard he was dead, all I could think was, for what? I couldn't even feel a sense of pride for my son who died in battle. I knew in his heart that he did not agree with it."

Richard tried to hold on to his contempt for the man, but, as Creed spoke, Richard relived the feeling of losing Keegan. He never thought he would share anything with the man he had hated most of his life, but he felt compassion. He knew what it felt like to lose a child, even if his loss seemed to be reversed.

Maybe Thaddeus was right; maybe they weren't so different after all. He had let his contempt for the dark consume him. He never thought of them as individuals.

"Creed, you know that the prophecy marked my son as the only chance the light had to survive. I think we should heed his advice and his vision. Being a great warrior, you know that sometimes calling a truce can be necessary, the right thing to do. I believe this is the time and place."

Creed grimaced. "I've always heard you're smooth. I actually felt a sense of pride just now, when I heard you call me a great warrior. Do you know I have spent most of my adult life hating you? I have lain awake countless nights waiting for this moment, for us to be face to face. I'd go over all the different ways I would kill you if given the chance. Yet, here we stand, both complimenting each other. And I admit that my hatred for you always included a hint of admiration as well."

The two men stared at each other, and Richard extended his hand. Creed grasped his hand and they shook.

"A truce it is," Creed said.

Richard clasped his hands behind his back. "Now that we don't plan to fight each other anymore, we have to do something. The humans sure could use some help."

Creed grunted in agreement, his eyes thoughtful. "Did you have something in mind?"

Thaddeus could see the idea growing in his father's mind. "We could combine our skills to protect them."

Creed nodded. "Yes, I miss the days when you could kill at night."

"True. The laws governing out battles do not apply in the human world." Richard smiled as he spoke.

Creed replied. "The humans seem to be on the brink of causing their own extinction. I think directing our talents and energy in that direction sounds like a good idea." Creed looked warmly over at Thaddeus. "Thank you, son. Your gift as a seer has saved us all. I will strongly consider your words. The hatred that has grown between us will not go away overnight. Probably not even in our generation. Perhaps, one day, dark and light elves will see each other as elves and nothing more. Now, go. Spread the word—the battle has ended in a truce due to your vision. We all respect magic, so I think everyone will rejoice to know the gods have decided to bring this to an end."

Thaddeus mostly felt relieved that it had ended. He didn't know anyone could be as stressed as he'd been, wondering if his plan would work. Richard put his arm around his son and they left the camp in silence.

Once they entered their own camp, Richard stopped and looked at his son. "There was no vision, was there?"

An impish grin spread across Thaddeus's face. "Strategy Number Twenty-Three from *The 33 Strategies of War* by Robert Greene: Weave a seamless blend of fact and fiction."

Richard pulled his son into a hug. Thaddeus continued, "You always taught me that your mind was the best tool during a battle. It finally dawned on me that I could affect the outcome of the battle, not because I have the gift of sight, but because of I have the mind of a warrior. For that, I thank you."

"And I believed everything I said to him about my thoughts on the light and dark."

Richard stared at the ground for a minute. "Thaddeus, you opened my eyes to a new line of thought. With all my knowledge, I somehow managed to overlook the obvious. I am humbled to be your father."

Thaddeus chuckled. "Let's not go overboard, Dad. You and humble do not go together."

Chapter 26

The next morning the sun rose, and the camp bustled with activity. Elves took down tents and headed home, laughing and chatting. Keegan's family sat patiently waiting. No one spoke; no one knew what to say. Three more hours passed, and then it happened.

Opening her eyes, Keegan rubbed her face and stretched.

Thaddeus jokingly said, "Leave it to you to sleep in on the day you come back to life."

Keegan looked puzzled. Looking over at her mother, she said, "Is there anything to eat around here? I'm in the mood for bacon and eggs." Everyone laughed, and the tension in the room lifted.

Rourk still looked concerned. "Bacon? You're a vegetarian."

Keegan glanced over, eyeing him speculatively. "Who are you, and why would I be a vegetarian?"

Her words stabbed Rourk through the heart. His worst nightmare was coming true. His mind scrambled for a solution. Maybe she just needed time to adjust. "I'm…my name is Rourk. I—I work with your father, and your brother was one of my students."

This seemed to bore her. She looked over at Anna's mother. "What are you doing here?"

Jennifer stood up and walked over to her. "Your mother will explain. I am glad you are okay. If you need anything, or just want to talk, you know where to find me." Then she left.

Anna's mother was a creature of the light? Why was everyone staring at her? Practically her whole family had piled in the crowded tent. Kat looked like she wanted to cry, and Brigid looked like she had something to say, but wasn't sure how to say it. Even her grandmother seemed at a loss for words. Keegan felt herself starting to freak out.

At a loss for what to do, Emerald smiled brightly. "Why don't you get out of bed and come get something to eat? You might feel better when we are outside."

Keegan got out of bed and wrapped her arms around herself. She was so cold. "Okay, but let me grab a sweater."

They all walked out in silence. Keegan looked around at all the elves packing up their tents. "What is going on? Did we win?"

Richard stepped in. "Long story short, we called a truce. The war is over."

After taking a second to process the information, she said, "That's good." Her mind felt fuzzy. She figured she would feel better after some coffee and food. The bacon tasted so good that she wanted to eat a plate full. She downed three cups of coffee.

Concerned, her mother reached over to place a hand to Keegan's forehead. "How are you feeling?"

Surprised, Keegan pulled away, wrinkling her nose. "I feel fine. Just a little cold and tired. Why is everyone coddling me?"

"What is the last thing you remember about yesterday?" Emerald asked her softly.

Keegan thought that was an odd question to ask. Concentrating, she thought back. "I remember Donald almost dying—but you saved him, right? How is he?"

Taking a deep breath, her mother moved closer and put a hand on her daughter's shoulder. "There is something we need to tell you."

"Okay. What is going on, and why is everyone acting so strangely?"

"As we were walking away from the battle after healing Donald, you were struck by an arrow."

Snapping her head towards her mother, Keegan said, "I was what?"

"You have been unconscious for over twenty-four hours. Keegan, the arrow went through your heart and killed you."

Keegan looked at her mother as if she had lost her mind. "What in the world are you talking about? Dad, is there something wrong with Mom?"

Giving her a tender look that could only be described as empathy, he said, "She is telling the truth. Anna's mother brought you back to life."

Standing up quickly, Keegan knocked over the chair, trying to wrap her mind around what they were saying. "You can only be brought back from the dead with black magic. Are you saying that Anna's mother is a dark witch?"

"She is not a dark witch, but her grandmother was and taught her spells. We are very grateful that she gave you a second chance at life." Her father watched her carefully, gauging her reaction.

"How long was I dead?" Her voice shook with disbelief. She half expected them to tell her it was a practical joke.

"Only a few moments or, at least, that's how it seemed. Anna's mother appeared, already chanting and, the next thing we knew, your eyes opened," Richard told her, rubbing a hand over his forehead without looking at her.

"Keegan, do you recall anything during the time you were…passed out?" Her mother looked at her curiously, like she was some kind of science experiment. If Keegan hadn't felt so weird and out of sorts, she probably would have been mad.

"I had a dream. I was in a field of flowers, I felt free and happy. A tiger was with me."

Rourk flinched. "Keegan, do you really not know who I am?"

She stared at him, trying to feel a twinge of recognition, but she felt nothing. *He was cute though, that was for sure.*

"Should I know you?"

Rourk inhaled sharply, closing his eyes he sat back in the chair. "I am your chosen."

"That's impossible; I'm not eighteen."

Deeply concerned, Emerald kept her voice calm. "Keegan, he is telling the truth. Under unusual circumstances, you met early. You even spent a weekend with him at a cabin with me and your father."

Weirder and weirder. Maybe she was still dreaming. As if her parents would allow her to spend a weekend with a guy. "I asked you how Donald was doing, and no one has told me."

Rourk got up and walked out of the tent. He had to get out of there before he lost control. He felt like throwing things and screaming at the top of his lungs. He wished the battle was still on; he felt a deep need to destroy anything and everything in his path.

Calm down, he told himself. *Don't let your emotions take control of your mind.* He knew he had to take a step back.

Thaddeus walked out of the tent and joined Rourk. He stood silently beside him, not knowing what to say.

After a while, the family packed up their belongings and headed back home. Normally, they would have stayed and traveled since they were in Ireland, but they wanted to get Keegan home. They hoped that, back in her own environment, she would feel better.

In her room, Keegan lay on her bed, staring at the ceiling. It was too much to digest. She had spent a weekend with a guy she didn't remember? Looking over at her camera laying innocuously on her desk, she jumped up. If she had gone away for a weekend there had to be pictures.

She scrolled through her latest photos. What she saw made her feel sick to her stomach. The camera held tons of photos of an apparently amazing weekend that she had no memory of. She looked so happy. There were several goofy ones of them where she must have used her self-timer to take them. They were obviously crazy about each other. So why couldn't she remember him? Ever since she was a child, she had dreamed of meeting her chosen. She had woven fairy tales in her head of how perfect their life would be.

When she looked at Rourk, she had felt nothing, none of the connection or the chemistry she'd been promised. The pictures proved that they'd once shared a lot of feelings. Could it come back or was it gone for good? What must he be feeling? It had to be frustrating for him.

More than any of those questions, Keegan couldn't stop wondering. *Why do I keep thinking about Donald?*

Conflicted

Book Two

*For my husband
who never doubts and always supports me.*

Chapter 1

Keegan unpacked her things, her mind on the photos of the weekend she had supposedly spent with Rourk. She wished she could remember him and the weekend at the cabin from before the trip to Ireland—a trip that had changed her life and erased her memories of him. The two of them looked so happy. So in love. As she picked up a pile of dirty clothes to toss into the laundry, a piece of paper fell out and drifted slowly to the floor.

She stared at it a moment, an inoffensive square of paper laying on the floor. Curious, she reached down and picked it up, her brow furrowed over her bright blue-green eyes. She opened it, smoothing the creases, and read:

Keegan, I am sorry I could not spend your special day with you. I will make it up to you. Forever Yours, Rourk

First the pictures and then the note—undeniable proof that she did, at one time, have a relationship with Rourk.

Keegan sighed, dropping the laundry to the floor without a thought as she flopped onto her back on the bed. Her pillow still smelled like her shampoo, despite the fact she had been gone for just over a week. The cool October breeze ruffled the sheer purple curtains at her window, making her shiver. She could smell the pine trees from the forest. It was so good to be home.

A thought struck her, and she leapt to her feet, rushing to her desk to grab her phone. It sat by her bendy desk lamp, between her camera and a couple of school books. She scrolled through the list of contacts and was annoyed to find Rourk's number was not on it. Strange. *Why wouldn't they have texted if they'd already met?*

Before she could talk herself out of it, she sent her father a text and asked for Rourk's number.

Rourk was miserable.

He hadn't bothered turning on the lights in his bedroom before he fell onto the bed, boots and all. Staring at the ceiling with his hands under his head, Rourk couldn't stop thinking about Keegan.

The battle in the fight for his kind was over, but it seemed yet another had just begun. He couldn't possibly accept the fact that his relationship with his chosen was over before it really began. There was no one else for him. Keegan was the only one.

He had to win her back.

Rourk ran his options through his head and realized there were only two. He could do nothing and hope Keegan's feelings for him would return, or he could take the human route and try to win her affections. He was not one to sit around and do nothing, so obviously it had to be option two.

His phone dinged on the nightstand and he reached over to grab it, flipping it open. It was a text from Keegan: *I'm sorry I don't remember you. I was looking at my photos and it looks like we had a gr8 weekend.*

Rourk sat up in bed and stared at the screen that held her message. His heart beat just a bit faster as he wracked his brain for the right words. The fact she had reached out to him first gave him hope.

Finally, he texted back: *It was the best weekend of my life. Would you like to go on a date this weekend?*

Her response was almost instantaneous. *A date? What did you have in mind?*

Rourk dropped his phone to the bed and groaned, shoving both hands through his hair as he stood. Glancing around his room, he hoped for sudden inspiration. He paced a couple steps, hating how awkward he felt, and tried to think of something to say that didn't sound lame. It had been much easier when the bond was there and no thought was required. But he knew anything worthwhile took effort, and Keegan was worth it.

He paced back and forth three times in his small bedroom before he finally picked up his phone and tapped out his response: *I know it's not original, but how does dinner and a movie sound?*

Almost as soon as it left his screen, she answered: *GR8 :)*

I'll pick you up Friday at 6. Goodnight.

Night.

Texting would take some getting used to. Rourk wondered how she texted so much and so fast. Before the great battle, when he had watched Keegan to keep her safe, she was always attached to her phone. In his opinion, picking up the phone and having an actual conversation would be easier. *The things you do for love,* he thought with a grin.

He could do this. After all, Rourk thought with a wry grin, he was a battle-hardened warrior.

Back in her room, Keegan laid her phone back down with a smile.
    This could be fun; after all, he was cute.

Chapter 2

It was strange for her to go back to school after so much had happened. She had battled and she had *died!* *How does a girl go back to normal after that?*

Walking through the front doors of the school felt surreal. Her classmates mingled at their lockers, chatting and laughing like average students. Keegan felt so disconnected. She was positive they'd never taken part in a battle or watched men and women die in the fight for their race.

They had never killed others to save themselves.

Keegan's brother, Thaddeus, had filled her in on the outcome of the battle, so she was aware now that many of her friends were also creatures of the light. They weren't elves, but they weren't human either. She wasn't sure if she felt relieved by that fact or upset. She had liked thinking she was the only special one among all the humans.

Keegan walked down the fluorescent-lit hall and felt as if everyone was staring at her, but she convinced herself it was all in her head. She was self-conscious, absently smoothing her auburn hair and tugging at the hem of her school skirt. When she got to her locker, she was happy to see things looked as they always did and for the first time since she arrived at school, she felt like herself.

Lauren, Anna, and Katie were gathered by her locker, books in hand while they gossiped, and the boys were messing around as usual. Keegan couldn't help but steal a glance at Donald as she walked by, and she noticed his eyes were on her as well. They both laughed and looked away, Keegan's face flushing. Was it just her imagination or had he gotten even hotter since she saw him last? He was tall and lean with a runner's build, and his orange hair was just so cute standing up all over the place, the craziness punctuated by the fact that his white Oxford shirt wasn't buttoned right. His eyes were a crazy blue. What was she thinking?

Forget about Donald, he's not even interested in you.

Keegan had managed to run late for school. No sooner than she had opened her mouth to greet her friends, the bell rang to signal the start of classes. She frowned.

"We'll talk later," Anna told her. Keegan's best friend was rocking her individuality with a purple and lime green striped scarf over her school sweater and white tights. Her pretty, oval face was perfectly made up with shimmery lavender eye shadow and pale pink lip gloss; her cat-like eyes were lined with silver.

Keegan leaned to give her a quick hug before she ran off to class.

"It's good to see you," Lauren said and squeezed Keegan's arm affectionately. Keegan noticed her friend had gotten her dark, curly hair cut; not much, but just noticeable. Lauren was in her cheerleading uniform, her long legs still tanned from the summer. "We'll meet you at lunch."

"Bye, Keegan." Katie gave her a shy wave and followed after Lauren.

Homeroom passed in a blur. Mrs. Harris had to repeat Keegan's name three times during attendance at the beginning of class. The student seated next to her, a slight girl with mocha-colored skin and huge, dark eyes, had to elbow Keegan to wake her from her thoughts.

Donald cornered her in the hall before first period so they could talk in private. "I never got a chance to thank you for saving my life," he said. He looked down as if he were embarrassed, the toe of one of his Chucks scuffing the floor.

"It was my mother that really saved you," Keegan shrugged. "I was just the foolish one to rush into the middle of a battlefield."

His incredible blue eyes moved to hers. "So you really died, huh? What was that like? Did you see the other side? Do you feel different now that you're back in our world?"

Keegan knew those were the questions everyone wanted to ask her, but didn't dare.

"I don't recall it at all," Keegan told him apologetically. "I know that's not the exciting answer everyone would like to hear. But if I hadn't been told I died, I would have never known. I do feel a little different. My body temperature seems lower now, and I'm always cold. And apparently my bond to my chosen has been broken. Other than that, I feel like the same old Keegan."

Donald stepped back, his eyes widening. *Did he just hear correctly? The bond was broken?* Suddenly, he felt very nervous and unsure of himself. His palms were sweating. He didn't even trust himself to speak.

"Are you okay?" Keegan asked with a frown. "You don't look so well."

"Sorry, I need to go. I'm glad you're alive, and thanks again for saving my life." He stumbled away.

Donald shoved his hands in his pockets, his eyes on the dirty linoleum floor as he hurried down the hall. He had dreamed of this moment; a chance with Keegan. Yet, when it was staring him in the face, he ran away like a scared, lovesick loser. *Real smooth, Donald.*

Chemistry class passed slowly. Usually, it was Keegan's favorite class, but she just felt antsy. There was too much on her mind. She sat and watched the second hand go around and around, wondering what in the world had gotten into Donald.

She really needed to catch up with Anna and Lauren because it seemed like forever since they had talked. They always sat together at lunch; she was eager to reach them. After suffering through a boring history lecture, it was finally lunch time.

She practically ran for her locker to get rid of her books, and slammed into Spencer and Sam in the hallway.

"Whoa, slow down Keegan. I feel like I've been hit by a bulldozer." Spencer rubbed his shoulder. He was a skinny guy whose long limbs made him seem tall, and a head full of black hair. He crossed his bright green eyes.

Sam, a good-looking blonde, laughed.

"Hey guys, I can't talk right now! I'm in a hurry," she told them quickly, waving as she dashed off once more.

They stared at her as she sprinted down the hallway to her locker. Other students parted to make way for her. Spencer and Sam glanced at each other and shook their heads.

Once at her locker, Keegan impatiently waited for Anna and Lauren. She drummed her fingers on the beige metal and looked at her watch. *Where were they?*

Anna got there first. She gave Keegan a cheesy grin as she walked up.

"Oh thank God, I didn't think you were ever going to show up," Keegan said with a sigh, leaning against her locker wearily.

Looking at Keegan like she was crazy, Anna responded, "I got here as soon as I could. The bell just rang. Chill out."

Lauren sauntered down the hall a second later. Anna and Keegan laughed as they watched all the guys turn and stare at her legs as she walked by. Lauren shook her hips deliberately—she loved the attention.

"Hey. Ready for lunch?" she asked with a grin.

"Let's go outside to eat so we can catch up in private," Keegan said. She grabbed them by the arms and pulled them towards the door.

Keegan noticed a glance exchanged between Anna and Lauren, and wondered what that was all about. Shrugging it off, she led the way through the back doors of the school.

It was a brilliantly bright day with not a cloud in sight. Some of their classmates lounged around the quad with their lunches and sodas, enjoying the mild weather and sunshine. Laughter and the distant thrum of cars on the main road were the only sounds as the girls headed for the shade of an old oak tree.

Once they were hidden behind the bushes surrounding the tree, Keegan turned with her hands planted on her hips. "So. How long have you guys known I wasn't human?"

Lauren looked down sheepishly, unable to make eye contact. Anna's smile was ear to ear. "Finally! Do you know how hard it's been *all these years* to not be able to talk about the elephant in the room?"

Keegan wasn't sure if she should laugh or cry, or stomp her feet like a little kid while screaming not fair! She settled for crossing her arms over her chest and narrowing her eyes at her friends. "You've both known all this time?"

Anna shrugged her shoulders. "Hey, it's not our fault that elves like to be so secretive."

"So, you're a fairy?" Keegan turned her attention to Lauren.

Lauren looked from side to side to make sure no one was looking. Suddenly, star-like flecks appeared in the air and translucent wings flapped open behind her. Flapping her wings, Lauren floated into the air with a big grin across her face.

"Wow, that is really neat!" Keegan turned to Anna. "What's your story? I hear people aren't quite sure about you because your dad is human?"

Anna lifted her hands in the air and closed her eyes. Keegan's mouth dropped open as flames appeared in her palms.

Keegan jumped up and down, clapping, and squealed, "We are like the coolest kids ever!"

Anna's face scrunched up. "I don't know. I think Calvron might be the coolest kid ever."

Lauren nodded her head in agreement. "He is awesome!"

Keegan crossed her arms tightly across her chest and stared back and forth at them. It wasn't fair that they all knew about each other and she was the only one left out. They were supposed to be her friends! She gave in and asked, "Why is he so cool?"

Smiling mysteriously, Lauren said, "He's a very powerful wizard, and they're rare these days. He can do almost anything; at least, that's how it seems."

Anna looked wistful. "I wish I had a quarter of his power."

"What exactly are you, Anna?" Keegan raised an eyebrow. "You're not a spirit walker like your mom, are you?"

Anna's eyes narrowed. "How did you know my mom is a spirit walker?"

Keegan was momentarily stunned into silence. "You guys didn't hear?"

They exchanged another glance, this time a confused one. Anna shook her head. "Hear what?"

Taking a deep breath, Keegan told them the long version of how she lost and regained her life. They both stared at her with their mouths hanging open.

"You guys know about the battle between the light and dark elves, right?"

Anna's face fell and she nodded. "Yeah, we heard something about it."

"Well, I was there," Keegan said. She gave them a wry grin as they both gasped.

Lauren covered her mouth with one hand and touched Keegan's shoulder with the other.

"So were Donald and the other guys. Donald was hurt, and I ran onto the field to help him. My mom is a Healer, and she was able to treat his wounds, but we were in the middle of the fighting." Keegan paused, clearing her throat as she remembered the clash of old-fashioned weaponry, the stench of hundreds of sweating bodies, and the ground drenched in blood. "I was hit by an arrow and killed."

Anna and Lauren looked at her in horror, but Keegan plunged on. "Anna, your mom somehow knew I was dead and showed up. She brought me back to life with dark magic."

When Keegan finished, Lauren spoke first. "Oh my god, you were dead? Keegan, you were dead!" She pulled Keegan into a tight hug. "I can't believe we could have lost you for good."

Anna was quiet for several moments before she whispered, "My mom knows dark magic?"

Neither Lauren nor Keegan knew what to say. The look on Anna's face made Keegan swiftly change the subject. "What do you guys know about elves?" She was curious if they really knew anything, and if so, whether any of it was accurate. She also wanted to clear the gloom that had followed her story.

Lauren bounced up and down. "I've heard that elves put on a front that they live among humans, but in reality they live underground. Is that true?"

Keegan couldn't help but smile. "There is a sliver of truth. We have underground safe houses in case of emergencies. Elves prefer living in nature over living in a city."

Anna finally spoke up, her voice a little clearer than it had been moments before. "Well, we're all envious that elves have the key to finding your perfect partner. We think that is the real reason you're all so secretive. Although, we really wish elves would share what they know. It doesn't seem fair they're the only ones that know their soul mates without the search."

Anna's observation brought all of Keegan's problems back to the surface, and she pouted.

What's wrong?" Anna demanded, reaching to shake Keegan's shoulder gently.

"It's true about the perfect partner. We call them our 'chosen' since they are chosen for us at birth. We aren't supposed to meet them until we turn eighteen. Apparently, I have already met my chosen, but because of the dark magic I don't recall him." It felt good to finally have someone to talk to about it all; it was so confusing for her. She pulled out her phone and showed them a picture she had saved on it of her and Rourk near the waterfall. She explained how they had spent the weekend together and she couldn't remember.

"When I was brought back," Keegan said, shooting a glance at Anna. "I met him, and I felt nothing for him." Keegan could tell by the looks on her friends' faces that they felt badly for her. People searched high and low for their perfect match. To have it handed to you and then taken away seemed too cruel.

"He's hot." Anna grinned and handed the phone back to Keegan, who managed a weak smile. Dropping her eyes, Anna continued. "You asked what I was, because of my parents. Well, I'm a witch." She fidgeted with her sweater. After a brief pause, she added, "On the side of the light."

Keegan could tell Anna was bothered about her mother knowing dark magic.

"I wonder if there are any spells to bring back the bond?" Anna said. "It would seem if it was taken away that it could be given back."

For the first time, Keegan allowed herself to feel hopeful. "Do you really think that is possible?"

"I will have to look into it. There is still so much I don't know, and I've never had anyone to teach me. Maybe I can talk to Calvron; he might be able to help or at least point me in the right direction."

Keegan glanced down at the photo one more time before she put her phone away. "Thank you, Anna; you have no idea how much this means to me."

Keegan was excited and relieved that she could finally share who she *really* was with her best friends. She wondered if this was why they had stayed friends no matter how different their personalities were. Perhaps creatures of the light could sense one another. Keegan smiled and thought of all the times she had made up stories in her mind of people and guessed whether they were creatures or human. Not once had she given thought to the fact that her friends might not be. Oh, the irony of it.

A huge smile spread across her face. She couldn't wait to see what adventures they would share together now that their powers were out in the open.

Chapter 3

Rourk looked through his closet trying to decide what to wear. It was their first date and he wanted it to be perfect, but he had no idea what humans usually wore for such things.

He pushed his hangers further to the left. Then again to the right; his wardrobe was useless. There had to be something for him to wear. All of his clothes looked alike: the shirts were all earth tones and he had a few pairs of jeans and khakis. He smiled and thought, *Keegan would probably love to take me shopping.*

His father came to the door and stared in at Rourk. The gray hair at his Greg's temples had gotten lighter since the battle, though it only heightened his movie-star good looks. Every time he looked at his dad, Rourk marveled at how different they were.

His father pointedly stared at the clothes strewn across the bed. "What are you doing?"

Embarrassed, Rourk answered, "Trying to figure out what to wear."

His father's booming laugh filled the room, shocking him. The man barely ever smiled, let alone laughed. "Son, in eighteen years I have never seen you debate on clothing choices."

Rourk's shoulders slumped. He took a deep breath and closed his eyes. "Dad, this sucks. How do humans deal with this on a regular basis? I'm nervous, what's up with that? I'm a warrior, we do not get nervous, let alone over a silly date."

Greg placed a hand on Rourk's shoulder, catching his son's gray eyes with his own intense blues. "I'm sorry this isn't going as easy as you expected. Just know that it will be worth it in the long run."

His dad walked away with a knowing grin on his face, which rather annoyed Rourk.

Finally, Rourk decided to play it safe and picked a pair of khaki pants and a plain black t-shirt. Looking in the mirror, he ran his hand through his rust colored hair; he needed a haircut. He rubbed his face vigorously and thought, *Well, there isn't much I can do about my looks.* Keegan had found him attractive before the black magic, so hopefully that hadn't changed.

Grabbing his keys from his dresser, he headed out. As he drove towards her house, his stomach was in knots. *What's wrong with me? It's just a date.*

The doorbell rang, and Keegan's father yelled out his usual line: "Don't forget the first rule of dating."

"Dad, you say that every time I go on a date. You know it gets old." Laughing, she added, "If he breaks that rule, it's your fault since you trained him."

Keegan glanced at herself once more in the mirror and thought, *Not bad.* Her auburn hair was behaving itself. She had on just the right amount of makeup to bring out her features. She had chosen to wear a form-fitting blue sweater and a pair of jeans that flattered her figure.

She opened the door, hoping to feel a spark or something. Yet again, she felt nothing.

He was hot, she would give him that. They made eye contact. His grey eyes were so intense, and she loved how strong his jaw line was. She gave him a once over, thinking to herself, *Nice.* She always thought guys looked hot in khakis. His shirt was just tight enough to show off his defined chest. The sleeves looked a little snug; she tried not to stare at his muscled arms.

"Keegan, you look...um, you look good." He stared at the porch at his feet as if he were embarrassed. The sky was rose-colored behind him, a beautiful contrast to the trees surrounding the house. Keegan loved the way it smelled outside when fall had arrived.

She smiled at him. "Thank you." *You look good? That was the best he had? Ugh, this might be a long night after all.*

"So, where are we going to eat?" she asked, twirling a piece of her hair. She hadn't stepped back to let him in the house, nor had she moved forward to the porch. Of course, she didn't notice his confusion over it.

"I figured we'd keep it low key and grab a pizza. If that's ok with you?"

"That sounds great!" Her smile reached her eyes causing them to sparkle.

Rourk didn't think he would ever get used to her overwhelming beauty. She was perfection. Why couldn't he say the words? *Good?* That didn't begin to do her justice. He was going to have to do better than that if he was going to win her back. Why did he feel so awkward? It was not supposed to be this way. When they had been together before it felt so natural, as if they had known each other their entire lives. He would do anything to get that back.

They rode to the restaurant in silence, and not the pleasant kind. Rourk tried to think of something interesting to talk about. Finally, he thought of a topic he knew interested her. "How is your photography going? Have you gotten any good shots lately?"

He was relieved to see her face light up. When she excitedly started rambling on about how much she loved taking pictures, Rourk knew he'd found the right conversation starter.

"I really want to get a new lens so I can get better pictures of animals in their natural environment," Keegan said, her words coming fast. "My parents have been talking about going to Sri Lanka, and I'd love to get some good shots of the elephants. If I'm lucky, maybe a tiger."

Rourk tensed at the mention of a tiger, even though he knew it was a well known fact there were tigers in Sri Lanka.

"When are you planning on going to Sri Lanka?"

"I'm not sure. My parents tend to spring trips on us out of nowhere. Hopefully soon."

"How many countries have you been to?" It was hard to keep his eyes on the road when he wanted so badly to watch her face as she spoke.

Keegan paused to think and counted off on her fingers silently. "At least fourteen, but I've probably missed some. I only count the ones I can remember and not the ones from when I was a baby. What about you? Do you like to travel?"

Rourk shook his head. "I haven't been many places. My father doesn't enjoy traveling anymore. Not since my mother died." He didn't want to travel down that path. Glancing at Keegan, he went on. "Do you have a favorite place you have been?"

Keegan tapped a finger to her lips. "Hmm, I think that would have to be Nepal. It's so beautiful there, and the people are so friendly even though they live in poverty. It's cool to see how the women dress in bright colors and always have smiles on their faces. The hiking is amazing there too. I think you would love it."

Her thoughtfulness touched him. "I'm sure I would. I love hiking. I think that's pretty common among elves."

"That's true." She settled back in the seat. "Although, after the first time I went to Nepal, I couldn't eat chicken for a long time. They slaughter them right in the open, like on the sidewalks. Probably one of the reasons I went on that vegetarian kick you mentioned."

He could listen to her talk for hours.

Rourk pulled his truck into the parking lot of the pizza shop and put it into park. He hurriedly walked around to let Keegan out, but she had already hopped from the cab and was waiting for him next to her door.

Michael's Pizza was one of Keegan's favorites, though she didn't think Rourk knew that. It was packed with people she recognized from school. The servers bounced from table to table amid the chaos, white smiles plastered across every face. Keegan took a deep breath and felt her stomach rumble.

Once they were seated, Rourk asked, "What kind of pizza do you want?"

"Meat lover's. I'm starving."

Rourk wasn't sure why this bothered him so much. He had found it somewhat annoying when he had first learned she was a vegetarian. To have her forget about that reminded him how she had forgotten about him, as well. If only he could turn the clock back to their time in the cabin, when he had gladly cooked her vegetarian meals, and she had looked at him as if he was the only person on the planet. Now, she was glancing around the room as if she was bored.

Rourk watched as Keegan devoured four pieces of pizza. "You weren't kidding when you said you were hungry."

"It's just sooo good." Keegan wiped her face with the napkin. "I love pizza. Actually, I love most food."

Looking up from his own slice, he smiled.

"You have earned my father's approval for a second date, by the way."

Somewhat surprised, he said, "Well, I would hope so." He was her chosen after all, and he had fought alongside her father in the Great Battle.

Keegan let him in on the inside joke. "He tells me that if I'm on a date and the guy sits with his back to the door, I'm supposed to get up and leave."

Rourk laughed. He could clearly picture Richard making up this rule. He was a character—and a great man. "Well, you don't have to worry. I will always make your safety my number one priority."

Keegan liked the sound of that. She really needed to give him a chance. Just then, while the two of them were having what felt like a great moment, her phone buzzed in her purse. She was surprised when she saw the text was from Donald, and her heart skipped a beat. He rarely texted her.

The text said, *A bunch of us are going to play laser tag. Do you want to come?*

Grinning, she replied, *Wish I could but on a date.*

Date? Who's the lucky guy?

Feeling herself blush, she replied, *My chosen.*

How's that going?

Keegan looked across the table at Rourk who was eyeing his piece of pizza. She replied, *Strange*

Have fun, maybe next time you can join us.

Love to, she replied, sad to stop the conversation.

Rourk took a sip of his drink. "Was that Anna or Lauren?"

After a brief pause, "Yeah, it was Anna. She was just seeing what was up." *Why did I just lie to him? You're never supposed to lie to your chosen.* Keegan felt like crying. Why was this not going as it was supposed to? Was she ever going to have feelings for this stranger sitting across from her?

They went to the movies after eating. She had to admit the movie was funny, and it was nice to know Rourk had a sense of humor. She eventually managed to relax and enjoy herself.

After the night was over, Rourk pulled down the long drive to her house and parked out front, cutting the engine. He jumped from the car and hurried to her side. Taking her hand, he walked her to the door.

Keegan wondered if he was going to try to kiss her. She didn't have to wonder long.

Stopping before they even reached the doorway, he put his hand under her hair, and pulled her towards him. He kissed her softly at first, and then with more force. Abruptly he pulled away. As he stared down at her, he almost looked frightened. "Did you feel it?"

Startled, she asked, "Feel what?"

Rourk groaned inwardly. A part of him had hoped that kissing her would make her feel the electricity they had felt before. His mind was reeling.

The bond was actually gone for her. He recalled their first kiss and her reaction. *"Wow, did you feel that?" she had asked.* Now, she felt nothing.

Of course, for him it was still the same as before.

Keegan patted him awkwardly on the arm. "Ok, well, I had fun. Maybe we can go out again sometime?"

"I hope so," he murmured, bereft as she pulled away from him.

Rourk watched as she walked into her house—she didn't even look back.

Keegan went straight to her room through the darkened house; everyone was already in bed and she didn't want to wake them.

She thought about the evening as she got undressed. He truly wasn't *that* bad. But, could she see herself spending the rest of her life with him? That—she wasn't sure of. She figured time would tell. There was no precedence for their situation as far as she knew. Would she still be expected to marry him when she turned eighteen, even if there was no bond? She couldn't picture her mother making her marry someone against her will. She pulled on her favorite polar bear pajamas and threw her hair in a pony tail.

She pulled out her phone and stared at the screen; she still couldn't believe Donald had texted her. After a slight internal debate, she sent him a text.

How was laser tag?

Fun, we dominated.

Of course, you are magical creatures.

Not as magical as you.

Keegan had to physically stop herself from squealing, bouncing on the tips of her toes in the dark and clutching the phone to her chest. *OMG*, he said she was magical, and at the pizza place, he had asked who the lucky guy was. Could he possibly be interested in her?

Okay, calm down; she knew Donald liked to joke around. Maybe he was just being funny.

I wish I had been there, Keegan wrote.

Me too, see you on Monday at school.

Keegan finished getting ready for bed and finally got under the covers, turning over on her back to stare at the ceiling in thought. So much had changed in such a short period of time. She felt as if her whole world had been turned upside down.

Why did things have to get so complicated? This was supposed to be easy! She was supposed to turn eighteen and marry her chosen—something she had been planning on since she found out his name was Rourk. She had lain awake many nights dreaming about their perfect home. They were going to have a dog—a fat, lazy English bulldog and his name was going to be Santa. She liked to humor herself and thought it would be funny since humans think Santa and elves go hand in hand. She figured they would have at least three kids. It was going to be perfect.

Why did this have to happen?

Now, without the bond, the thought of getting married at eighteen seemed absurd. That was only a year away. She had college to think about. She'd dreamed of going to college in Alaska, because they had one of the best marine biology programs and her dream was to work with dolphins. It had never crossed her mind whether Rourk would even want to move to Alaska.

Closing her eyes, Keegan let sleep take over; she would worry about it all later.

Chapter 4

Anna was nervous, but she needed answers. She had already put it off too long.

Thankfully, her mother seemed to have come out of her depression fog. It felt like it hadn't been all that long since her mom had been nearly frozen with despair, unable to function or even smile. She had done a complete turnabout.

Actually, Anna could not recall a time when her mom had seemed as happy. Maybe she was on a new medication or something. Whatever it was, Anna was glad for it. Her mom was back to doing her hair and make-up, and she had even been going for morning runs like she used to before things got bad.

The idea of upsetting her mother made Anna's stomach roll, but it couldn't be avoided. She took the stairs slowly, dreading the confrontation and what it could bring.

Her mom stood in the kitchen arranging an assortment of red and yellow flowers in her favorite blue glass vase. A private smile crossed her face as Anna watched, and she wondered what her mother was thinking. "Hey, Mom."

Jennifer glanced up at her daughter, standing in the doorway. Anna was more subdued than usual, wearing only a pair of blue jeans and a tank top. Her pink hair was secured with a bland gray headband.

"What's wrong?" she asked, not bothering with pleasantries.

"We need to talk," Anna said softly.

Her mother's smile disappeared as she turned to face Anna fully, her hands moving away from the flowers. "I take it you've talked to Keegan?"

Anna was surprised. She thought she was going to have to pull it out of her mother one word at a time. "Yes, and she told me you know black magic? Mom, how can that be? I don't understand any of this."

Sighing, Jennifer walked forward and grabbed her daughter's hands, squeezing them tightly. Her dark eyes were haunted. "Let's sit down."

Anna let her mother lead her to the table. She watched as Jennifer bustled to the refrigerator and pulled out a glass pitcher of juice.

Anna tried to remember the last time she'd seen her mom look so youthful. Even just wearing a pair of gray cotton yoga pants and an old, worn out T-shirt on her tall, willowy body, Anna's mom was beautiful. She had her long brown hair pulled into a high ponytail that swished around her neck when she moved. Her toenails were painted pink.

Jennifer put a glass in front of Anna and sat across from her. "Anna, you know I was raised by your great-grandmother and that she was also a witch." She cleared her throat, shifting uncomfortably in her seat. "What I failed to mention was that she was a dark witch."

Anna stared at her mother in disbelief, her hands wrapped around her glass even though she hadn't picked it up yet. "My great-grandmother was a dark witch? How is that even possible?"

"It's a long story, or at least the story unfolded over a long period of time." She paused, and then held up a finger. "One minute."

Raising an eyebrow at her mother, Anna watched as she hurried from the room, her flip-flops making slapping sounds on the linoleum. She returned a minute later with a large leather-bound album and opened it on the tabletop. She flipped forward a few pages until she came to a picture of a handsome young man in old-timey clothes. "Your great-grandfather, as you know, was also a spirit walker."

"That's him?" Anna murmured, leaning forward to stare at his face. He had a mischievous glint in his dark eyes and hair the exact shade of Jennifer's.

Jennifer nodded. "Yes. His name was Patrick. As a spirit walker, his body absorbed the spirits he took over to the other side. He was unable to protect himself from it because he was never taught to shield himself, or at least that's what we liked to believe." Her mother's eyes darkened. "Some wondered if he let his guard down on purpose because he enjoyed the power of absorbing souls. One man with thousands of souls. You can imagine all the demons that came along with that. It was feared he was going mad. He started acting irrational. His mind shattered, and he became a deranged lunatic that could no longer live among the humans. It was as if the souls were speaking through him, comparable to someone with split personalities. Of course, your great-grandmother, Grace, loved him very much and it killed her to see him fall apart. She tried every spell she could think of and nothing worked. She searched near and far trying to find a cure." Jennifer flipped a few pages in the photo album to show Anna a picture of a vibrantly beautiful young woman in a long black dress. She looked just like Jennifer.

Her mother stopped and looked out the small kitchen window, her eyes distant, before she continued. "She heard about a dark witch that could help her. Light and dark witches do not communicate with each other. So, Grace cast a spell on herself to appear as if she were a young dark witch. She begged the dark witch to teach her the ways of the dark. The witch was so impressed with your great-grandmother's skills at such a young age that she took her under her wing."

She leaned over and grabbed Anna's hand. "I know this is a lot to take in."

"Just finish the story, Mom." Anna pulled her hand away.

"She was gone for years, and when she returned, Patrick was dead. She went berserk and cursed the light. She swore never to return, and she remained a dark witch until her death. Unfortunately, she passed on her skills to me. I was not told of her story until after she passed away. A kind, light witch took care of me until I was of age. She taught me the beauty of the light."

Anna sat with her mouth open, staring dumbfounded at her mom. "You should have told me. How could you have kept this from me all these years?"

"What good would that have done? I am not a witch. I am a spirit walker."

Anna glared at her. "All these years, you have left me on my own to deal with my power. You have given me no guidance." She pushed back from the table and crossed her arms.

Her mother's anger filled the room, though she tried to hold it in. "What did you expect me to do? Teach my daughter black magic?"

"Well, no, but it would have been nice to have known about all of this." Anna shifted uncomfortably. "Mom, I need to learn about my powers. I'm almost eighteen and this is crazy. I don't know what you're trying to shield me from. Avoiding it isn't going to make me human."

Jennifer's face was pained. She looked away quickly, but not before Anna saw the tears gathered in her mother's eyes. "I'm sorry, Anna, I know I haven't been fair to you and my reasons have been purely selfish. I was really hoping you were going to be a normal human. I thought maybe since your father was human…"

"We've known for years that I'm not *normal*, as you say." There was a lot more bitterness in her words than she meant.

"We'll sort this out, Anna. I'm sorry, and you are right. You need someone to guide you in your abilities."

There was an awkward pause while the two of them stared across the open album at each other.

"Mother, the real reason I wanted to talk to you is because of Keegan," Anna started slowly, her hands clasped on the table. She stared down at her chipped blue nail polish. "When you brought her back, you took away her bond to her chosen."

"I know, and there is nothing I can do about that."

Looking at her mom searchingly, Anna said, "Are you sure? If you can take something away, there must be a way to give it back?"

"Anna, I'm sorry. Dark magic is not known for its kindness. Losing her bond is a small price to pay for her life. She will be fine." Jennifer took a sip of her juice, entirely too calm and collected for Anna.

"Sure, just like *you're* fine? Look how great your marriage is working out for you. Elves are the only ones that have this secret to finding their perfect match. Do you really think it's fair to take away Keegan's chance at happiness?"

Her mom stared intently at her fingers, avoiding her daughter's gaze. "Anna, I truly am unable to help her. I wish I could." She looked up, her soft brown eyes catching her daughter's. "However, there might be someone that can. The light witch that took me in has since passed to the other side. She does have a daughter, Magdalena, who happens to be an extremely powerful witch. She might know of a spell that could reverse the damage I caused to the bond."

Anna breathed a little easier, closing her eyes as she allowed herself a bit of hope that she could help her best friend. Not only might she be able to help Keegan but she was finally going to meet a light witch. Perhaps the woman would give her the guidance she had ached for.

"Where does she live?"

Jennifer frowned. "Well, that's the tricky part—I am not sure. It might take me a while to track her down. I will start making inquiries right away. Anna, don't get your hopes up. It is very likely that it's not reversible. Please don't tell Keegan and give her false hope. She needs to start accepting the fact that it may never return. It would be cruel to make her think otherwise until you have concrete information."

"I won't say anything to Keegan." Anna looked over at her mom. "I'm really glad this is all out in the open now. I have so many questions, I don't even know where to begin. I have to say it's kinda cool that my mom knows black magic."

"As much as I've wanted you to think I'm cool over the years, this is not the way I wanted it to happen," her mother answered wryly, raising an eyebrow at her daughter pointedly. "Black magic can be very dangerous, Anna."

"I know, Mom. I don't want to learn black magic. I want to learn the ways of the light witch. I want you to be proud of me." Anna was kind of embarrassed to admit it.

"Honey, I have always been proud of you."

Anna smiled, relieved. She went on, "You seem to be happier lately. Are you and Dad doing better? I haven't heard you fight in awhile."

"No, actually, we aren't. I just feel better about myself and have realized I don't need to be married to be happy. Keegan's mother gave me a healing, and I feel like my old self again. It's such a wonderful feeling." Jennifer reached across the table to touch Anna's hand. "Honey, there is something you need to know."

"What?"

"Your father and I will be filing for divorce soon."

Anna took her hand away from her mom's and crossed her arms across her chest, her heart pounding. "That sucks, Mom."

"I'm sorry, Anna. I *have* tried."

"I know you have," Anna sighed, resting her elbows on the table and putting her face in her hands. "I've been expecting you guys to divorce for years. I wish Dad wasn't such a jerk to you."

"It's not really his fault. It isn't easy for humans to be involved with the gifted."

"That's a lame excuse. Why are you still sticking up for him?" Anna looked up with a glare, letting her palms rest on the tabletop.

"He's your father, and I will always love him," Jennifer said simply, shrugging. "Speaking of humans, any progress with Xavier?"

"Nice job on the subject switch. There hasn't been any progress. He just doesn't see me as anything more than a friend. I think he's interested in a cheerleader at school." Anna's lower lip jutted out in a pout.

"I'm sorry, honey. I know you care about him. Maybe you should start dating someone."

"Sure, the guys are knocking down my door." Anna rolled her eyes at her mom.

"Why wouldn't they be? You are beautiful, intelligent and original."

"It's the last one, Mom. Not all guys are into chicks that change their hair color at the drop of the hat and don't conform to society." Anna pushed her recently dyed pink fringe behind her ear.

"Well, it's their loss." Jennifer gave her a beautiful grin.

"Of course, you aren't biased or anything," Anna joked, taking a sip of her juice. It was some kind of grape juice, and it had gotten warm while they talked.

"Of course not. Do you want something to eat?" Her mom stood and moved to the fridge, opening the door and bending to shuffle through its contents.

"Sure, what are you making?"

"How about a grilled cheese sandwich?"

"Ah, yeah! How could I turn that down?"

Jennifer was silent as she pulled out the cheese, bread, and butter. As she put the skillet on the burner and turned it on, she said, "Anna, I'm glad we had this talk. I really hope Magdelena can help you get the bond back. Keegan does deserve to be happy. Although, I really think she can find happiness without the bond."

"It's worth looking into," Anna replied. "I feel kinda responsible since my mother is the one that broke the bond."

"Don't forget I also saved her life."

Anna watched her mom butter two slices of bread and slice the cheese, before tossing the sandwich in the skillet. She told her mother, "I can't imagine life without Keegan. It still doesn't seem real that she died. It's just so bizarre. Thank you for brining her back."

"I'm glad I was able to help. Keegan is a good girl."

When her grilled cheese was done, Jennifer placed it in front of her and they chatted about school while Anna finished off the sandwich.

On the table at her elbow, her phone buzzed loudly. It was a text from Calvron. *Time to play.*

"Thanks for the food and the talk, Mom. I'm so excited to meet Magdalena. I'm going to go hang out with the guys."

Jennifer waved her off. "All right, well have fun, and I will let you know as soon as I hear anything. We'll talk more about this later."

Grabbing her phone as she ran up to her room to change, Anna replied, *Can Keegan come?*

Of course

K, see you soon

She sent a quick text to Keegan, *On my way over, we're going on an adventure.*

Chapter 5

An adventure? Keegan loved surprises. She got up from the couch where she had been idly flipping through television channels and ran upstairs to change.

Adventures usually required sneakers. Keegan grabbed her Puma trail shoes and threw on a pair of jeans along with a band tee. She grabbed a hoodie since she was always cold. She didn't bother with make-up.

Running down the stairs, she yelled to her parents, "Going out with Anna!"

As she opened the door, Anna's old, rusty Buick pulled into the driveway. Keegan yanked open the door and said, "Good timing!" Jumping in the car, she excitedly asked "So, where are we going?"

"Right now, we're going to get Lauren, and after that you will officially be invited into the club." Anna had her pink hair tucked under a lacy white beret and was wearing an electric red cardigan sweater with black skinny jeans that had glittery hearts on one leg. She signaled as she turned out of the long, gravel driveway that led back to Keegan's house and took a left onto the main road.

Keegan glanced over at her profile. "What club?"

"We call it the ABC club," Anna flashed a grin. "Amazingly Beautiful Creatures."

They had a club and she wasn't aware of it? *How could they keep all these secrets from her?* Keegan's anger began to build; she had noticed she got angry more often lately. When she started to get mad, her body felt colder. She normally tried to think happy thoughts right away, which warmed her back up. Reminding herself that at least she was invited now, she was very curious to see what it was all about. Instead of responding, she just turned to stare out the window at the passing scenery.

Lauren was waiting in her own driveway, looking like a star as usual. Her Hollister sweater was pale peach and form fitting and her khaki corduroys were perfectly pressed over her leather slip-on shoes. She slid into the backseat with a bright greeting.

They headed out of town down a winding, two-lane road beneath a bright and clear autumn sky. In the distance, Keegan watched the Appalachians draw nearer, a never-ending sea of fiery, rolling hills. Every so often, her family would pack a lunch and drive to the mountains to go hiking for the day. The Appalachians always felt so magical and surreal, standing like soldiers over their town.

Anna turned into a hidden drive in a grove of trees and the car crunched down a long unpaved road for several minutes. Eventually, they pulled over into a large clearing, and Keegan noticed Spencer's truck along with Calvron's red mustang. There were also several others that she didn't recognize.

"Where are we going?" Keegan asked as they stumbled down the rocks of a small hill. Anna and Lauren just laughed, not answering her as they came to the bottom. Keegan was entranced to find that, oddly, there was a wooden door standing seemingly on its own in the grass.

"Keegan, open the door!" Lauren practically yelled at her, shooing her towards the door.

Fascinated, Keegan peered around the wooden frame; nothing but more grass and woods behind it. She circled around it before turning back to her friends questioningly.

"Just open it," Anna giggled.

Grabbing the handle, Keegan yanked the door open.

What she saw left her speechless.

It looked like a magical wonderland. It was like stepping onto the page of a make-believe land in a novel or a movie. *Yeah, that's what it's like*: walking into the movie "Avatar." Everything was bright and cheerful. The plants and the flowers were lush and exotic, while the trees soared high over her head and the distant patter of rain on the canopy met her ears.

Lauren put her hands on Keegan's back and gave her a shove. "Yeah, yeah it's magical, just get in there."

Anna stepped through with Keegan, nudging her shoulder, "I told you Calvron was amazing."

Keegan turned wide eyes to Anna, her mouth open. "He did this?"

"Yep," Anna nodded, her incredibly bright green eyes surveying the landscape. "He can create a whole alternate world. We come here to play and be ourselves." She gestured around them.

Keegan looked closer to where Anna had indicated and could see there were several different magical creatures already there with them. Of course, you couldn't miss the three huge, beautiful cats that sauntered their way. She laughed when they rubbed up against her legs as if they were pets. She could have sworn the tiger was purring. That would, of course, be Donald. She reached down and rubbed behind his ears, catching his big eyes with her own as he leaned his soft face into her hands.

Keegan watched Spencer in his panther form. His green eyes were shocking next to his black fur. Sam, even as a lion, was the most beautiful of the group. They nudged on Lauren and Anna playfully, trying to get them moving.

"One minute, let her take it all in, we don't have to start right away," Lauren chuckled, talking to Sam as she ran her hands through mane.

The big cats laid down and stretched out lazily, Spencer and Sam batting at each other with their giant paws. Lauren's wings unfurled behind her. Keegan reached out to touch one of the stars that danced around them, but her finger went right through it.

Glancing over at Anna, Keegan thought, *Wow*. Both of her best friends were so beautiful, there was no doubt about that. Calvron's magical land only seemed to enhance their beauty, just like the flowers and the rest of their surroundings. Anna's eyes were always a startling color of green, but they were even more so here, almost a match for the vivid green color of the foliage. It was as if she were staring into emerald jewels instead of eyes. Everything about them was different. They almost looked like animated versions of themselves, their eyes larger and skin glowing.

Neither were in their regular clothes any longer, either. Lauren wore a sparkly dress that fell in pretty pink strips to her knees, while Anna wore a satiny, black sheath with bell sleeves.

Keegan couldn't help but wonder what she looked like. Too bad there wasn't a mirror around. She looked down, surprised to find that she wasn't in her jeans and t-shirt anymore. Her dress was an ankle length green affair with a form fitting bodice and a flowing skirt. She smiled.

They looked awesome.

Donald wasn't sure he could handle this.

Seeing Keegan always left him slightly in awe of her beauty, no matter where they happened to be. In this magical world with her beauty enhanced to its fullest potential, being near her was almost too much to bear.

He tried not to stare, really, but it was like he could sense her everywhere. Whenever he turned to find her, he couldn't help but get lost in her, only able to shake himself out of his daydreams when he realized she was looking back. He battled with himself not to watch her every move.

The excitement was clearly written all over her face. It was obviously hard for her to sit still as she flitted from flower to tree to rock, touching everything as she exclaimed over them. With the background of the forest and her auburn hair over that long, green dress, Donald thought she looked like a nymph of autumn. She was magnificent.

Slowly, Donald rose to all fours and gave his head a good shake. He circled around Keegan and wrapped his tail around her leg trying to tug her forward. A loud roar escaped from deep within him as he took off running. He could hear Keegan laughing as she chased after him down towards the water.

Submerging his powerful body under the water felt wonderful. It was the perfect temperature, like a warm bath. Eventually, Keegan made it to the edge of the lake, a little out of breath after chasing him. She had a mischievous grin on her face when she saw him in the water.

"Is it deep enough to dive?" Keegan yelled, her hands on her hips.

The tiger nodded his head yes, and she dove in, graceful as a dolphin. His heart was racing. Just the sight of her had such an effect on him.

She swam up to the tiger, her arms splashing gently through the water. "It's freezing."

"You're crazy. This water is warm," Donald answered, treading water with all four legs.

"Maybe when you're covered in fur, it's warm." Keegan stuck out her tongue, and then paused. "Hey, wait a minute! I didn't think you could speak?"

"In here we can pretty much do anything we want."

Keegan cocked her head at him, her hair plastered to her head in a way that was more endearing than unflattering. "I have to admit this is probably the most amazing place I have ever seen."

"Yeah, Calvron is something else. He can pretty much do anything. I can't imagine having that kind of power."

"Do you think he could bring the bond to my chosen back?"

Donald's whole body tensed. "No idea, why don't you ask him?" After a slight pause, he added, "Are you even sure you would want him to?"

Keegan stared at him like he was crazy. "Why wouldn't I want him to?"

"Well, don't you think it's a little strange that you are not comfortable around the person who is supposed to be your perfect match? Wouldn't you rather know that it was real and not just some magic bond that made you want to be with him?"

Her eyes on the large tiger before her, the water beading on his fur, Keegan realized had never thought of it that way. What if he was right? She would rather have true love than a magic spell that made them believe they were perfect together. Shouldn't she feel something for Rourk even if the bond was broken?

Ugh, it's all so confusing. She lay back in the water, her body floating as she put her head on the tiger. She was always so comfortable around Donald; too bad he wasn't interested in her more than a friend. "You know, you really are very smart for a tiger."

He wasn't sure if it was the place that gave him the courage, or the fact that he was in his tiger form. Before he could stop the words, they spilled out. "I think you should give me a chance. What if we're perfect together *without* a bond?"

"Donald, stop joking around," Keegan said with a sigh, treading the water. "You already made it clear that you're not interested in me."

"That was before your bond was broken. Keegan, I've always been crazy about you. I just didn't want to get hurt. I knew you were an elf and that you were bound to another."

She stared across the expanse of water into the bright blue eyes of the talking tiger. *This is absurd*, she thought. *I'm talking to a tiger who wants to date me.*

Well, then why is your heart beating a mile a minute? she wondered. This did feel perfect. "Are you serious?"

"I have never been more serious about anything in my life. I know I joke around a lot…"

Keegan thought, *It is so weird to hear Donald's voice come from a tiger.* She giggled.

"This is not a laughing matter." The tiger cocked his head and glared. "Keegan, every time I see you I feel like I am on an elevator that has dropped. I think about you constantly. Maybe fate has stepped in and broken the bond so we can be together."

Keegan backed up enough to find the ground and stood. "I'm sorry, I need to think."

She disappeared before his eyes. Her main power was invisibility; it was the first time he had seen her use it. Donald hoped he hadn't pushed her away. He couldn't imagine not having her in his life, even if she only wanted to be friends. Rolling over, he looked up at the sky. He had done all he could; it was up to her now.

Keegan was so confused and, oddly, a little angry. She tried to think positive thoughts to warm herself up as she trudged out of the water. Her dress and skin dried instantly; she guessed it was Calvron's magic that did it. Sitting down on a large, flat rock in the warm sunshine, she recalled the photos of her weekend with Rourk. They looked so happy together. Was she ready to give up on her chosen to give Donald a chance? Could she ever be that happy again without the bond?

She always knew there was something special about Donald. He was the only boy that kept her interest more than a couple of weeks. However, she really did need to think it over. Donald was a shape shifter and she was an elf. What if she fell in love with him and they got married? What would that mean for their children? She thought of her cousin, Keara. She was the only half elf that Keegan knew. Keara always felt so out of place among the rest of the elves. Did Keegan really want to do that to her own children? Ugh, she was ashamed of herself. She was a hypocrite. How many times had she sat down and told Keara how special she was for being different? And she truly meant it: Keara was amazing. She was obviously just looking for an excuse, an easy way out of this predicament.

What if she did lose her bond so she could have a chance with Donald? Could she really turn her back on that?

The real question was could she turn her back on Rourk? He was her chosen after all.

Chapter 6

A voice shook her out of her thoughts. "Keegan, you're it. You could have picked a better hiding spot." Sam gave her a strange look, his blonde mane windblown from his romp through the woods. He was a magnificent lion, but she was still really fond of certain tiger.

She hadn't even noticed that she'd become visible again. "Hide and seek? Well, you guys are about to lose," Keegan answered, smirking as he roared and ran away.

Keegan leapt to her feet and took off running, deciding she would try playing the game without magic at first. She looked everywhere for several minutes, but could find no one. She was passing through a small clearing near a clear, trickling brook when she saw movement from the corner of her eyes. Wait, were those stars she had seen? She changed directions and headed towards a group of large, freestanding boulders. Yes, she saw them again. She closed her eyes and with her mind, she saw Lauren, her best friend, the fairy. Once again, Keegan was struck by her beauty. "Lauren, you're it."

Lauren came out from behind the huge boulder, putting her hands palm up as she shrugged. "I let you find me. I know you are not used to playing in the big leagues."

What the hell did that mean? Keegan wondered. Whatever, she would just disappear if anyone came close to catching her. She sprinted towards the forest searching for a great hiding spot. The trees were huge, their trunks the biggest she had ever seen. The colors were so vibrant it was mesmerizing.

Something compelled her to keep heading further into the woods. She kept going deeper into the shadows, the brush under her feet cracking, and she didn't want to stop. There was no way they would find her way back here.

She was sidetracked by the sound of whispers coming from the large hot pink flowers that lined the path upon which she walked. *Were they talking?* Keegan leaned down to put her ear next to the largest, and she heard Calvron's voice say, "You're it again." His laugh could be heard throughout the forest.

"Calvron, is that you? You're a flower?" Keegan was aghast. She poked one of the silky petals. The flower swayed back and forth a couple times, and vapor slowly appeared. It hid the flower and grew larger as Keegan stepped away from it.

In just a few seconds, Calvron was standing before her. He was a tall, lanky guy with shaggy dark blonde hair and pale blue eyes. Keegan had always thought he was kinda cute, but he was also too arrogant. "You really suck at this game, Keegan."

"What? How can you say that? You cheated!"

"I cheated? How is that?" He crossed his long arms over his chest. He looked rather outlandish, but somehow suave, in a pair of black cotton pants tucked into high leather boots, topped with his white cocktail jacket. The collar of a satiny shirt was open under his coat and there were white gloves on his hands.

"You were a flower."

"Keegan, this is the land of magic, of course magic will be used. Are you going to tell me you didn't think your little disappearing act would give you a leg up?"

She could feel the anger rising in her as coldness seeped through her body.

Calvron shook his head. "Keegan, you need to stop being a baby. I got you fair and square. You are no longer playing with a bunch of elves and humans. We all have powers here and we use them."

Hearing laughter, she glanced around to find there were at least twenty creatures of the light of different varieties staring and laughing at her. They popped out from behind trees and morphed from inanimate objects of the forest, just as Calvron had done from the flower. *How dare they!* They had some nerve making fun of her. Her fingernails dug into her palms. Suddenly, one by one they started disappearing and reappearing, blinking in and out of existence before her while their muffled laughter filled the air. Even Lauren and Anna were laughing.

"Elf, you're not so special in here," echoed through the forest.

Keegan was getting colder by the second, her lips quivering and her body shaking. A cracking sound startled her, like a gunshot through the woods, and when she looked down, the ground had turned to ice. The laugher had stopped.

Everyone had been turned to ice! *Oh my god, did I do this?*

A loud pop sounded, and the ice shattered around Calvron. He shook himself, brushing ice shards from the sleeves of his white jacket. His voice was serious when he asked, "Keegan, have you always had the ability to turn things to ice?"

She covered her mouth with her hand, her eyes wide. "No, this is the first time it has happened. I don't even know what I did."

"Well, it has to be a pretty strong power to work in this place," Calvron said softly, his jaw set in a hard line. "Negative or destructive magic is forbidden in here. What were you thinking when it happened?"

"I was angry that everyone was laughing at me."

"So, it's probably brought on by your temper. I don't recall you ever having a bad temper."

"I didn't, but since I was brought back to life, I seem to get angry easily and when I do, I get really cold. I can usually warm myself up by thinking positive thoughts. I guess this is the first time I've gotten so mad."

Calvron looked at her with interest. He had never come across something like this before; he loved puzzles.

Keegan returned his look with pleading eyes. "Can you please help me?"

He paced around for several minutes as if he were deep in thought, intrigued by her newly revealed power. Finally, he came to a pause and shook his head at her, his hands clasped behind his back. "Keegan, I'm not sure I can. Whatever dark magic is in you is stronger than me. Not to brag or anything, but I'm pretty damn powerful. I will certainly look into it and see if there is anything I can do. The easiest thing is to try to avoid situations that make you angry."

She wanted to cry. *How could I have done this?* "Can't you at least unfreeze them?"

"Nope, that's on you. I was strong enough to break myself free. You need to figure out how to set them free."

"Calvron, this is *your* made up world. You fix it!" She yelled, watching in horror as the ice begin to cover him again. Hurriedly, she told him, "No, I'm sorry! I didn't mean it. Please stop. I'm not mad at you. You are one of my best friends. I know you would help me if you could."

The ice melted and Calvron was once again free, though wet.

Just then, Donald strolled up in tiger form, his tail flicking behind him. "What happened to them?" His big head jerked in the direction of the icy creatures.

"Why is he not frozen?" Keegan's voice sounded panicked.

"Hmm, if I had to guess it's because you weren't angry at him at the time." Calvron turned and explained to Donald what had happened.

Donald started intently at her. "Keegan, this is not who you are. Don't let your anger turn you into something you are not. You need to learn to control this. Before, you told me when you started to get cold you would think good thoughts to warm up. So, think of something that warms your heart."

She was still so angry that they had mocked her and laughed at her. Taking a deep breath, she tried to think of something that would make her happy. Why was she drawing a blank? It shouldn't be so hard.

Donald sprawled out next to her, using his back paw to scratch his ear. "I can still picture the first time I saw you and it always makes me smile."

Looking skeptical, Keegan responded, "You do?"

Laughing, he replied, "It was the first day of high school, and I believe it was in Latin class. The teacher was giving a long speech. She was going on and on about how we were freshman and had no idea what we were going to do with our lives. That we were scared and not sure of ourselves. Inside, we were all mentally agreeing. You raised your hand." The tiger laughed and shook his head. "The teacher called on you, and clear as can be you said, 'I'm going to be awesome.' I looked over at this auburn-haired beauty and couldn't help but laugh. I knew in that moment that I had to meet you. I needed to know who this girl with such unabashed confidence was."

She could feel her face flushing and a smile slowly crossed her face. The loud sound of ice cracking startled her. Looking around in relief, she saw all the creatures breaking free from the icy prison she had put on them. She felt light and happy. How was he able to have that affect on her so quickly? She was actually able to laugh at herself for getting angry over something as silly as a game of hide and seek.

"I do believe that's enough for today, everyone," Calvron called out. Right before her eyes the magical land was gone, and they all stood at the bottom of the hill below where the cars were parked. Donald, as well as the other creatures, were back in their human forms.

The door was gone.

Walking to his truck, Calvron yelled, "See you guys next week."

Keegan turned to Donald, "Thank you." She paused, started to talk, and stopped again.

"What is it, Keegan? You can tell me."

"It's just, I'm really scared, Donald. I'm glad you were there to help me fight through the darkness." She wrapped her arms tightly around herself and stared into his cerulean eyes.

"You will figure this out. There is so much good in you, the dark doesn't stand a chance. When you feel yourself getting angry, try to focus on something or someone that makes you smile."

Keegan looked down at her shoes and then back at Donald. "Thinking of you makes me smile."

Donald grinned and he quickly responded, "Would you like to go out with me sometime? Maybe we could go on a hike, or just hang out and watch a movie? "

"I think I would like that. Text me later and we'll make plans."

Keegan walked slowly over to Anna's car, her mind racing. She was still so confused. However, she couldn't deny that she felt happiest when she was around Donald. Rourk was always in the back of her mind, but she still could not remember what if felt like to want to be with him.

Once she got to Anna's car, Anna started blasting out questions. "What happened? I feel like I lost time, but I have no idea why. All I remember is teasing you and next thing I know Calvron is telling everyone to go home." She looked down at her sweater. "What the heck is up with my clothes? They're wet!"

"So are mine," Lauren added from the backseat.

Sighing, Keegan told them about her temper leading them all to be frozen. How it seemed to be an unfortunate side affect of the dark magic.

Her friends' silence worried Keegan.

Glancing at Anna, Keegan saw the girl's jaw clenched. Keegan said, "I'm not mad at your mom, Anna."

Anna just nodded, her pink hair swishing. She didn't answer.

They drove to Lauren's house in silence. After they dropped her off, Keegan turned in her seat to look at Anna. "What do you think of Donald?"

"Well, that's an odd question." Anna's brow was furrowed when she glanced at Keegan. She turned her eyes back to the road. "I think he's a great friend. And he's hilarious."

"Do you think I should date him?"

Anna raised an eyebrow in her direction. "Where is this coming from? I know you used to have a crush on him, but I thought your focus was Rourk?"

"I feel nothing for Rourk," Keegan said, turning to look out the window. "There's just *nothing*. But when I'm around Donald, I feel happy and excited."

Anna stared at her friend, not sure what to say. Her mother's warning was ringing in her ears. "Well, you did used to date a lot before so I really don't think it's a big deal if you want to hang out with him."

"Yeah, that's what I was thinking too. I just don't want to hurt Rourk's feelings."

They drove the rest of the way home in silence. Anna needed to find the light witch quickly. Hopefully her mother had made some progress on her search.

After dropping Keegan off at home, Anna pulled out her cell and called her mother.

"Mom, have you found her yet?"

Her mother's sigh was weary. "Not yet, it's not as easy as you would think."

"Well, Keegan is already moving on from Rourk; she wants to date Donald."

"Anna, you have to let Keegan make her own choices. Don't try to talk her out of anything."

"As if that would be possible. Keegan is stubborn."

"Ok, well, I'll see you when you get home."

"Bye"

Anna was deep in thought. Sure, Keegan could probably be happy with Donald, but she deserved her chosen. Anna would do anything to know who her own perfect match was. Keegan had been handed hers, and then had it ripped away.

She had to figure out a way to get Keegan's bond back.

Chapter 7

Keegan walked through the door, energized from her time in Calvron's world and itching to share it with someone. Her mother was sitting in the living room with a book open on her lap, sipping a mug of something steamy.

"Hey, Mom!" Keegan said brightly.

Emerald looked up, one hand resting on the pages of her book, and smiled at her daughter. "Hey. Where have you been?"

"You will never believe! Calvron made this incredible magical land. We actually had to walk through a wooden door that was suspended in the air. It was amazing. I wish you could have seen it." Keegan's words rushed out quickly.

"Slow down, Keegan. Why don't you come sit down and tell me all about it?" She patted the seat beside her and turned to face Keegan.

Smiling, Keegan skipped over and sat beside her mom, chatting away as she described Calvron's world. After a while, she paused, biting her lip. She almost forgot to tell her about the freezing issue. "Mom, I learned of another side effect of the dark magic today."

"What?" Her mother gave her a concerned look, her blue eyes dark.

"Well, I have been noticing that when I get angry, I start to feel cold. Today, they were teasing me during a game and I got so mad that I froze them all on the spot...even the ground. Calvron and Donald were able to help me. When I think positive thoughts, the coldness goes away. So after Donald told me some stories that made me happy, the ice melted. I was really scared."

Her mother stared at Keegan without saying anything for several seconds. "Interesting," she finally murmured. "I guess it could be worse. You will just have to learn to keep your anger in check, Keegan. Believe me, I've been dealing with learning to control my temper most of my life. It is not an easy thing to do." The corners of her mouth turned down and her brow furrowed.

She sighed, reaching to brush Keegan's hair behind one ear. "It is, of course, possible. Your father can work with you on breathing exercises. It also helps that you know how to keep it at bay through your thoughts and emotions. Obviously, trying to avoid situations that increase your anger is the easiest thing to do. Prevention is the best medicine, as they say. I just hope other side effects don't pop up." She put her arm around Keegan and gave her a squeeze.

"Mom, I think I like Donald." Keegan spit out before she gave it too much thought. She really wanted her mother's thoughts on it.

"What do you mean you think you like him?" Emerald asked, pulling away to catch her daughter's eyes. "As in more than a friend?"

"Yes. He makes me happy. I feel special when he is around." Her cheeks flushed as she looked down to where her hands were clasped in her lap.

"Keegan, you've met your chosen. You cannot be interested in others."

"Mother, I can't even remember Rourk. He's literally a stranger to me," Keegan said softly, rubbing her arms in an attempt to warm herself up.

Reaching over her daughter, Emerald pulled a throw blanket from the back of the couch and handed it to Keegan. "You really should give Rourk a chance, Keegan. But, if you are interested in Donald then perhaps you should see where it goes. I do suggest that you take it slow. I don't have to remind you that elves are supposed to partner with elves. You *have* been dating humans for years so I guess dating a shape shifter is not the end of the world." Emerald gave her a wry smile.

Keegan reached over and hugged her mother. "Thank you for understanding."

Slowly, Keegan headed up the stairs to her room, the blanket still draped tightly around her shoulders. She was actually pretty sad at the thought of moving on from Rourk. How many hours had she sat around daydreaming about meeting her chosen and their perfect life? He was incredibly cute, too.

Her phone vibrated and she looked down to see it was a text from Donald.

Night beautiful.

Smiling she replied back. *Night and you're not so bad yourself.*

A goofy grin spread across her face as she changed into her pajamas and crawled into bed, adding the blanket from downstairs on top of her comforter for extra warmth. She was excited to see Donald at school tomorrow.

When she rolled out of bed the next morning and looked at the clock, Keegan noticed she had better hurry up unless she wanted to be late again. At least she had her Jeep now so she could speed if needed. Of course, she couldn't find her sweater. She misplaced at least one piece of her school uniform everyday.

"Mom, where's my sweater?" Keegan yelled out her bedroom door, tearing through the pile of clothes in her desk chair.

"Did you look in your closet?" her mother called back, her voice thin and reedy from down the hall.

"Ugh, of course I did!"

Her mom's footsteps sounded down the hall and she walked in, moved a couple of things around, and pulled the sweater off the back of the chair.

"I looked there."

Raising an ironic eyebrow, Emerald replied, "Obviously."

Keegan rushed out of the house a few minutes later. She still had enough time to make it to school before the bell rang. She wanted to get there a little early to see Donald.

She pulled into the lot of school after breaking several speed limits to get there and went inside. As she was walking down the hall, one of the teachers yelled out, "Keegan, your sweater is inside out."

Looking down, Keegan saw the little tag hanging from the inside seam at her waist. She shrugged and waved to the teacher where he was grinning outside his classroom. "Thanks."

Where is he? she thought as she scanned the halls. She didn't see Donald anywhere. Spencer and Sam were deep in conversation, so she didn't want to bother them to ask.

Lauren and Anna were waiting at her locker. "Hey, guys."

"Keegan, your hair is a mess. Get over here so I can fix it," Lauren said with a puzzled look.

Keegan ran her hand over her hair and realized she hadn't even brushed it. It was official; she was going mad.

"Just put this clip in it and it'll be fine." Anna reached into her big purse and pulled out a clip with a huge blue flower on it, passing it to Lauren.

"Let's hope there are no bees in here 'cause I'll surely be attacked" Keegan joked.

"You're just *so* funny, Keegan." Lauren rolled her eyes, adjusting the clip in Keegan's hair. "You'll see. It's actually really cute."

"If you say so."

"Voila!" Lauren dramatically moved her hands as if Keegan was a piece of art on display.

Keegan glanced in her locker mirror, turning her head from side to side. "It *is* kinda cute."

The warning bell rang. Keegan waved to her friends as they all ran off in separate directions to their classrooms.

She was bummed she didn't get to see Donald.

The morning seemed to drag on. Donald was nowhere to be found between classes and she started to wonder if he was avoiding her. It didn't make any sense, though, because she hadn't done anything wrong. Maybe he was sick? Hopefully she would find out at lunch.

She was relieved to see a flash of orange hair when she entered the cafeteria. Her pulse quickened as he walked towards her.

"Hey Keegan, nice flower."

She self-consciously touched her hair. "Thanks, I think. I thought you might be sick or something. I haven't seen you all morning."

"Nah, I just woke up late. Let's go grab something to eat."

"Umm, sure." He had never asked her to eat lunch with him before. She wanted to run over and tell Anna and Lauren, but that would be silly. They would figure out it out on their own.

Keegan grabbed a hamburger, fries, and some chocolate milk. She hesitated and then grabbed a slice of cake.

"You eat a lot for a girl."

"I hear that all the time. One of the perks of having pointy ears is I have a high metabolism."

"Yeah, same for me. No matter how much I eat, I can't seem to keep on any real weight."

She looked him up and down. "You look fine to me."

"Well, thank you." His face was bright red, making his blue eyes seem even brighter.

Keegan had an odd urge to reach up and kiss him. *Sure, great idea in the middle of the cafeteria.*

"Are we going to sit with the guys?"

"Nope, I want you all to myself today. If that's okay with you?"

"Of course it is." Keegan smiled up at him.

Keegan couldn't believe this was happening. After all this time, Donald was into her.

Her tray went flying as she tripped and started to fall. Luckily, she caught herself on the corner of a nearby table as she fell. *What the heck! What did I trip over?* Well, if people hadn't noticed them together before, they did now. The kids at the tables around them were snickering as Keegan tried to clean up the mess.

"Keegan, it's no big deal. I'll go grab you another tray of food." Donald set his tray on the table. "You look super cute when you're clumsy." He winked at her and walked off.

Keegan found herself smiling as she picked up the splattered cake. Donald seemed to have a knack for defusing situations.

He came back with a tray that had twice as much food as the last. "We can't have you hungry with the big chemistry test at the end of the day."

"Thanks." Keegan looked around to see if anyone was staring at her. Everyone had gone back to eating and chatting, oblivious to the two of them.

"Are you ready for the test?" he asked her as they took seats across from each other at an empty table.

"Sure. I don't have to study for science and math." Keegan shrugged and shoved a fry in her mouth.

"Must be nice," Donald laughed, pulling the top bun off of his hamburger before ripping open a packet of ketchup. "I have to study a lot. My mom would kill me if I got bad grades."

They were silent as she finished off her fries and watched him pile his burger high with vegetables and condiments.

He took a bite and seemed to barely chew it before swallowing. "Keegan, do you want to go for a bike ride with me on Saturday? I'd like to show you one of my favorite places."

"I would love that. I'm not a very good at it so I hope you don't need me to go mountain biking." Keegan made a face at him then took a drink of her milk.

"Well, it *is* in the woods, but we can hike from the road."

"I can't wait! Do you want me to bring lunch for us?"

"Leave it to you to think of food." He chuckled, shaking his head. "Of course, that would be great, we could make a day out of it."

She tried to be nonchalant about it, but inside she was dancing and jumping around. *Donald asked me out!*

Chapter 8

Keegan was super excited. Today was her first date with Donald; they were going for a hike and picnic. She looked around her room trying to think of what to wear. It was starting to get cool out so she knew she should dress warm. Of course, she still had to look cute.

Keegan sent Lauren a text: *What should I wear on a hiking date?*

With your chosen? :)

No, with Donald.

What!?? When did this happen, and why am I just finding out about it?

I'll fill you in later, what should I wear?

I hope you know what you are doing. Wear your new black skinny jeans and that teal tight sweater to show off your curves.

Oooh great choice! What would I do without you?

Uh huh. Let me know how it goes. Donald? I still can't believe it.

Keegan got dressed and ran down the stairs, jumping the last two with a grin.

"Where are you off to all excited?" Her mother asked with a smile. She was tapping away at the keyboard of her Macbook.

"I have a date with Donald. Can you throw me together a picnic lunch?"

The smile faded. "Keegan, so soon? Don't you think you should give Rourk more time?"

"It's just a hike, Mom, don't worry." Keegan opened the fridge and pulled out a couple of drinks. "What should I bring for food?"

"Well, I would have needed more notice for something fancier, so you're stuck with sandwiches and chips." Leaving her computer with a sigh, her mother opened the bread box and pulled out the loaf.

"That works. Make us both two sandwiches. I'm really hungry."

"Aren't you always?" Her mother threw together the sandwiches and sealed them up, and then grabbed some chips and threw them in a bag. "Here ya go. I hope you aren't gone all day. Your room is a mess."

Keegan rolled her eyes. "I'll see you when I get back." She blew her mom a kiss and slammed the door behind her.

Donald didn't have his own car so she drove over to pick him up. She blared her radio, and sang along to the latest Lady Gaga, tapping her fingers on the steering wheel. As soon as she pulled in, Donald sauntered out, his hands in his pockets.

Keegan's heart fluttered as he slid into the passenger seat and closed the door. She smiled. "So, where do you want to go hiking? I guess we're skipping the bike ride?"

"You'll see. It's my special spot. I've actually never taken anyone there."

Keegan grinned. "Really? Not even the guys?"

"No one. I like to go there and think sometimes or just be alone."

"I have a spot like that, too. It's my favorite place to take photos." Keegan slammed her hand on the steering wheel. "Shoot, I forgot my camera."

"No biggie, you can bring it next time." He pulled his cap a little lower and gave her a lopsided grin that made her heart flutter.

Keegan followed his directions until he prompted her to turn into a hidden driveway. They parked in an empty field, jumped out, and grabbed their lunch.

It was a long hike and Keegan quickly became tired. "Are we almost there?"

"Yep, just about five more minutes."

Donald grabbed her hand and pulled her up the last bit of the hill. They crested the top, and Keegan stared out over the scenery, wide-eyed. "Wow, it's amazing." She looked down over the cliff at the assortment of colors from the leaves changing. "I feel so small up here." She whispered. "I really wish I had my camera."

Rourk was out on his daily trek in the woods trying to enjoy what was left of fall before winter took over. He still hiked in the winter, it just wasn't as enjoyable. He stopped in his tracks and listened intently. He could hear someone talking, which was odd since he couldn't remember the last time he saw anyone in this part of the woods. It was very secluded.

He heard laughter and his heart dropped. He must be losing his mind. He could have sworn that it sounded just like Keegan's laugh. But what would she be doing way up here? Rourk silently went in the direction of the voices, careful not to make a sound so he didn't startle anyone. He wanted to prove to himself he wasn't going crazy.

As he got closer, he stopped dead in his tracks. His heart rate skyrocketed. It was Keegan, and she was there with the shapeshifter. Rourk clenched his fist and closed his eyes, trying to compose himself. He opened his eyes and stood eerily still, watching the two. He had to will himself to stay in place. He felt like a cave man—he wanted to throw her over his shoulder and drag her away from the cat. He knew he couldn't do that. He should turn and leave; it was as if he was frozen in place.

He watched as Keegan smiled up at the shifter and played with her hair. He cringed when she leaned over to wipe something off his face. Rourk could feel the rage building in him. He didn't know how to bring it down.

He's so cute. Keegan thought, smiling as she wiped mustard from the side of his mouth. His skin was warm even though the air was cool.

Donald lightly wrapped his hand around her wrist as she touched his face and pulled her towards him. Keegan's heart pounded. She reached up and wrapped her hands around his neck to pull him forward. As she leaned down, her head hit the bill of his cap. She giggled, embarrassed, and pulled back. "I'm sorry. I don't know what came over me," she gasped, her face flushed as she looked down at her hands.

Donald chuckled, and threw his cap to the side. His bright blue eyes were such a contrast to his pale skin and orange hair as he stared at her. "Come here."

She let his arms encircle her waist, his hands were hot even through her shirt as scooted closer to him.

Keegan's pulse quickened as he leaned down and kissed her. This time their lips met his, and their kiss was soft and light. Keegan pulled him a little closer causing him to intensify the kiss.

Suddenly Keegan pulled back looking around nervously. "Did you hear that?"

"It was probably just a deer." Donald smiled and pulled her back into him.

Chapter 9

Rourk decided to check up on Keegan. Seeing her kiss the tiger on Saturday had nearly destroyed him, but he'd managed to convince himself she was living in the moment. He had felt unbearable jealousy when he found them together in the woods, but had managed to escape back into the wilderness before they saw him. He longed for a hint from her that she still cared for him. Anything, really.

He closed his eyes and of course, that didn't work. All he saw was darkness. His hands clenched into fists. He hated feeling so helpless.

Keegan hadn't contacted him since their date. He didn't want to put pressure on her because he knew she needed her space, but it was just so hard to sit back and do nothing, especially when he knew Donald was having success where he'd failed. He wished someone could find a way to bring back their bond. He was obviously doing a poor job of winning her over on his own.

They weren't even supposed to meet until she turned eighteen, anyway, so he had to remind himself to just be patient. He had been given a gift in being able to be with her before their time.

He knew he shouldn't do it, but he couldn't help himself. He closed his eyes and thought of Lauren, and as he suspected, Keegan was with her. She was laughing at something, which brought a smile to Rourk's face. He wished his ability allowed him to hear what was being said and to hear her laughter.

He watched as Keegan jumped up from her chair and ran over to the orange-haired boy. She looked so excited. It was like a knife driven into Rourk's heart. He opened his eyes; he couldn't watch any longer.

Grabbing his pack, he decided to go on a long hike to clear his head.

He felt at home in the woods. He was grateful to have work to keep him busy. At least all the training kept his mind occupied and gave him a reprieve from his thoughts of Keegan.

Rourk couldn't help himself; eventually he checked in on Lauren again. Keegan was still there, and she seemed to be hanging on to every word the shapeshifter said. He wished he wasn't capable of feeling the jealousy he felt. On an impulse, he pulled out his phone and sent her a text. As he hit send, he closed his eyes to see her reaction.

He watched as she looked down at her phone and put it back in her purse without replying, turning back to the other boy. Rourk's eyes snapped opened, his heart racing. She really felt nothing for him.

It was starting to feel as if he didn't stand a chance of winning her back. Maybe he should just leave her alone until she turned eighteen. After all, it was one of the elfin rules. She was obviously not interested in him. He didn't exactly have skills in the romantic field. Perhaps if he let her obvious crush on the boy run its course, she would be ready to give him a shot later on. It really wasn't fair to her to make her choose. He was quite sure if he asked her to pick he would lose, and he couldn't handle that right now.

Rourk finished his hike and headed back home. After taking a quick shower, he grabbed a sandwich and read for a little while, trying to banish the memory of Keegan's lips touching the shapeshifter's. Finally, sleep washed over him

He woke with a start some time later and knew what he had to do. Throwing on a pair of jeans and a t-shirt, he grabbed the keys to his truck and headed out the door.

He wasn't quite sure where he was going, so he looked it up on his GPS. The drive wasn't long and he didn't allow himself to think too much. He was afraid he would change his mind.

It was nothing special. A single glass door and picture window in a strip mall near the center of town. The bell went off as he strode into the room. Without even bothering to look around, he walked straight to the man behind the desk.

"I'm here to enlist. I will be joining the 18X program." Rourk stated in a clear, concise manor.

The sergeant looked up from his paperwork with a smirk on his face. "Is that so? You think you can just waltz in here and tell us what you want to do? You think you can walk in here and tell me you are going to try out for the Special Forces off the street?"

"Actually, I know I can. I am more than qualified. Of course, I will have to jump through hoops and take your assessments. I have no doubt I can pass anything you throw at me with flying colors."

The sergeant stared at him in silence for a moment as if he were studying him. He leaned back in the cheap office chair and tapped his pen on the desk.

"Normally, I would kick a punk out for coming in and acting all arrogant in my office. However, you don't really sound arrogant. You might as well have stated the sky was blue."

Rourk met his gaze and remained expressionless.

"What is your name son?"

"Rourk."

"Rourk, do you have a last name?"

"My last name is Kavanagh."

"Rourk Kavanagh, how old are you?"

"I'm 18."

"Do your parents know you are here?"

"No, but it has been expected. My family has always known I would be a soldier, following in my father's footsteps."

"So your father was in the Army?"

"Actually, he was a Marine Recon."

This brought a loud laugh form the recruiter. "You don't think he will mind his son joining the Army?"

"No, he will understand my reasons. Currently the Army is the only service with the option to go straight into special operations. Now, if I told him I had joined the Air Force, he might have issues."

The sergeant laughed loudly. "What is your father's name?"

"Greg Kavanagh"

The recruiter quickly typed the name in the computer. Scanning quickly through the files, he finally said, "It seems as if your father had quite the career. Almost everything is classified."

Rourk looked him in the eyes but said nothing.

"Did he prepare you as you were growing up?"

"You could say that."

The recruiter slapped his hands to the desk as he stood. "Ok, Rourk, I have to say you have piqued my interest. Let's see how well you can 'jump through the hoops'. First, you are going to have to take the ASVAB, and a PT test, and we will go from there."

"I would like to leave ASAP. The faster we can get this over with, the better it will be. I would like to leave for basic before the month is out."

The recruiter stared at him. Finally, his lips twitched as if trying to hide a smile. "Go in the back room and they will proctor your ASVAB. The results will be almost instant because it's all done through the computer now."

Rourk nodded his head towards the recruiter and walked to the back of the room. The test was a joke. He finished and walked back to the recruiter's desk.

The sergeant looked at his watch. "You're already finished?"

"Yes."

"I'll be right back."

Rourk could see him talking to the woman in the office. He seemed agitated as he walked back towards his desk. "Rourk, would you mind taking another test?"

"I'll do whatever is required."

After the second round, the recruiter made a phone call. "Sir, we have a young man in here that just aced the ASVAB in record time." After a slight pause "Yes, I made him take another version. The same result. No, he is not interested in any of those fields. He wants to join the 18X program." He listened some more and after the call was ended, he looked at Rourk as if he was trying to understand him.

"I can't change your mind can I? How about the intelligence field?"

"No, 18X or nothing."

"Well, let's get the PT test over with. I'm sure that won't be an issue for you."

After scoring a perfect score of 300 on the PT test, the recruiter asked if Rourk would go to the range with him. The recruiter explained this was not something that was normally done. However, he was interested and wanted to see with his own eyes if Rourk would live up to the expectations that had formed in the recruiter's head.

Rourk loved shooting, so it was fun for him.

The recruiter shook his head when he looked at the dime sized hole in the target paper. "Very impressive. The Army will be proud to have you as one of their own. We have a group shipping out to basic on Friday if you are serious about wanting to go right away."

"Thank you. I will be ready."

The recruiter shook his hand. "I'm going to keep my eye out for you, son. I think you will make quite the name for yourself."

Rourk shook his head roughly. "I'd rather remain anonymous."

"Too late for that. The instructors will easily pick you out. Soldiers like you will always stand out. They will try to break you. For the record, my money is on you."

Rourk grabbed all the info he needed and headed back to his house.

It was going to be so hard to leave Keegan. He only had three days before he left. He wasn't sure if he should see her or just make a clean break. She deserved the chance to be happy.

He knew it wouldn't do any good but he tried anyway. Closing his eyes, all he saw was darkness. It killed him that he could no longer see her or sense when she thought his name. He wondered what she was doing right now. She was probably with the tiger. Just thinking about it made him clench his jaw.

Once in his room back home, he sat at his desk and wrote her a letter. He folded the paper and put it in an envelope; he would leave it in her mailbox on his way to the airport.

Now, he had to tell his father.

Rourk walked into the living room and sat across from his dad. "I will be leaving on Friday. I am joining the U.S Army and going through the 18X program."

His father glanced up, mouth set in a grim line. "I think that is a wise decision. Have you told Richard?"

"No, I will inform him tomorrow at work."

"What about Keegan?"

"I wrote her a letter."

"Are you sure you don't want to tell her in person?"

He hesitated for only a second. "I can't handle that right now."

"I understand." His father clasped his hand on Rourk's shoulder with nothing more to say.

Rourk stood up and headed back to his room. He went over his packing list and started preparing to leave.

Early the next morning he found Richard and asked if they could speak in private. Richard led him to his office and gestured for him to sit down.

He was a large man, made even more impressive by his thick head of bright red hair and bushy beard. Rourk was impressed by the man's collection of visible scars, wounds from previous battles. He looked up to his commander.

"Richard, I am leaving on Friday. I have decided to go ahead with my plan of joining the U.S military."

"I see. Are you sure this is the route you should be taking?"

"I believe it is the right thing to do," Rourk said diplomatically. "I would love nothing more than to stay here and be with your daughter. After careful thought, I have realized the only thing I can do is leave. She deserves the time and space. We were brought together before we were meant to be. She should be able to enjoy her last year of high school without worrying about me. I will return when she is eighteen and we can decide where to go from there."

Richard peered intently at him, his arms crossed on the surface of his desk. "I don't have to tell you that the training will take a couple of years."

"No, you don't. I'm well aware of the schedule. I have been planning this since I was a young boy. Until you gave me the opportunity to stay on with the Army of the Light, this was always the plan. We strayed from the plan by allowing me to meet Keegan early, and that didn't go over so well. I think it's time I get back on course."

"Valid arguments. They will be lucky to have you. It is an experience that you will learn and grow from. Do you know where you want to go? Will you try to stay close by and opt for 5th Special Forces Group? Your Arabic is well above the requirements."

"Actually, I have been brushing up on Chinese since I learned Keegan's dream was to go to college in Alaska. That would allow me to be in Washington state which is the closest I can get to Alaska."

"Very well, you have obviously thought this through. It saddens me to see you go. You are an exemplary soldier."

"Thank you for putting your faith in me. I hope someday I can be half the warrior you are."

Standing up, Richard patted him on the shoulder, "You already are, son."

Rourk walked out of Richard's office and into the camp. Glancing around, he realized he had no one else to tell. He had always been a loner. Even so, he would miss this place; it was like a second home to him. But, he was determined. He strode off without looking back.

Chapter 10

Keegan pushed through the door and threw her backpack on the floor. She was glad it was Friday. She was looking forward to a break from school. Hopefully, they were going to be able to go back to Calvron's magical land over the weekend. It had been on her mind all week.

Walking into the kitchen, she saw a note propped up on the kitchen counter. It had her name written on it in neat block letters. Curious, she opened it and read

Keegan,

When you read this letter I will be on my way to basic training. I have decided to go ahead with my life-long plan. I will join the human military like the elves before me. I know I have been offered a position in the Army of the Light, however, I feel it is best I leave and continue with the path that was set from the day I was born. We shouldn't have even met yet. You should be enjoying your high school years and having the time of your life with your friends. When you turn eighteen, I will come back for you. Perhaps you will have found a way to get our bond back. If you have not, and you wish me to let you go, I will do so. Just know Keegan, you are the only one for me. I will wait forever. Leaving you is the hardest thing I have ever had to do. Not a day will pass that I will not think of you. Every night when I close my eyes I will hope that by some miracle I can see you with my mind's eye again. Even if you decide you do not wish to be with me when you are of age, I will be forever grateful to you. The short time I spent with you were the happiest moments of my life.

Forever Yours, Rourk

Keegan reread the letter three times. She wasn't sure what to think. She felt sad that he was gone. She was also really annoyed that he didn't try harder to win her over. The more she thought about it, the angrier she got. The paper turned to a sheet of ice in her hands. Keegan dropped the note on the counter and pulled her sweater tighter. Why was she so angry? She should be relieved. Now she could date Donald and not worry about hurting Rourk's feelings. For some reason, that thought didn't bring her much comfort.

Thaddeus came downstairs, took one look at his sister sitting in a chair at the kitchen table, and asked, "What's the matter?"

Keegan gestured down at the paper which was now in a puddle of water at her feet. Leaning to pick it up, she shook the water off of it and thrust the soggy note into her brother's chest. "Let me guess, you didn't see this coming?"

He grabbed the letter and read it. As he was reading, he had flashes of a vision. *Rourk was in uniform with a look of indifference on his face, getting screamed at by an instructor. Rourk lying on his cot looking at the ceiling. The tiger in the woods. Anna holding a ruby ring in her hand.*

His visions drove him crazy. What did Anna have to do with all of this and why were they showing him a ruby ring? It was pretty obvious why Rourk and the tiger were in the vision. Leave it to Keegan to create a love triangle between an elf and a shape shifter.

Thaddeus mentally scanned books he had read, looking for rings. He could have smacked himself in the head when it finally dawned on him. How could he have missed something so simple?

Thaddeus handed the note back to Keegan. "I can't say I blame him for leaving. Probably a smart move on his part."

"Thaddeus, please tell me." Keegan pleaded, reaching up to tug on her brother's black t-shirt. "Am I going to get my bond back with Rourk?"

"Keegan, I couldn't tell you even if I knew, which I don't." Thaddeus gave her a look of pity. "I haven't had any visions of you since you came back from the dead. You are closed off from me as well."

Keegan walked across the room and plopped down on the couch like the drama queen she was. "This sucks!"

"Keegan, do you want your bond back with Rourk?" Thaddeus asked, following behind her to stand next to the arm of the couch.

"I don't know. I'm an elf. I'm supposed to be bonded to my chosen. It's what I've always expected. It's really not fair." She crossed her arms over her chest with a pout and leaned her head back on the couch.

"It could be worse. You could be dead," Thaddeus reminded her.

"Ugh!" Keegan groaned, whipping a pillow from the couch beside her and throwing it at him.

Thaddeus dodged it with a chuckle. "How's Anna?"

Keegan looked up at her brother, narrowing her eyes suspiciously. "Since when do you care about my friends?"

"I don't know. I was just curious as to how she took finding out about her mother and the black magic. Did she already know about it?" He needed to find a way to get Anna alone so they could talk.

Keegan sat up. She loved to gossip. "She had NO idea, and she was quite upset with her mother. It seems her mom has not helped her at all with her gift."

"What's her gift?"

Keegan looked taken aback. She always expected him to know everything before she did. "I thought you knew. She's a light witch."

Interesting, maybe there is hope after all.

"Thaddeus, you should come with us this weekend to the magical world that Calvron created, it's amazing. You could probably bring Sam."

Distracted, he said, "Sure, sounds like fun."

"Can't you do something about this whole frozen thing I have going on?"

"No, I can't. Just stop getting angry over stupid things."

"Easy for you to say." Keegan kicked her legs up on the table and glared at her brother.

"I'm going for a run." He walked out without looking at her.

About twenty minutes later, Keegan's mother came through the door with a couple of reusable grocery bags in her hands. Keegan peeked out of the blanket she was wrapped in.

"What's wrong, Keegan?"

"Rourk left." A hint of sadness was in her voice.

"What do you mean he left?" Emerald asked, walking past Keegan on her way to the kitchen to deposit her bags on the table.

"He's gone off and joined the military. The human military." Pulling the blankets closer to her chest, Keegan sat up and crossed her legs, staring at her mother.

"Did he come by to tell you?" her mother asked. She took off her green North Face jacket and hung it on the peg by the back door.

"Nope, he left me a note." She nodded towards the table.

"Can I read it?"

"Sure, why not."

Keegan watched as her mother read through the note. Her expression gave nothing away.

Finally, Emerald laid the paper on the table and glanced over at her daughter. "Keegan, this is a very sweet letter. You must realize how hard this was for him. I know you can no longer feel the bond to him. However, for him it's as strong as ever. To walk away from your chosen is no easy feat. He obviously cares deeply about you."

"What do you think I should do?" Keegan hadn't meant for her voice to sound so small.

"That's up to you. I think Rourk is very wise. He realizes you need your space to figure this out. You did meet before your time. I think this is for the best. Enjoy your time with your friends just as you did before you met him."

"I wish I remembered him, Mom."

"I know, sweetie. I wish you did too."

In the silence that followed, Keegan and her mother felt Richard arrive home at the same time and said simultaneously, "Dad's home." They laughed.

A few moments later, Keegan's father came through the door with, of all people, Creed. Keegan wasn't sure she'd ever get used to seeing them together. The leader of the light and the leader of the dark working together, friends even. It shocked everyone involved.

Her father walked over and kissed her mom. "How was your day?"

Her mother smiled up at her father. "Better now."

Richard grinned like a fool. It was almost sickening to see elf couples together. Ugh, she was supposed to have that with Rourk. Keegan wanted to cry.

"Did you know Rourk has left and joined the human military?" Keegan blurted out.

"Yes, he came and talked to me," Richard answered, stroking his red beard and not quite meeting her eyes. "He's just trying to do what's best for you, Keegan. Joining the human army is a long tradition for elves. I think it's the right thing for him to do."

Neither Keegan nor her mother said anything.

Richard addressed his wife. "Creed and I are going to be going out of town for a few days. We have some business to take care of."

"Saving the humans from destruction one day at a time?" Keegan rolled her eyes and cuddled back down under her blanket.

Her father ruffled her hair. "Something like that kiddo."

"Will you two be staying for dinner?" her mother asked.

Richard exchanged a glance with Creed, who had been respectfully silent during the scene. The leader of the dark grinned. "I can't speak for Richard, but I'm starving. I'd love to stay for dinner."

Emerald smiled and headed off to the kitchen.

"You might have made a mistake, Creed," Keegan said, shaking her head sadly. "My mom isn't much of a cook."

Her father chuckled. "Keegan, that's not true. Your mom is a great cook."

Her mother peeked around the corner. "I can hear you guys."

Keegan sat up straighter. "Creed, when you get angry do you turn things into ice?"

Creed laughed. "I can't say that I have that ability. Why do you ask?"

Keegan sunk back into the couch. "That's what happens to me. When I get angry my body starts getting cold and when I get *really* angry, I freeze everyone around me. I thought maybe it was a dark thing since you guys always have a lower body temperature."

"Why am I just hearing about this now?" Her father stared intently at her.

"I don't know, Dad, why am I just hearing about Rourk leaving?"

"Fair enough."

Creed was watching her from across the room. "I have to say that is very interesting, Keegan. I will ask around, maybe someone can help from the side of the dark."

"That would be great. I don't need to attract attention to myself by randomly freezing people."

They chatted for a while and then had dinner. Emerald had made chicken breast, rice, and corn and it was surprisingly good. Thaddeus still hadn't returned from his run. He could spend all day out in the woods.

Her father and Creed left, and Keegan sat at the table with her mom having a cup of hot tea.

"Mom, you don't mind Dad being gone all the time? That's what it would be like for me if I stayed with Rourk. I'm not sure I would like it too much."

Her mother looked over and smiled. "I don't think I could handle it if your father was home all the time. I like having my space. Plus, it makes us miss each other more."

"I can see that, I guess." Leaning back she crossed her arms like a spoiled toddler about to stomp her feet. "Mom, what am I going to do? This is so confusing for me."

"It will all workout. Life is funny. You don't always take the path you expected to take." Emerald stood, her mug in hand. "I need to make some phone calls. If you need to talk later, you know where to find me."

After her mother left, Keegan flipped through the TV channels. Nothing good was on. There were so many crappy shows out. She really didn't get the interest. Too bad *Vampire Diaries* wasn't on, now that was a good show. There was never enough Damon Salvator.

Looking down at her phone, she realized she had never replied to Rourk's text. She quickly typed. *Sorry I didn't reply earlier I was at school. I got your letter.*

Keegan waited for a reply, but it never came.

Touching her lips she thought of the kiss with Donald. She was so confused. She really liked Donald, but she also felt sad about Rourk leaving. *Why did things have to get so complicated?*

She felt like she was about to go stir crazy staying in the house. She went up to her room to go through some photos. Editing usually kept her mind busy.

On an impulse, she looked through the photos of her and Rourk. She did this at random times hoping it would bring back some feelings. Sadly, it did not.

After a couple of hours of manipulating photos, she got ready to go to sleep. She pulled her covers over her head and fell back on the bed. She wasn't tired. She would probably be up all night going over everything in her head. It was ironic that saving Donald severed her bond to her chosen. Maybe fate really had stepped in.

Her phone beeped, bringing a smile to her face. It was Donald.

Goodnight, I can't wait to see you tomorrow.

Ditto, sleep well.

Chapter 11

It was early morning when Rourk walked through the doors at the Military Entrance Processing Station. Glancing around, he saw many young guys and girls that appeared nervous and unprepared. The building was sterile and drab. The grey walls with the peeling paint reminded him of a prison. In a way, it was.

They were all at the MEPS to sign away a few years of their lives.

After signing in, Rourk waited his turn for the medical exam which he passed with flying colors. He already had an 18X slot, so he got to bypass some of the steps. However, it was still a lot of the "Hurry up and wait" for which the Army is famous.

Rourk could have laughed when he was brought into a room and taught how to stand at attention. They obviously didn't know he'd been going through the motions for several years already. He knew he had more experience than the others, but he just sat back and did what was asked of him, regardless of expertise.

A young officer went over the Oath of Enlistment with him. Apparently, they were afraid someone might stand incorrectly or not repeat the correct words. It was a joke. After they thought he was fully prepared, they sent him to sign his contract and take the oath. They seemed surprised that he didn't have any family members there to take his photograph. Whatever.

It turned out to be a long day, but rather painless. As he walked out the door and felt the crisp air hit him, he thought about Keegan. He wondered what she was doing and if she was angry at him for not seeing her before he left. Hopefully, he had made the right decision, because he would not see her again for almost a year. Just the thought of it made physical pain shoot through his body.

Grabbing a taxi to his run-down hotel, he forced himself to move forward. He could do this. He was doing this for her. If his unhappiness is what it took for her to be happy, he would endure the pain.

Rourk walked in the door of the hotel for which the military was paying, and the smell of mildew and cigarette smoke hit him. *Great. Oh well, it could always be worse.* He hung the *do not disturb* sign and locked the door. Rourk tossed his bag on the stained chair and headed for the shower.

The water pressure was pathetic, but at least the water was hot. He turned it on as hot as it would go and just stood there with his eyes closed. Finally, he washed up and got out, drying off before he walked back out to the room. He wasn't tired, but knew he would need his sleep.

He lay in bed and replayed scenes in his mind of Keegan. Her laugh, the way she skipped all over the place, her eyes that he could stare into forever, her hair that was almost always a mess, the way she kissed. He had to stop himself before he drove himself crazy.

He took some deep breaths and cleared his mind. Every time she crept back into his mind he pushed it away. After hours of fighting it, he drifted off to sleep.

Yelling woke him up. He looked at his watch; it was 3am. *That's what you get when you stay at a cheap hotel in the ghetto.* He didn't even bother to pay attention to the argument. It was none of his business. He might as well get up. The bus would be there at 4:00 to take them to Fort Benning, Georgia. After he did his morning workout, changed clothes, and ate a protein bar, he strolled out to wait for the bus.

There were a few others already waiting. He looked over the recruits, and they mostly looked tired. One young kid was pacing around, obviously nervous.

About twenty minutes later, a bus pulled up and the 30-50 waiting soldiers were on their way to basic training. Rourk walked down the aisle and sat in the first outside seat, next to a skinny boy with blond hair, pale skin, and light blue eyes. The kid started rambling immediately. Rourk wished he had picked another seat.

"Hey, so are you also going into the 18X program to try out for Special Forces?"

Rourk looked over at the kid and thought, *You have to be kidding me.* "Yes."

"That's awesome. It will be nice to already know someone. My name is Tommy, by the way." He stuck his hand out and Rourk grasped it tightly.

Rourk was surprised to see the kid had a firm grip. That usually told a lot about a person. "Rourk."

"Rourk? That's a pretty cool name. Is it your last name or first?"

"First."

"Are you nervous? I'm so nervous I can barely sit still in this seat."

"No."

"You're not nervous? How is that even possible?"

"I've been training for this my whole life."

"Your whole life? You're a funny guy."

Rourk thought, *Sure, I'm a laugh a minute.* "How long have you been training, Tommy?"

"On and off for about three months. The last 6 weeks I finally took serious. I did a lot of running and push ups."

"Did you run with a weighted rucksack?"

Tommy looked at him like he was crazy. "No, I just ran."

This kid doesn't stand a chance.

"So Rourk, do you have a girlfriend?" Tommy asked, swiftly changing the subject. "I have one and we plan on getting married once I graduate. Here, you want to see a picture?" Tommy scrolled through some pics on his phone and stopped at a pretty girl with brown hair.

"This is Jessica. We've been dating about four months."

"She looks nice."

"What about you, do you have girl back home?"

Rourk thought of Keegan and what a mess that was, then replied. "No." It was no one's business what went on in his personal life. He wasn't about to tell his life story to a stranger.

"That's too bad, Rourk. Maybe you'll meet a girl after we're done training."

"I don't care about girls, Tommy. Right now my sole focus is earning a green beret."

"Sure, that would be nice. You still need a girl, though." Tommy laughed and jovially hit Rourk on the side of his arm.

Tommy rambled on for another twenty minutes. Rourk just nodded when it seemed appropriate.

Finally, Rourk leaned his head against the glass and pretended to be asleep. In the darkness behind his eyelids, he tried to locate Keegan, but it was impossible. He missed seeing her. The longer it went on, the more he felt he would do anything to bring their bond back. He tried not to think about her with the shape shifter; it upset him too much.

Instead, he thought about what lay ahead. He would be spending at least sixteen weeks at Fort Benning, Georgia. Nine weeks of initial infantry training, four weeks of advanced individual training, and three weeks of airborne training. That was just the beginning. He wasn't concerned, although he did feel bad for the kid sitting beside him.

He must have dozed off, because the next thing he knew the bus had stopped and they were being herded off like a bunch of cattle.

The screaming started as soon as they got off the bus.

"Throw your bags in a pile. You guys are pathetic!" one of the drill sergeants yelled.

A few minutes later, a different drill sergeant screamed, "Pick up your shit, and you better not get it messed up!"

It was complete chaos. Rourk stood back and watched as all the recruits ran around like chickens with their heads cut off. One of the drill sergeants yelled at Rourk to grab his stuff, so he just picked up anything and walked over to the line. He had to hide a smile as he watched them all run in circles.

He had done many such tricks with his own soldiers when he was an instructor for the young boys training for the elfin army. There was no way they could get the right gear. It would be sorted out later. He noticed Tommy was looking lost and scared. Rourk walked over to him and handed the kid the gear he was holding then told him to get in line.

"Thanks so much, Rourk. I owe you. This shit is scary man." The poor kid's face was white and his hands were trembling.

Rourk laughed. "Tommy, you haven't seen anything yet."

Rourk grabbed another set of gear and took his place in line next to Tommy. He'd try to look out for him, at least for a little while. Right now, all that was going on were mind games. It would be interesting to see how many of the guys broke before the week was over.

When they went to their assigned rooms, Rourk could have laughed when he saw that Tommy had the bunk under his. *It's funny the way life throws someone in your path.* That cemented it. He would do everything he could to try to help Tommy make it through this nonsense.

"Hey, Tommy. Looks like were stuck together for a while."

"Rourk, I have never been so happy to see someone in my life," Tommy answered, clapping Rourk on the shoulder. "Thanks again for helping me earlier."

"Listen, Tommy, everything they're going to do for the next few weeks is nothing but mind games. They want to break people so they can sort out the weak from the rest. Every time you are scared or don't think you can make it, remind yourself: It's all mind games. Countless others have made it and so can I. Repeat that to me."

Tommy repeated, "It's all mind games. Countless others have made it and so can I."

"That is your mantra for the next few weeks. I want you to say it to yourself before you go to bed, when you wake up, while you eat, and whenever you doubt yourself during the day. When you're being screamed at, just look straight ahead and repeat your mantra. Do you understand?"

"Umm, sure Rourk. If you think it will help. At this point I'm willing to try anything and we're only at day one. I'm glad you're my buddy."

"Get some sleep. We'll be woken up before the sun."

"Night Rourk, and I meant it man, we are going to find you a girl once we're out of here."

"Goodnight, Tommy."

Rourk didn't bother to get under his blankets because he knew it would be a waste of time to make up the bed in the morning. He closed his eyes and willed himself to fall asleep.

Inhaling deeply, he swore he could smell a hint of sandalwood and vanilla, Keegan's smell. He needed to pull himself together. Rourk placed his hand behind his head and closed his eyes, thinking about when he would see her again. On her birthday. He wondered if he should give her the present he had planned on or if that would upset her. Maybe he should just find a normal gift instead of giving her something that once belonged to his mother. He could always get her the new lens she wanted. Rourk smiled and pictured her on the rocks in the creek, taking photos.

It helped him drift off to sleep.

Chapter 12

Keegan woke up thinking about Rourk. It had been six weeks since he had left, and it was still hard for her to believe he was gone. She wondered how he was doing and if he had already started basic training. She had a feeling she would not hear from him again until her birthday. The thought made her sad even though she wasn't sure why.

Her mood lifted when she thought of the date she had with Donald later that evening. He was so funny. They had been spending a lot of time together, and she hadn't had an anger incident since the first time in Calvron's world. It was hard to get angry when Donald was around because he always kept her laughing. He made her feel like the most important person in the world. He was obviously crazy about her and not afraid to show it or let the whole world know.

They were now officially a couple. She had to admit they did look cute together. Though, there was still a nagging feeling in the back of her mind that she wasn't being fair to Rourk.

Tonight, they were going to go ice-skating. Donald thought it was funny when he told her that if she got angry on the ice, no one would realize. She smiled to herself as she tossed her blankets to the side and crawled out of bed. Checking her phone, she found a couple of texts from Lauren and Anna. They were finally going back to the magical land!

Keegan was super excited and ran to tell her brother.

She skidded to a stop at his doorway, not bothering to knock as she threw it open. "Thaddeus, we're going to the magic land I told you about. Do you want to come? You can even bring Sam. Calvron isn't grounded this weekend."

Thad looked up from his Xbox, totally unfazed. "What time are you going?"

"Around noon."

"Sure, I'll go. Can we pick up Sam on the way?"

"Of course. You know I love Sammy."

Keegan had about two hours to waste so she headed downstairs to see what her parents were up to and to play with Warrick. She had forgotten her father was gone, so it was just her mom and Warrick.

Warrick was in his corner playing with blocks, as usual. He was obsessed with those things. When he saw Keegan he jumped and ran squealing into her arms. "Kee-Kee!" She loved that kid.

"Vroom Vroom." She started running in circles with him. Warrick giggled loudly. Finally, she let him down which made him very unhappy, and he screamed at the top of his lungs to show his displeasure. She left him for her mother to deal with.

What to eat? Opening and closing the cabinet doors, Keegan found nothing that looked appealing. "Mom, can you make some french toast and bacon?"

"Keegan, you need to learn to cook. How are you going to survive college next year?" Emerald was at the kitchen table with Warrick in her lap and her laptop open in front of her as she paid bills online.

Keegan shrugged. "Pizza and canned food."

"That's healthy." Her mom stood up with Warrick on her hip and handed him to Keegan before gathering what she needed to make breakfast.

"So, what are you up to today?"

"I'm going to take Thad to that magical land Calvron creates." She tossed her brother in the air, and he had a giggling fit.

"Really? Well, that's nice of you to include your brother." Her mom glanced at her with a smile while she was cracking the eggs.

The bacon was sizzling on the stove. Keegan loved the smell. "Yeah, it should be fun. I wish you could come see it, but I don't think adults are allowed."

"Too bad you couldn't take pictures."

"Yeah, I asked Calvron and he said they would just show up blank." Keegan put Warrick in his high chair and got out his favorite snack, Cheerios, which he immediately started tossing on the ground.

"Magic and modern technologies don't work well together."

"It sucks. How cool would that be to have pictures of that amazing world?"

Emerald dipped the bread slices in the egg mixture as she asked, "Is Calvron still going out with Lauren's sister?"

"Yep, they seem to really be into each other. Calvron probably cast a spell on her or something." Keegan grinned.

After dropping the french toast in the skillet, her mom turned to face her. "How are things with Donald?" Her voice was nonchalant and her face carefully empty of emotion, but Keegan knew her mother didn't approve.

"Fine, we are having tons of fun hanging out. Tonight we're going ice-skating."

"Is it serious?"

"Mom, it hasn't even been that long. Who knows what will happen? Don't worry, I haven't forgotten about Rourk." Keegan could feel the annoyance rising in her.

Her mother must have noticed too because she changed the subject. "I haven't seen Lauren and Anna lately. You should invite them over for a sleepover. We could have a cookout, make S'mores and learn more about their magical abilities."

"Sure, I'll invite them over soon. We haven't had much girl time lately. I've been spending all my time with Donald, and Lauren has been with Josh."

"Anna is probably feeling left out," her mom said as she finally set the plate of food down in front of Keegan.

"Oh my god, Mom, this is amazing," Keegan groaned, her mouth full of food.

"Keegan, don't talk with your mouth full. It's gross." Emerald rolled her eyes as she placed her cup of tea on the table and sat next to Keegan. The baby was still tossing Cheerios all over the floor. They both pretended not to notice. "How is Anna handling everything with her mom?"

"I don't know. She hasn't really talked about it."

"Maybe I should call and check on Jennifer. I can never repay her for bringing you back to us."

"I'm sure she'd like that." Keegan got up and put her dishes in the sink. "I'm going to jump in the shower and start getting ready."

"Well, have fun. I'm meeting Brigid and Katrina for lunch. I should be home before you get back. If not, make sure to text me when you get home."

"Yeah, yeah." Keegan took the stairs two at a time, excited to go back to the magical land. She really hoped she didn't have any issues with her temper today.

After a swift shower and change of clothes, it was time to leave. The weather was starting to get cold so Keegan grabbed her pea coat before heading out the door with Thaddeus. "We have to pick up Donald on the way to get Sammy."

"He hates when you call him that." Thaddeus sighed, tugging his gray hooded sweatshirt over his head as they opened their car doors.

"I know." Keegan laughed.

Keegan pulled up in front of Donald's house a few moments later, and he came out before she had time to text him to let him know she was there. Her face lit up when she saw the door open. She loved his lazy gait. He looked so cute in his Green Lantern t-shirt that was pulled snugly across his chest. As he approached her side of the Jeep, she rolled down her window. He leaned in and gave her a quick kiss.

"You're looking even more beautiful than usual," he said, grinning. Keegan could feel the blush creep up her face.

"Gross! Just get in the Jeep," Thaddeus said from the backseat.

Donald climbed in, shooting an apologetic look over his shoulder. "Sorry, I didn't know you were back there."

"Whatever, let's go get Sam."

Once they picked up Sam, they headed back to the same spot as before. The big wooden door had been replaced with what appeared to be a mirror just hanging in the air by itself.

"That's pretty cool." Sam said from the backseat. He was a tall, lanky kid with sandy blonde hair and pale green eyes. Keegan wondered if he and Thad had planned their clothes because they were both in plain gray hoodies and blue jeans.

"Come on, let's get out there." Keegan jumped out of the Jeep and rushed for the mirror.

No one else was around. Donald reached forward and touched the glass with his hand, and his fingers when straight through. "Well, this is new. Calvron is always coming up with the oddest things. Let's go through and see what awaits us on the other side." He waggled his fingers in the air, making spooky noises.

Donald went first. Keegan made Thaddeus and Sam hold her hands so they could all go through at the same time.

Calvron had outdone himself once again. Even Thaddeus was impressed.

It was as if they were walking on clouds and there was a huge ancient city suspended in the air. Golden temples and buildings stretched as far as they could see, the sun brightly shining. Every step they took it felt like they were going to fall through.

"Don't worry, you're safe. Calvron would never let anyone get hurt in his land," Donald reassured Keegan as he noticed her hesitation.

With that Keegan took off in a run, her laugh echoing. Donald morphed swiftly into a tiger and chased after her, the two of them disappearing in the clouds.

Thaddeus and Sam looked at each other, shrugged and headed towards the main building. Thaddeus was hoping to run into Anna. They had to discuss some things, but for now, he might as well enjoy hanging out in this alternate world.

"Hey, look at your clothes." Sam pointed at Thaddeus.

Thaddeus looked down. "Awesome."

They were dressed in ancient gladiator wear.

"Come on, let's go see what is inside!" he told Sam, beating on his armor.

He completely forgot about Anna.

Chapter 13

Anna walked through the door at home, exhausted after being out all day with Keegan and the rest of the crew. All she really wanted to do was grab a sandwich and trudge up to her room.

"Anna, guess what?" Her mother walked in from the kitchen. Anna groaned inwardly. She just wanted to be left alone.

"No idea, Mom." She hung up her jacket and sunk into the couch. She knew she couldn't run up to her room if her mother was in talkative mood.

"I've found Magdalena, and you will not believe the luck. She lives only thirty minutes away." Her eyes sparkled when she was happy. Her laugh lines were well-earned.

"You mean you found the light witch?" Anna clasped her hand over her mouth. She was no longer tired. "Did you talk to her? Does she know about me? Did she agree to see me? I wonder if she'll like me."

"Slow down sweetie. Yes, yes, yes, and yes. She wants to meet you right away, as soon as possible. I told her you could come over tomorrow around ten. I hope that is ok with you?"

"Is that ok with me? Ah, yeah! I've been waiting so long for someone to help me. I really hope she likes me. What am I going to wear? I can't believe I just said that, I sounded like Keegan. Speaking of Keegan, I need to call her." Anna hopped to her feet.

"Not so fast. Remember you can't get her hopes up. Do not say anything to her about trying to get the bond back. You promised me, Anna." Her mother looked at her with pleading eyes.

"I won't say anything. I just want to tell her that I have someone that can help me develop as a witch." She walked away, already on the phone with Keegan. They talked for a few moments. Anna had to pull the phone away when Keegan was squealing with excitement on the other end.

Keegan said, "I'm just happy for you to have someone to help you with your gift. This is so exciting."

After she said goodbye to Keegan, Anna made herself a ham and cheese sandwich with mayo and pickles. Grabbing a bag of chips, she sat on the stool and imagined how awesome the next day was going to be.

Her mind filled with images of meeting her first, real light witch. What would she look like? Would she be able to tell that the woman was a witch? She wanted to tell Xavier about it, but he was a human and unaware of her lineage. *Probably not a good idea.*

When she finally went to her room to try to get some sleep, she ended up tossing and turning all night. She was too excited to sleep. She must have dozed off because the next thing she knew, her mom was knocking on her door telling her it was nine. She only had thirty minutes to get ready!

Okay, calm down, she told herself. *Just throw on some clothes.* Anna tossed almost all of her clothes on the floor—nothing seemed right.

Just as she was about to scream into her pillow, her mother walked in the door and smiled.

"It's okay, Anna. Breathe." She glanced around the room, zeroing in on a pair of black skinny jeans. Picking them up, she handed them to Anna. "Here, wear this. And..." Perusing her daughter's closet, she found a flowing, green shirt and tossed it to her. "And that."

"Thanks, Mom." Anna gave her a grateful smile, clutching the clothes to her chest.

"Breakfast? You should probably eat something."

"I'm too nervous to eat," Anna replied, yanking the shirt over her tank top.

Narrowing her eyes, her mother said, "I'll get you a granola bar and some OJ."

Anna was so nervous she could hardly sit still on the drive. Her mom had plugged the address into the GPS so she wouldn't get lost, which meant Anna was able to arrive promptly and with minimal effort.

Anna pulled up to the house and put the car in park and stared. *You have to be kidding me.*

There was a mini-van parked in the driveway and a white picket fence, complete with flowers, surrounding a two-story, ranch home. It was not at all what Anna had expected. She thought it would be some cool hidden house off the beaten path, maybe bats in the attic and cobwebs on the front porch.

Not Suzie Homemaker in the suburbs.

One last look in the mirror, and she jumped out, heading for the door with her stomach in knots. She rang the door bell.

A stereotypical soccer mom answered. The woman had short, wavy dull brown hair, and a plain face. Her nose was slightly too large, her lips were thin, and her eyes were too close together. She did have a beautiful smile that somehow smoothed over the flaws. She was even in soccer mom clothes: a matching, pink velour jumpsuit.

"You must be Anna," she said with a lovely smile. "Please, come in." She held the door open to allow Anna to pass through.

Anna knew she was staring at the light witch but she couldn't help it. It was so far from what she'd thought that she couldn't wrap her head around it.

Magdalena laughed as she closed the door behind Anna. "You look surprised. Not quite what you expected?"

"Umm, I'm not sure what I expected, but you're right. I am a little surprised."

"Were you expecting something more along the lines of this?" Magdalena snapped her fingers and was replaced instantly by a beautiful woman with long dark hair, perfectly proportioned face, and a smile that could light up the room. She still looked similar to the woman that opened the door, just a beautiful version. She was wearing a long flowing black robe, with purple and gold cords hanging around her neck.

"Yes, I was expecting you to look exactly like this." Anna's cheeks flushed a deep red.

"It's okay, Anna. I have just toned myself down to blend better with the humans. When I am home and the doors are locked, this is how I look in my true form. Let's go into the den."

Anna followed her into the den, looking around the immaculate house still in awe by what had transpired.

Magdalena's home was pretty normal. Her walls were painted in warm earth tones and her furniture was a mish-mash of well-worn antiques. Beautiful nature paintings adorned the walls, lit by the overabundance of natural light that came through the windows. It was pretty and serene. She still had a flat-screen television in front of the couch and a laptop on a corner desk.

Magdalena gestured for Anna to sit at the large wooden table as they passed through a swinging door into the kitchen. "Would you like something to drink? I have iced tea and sodas."

"Iced tea would be great."

The light witch drifted to the refrigerator on silent feet, pulling out a pitcher of dark tea. She filled a glass and sat it before Anna with a plate of cookies.

"Anna, I would like you to show me what you can do with magic," she finally said as she took a seat across from Anna and looked at her expectantly.

"Um, okay. I really can't do much. I haven't been trained." She opened her palms and smiled as the flames appeared. Surely, that would impress Magdalena.

"What else can you do?"

"That's it." Anna shrugged.

Magdalena's mouth pursed as she studied her. "What do you mean, that is it?"

"That's all I can do." Embarrassed, Anna looked away, taking a sip of her tea. It was some kind of fruity tea, and it was delicious.

"How did you learn to conjure the fire?" Magdalena inquired, sitting forward with her elbows on the table.

"I'm not sure. I saw a witch on TV do it so I figured I'd give it a try. It took about a dozen times till I could finally get it to work."

"What were you thinking when the flames came out?"

"Well, for a while I tried chanting *fire fire come alive*. That didn't work. I tried screaming and jumping around but that didn't work either. Eventually, I gave up and sat on my bed to read. I figured I'd give it one more go, so I closed my eyes, took some deep breaths and relaxed my mind. I visualized the fire and there it was. It was quite amazing, if I do say so myself."

"Anna, you have so much to learn," Magdalena sighed, rubbing her forehead. "I wish I had met you years ago."

"You're not the only one," Anna mumbled under her breath.

The light witch stood abruptly and held up a finger before walking out of the room. Anna drank the rest of her tea while she waited, gazing around the kitchen. What little wall space that wasn't covered by white cabinets was pale purple. A small window over the sink looked out over rolling hills, and a pair of glass double doors opened out into a small backyard.

When Magdalena returned a moment later, she had a satchel in one hand. Pulling out a notebook and pen, she opened both and said, "I'm going to give you some exercises, but first I want to know something. Is there anything in particular you would like to learn or study?"

"Actually, there is," Anna said, rotating her empty glass absently on the table. "I'm not sure if my mom told you that she brought my friend back to life by using black magic?"

"Yes, she mentioned that when we spoke." Magdalena's face was empty of emotion.

"Well, my friend, Keegan, is an elf. I was kinda hoping you could teach me how to get back the bond between her and her chosen. The black magic seems to have broken it."

"I see." Magdalena nodded slowly, making a note in her notebook before looking up at her seriously. "Anna, I am going to tell you right now. I will not help you get your friend's bond back. I will teach you the way of the witch, if you are willing to follow my instructions and really want to learn."

Anna tried to compose herself though the anger filled her. "Why won't you teach me about the bond?"

"Because, that is not the right reason to learn the way of the witch, especially the way of the light witch." Magdalena put her palms flat on the table. "I don't teach or practice dark magic, and any kind of spell dealing with dark magic is far out of your grasp right now, anyway. You will be starting from the beginning. The first thing you need to understand about magic is there are certain rules you must follow. One of those is that you mustn't interfere with others' free will. Sometimes, you just need to let life take its course."

"Fine," Anna answered shortly, peeved at the change in plans but determined to see her training through. She couldn't understand why everyone was making such a big deal about it. Was it really so horrible that she wanted to help her friend? "So I guess you won't tell me how I can win over Xavier? My best friend I've been crushing on forever?"

"Anna, you need to take this serious."

"I was just kidding." Anna sighed. "What do you want me to do first?"

"The most important part of your training," Magdalena told her, gesturing for Anna to follow her to the living room. "Will be keeping a Book of Shadows."

"I get my own Book of Shadows? Like on *Charmed*? Cool!"

"This isn't a game, Anna, or a television show. A Book of Shadows is like a witch's diary." She gestured at a small bookcase near her computer desk. It was full of small journals, some of them with cracked and broken bindings while some looked shiny and new. "In it, you record your thoughts, feelings, poetry, successes and failures in spellwork, and anything else for which you need it. Consider it a journal of your magic."

"Are these all yours?"

Magdalena nodded. "All of them except this corner of the top shelf. These are blank. I want you to pick one that speaks to you."

"To keep?" Anna looked up at her, puzzled.

She laughed. "Yes, to keep. You must start using it right away."

Anna stepped forward, kneeling to run her fingers across the spines of the empty notebooks. She slid a few out to see their covers. "They're so plain."

"The inside is what matters, Anna. You'll find that to hold true across all aspects of life." Magdalena gave her a beautiful smile, the kind that reached and crinkled her eyes. "A simple Book of Shadows isn't ostentatious. A witch should never draw attention to herself."

There was one book, a thick, black leather-bound to which she kept returning. It seemed to hum beneath her fingertips. Pulling it from between the other books, she held it in both her hands and smiled.

"This one. Though, I really expected it to look different."

Magdalena shook her head, amused. "Oh, Anna. You have so far to go. Let's talk about what you need to do first, okay? Bring your journal."

They headed back to the kitchen table, where Magdalena handed her a pen. "I have two things for you to do over the next week, and you have to promise to remember to do them."

Anna nodded, opening her journal and putting the day's date in big block letters at the top of the first page.

"Every day for the next seven days, I want you to experience the sunrise and sunset."

"Um, what?"

"In the morning, you are to get up before sunrise and find a spot outside where you can easily see the sun crest over the horizon. Stay until it has fully risen, marking down in your Book of Shadows every sensation and every thought you have while you observe. Consider all five of your senses and write down every thought, no matter how mundane."

"Oka ay." Anna drew out the word, confused, but made a note in her journal.

"Then, you will do the same each evening with the sunset. Seven sunrises and seven sunsets. I expect you to have many pages of notes to go over with me when we meet a week from today. You can begin with the sunset tonight."

"That's it?"

"That is it, for now. Believe me, Anna, your journey has only just begun."

Chapter 14

Keegan came down the stairs in her pajamas, still yawning. Her mom was typing away on the computer at the kitchen table, her ever present mug of tea at her elbow. Her mother glanced up, giving her a brief smile. "We're going to Italy next week."

"What? I thought we were going to Sri Lanka." Keegan opened the refrigerator, hanging on the door as she searched for something to drink.

"It's too unstable there right now. We haven't been on a cruise in a while. You know that's your brother's favorite, and it's his turn to choose."

"Well, Italy sounds cool. When are we leaving?"

"Thursday, since you have some time off from school for the holidays."

Keegan suddenly got an idea as she grabbed the orange juice and closed the door. She carefully avoided her mom's eyes as she grabbed a cup from the cabinet and said, "Can Donald come with us?"

"Of course not," Emerald answered sharply. "Have you lost your mind, Keegan?"

"Why not? You let Rourk go away with us to the cabin."

"That was under different circumstances. Besides Rourk is your chosen, not just some boy you're dating. You are not eighteen yet." Her mother went back to typing on her computer, dismissing Keegan.

"You are being so unfair, Mom. He could stay in Thaddeus's room. It's not like we're doing anything."

"I said no, Keegan, don't ask again."

Keegan was getting cold as a familiar anger began coursing through her veins. "He's not just some boy, Mother."

"He's no different from the countless others you have dated."

Keegan glared at her mother. "Donald is important to me. You need to accept it." She crossed her hands over her chest and rubbed her arms, her body becoming increasingly colder.

"He's not going, so just forget you brought it up."

"You are such a hypocrite..." Keegan started, only to stop speaking as she stared, her mouth gaping open. Her mother was frozen to the computer like a huge block of ice. "Mom, Mom! I'm sorry!"

Keegan ran to the stairs and yelled, "Thaddeus, help me!"

Something in her panicked voice must have gotten through to him because he came running down, almost stumbling over his own feet as he slid to a stop next to Keegan and his mother. "Damn it, Keegan. I told you to keep your anger in check. What were you fighting about?"

"She won't let Donald come on vacation with us."

"Imagine that. She doesn't want her teenage daughter to go to another country with her new boyfriend. Shame on her. Such bad parenting skills."

His sarcasm struck her painfully, and she started crying. "Thaddeus, what is wrong with me? I feel like some kind of freak. Our mother is frozen, and I don't know how to get her unfrozen."

Thaddeus stared at his mom for a few moments. "What did you do last time?"

"Donald helped me. He just told me stories about myself to make me feel better."

"Any story I could think of right now would not make you happy." Thaddeus gave her a dirty look. "Call Donald."

Keegan was skeptical, but she picked up the phone and dialed his number. She filled him in on what had taken place, and he laughed.

"Keegan, I'm glad you want me to go with you, however your mother is right. That is asking too much from her."

"You don't want to go?"

"Don't be ridiculous, of course I would love to go. But we're still in high school and taking your boyfriend on vacation with you isn't something most parents would approve of. To be honest, I don't even think my parents would allow me to go." He paused. "How long are you going to be gone for?"

"I don't know. I got angry at her before I found out the details."

"Even if you were only gone a day, I would miss you."

"Aww, you're so sweet."

From his post beside his mother, Thaddeus rolled his eyes.

"Are we still on for tonight? I'm looking forward to beating you on our dance off. I know how you love *Dance Central*."

Keegan burst out laughing as Donald started singing in her ear.

"Of course, we're still on. I was going to have Anna, Lauren, and their boy toys join us." Keegan smiled.

A loud cracking noise filled the room as her mother broke free from the ice.

"Keegan, this has got to stop," she snapped. "You need to stop having little fits for no good reason. I swear, you act like you're three sometimes." She brushed the ice off her. "I'm going to take a hot shower and change."

"Donald, I have to go," Keegan said quickly before she hung up the phone. Her mother stood to walk out of the room and Keegan reached for her, horrified. "Mom, I'm so sorry. I didn't mean to."

Emerald just eyed her silently for a moment, then left.

"Keegan, you never make things easy," Thaddeus said, rolling his eyes as he walked out of the room.

She was disgusted with herself. Falling into a chair at the table, she stared down at her cell phone, her cheeks hot.

A couple of hours later everyone showed up at Keegan's house. Anna brought pizzas, Lauren brought soda, and the guys just brought themselves. The six of them headed down to the basement. It was a large space set up like a game room even though it rarely got used.

"Who wants to go first? Dance battle mode. Oh yea!" Donald did a little Michael Jackson spin and looked at them expectantly. He was obsessed with the new Xbox Kinect game *Dance Central.*

"I vote we eat first," Josh said and everyone agreed.

After everyone had eaten, Donald couldn't be put off any longer.

"Let's see what you got, Donald." Keegan turned on the TV and Xbox.

"Yes! You are so going down, Keegan. We'll start with an easy one, 'Funkytown'."

Within minutes, they were all cracking up. Keegan didn't stand a chance. She could barely dance because she was laughing so hard. What made it even funnier was the fact that Donald was so serious about it. He was good, even though he did look ridiculous. It just made him even cuter in her eyes. Xavier took a video and said he was going to put it on YouTube with no sound.

They were sweating by the end of the song and Donald was still dancing when Anna and Xavier went. Keegan pulled him down on the couch with her. "That was fun."

"I told you." He reached over and gave her a quick kiss.

Keegan and Lauren were loudly singing "Can't get you out of my head" while Anna and Xavier were fumbling around with the steps. The game was no joke.

Josh didn't stand a chance against Lauren. All of her years as a cheerleader meant she could pick up dance moves quickly. They decided

Lauren and Donald should have a big dance off with a level five song, "Satisfaction."

Lauren won. Donald was seriously impressed with her skills. He said he'd have to do some more practicing and have a rematch.

Richard came home and Emerald filled him in on what had happened with Keegan earlier.

"I wish there was something we could do to help her." Emerald stood up and got her husband a drink.

"Maybe we should just let the boy go with us. I could threaten him, and I doubt he'd do anything inappropriate."

"Richard, we can't just keep giving in to her."

"Listen to them all downstairs. How long has it been since we've heard her laughing like that? Maybe he is good for her."

"What about Rourk?" Emerald wanted to know.

"Rourk is a big boy, he can take care of himself. And he's the one that decided to leave. Of course, I would much rather Keegan be with Rourk than a shapeshifter. However, the bottom line is, it's Keegan's choice not ours. She's not a little girl anymore. She will be eighteen before we know it. Maybe if we act like we approve of Donald, she'll get over him quicker. You know forbidden fruit is always sweeter."

"You're probably right. I just wish we could figure out how to get her bond back."

Richard reached across and grabbed his wife's hand. "Emerald, we are so lucky to have her alive. I really just want her to be happy and enjoy the chance she has been given."

"You always know the right thing to say. It's one of the reasons I love you so much."

"I love you. So are we in agreement?" He raised his eyebrow.

"I guess so. I hope I don't regret this."

Donald stayed after everyone else left, the two of them sitting close together on the couch in the basement. They were just talking when Keegan's father yelled down for them to come upstairs. He probably didn't trust them to be alone together.

"Okay, Dad, we'll be right up," Keegan called. Glancing over at Donald, she saw that he looked nervous.

"Don't worry it's probably nothing. My mom probably just wants me to clean up something."

When they got upstairs, Keegan saw her father sitting at the table and thought, *Oh, no.*

Nothing good happened when her parents called for her to meet them at the kitchen table.

"So, I heard about your little incident today, Keegan." Richard had his hands clasped on the table top. He was still in his uniform from camp. With the camouflage and his size, not to mention the bushy beard, he looked threatening. Keegan could feel how nervous Donald was beside her.

"I'm sorry. I didn't mean to." Keegan sighed and sat down at the table. Donald stayed standing by himself.

"Have you been doing the breathing exercises I went over with you?" her father asked. "You're not supposed to do them just when you are angry. You can do them throughout the day."

"Not really. I always forget."

"You need to remember. This cannot happen out in public, Keegan. I'm sure you don't want us to pull you out of school because you can't control your temper."

Panic raced through her. It was her senior year—she couldn't imagine not finishing school with all her friends. "I'll work on it, I promise. Please, don't take me out of school."

Her father turned his attention to Donald, who was trying to appear as inconspicuous as possible. Richard eyed him. "Donald, I heard my daughter wants to bring you on our little vacation. Do you think your parents would allow it?"

Donald stared at Richard. It took him a minute to compose himself. "I'm not sure. To be honest, we don't have a lot of money, so I'm not sure they would."

Richard stood up and walked over to Donald, putting his hand on his shoulder. "We would never take a cent from you or any of Keegan's friends. She often brings Lauren or Anna on trips. If your parents will let you, we would like you to join us. I think we need to get to know more about the person that has caught our daughter's attention."

"I'll talk to them tonight and let Keegan know."

"Donald, I don't think I need to say this out loud. We are trusting you not to do anything inappropriate with our daughter. She has not yet left this house."

"Of course not, sir. I hope you don't think that is why I'm interested in Keegan." Donald's face flushed a deep shade of red.

"You would be a fool not to be interested in Keegan, she's a terrific girl. Call me Richard. I hate being called sir."

Keegan ran over and hugged her dad. "You are the best dad ever!" Her squeals echoed off the walls as she jumped up and down, "We're going to Italy. I can't believe we are going to Italy! When are we leaving? How long are we going to be gone?"

"Thursday night. You'll have to miss a day of school, but I'm sure you'll get over it," her father said sardonically. "We'll be gone ten days, I believe. Seven nights on the cruise and a couple of nights on land. Your brother is very excited. Now that you are bringing Donald, I'll have him invite Sam. This might actually be a good trip. Hopefully, we won't have to hear you and your brother arguing."

"I think we can manage." Keegan bounced around again. "Ack, I can't believe you are letting Donald go! We'll be good, I promise."

"Famous last words." Richard tried to be surly but he was smiling. His daughter's happiness was infectious.

"Donald, you need to go home and ask your parents. Make sure you text me right away. If they need to talk to my parents, just call my phone." Keegan practically pushed him out the door.

"Where's Mom? She's OK with this?" Keegan asked after she'd waved Donald down the driveway.

"She's not thrilled, but I convinced her. You owe me one."

"Sure, Dad!" Her mind shifted gears. "I wonder if Mom would like to go shopping. I love shopping for new trips."

Keegan ran up and hugged her dad again, and then barreled up the stairs. She had to text Lauren and Anna to let them know. She was so excited that she could hardly stand it.

She jumped online and searched Italy, even though she wasn't even sure what part they were going to. She really should have asked more details but she was just too excited. Cruises were a quick way to add more countries to her list, so she loved taking them. Keegan walked over to the map on her wall and ran her fingers over all the pins that were sticking out. Ever since she was little, her parents had kept a map of all the places they have visited. Soon, she would have a pin on the big boot.

Keegan headed down the hall for her mom's room so they could talk about the trip.

Chapter 15

Seven weeks had passed since Rourk started basic training. His days were long and somewhat irritating because he often didn't agree with the instructors' methods of teaching. Even more irritating was the fact he had to sit back and act like he was learning all of it for the first time when he could probably teach it better himself.

He had managed, however, to stay out of trouble and go virtually unnoticed, which was his goal. Well, maybe not completely unnoticed. It was hard to stay invisible when he consistently finished first in everything.

On the diagnostic PT test, only four trainees scored a 300, Rourk being one of them. In both unarmed combatives and pugil stick fighting, Rourk was undefeated. On the rifle qualification, Rourk and one other soldier scored a perfect 40 out of 40 hits.

Tommy on the other hand had not been so lucky. He was always doing stupid things to draw attention to himself, and there was only so much Rourk could do to help him. Truth be told, he would be shocked if Tommy made it past the first nine weeks.

The kid wouldn't shut up about his girlfriend and how wonderful she was, which was starting to irk Rourk. Every time Tommy mentioned his girlfriend, it was a painful reminder to Rourk that Keegan was no longer his.

Rourk's thoughts were constantly centered on Keegan. He was unable to escape the memories of their short time together and constantly wondered how she was doing. Through Anna and Lauren, he tried to check on her a few times but the three girls were never together.

He needed to practice more restraint because he was starting to feel like a stalker.

As he pushed himself from where he rested on his bunk, he vowed that he would not check up on her any longer. His heart sunk at the idea.

Rourk headed to the shower and quickly hosed off before the water turned cold. When he came back to his bunk, Tommy was sitting on his bed crying. *Now what...* "What's wrong, Tommy?"

"My girl broke up with me. In a god damn letter. She said she had met someone else and didn't think she could wait for me." Another sob ripped from him, and Rourk couldn't help but understand his pain. "I wish I knew who the jerk was, I would beat the shit out of him."

"I'm sorry, Tommy," Rourk said, standing awkwardly over him. "I really am. Don't waste your time being angry at the guy. It's probably better this happened sooner than later. Now you can focus on your training."

Tommy looked down, picking at the blanket and unable to meet Rourk's eyes. "Rourk, I could give a shit about this training. I feel like quitting and running back to her. Maybe she'll give me another chance if I don't join the Army."

"Tommy, would you listen to yourself? You want to give up on your dream for a girl who hasn't even waited a few weeks for you. If she cared about you, she would have waited. You need to make a choice. You can quit now and run home with your tail between your legs or you can act like a man and finish what you started."

Tommy wiped his nose with the back of his shirt, gazing pleadingly at Rourk. "I've wanted to be a Green Beret since I was a little boy, but do you really think I can even make it? I keep messing up and getting in trouble."

"If you want to make it you can, Tommy, but you need to decide here and now if this is what you want. You can throw it all away for a girl who cheated on you or you can move forward with your life-long dream. That is your choice to make."

Tommy laid back on the bed and kicked his feet up on the metal bar. "I want to stay. As much as it sucks, you're right. If she hadn't cheated on me now, she would have sooner or later." He became quiet, and his jaw hardened. "I just really love her. I thought we were going to get married. When we graduated, I was going to buy a ring."

"That's good that you want to stay. Now you need to direct your anger towards your training. I know it's easier said than done. Do this for yourself. I can tell you one thing, a Green Beret would not run home crying because his girl left him. You need to change your mentality starting right now. Let this lesson harden you. Use it to your advantage."

"You sure talk funny, Rourk. I don't know what I would do if you hadn't been here. If you see me off crying in the corner, hit me."

Rourk laughed. "I hope I don't have to do that. Now let's get prepared for tomorrow. Sleep on top of your blankets so you don't have to make it in the morning. Go jump in the shower now so you are not fighting in line in the morning. When you get back, we'll make sure you have everything in order."

"Thanks, Rourk."

Rourk watched as Tommy headed off to the shower, his shoulders slumped and his head down. The boy needed a lecture on perception. He should be holding his head high and back straight, no matter what was going on in his heart and mind. Rourk couldn't help but feel bad for him; he knew what it was like to love someone and not have the feelings returned.

They only had two more weeks of basic training. Rourk would be glad when it was over, although he still had a long way to go before it was really over. They had lost a few guys—some to injuries, some for reasons like Tommy's, and even one who had been considering suicide—but most of them had managed to last.

Thinking of the guys who had left to return home to their women, Rourk thought, *it's crazy how much a girl can mess up a guy's plans*. The more he thought of it, he realized even most wars were started because of a woman. Tommy had made the right decision. At least now he had a goal which would help keep his mind off the pain.

Rourk knew that having a goal didn't always help. No matter what he was doing, Keegan was always in the back of his mind. He wondered if the loss of a human love was felt as deeply as the love of a chosen.

Just looking at Tommy, he figured it had to be pretty close.

Chapter 16

Keegan lugged her bags down the stairs, grunting from the effort as she griped, "This is ridiculous, Mom, I really don't see why we can't teleport. We are wasting so many hours when we could be there in seconds."

Emerald glanced up from where she was clipping her luggage tag into place on her plaid suitcase. She raised an eyebrow at Keegan's load. "I told you, Keegan, we shouldn't misuse magic. We are perfectly capable of flying like normal humans. It will be fun."

Richard appeared in the open front door and looked up, frowning at his daughter. "Keegan, what in the world? I told you that you could only bring one bag."

Keegan rolled her eyes, letting her bags *thunk* on the floor as she came off the staircase. "As if I could fit everything I need in one bag, Dad. It's not like we're just going away for the weekend."

He closed his eyes and sighed, rubbing his beard. "Well, don't ask us for help. You are responsible for your own luggage."

"Whatever. When are we leaving?"

"In about thirty minutes."

"Where is the itinerary, Richard?" Emerald called from the living room. Keegan stepped over to the archway leading from the foyer. Her mother was on her knees, frantically moving papers around on the coffee table.

"It was right on the table a minute ago," Richard replied, pushing past Keegan to go help her look.

"Well, it's not there now!"

They heard giggling and the three of them looked over to find Warrick in the corner, chewing on the itinerary as if it were candy.

"You have got to be kidding me!" Emerald slammed her hand down on the table, making a crystal candle holder rattle.

"Emerald, just print out another, it's not a big deal," Richard soothed.

"Hello?" Donald called, coming through the still open front door with nothing more than a backpack on his shoulder.

"I like you already, Donald," Richard said, walking over to clap a hand to the boy's shoulder. He glared at his daughter as she came back into the foyer, smiling at Donald. "Keegan, take note. This is how you are supposed to travel. And Donald, not matter how much she pouts, do not help her with her bags."

"Yes, sir. I mean, Richard. Sorry that is going to take some getting used to." Donald grinned nervously.

Keegan thought it was cute how Donald stuttered when he spoke to her dad.

Once the bags were loaded into the Land Rover, they were on the way. It was an hour's drive to Nashville, and Keegan was peeved that Thaddeus sat between her and Donald. Poor Sammy was stuck in the back with the luggage. It passed quickly, and they arrived at the airport two hours early.

After waiting thirty minutes in line to check-in, the service representative said there wasn't a ticket issued for Warrick. Keegan watched her dad's eyes narrow and his lips tighten as he spoke with the representative, sure signs he was pissed. He had to go through the hassle of getting another ticket issued, a process that took almost an hour.

When they finally made it through security and to the departure gate, the agent frowned at the tickets. "Sir, there's a problem. Are you aware that Warrick's ticket has been issued for economy class while the rest of your party is in business?"

"That is ridiculous," Emerald spat. "He's still under two, so he sits on my lap. He doesn't even have his own seat."

"I'm sorry, ma'am," the agent responded, not sounding sorry at all. "It's going to have to be taken care of before you can board."

After too much back and forth, the ticket was fixed, and they were allowed to board right as the airline made the final boarding call.

"I told you we should have teleported," Keegan said gleefully as they were hurrying down the jetway.

"Shut-up, Keegan," three voices chorused, making her giggle.

Sliding his hand into hers, Donald grinned at Keegan as they walked. "I'm really excited about this trip. We don't get to travel a lot."

"What is it you want to see while we're in Italy?" Keegan asked. They paused to greet the flight attendant, an older blonde woman with a pretty smile, and slowly followed the late boarders down the aisle.

"The Colosseum, I've always wanted to see that. Oh! Will it matter that we don't speak Italian? What do you want to see?"

Keegan quickly got caught up in his excitement and they chatted, holding hands, during the entire flight.

During the layover in Paris, they were told that Warrick's stroller was going all the way to Rome. That meant they had to carry all the bags and the baby instead of using his stroller as a cart, and the Charles de Gaulle airport was huge.

Emerald was not happy.

"Is it too much to ask for some competence in customer service?" she snapped, shifting Warrick to her other hip as they searched for the gate for their connecting flight.

Warrick started screaming, unprovoked, and threw his bottle, which hit a nearby man in the head. After profusely apologizing to the man, in a fit of exasperation, Emerald said, "Fine, you win Keegan. We are teleporting back home."

"Yes!" Keegan was so excited. She had never teleported before. Not to mention she was dying carrying all her luggage, but she wasn't about to admit that to her father.

Of course, her mother was just being sarcastic.

They arrived in Rome much too early to check into the hotel, so they decided to go for a walk. Thankfully, the hotel had a check room for baggage.

At first, Keegan wasn't very impressed. The hotel seemed run down and even the neighborhood was a bit on the dingy side. It was nothing at all like she had imagined. However, the deeper they walked into the city, the more its beauty started to emerge. She quickly forgot about the long flight, her tired feet, and her aching back and allowed the magic of the ancient city to take over.

"Isn't this amazing?" Keegan murmured, squeezing Donald's hand. "Imagine all the artists and masonries that were involved in building this city."

Donald's whispered answer was awed. "I am speechless. I expected it to be pretty since I've seen pictures, but this is magnificent. I feel so small, as if I don't belong here. This is a place fit for the gods."

Thaddeus and Sam were anxious to go to the Colosseum, so they grabbed a taxi instead of making the hour-long walk. Keegan had to admit it was a breathtaking site. She found it incredible that it was still standing and that so much took place beyond its walls. They signed up for a guided tour, but quickly ditched it when they realized the guide was boring. Everyone wanted to explore on their own.

Keegan could tell the guys were in awe, and as she wandered, she had the fleeting thought that Rourk would have enjoyed it, too. *Where did that come from?* she wondered, remembering a flash of Rourk's soft gray eyes and his tousled dark hair.

She shook herself from her counter-productive thoughts, looking around for the others, and noticed Thaddeus. He was standing as still as a statue with his eyes closed and his face slightly tilted up to the sky. Keegan watched him curiously for several minutes as he did nothing but breathe. She wondered if he was having a vision.

Donald's eyes were large, trying to see everything at once. When he drew near her and spoke, his voice was low and hallowed. "I feel like their ghosts are still here."

Thaddeus, with his eyes still closed, smiled and said, "They are. Some of them couldn't let the place go and still wander around. They seem annoyed that tourists have taken over the grounds."

Eventually, he opened his eyes. Keegan asked, "Were you having a vision?"

"More like a flashback. It was insane, I was actually watching a gladiator contest. You think elves are cool? Those guys were ridiculously crazy. I could feel the ground shake from the roars of the crowd. It was a whole different world back then. Humans have gotten soft."

"I envy your gift, my son," Richard said, walking up in time to catch Thaddeus' explanation. "I would do anything to go back in time and witness what took place here. You can feel the electricity running through even now." He took a deep breath and closed his eyes, a smile on his face as he placed his hand on the marble pillar. With his large, imposing form and thick beard, he could have passed for a gladiator.

"Donald, I also sense the spirits that walk amongst us today. I have traveled far and wide yet I have never felt anything as magnificent as the energy that claims these grounds." He put his arms around Donald and Thaddeus. "Remember this day. This is what we strive to live up to. The history of great warriors."

"Well, warriors," Keegan said with a chuckle as she took Donald's hand. "I'm starving so I think it's time for some pizza. We can't visit Italy and not have a slice or two."

Emerald nodded her agreement. "I agree. Warrick is getting fussy and needs to eat. This was definitely worth the trip. I hope we come back here someday. Perhaps when Warrick is old enough to understand." They all looked over at the baby. He was walking around with a twig, striking the ground with it at odd intervals.

"Perhaps, he already understands." Richard smiled down at his youngest son.

The rest of the day went by in a blur. They walked many miles and saw many beautiful monuments, fountains, and statues. By the time they made it back to the hotel, everyone was ready to crash. There was one more day in

Rome and then they were headed to Venice, where the cruise ship would depart.

Chapter 17

They took a train to Venice, which Keegan loved. There was something about a train station that she found very romantic as she watched the people bustling around, getting ready to head off on their own adventures. She thought she probably enjoyed train stations even more than coffee shops.

Keegan pulled out her camera and started snapping pictures of the travelers. She always felt a little odd taking photos of people without their permission, but they were in a public place after all.

As they took their seats on the train, Keegan noticed another elf seated near them. She was beautiful, with long curly red hair to her waist. She had the sides pinned back as if she were trying to show off her pointed ears. She looked very elfish, so Keegan thought her bloodline must be strong.

Keegan glanced over at Donald to see if he had noticed her, but he was deep in conversation with Thaddeus. Keegan made eye contact with the elf and they exchanged knowing smiles.

Thankfully, Warrick slept almost the whole train ride so they didn't have to listen to him screaming at completely random times as he usually did. Keegan spent most of the ride snapping pictures through the window. She wished the windows had been cleaned. They were so dirty it would take forever to clean up the images on photoshop.

After a while, it was hard to keep her eyes open so she laid her head on Donald's shoulder and dozed off. The next thing she knew, Donald was shaking her awake and laughing as she wiped the drool off her face.

"You missed some." He wiped the corner of her mouth with his sleeve.

"I've always wanted to go to Venice!" she told him excitedly. "I have to get a mask to add to my collection." Jumping up a little too quickly, she hit her head on the overhang. "Ouch."

A parade was passing as they left the train station via a small side road. People were dancing and singing, wearing brightly colored robes and dresses. Some were playing instruments, the music carrying over the exclamations of the crowd lining the street to watch, while some held signs and danced. It appeared to be some kind of festival.

Keegan laughed in delight, jumping out into the street to join them as they danced to the lilting music. She shared smiles with several of the parade members, who clapped their hands to encourage her.

"Keegan! Get back here!" Her mother yelled, irritation in her voice.

Pouting, Keegan danced back to the side of the road as she waved goodbye to the parade-goers.

The streets were lined with shops. Tons of people milled around, chatting and gesturing to one another. It was so bright and cheerful with so much going on around her, Keegan didn't know where to look first. She continued to take photos and thought of how easy it was to get good pictures when the scenery was so amazing.

Venice was beautiful, and exciting. The colorful buildings were so close to the edge of the canals, they seemed to shoot out of the water. Tourists clogged the streets, though Keegan didn't think they could be called streets. *More like a cobblestone maze,* she thought more than once as she followed her family.

The city was bisected by canals, so sections of it were connected by bridge. However, they weren't normal bridges; they were made completely of stairs. That meant Warrick and his stroller had to be carried over every one.

Keegan felt bad for anyone in a wheelchair.

"This place is not stroller friendly at all," Emerald remarked as they hefted Warrick over yet another set of stairs.

"If we ever return, it will be without children." Richard laughed.

"I agree," Emerald said, tossing him a smile, "but I'm glad the kids got to see it. Though it would be better if Warrick was older."

They had some time before they could check into the hotel, so they browsed shops and picked out some souvenirs and gifts. Keegan also got a mask for her collection.

Seeing all the masks lining the shop wall gave her a great idea. She sent Lauren a text. *Great idea. Masquerade theme for our prom.*

Lauren replied back. *Genius. How's trip?*

Amazing

Jealous have fun xoxo

Everyone was pretty tired, so they took a water taxi back to the hotel to get some sleep for the cruise in the morning. Keegan couldn't wait. Cruise ships always had the best food and you could eat as much as you wanted.

Their hotel was dirty and smelly, so Keegan was glad they only had to stay one night.

"Donald, can you come to my room and watch a movie?" Keegan wrapped her arms around his waist.

"I don't think so, Keegan." Her father gave her a stern look.

"Come on, Dad. We aren't going to do anything."

"Why don't you just go to the boys' room and watch a movie?" Her mother was clearly trying to keep the peace.

"Thanks a lot, Mom. As if we haven't had enough of Keegan for one day," Thaddeus grumbled under his breath. "Come on, Sam. Let's at least pick out the movie before she ruins that too."

"You'll live, sweetie," their mother said, rolling her eyes.

"Let's order some room service!" Keegan exclaimed, pulling Donald towards Thaddeus's room.

They stayed up till after midnight, snacking and watching movies, before Keegan headed to her own room.

Donald walked her to her door, their hands swinging playfully between them.

As they came to a stop at her door, he whispered, "Good night," and leaned down to kiss her. Her stomach filled with butterflies at the touch of his hands on her waist, and he pulled her close to him. She fell into his kiss, forgetting anything but how it felt.

When he was gone, Keegan closed the door and leaned back against it. *How can this be wrong when it feels so right?*

Racing across the room, she threw herself on to the bed. She had feelings for Donald, it was true, but despite the way she felt, Rourk still remained in her thoughts.

She thought of her chosen at the oddest times. He was probably doing well at basic training and was almost done by now, or at least the first phase. Her father explained the process to her, and it was a long one. He said Rourk would break many of the records while he was there because he was that good of a solider.

If only she knew more about her chosen. She couldn't even remember what he liked to do. *Maybe I should have given him more of a chance*, she thought, staring at the ceiling. *Too late for that.*

Besides, she had Donald.

Grinning at the thought of him, Keegan rolled off the bed and jumped in the shower. After such a long day of traveling, the hot water felt so good on her skin. She stayed in the shower until it turned cold and then went to bed.

The next morning she was awakened by her brother banging on the door and yelling, "You better get up. The breakfast bar closes in fifteen minutes."

That was enough to get her out of bed. "I'll be right out."

She threw on a pair of worn, blue sweatpants and a school t-shirt. Tossing her hair up in a ponytail, she ran down to eat. It was obvious everyone had been awake much longer than she since they were already showered and ready to go. Keegan wolfed down a couple of croissants, some ham and eggs, and coffee in record time. The food wasn't that good, but she couldn't expect the best from a stinky hotel.

The worst part about a cruise was waiting in the line to get on the ship. That took forever. "Come on, Mom, can't we use magic to skip the line?"

"Keegan, you are getting ridiculous. We'll be onboard before you know it."

An hour later, they were finally able to get to their room and settle in. They decided to grab lunch while they waited for the mandatory safety brief. Keegan refused to go. "I'll just stay in my room and disappear when I hear the door for the check."

Her mom was so fed up with her by that time that she agreed. Keegan grinned and went and laid back on her bed. She'd go through her photos while they wasted an hour or so on the drill. Thirty minutes later she heard the doorknob turn and she felt the familiar tingling as she disappeared. She loved her gift. Too bad she wasn't able to use it more often.

When everyone returned, they went and checked out the boat. It was huge; there were sixteen floors for the guests alone. They had a rock climbing wall, miniature golf, skating rink, basketball, and a cool teen room. Plus all the pools and hot tubs. It was too cold for swimming, but Keegan planned on spending a lot of time in the hot tub.

Later that night, Donald and Keegan decided to go check out the teen hangout. They were having a dance party which of course was right up Donald's alley. Keegan loved dancing with him even if it was somewhat embarrassing. She thought it was so cute that he really thought he was a good dancer. Her favorite part was when a slow song would come on and he would pull her close. The rest of the room seemed to disappear.

"I'm so glad you were able to come." She smiled up at him.

"Me too. I feel like the luckiest guy in the world."

"You are." Keegan laughed and tiptoed to kiss him.

The next morning they docked in Koper, Slovenia, a beautiful little coastal town. It was chilly on the water so they bundled up before they headed out. Keegan pulled on the green sherpa hat she had bought in Nepal that she loved so much, and her new tan mid-length wool coat. Her parents just wanted to go walking and explore the town. Thaddeus and Sam wanted to stay on the boat, big surprise there. They said they wanted to have the arcade to themselves. Her brother was a serious nerd at times.

Keegan looked around trying to figure out what they should do. "Donald, lets go on the horse drawn carriage. I've always wanted to do that."

Donald grabbed her hand and they crossed the street to where the woman was standing on the curb, running a brush over one of her horses. "Can we get a ride?"

"Of course, I can take you around the town if you'd like and we can stop at one of the cafés." Her English was pretty good.

Keegan looked up at Donald and smiled. "That sounds amazing!"

They jumped in and the woman handed them a colorful wool blanket to drape over their legs. Donald wrapped his arm around her, pulling her close to his warmth. Keegan rested her head on his shoulder and sighed. "This is the most romantic thing I've ever done. It's like something out of a movie."

Donald turned her face towards him and leaned down to kiss her softly. Keegan felt like she was floating on air. She didn't think she had ever felt so happy.

The town was beautiful and the cafe was nice and warm. They were friendly, even with the language barrier. Keegan really needed to work on her language skills. All she knew was *ciao*, which was hello and goodbye in Italian.

After the café, the woman took them by an old castle. It was pretty, but also a little creepy.

"Would you like to go on a tour of the castle?"

"Not this time, we just want to stay in the carriage as long as we can." Keegan smiled at the woman.

"I understand. Young love is a beautiful thing."

Keegan blushed. *Were they in love?* Keegan wasn't sure she even knew what it felt like to be in love. Donald squeezed her tighter and ran his hand through her hair, staring deep into her eyes.

Maybe they were.

The next day they got off the cruise in Croatia, another coastal town as lovely as the last. This time, they walked around town with the rest of the family. They stopped at a local café and had some pizza. It was really cold out so they didn't stay off the boat too long. Once back on the ship, Keegan and her mother went and spent some time in the spa.

As they walked through the glass double doors and into the warm reception area of the ship's spa, Keegan's mom put an arm around her shoulders and squeezed. "So what do you want to do, the works or just a massage?"

"Let's do the works since tonight is the formal dinner."

"Ok, but your Dad and I aren't going to the dinner. You know Warrick can't sit through something like that. We'll be eating at the buffet. I think you and Donald are on your own. You won't be able to bribe your brother into getting dressed up."

The spa receptionist escorted them to the relaxation area. Keegan loved being pampered. She figured her mother was just humoring her since this wasn't really her thing.

"I have to admit, Donald is a nice boy. I can see why you are interested in him."

Keegan blushed. "Isn't he so cute, Mom?"

"He is pretty cute. He's got the orange hair going for him." Her mother laughed.

After spending three hours in the spa, they went back to their rooms to get ready for dinner. Keegan loved to dress up. She pulled out her dress and held it up in front of her, spinning around.

They already did her hair and makeup at the salon so all she had to do was slip into the dress. It was a full-length, Grecian-style, dark green dress that flowed around her legs. Keegan slipped on her heels and checked herself out in the mirror. Her hair was up with a couple of loose curls and her makeup was pretty dramatic, especially in the eyes.

Keegan made her way to the boys' room to get Donald. When he opened the door, he took a step back and his eyes widened. "Whoa, Keegan, just when I think you can't get any more beautiful you show up looking like this. Wow."

"Thank you." She twirled around and smiled.

"You're so adorable when you blush from a compliment."

"Well, I guess you'll have to keep giving them to me."

"I don't think that will be a problem."

"Ok, let's go. You know they get cranky when we're late. I want us to get our pictures taken together, too."

Their time on the ship passed in a whirlwind of sun, lazy days, and Donald. Keegan couldn't remember a time when she'd been so happy or at peace. When the time came to return home, she wanted to hold on to him and Italy as long as she could.

Chapter 18

As they were getting into their class-A military dress uniforms, Rourk looked over at Tommy.

The kid was seated on his bed, putting on his boots. His face broke into a huge grin. "We made it, man. I wasn't sure I was going to at times, but thanks to you, we made it."

Rourk smiled. "Enjoy the moment, but don't get too excited. There is still a long journey ahead of us. We still have three weeks left here for airborne before we move on to the big leagues. This will seem like a joke once we start the Special Forces selection process."

Tommy went silent a moment as he buttoned his shirt, then cleared his throat. "Rourk, I'm not sure I'm cut out to be a green beret."

"Nonsense," Rourk said sharply. "Don't ever speak like that again around me. Confidence and a positive attitude will take you a long way."

"What if they separate us?"

"That's a possibility, Tommy. However I have a feeling we're stuck together through this. Life is funny that way."

"I sure hope you're right."

The barracks were filled with activity and excitement was palpable in the air. It brought a smile to Rourk's face. Human or elfin, soldiers were soldiers. Most were anticipating seeing their family members after so much time apart. Tommy's parents were coming and he seemed to be happy about that. Rourk wondered if he would be the only one without anyone. Probably not.

Because of Christmas, they had two weeks off after graduation. Rourk wasn't sure what he was going to do with his time off. He had debated going home to see Keegan, but he wasn't sure he could handle the rejection. He had been planning on hiking the Appalachian Trail, eventually. Maybe he'd start that to pass the time.

When they were all lined up and their uniforms were inspected, the soldiers were sent out to receive their certificate of completion. Rourk stood straight as a rod when they called his name. He was slightly taken aback when they announced he was the Distinguished Honor Graduate. They gave a speech about him being the top of his class and making them proud. Rourk's eyes scanned the crowd and he was surprised to see his father, Richard, and Thaddeus beaming at him.

His heart dropped; was Keegan there? He looked around but didn't see her anywhere. A wave of sadness washed over him, but he put one foot in front of the other and walked off the stage, hoping his emotions did not show. Everyone clapped and some of the guys chanted "Kavanaugh."

Rourk should have felt proud of the accomplishment, but all he could feel was a deep emptiness throughout his body. He wanted to be anywhere else.

Once Rourk was able, he walked over to see his father. Greg gave him a hug, much to Rourk's surprise. When they pulled apart, Rourk said, "I didn't expect to see you guys here."

"As if we would miss this day. You make me proud." His father's voice was gruff, as if he were trying to hide his emotions. Rourk thought the gray at his dad's temples was a little more prominent against the rest of his dark hair than it had been before he left.

"Thanks, Dad."

Richard stepped forward and extended his hand which Rourk shook firmly. Thaddeus did the same. Rourk noticed how much taller the kid had gotten in the weeks since he'd last seen him. "It was nice of you guys to come. I'm sure you are busy."

"Don't be ridiculous, of course we are here. Wouldn't miss it for the world. We'll be there when you receive your green beret as well."

"That means a lot." Rourk found himself unconsciously glancing around for Keegan.

Richard noticed and said gently, "I'm sorry, Rourk. She isn't here. We did not even tell her we were coming. Emerald thought it was best."

"I understand. How is she?"

Richard and Thaddeus exchanged a glance before the elder man said, "She is fine. Typical Keegan. We recently returned from a trip so she's settling back in at school."

"Rourk, is this your family?" Tommy came up behind Rourk and put his arm around his shoulder, breaking the gloomy moment.

"Yes, these are family friends Richard and Thaddeus, and this is my father, Greg." As Rourk introduced them, Tommy leaned forward to shake their hands jovially. "Guys, this is Tommy. He's been my bunk mate the last nine weeks."

"Rourk, your dad looks like an action figure," Tommy joked, causing them all to laugh. Greg's brilliant blue eyes sparkled merrily. Turning back to Rourk, Tommy pointed his thumb over his shoulder. "I want you to meet my parents, if that's ok?"

"Of course, Tommy. I'll be right back," Rourk told his father before striding off with his friend.

Richard nudged Greg with his elbow as the two boys walked away, Tommy's hand clasped to Rourk's shoulder companionably. "It's unusual for Rourk to make friends. Let alone with a human."

"I was thinking the same thing."

Thaddeus shifted on his feet. "I had a vision when Tommy approached us. If he had not met Rourk, his life would have ended shortly. Rourk changed his fate."

"Well, then I guess it's a good thing Rourk finally made a friend." Greg stared off at his son who was being introduced to a harmless-looking human family.

There was a cookout of sorts for the newly graduated soldiers, but Rourk just wanted to leave. When he returned from meeting Tommy's family, he grabbed his bag and they headed to the hotel. They were staying at a Crown Plaza so the room was clean and smelled good. It felt like paradise compared to the barracks.

"I'm going to get a shower before we go out to eat," he told his father. Greg just nodded, waving to him absently as he entered his own room.

Rourk tossed his bag on the chair and walked into the bathroom. He leaned his head against the wall of the shower and let the hot water ease his muscles. If only it was that easy to ease the pain in his chest. He closed his eyes and tried to picture Keegan's face and, of course, all he saw was darkness. At least he could take some comfort in the fact that she wasn't given the option of coming. He would hate to know she turned down the chance to see him.

It was hard to believe Christmas was right around the corner. Everyone was excited to have the time off. Rourk just saw it as a delay. He wanted it all to be over with.

As he rinsed off under the stream of water, he realized he hadn't gotten Keegan a gift for Christmas yet. Maybe the other men wouldn't mind stopping at a mall so he could send something home with Richard.

He had already decided he wasn't going to go home.

Rourk was relieved to be out of the uniform and in civilian clothes again. He grabbed his coat and winter cap, and then headed to his father's room, where he called Richard to meet them in the lobby. The food at the military base left a lot to be desired. Rourk wanted steak and potatoes, so they went to a local steakhouse.

"So Rourk, are you coming back home during your break?" Richard asked later as they ate, looking at him over his glass of soda.

"No, I'm going to stay here. I've been thinking of hiking the Appalachian Trail. I'll just start in Georgia, and head north for the two weeks. Once it's time to come back, I'll grab a flight back from wherever I end up, which should be near Virginia. I need some time to think. As you well know, it's easier to think in the woods."

"Would you like company Rourk? I am due for some time off," his father said.

This startled Rourk. His father never wanted to spend time with him anymore. He'd rather be alone, but he couldn't turn down his father. "I would like your company, Father."

"We'll have to make a trip to an outdoors store. I didn't bring the correct gear."

"I wanted to stop and get Keegan a present anyway."

"I wish we could join you but I don't think my mom would be too happy if we missed Christmas." Thaddeus laughed.

After they ate, they went to a mall and Rourk found a camera shop. He knew Keegan had a Nikon, but that was all he knew. He asked what lens was the best, and the clerk showed him three different ones. He got them all. He had nothing else to spend his money on.

The mall didn't have a decent outdoor store so they headed to the nearest REI. His dad bought the gear that was required to go hiking in cold weather. Rourk was starting to look forward to spending time with his father. It had been a long time since they had done anything together. When Rourk was a young boy, they had gone on many long hiking trips together.

The next morning Richard and Thaddeus left for home. They took the easy way and used magic. Rourk had given them Keegan's presents to put under the tree, signing the box Rourk and leaving it at that. He didn't know what to say to her.

Rourk was impatient to go. After they had seen their companions off, he turned to his father. "Want to head out, Dad?"

"Sure, might as well get an early start. Let's grab some breakfast, and then we will get our gear and go." His father smiled warmly.

Rourk took out his GPS and found the nearest opening to the trail as they were walking down to the hotel buffet. "We shouldn't have to worry about seeing too many people at this time of the year."

"I'm sure there were will be a few hard-core hikers out."

Sure enough, they did pass a few guys along the way.

At one point as they were trudging up a hill through ankle-deep snow, Rourk said, "I'm glad you decided to come with me, Dad."

Greg nodded, his hiking stick striking the ground as the crunching of their footsteps filled the silence. "Me too. It's been too long. I know I have been distant since your mother passed away. After the battle in Ireland, I did some deep thinking. I have missed out on so much since your mother died. I need to get back into the real world. I know I will be with her again when it is my time."

Rourk looked over at his father, surprised that he was being so open. "I'm glad to hear that, Dad."

They continued hiking in silence.

After a while, Rourk broke the silence once more. "Have you seen Keegan?"

"No, son, I'm sorry but I have not. I don't really get out other than going to work."

"Do you think I should give her mom's ring for her birthday like all chosen do?"

Greg seemed lost in his thoughts for several minutes as he tried to form an answer. Rourk waited patiently, watching his breath fog in the cold air until his dad finally answered. "I'm not sure that is a good idea. Maybe you should talk to her first and see what her thoughts are on the whole matter. It might be too much for her to handle, and you don't want to push her away."

"That's what I was thinking. I just wish this had never happened." Rourk kicked the ground with his boot.

"Don't give up. Hopefully, it sorts itself out."

"I hope so. Although, it's not looking too good at the moment."

His father put his arm around his shoulder. "I wish there was something I could do."

They hiked the full two weeks together. The weather was freezing, but neither seemed to notice. They mostly hiked in silence, but when they did talk it was never idle chit chat. Their words always had meaning.

When it was time to say goodbye, Rourk was sad to see his father go, but he was happy to have spent so much time with him. He really hoped that his father had meant it when he said he was going to try to enjoy life more.

Chapter 19

Her grandmother must have been over, because Keegan woke up to the smell of gingerbread.

Jumping out of bed, she was filled with excitement that it was Christmas. *Who doesn't love presents?* she thought with a smile.

She found it hard to believe time had passed so quickly. Keegan looked down and grinned, wiggling her toes in her footed polar bear pajamas. Ever since she was a little girl, her mother had given them Christmas pj's to wear to bed every year on Christmas Eve.

She stretched, went to the bathroom, and then headed downstairs. Halfway down, she realized she had forgotten her camera, so she ran back up to grab it. Once downstairs, she skidded across the wooden floor laughing.

Her father always went out to the woods, and picked the biggest, fattest tree he could find. He outdid himself this year—it was almost touching the ceiling. They had spent a full day decorating it. Even though they lived out in the middle of the woods, and no one could see them, he also went crazy with lights for the outside of the house. Her father always went over the top for Christmas.

Thaddeus was lounging on the couch in his hooded sweatshirt and new pj pants. He had been given black flannel pants covered in reindeer with strings of lights around their antlers. "Waiting on you as usual, Keegan."

"Well, I'm here now. Let's open some presents. I see Warrick already got started." He was playing with a box and had the wrapping paper covering his head. He was a little clown. She snapped a picture.

"Hey Nanny, I can't wait till you see the present I got you."

Her grandmother walked over and kissed the top of her head. "I'm sure I'll love it."

"Ok, dig in everyone." Her father tossed a present to Keegan.

She got the usual: tons of clothes and gift cards. Her father got her a cool tripod she could use in the woods. It would attach to almost anything.

One section under the Christmas tree was dedicated to their household, and there was one box left. There were still piles of presents for the rest of the extended family.

"Whose is this?" Keegan asked as she picked up the present and shook it. The room was oddly quiet. She looked at the card.

It said *To Keegan, From Rourk.*

Keegan sat down on the floor and crossed her legs, staring at the box in front of her. She felt bad that she didn't get him anything.

Slowly, she opened the box and started squealing at the three lenses. "I've wanted a new lens forever."

"That was really sweet of him," her mother said from across the room.

"I know, I feel bad I didn't get him anything," Keegan answered as she attached one of the new lenses to her camera.

"Well, maybe you can send him some photos you took. I know when I was in training, I loved getting mail." Her father smiled at the memory.

"That's a great idea. Let me get a picture of all of you near the tree."

A couple of hours later, Donald showed up for dinner. He had become a regular at their house. He gave her mother a new teapot, which she loved, and gave her father a book for his library. Thaddeus got a gift card with Xbox points.

"I'm sorry. I didn't know you were going to be here," Donald told Keegan's grandmother. He was obviously embarrassed.

"Don't be ridiculous. I'm old and have everything I want. Just come over here and give me a hug."

After hugging Mary, Donald pulled a small box out of his coat. "I got this for you, Keegan. I wish I could have gotten you more. But, there's only so much snow shoveling to be done in Tennessee to make extra money," he said, making everybody laugh.

Keegan smiled and slowly unwrapped the present. It was a pair of silver dolphin earrings with a small blue stones for eyes. "I love them! Thank you." She put them in her ears right away with a big grin.

"I know how you love dolphins. I'm glad you liked them. I wasn't quite sure what to get you."

"Can you take a picture of me with them on?" Keegan handed Donald her camera.

"Nice, I see you got a new lens for Christmas." He snapped a picture.

"Yes, I actually got three."

"I know you will have fun with that. Santa was good to you this year."

Keegan looked down, biting her lip. "Rourk sent them."

"Oh." Everyone was quiet.

Warrick squealed out to break the awkwardness.

"That was nice of him," Donald said as he handed the camera back to Keegan.

She could tell he was uncomfortable.

"Keegan, why don't you take Donald into the den while we finish cooking in here?" Her mother practically pushed them out of the kitchen.

Keegan put her arm around his waist as they walked into the den. "You don't have anything to worry about with Rourk."

"Are you sure, Keegan? He is your chosen, after all."

"My bond to him has not returned, and I don't think there is any possibility it will. He is a stranger to me. It's you I care about."

Donald paused just inside the door of the living room, turning to face her. His eyes searched her face as he brushed her hair back with one hand. He took a deep breath. "I love you, Keegan. I know I haven't said it before, but it's true. I've loved you for as long as I can remember. I'm terrified I am going to lose you to him."

Keegan didn't know what to say. She wrapped her arms around herself, staring wide-eyed at him. Why weren't the words rolling off her tongue as easy as they did his? "I really love the earrings you got me."

"Smooth change of the subject." Donald quirked an eyebrow at her, pulling on her elbows until she put her hands in his. "I understand if you can't say the words yet. I hope in time you will be able to look me in the eyes and tell me you love me."

Keegan thought about her words before she spoke. "I do care about you. I have been so happy during our time together. I love the way you make me feel."

They sat together on the couch in front of the tree. Keegan liked the way the colorful lights blinked on and off on his hair.

"I guess I will have to settle with that for now." Donald pressed a light kiss to her temple before saying quietly, "I applied for a couple of colleges in Alaska."

"You did?" Why did she feel so strange about this revelation?

"I just can't stand the thought of being so far apart from you. I really don't care where I go to school. I've never had a favorite college that I wanted to attend to. They have plenty of good engineer programs in Alaska."

"I hope you applied to other schools, as well, so you have a choice?"

"Yes, I applied to several. A couple in Tennessee, Florida, and California."

Keegan felt slightly relieved to hear this. She had already received her early acceptance to the college of her choice in Alaska. Her mother was going to take her to check it out soon.

"I think our conversation is much too serious to have on Christmas day. You haven't even opened your present from me." Keegan ran up to her room and came down with a box.

She watched as he tore open the present and a smile spread across his face. "Keegan, this is too much. I can't accept this."

"Shhh, how else are you going to beat Lauren unless you are able to practice?"

"Thank you." He leaned over and kissed her deeply as if it were their last kiss.

She had gotten him the Kinect for his Xbox along with the *Dance Dance Revolution* game. Keegan loved giving presents almost as much as she enjoyed receiving them.

"Guys, come on out. It's almost time to eat."

"Well, be right there, Mom."

They walked into the kitchen and saw the rest of the family had arrived while they were chatting in the living room. Keegan's aunts Katrina and Brigid stood at the counter with her mother while all of her cousins milled about, stealing food.

"Hey guys, come get your presents!" Keegan said excitedly, leading the rush to the tree. She started tossing presents at them, laughing as they all tore into them.

Donald put his arm around Keegan. "You seriously have the best family."

"Yea, they aren't so bad." She looked down to find Mackenna wrapped around her leg. Keegan laughed, pinching the little girl's cheek. "Go get your presents, Mack attack."

Mackenna ran off giggling.

The house smelled wonderful. Her grandmother always came over and cooked the holiday meals, so they had a huge turkey, ham, and a roast. Keegan always ate more food than she could handle and ended up uncomfortable for the rest of the night, but it was delicious, anyway.

Chapter 20

Keegan heard a knock at the door. She closed her eyes to see who it was even though she was expecting Anna and Lauren. It was them, and they looked like they were freezing. She ran down the stairs to let them in.

"Mom, can you make us some hot chocolate?" Keegan yelled into the kitchen.

"Of course." Her mom peeked around the corner. "Hi girls, it's nice to see you."

"Hello, Keegan's mom," they said in unison, stomping snow off their boots on the rug outside the door. Frigid air drifted through the door around them, so Keegan quickly ushered them inside.

"Just throw your bags on the floor," Emerald told the girls, disappearing back to the kitchen, presumably to make hot chocolate.

"It's been so long since we've had a sleep over." Keegan hugged them both and then brushed the snow off Anna's shoulder as they pulled off their snow boots.

"I can't wait for the party tonight," Lauren gushed, nearly tripping as she finally yanked her second boot off a little too roughly.

Anna rolled her eyes. "Yay, we get to go to a party at one of your lame cheerleader friends' houses."

"It's not just any house. It's more like a mansion. You will have fun, I promise."

"Don't forget Xavier is going to be there," Keegan teased her.

"I've given up on him. You would know that if you bothered to call me." Anna shot her a bored look.

"Sorry, I know I've been spending more time with Donald and less with you guys." Keegan pouted.

Anna rolled her eyes, hanging her scarf and jacket up in the hall closet. "I haven't even been able to tell you about Magdalena, the light witch that has been helping me with my powers."

"How has that been going?"

Suddenly, Lauren's hat flew off her head and hit Keegan in the face. "Well, I can do that now." Anna laughed.

"Good one." Keegan threw the hat back at her.

"We have so much catching up to do. Let's promise to spend more time together. Before we know it we will all be heading off to different colleges," Lauren said.

That sobered the moment.

Emerald came in with a tray full of hot chocolate and warm cookies. "Come and sit down in the den in front of the fireplace, girls."

They didn't have to be asked twice. They knelt around the coffee table, helping themselves to the goodies. "This is the best hot chocolate ever," Anna groaned, closing her eyes in ecstasy.

"It's Godiva from the can." Emerald shrugged and smiled.

Thaddeus came barreling down the stairs. "I have to talk to Anna about something."

The girls all looked at each other in surprise. Thaddeus rarely bothered with any of them.

"Um, ok." Anna stood up and followed Thad to the back of the house.

"Keegan told me you were a witch."

"More like a witch in training. Why what's up? You're like all powerful? What do you want with me?" She placed her hand on her hip and stared at him.

"Once again, I am going to break the rules for Keegan. Don't ask me why. She's such a pain. I do like Rourk though, and I want him to be happy."

Anna was getting excited. "I like where this is going. What do you need from me? I have been trying to find a way to get their bond back, but I am having no luck at all."

"Well, I had a vision and the answer came to me. It's so simple, it's almost laughable."

"What is it?" Anna's eyes were wide with excitement.

"It's the ring. The ring is the key to all of this. You know how elves get engaged as soon as the youngest turns eighteen? The ring is what cements the bond."

"Oh my Goddess, are you serious, Thaddeus?" Anna couldn't control her excitement. "Where do I come into all of this?"

"Well, I need you to implant dreams into Rourk's head that make him want to give Keegan the ring. It's the natural thing for him to do, but with the bond broken he might need a nudge in the right direction."

Anna's face fell. "I have no idea how to implant dreams."

"That's okay, I have access to a Book of Shadows. We can figure it out."

"You have a Book of Shadows? Thaddeus, can I kiss you?" She grabbed him by the shoulders and jumped up and down, her brown and purple hair bouncing.

"Gross, no." He gave her a horrified look.

"Okay, but what if Keegan doesn't want to take the ring?"

"That's also where I need your help. I could ask an elfin witch, but they know it's breaking the rules. You never follow the rules so I figured you would be the perfect witch. Not to mention I saw you holding the ring in my vision."

"That's so cool that I was in your vision," Anna gasped, grabbing his arm. "What was I wearing?"

Thaddeus shook her off, rolling his eyes. "Now you're being stupid. Just pay attention. We don't have much time before they wonder what we are up to. You are going to need to spell the ring. Some sort of enchantment spell so it will be impossible for Keegan not to want to try on the ring. Once the ring is on her finger, BAM. The bond is back and sealed."

"Is it really that simple? I have spent months trying to figure this out."

"Magic is often simple." Thaddeus grinned at her. "Of course you have to keep this to yourself or it won't work. This has to come as a total surprise to both Keegan and Rourk."

"It's going to be hard, but I will keep the secret. I feel like screaming it from the top of a mountain."

"It has to happen on Keegan's birthday," Thaddeus mused, leaning against the wall. "So hopefully the stars align and we can get Rourk back here in time."

"Well, we have a few months so I'm sure it can be worked out. Maybe you can contact his father. The dreams may be enough to pull him back."

Thaddeus nodded. "His father is a last resort. Rourk did tell Keegan he would be back for her on her eighteenth birthday. He is a man of his word. So I'm sure he will be, as long as his training does not interfere."

"When are we going to get to see the Book of Shadows?"

Anna's swift changes of subject were wearying. Thaddeus sighed. "I cannot remove it from the vault so I will have to take you there. It is forbidden for any non elves to enter. We will have to cloak you."

"This is the most excitement I've had in my life," Anna squealed, bouncing up and down again as she clapped. Thaddeus tried to shush her, but it didn't work. "I'm going to a secret vault, I'll be cloaked, and I get to read a Book of Shadows. Are you sure I can't kiss you?"

As she stepped towards him, he bounded quickly away. "Don't even think about it. Get back in the living room and tell them I needed your help on a computer program. They will buy that since you are a computer geek."

"I'm not a computer geek," she argued, but there wasn't a lot of strength behind it.

Thaddeus ignored her. "We'll get together next week and start working on the plan. Wait, what's your cell number? I've been waiting almost a month for you to come by."

"I feel so diabolical," she giggled, sending him a quick text so he would have her number. She gave a wicked laugh, patting him on the head before she headed back to the living room.

She walked casually into the room, hoping her face didn't give away the glee she felt inside.

"What the heck did Thad want you for?" Keegan asked, slurping her hot chocolate.

"He needed some computer help, and he knows I have mad skills. Of course I took care of the problem." Anna gave a low bow, and Lauren clapped.

"Well, we have more important things to talk about. What did you bring to wear for the party?" Lauren raised an eyebrow.

"I brought a short, one-shoulder black dress and sparkly heels. Don't even bother to ask, Keegan. I'm not wearing flats." Anna stuck her tongue out at her friend.

Keegan shook her head and giggled before answering. "Oh, I can't wait to see it on you. What about your hair?"

"Whatever our stylist, Lauren, wants to do with it."

Lauren looked over at Keegan "What about you? It feels odd that we didn't go shopping together."

"You'll have to wait and see."

A few hours later, they were getting ready for the party. Lauren came out of the bathroom wearing a beautiful, strapless purple and black dress. It was short and the bottom flared out with a tulle skirt.

"You are so hot it makes me sick." Keegan grinned to take the sting out of the statement.

"Ok, now go put on your dress. I'm dying to see what you picked out." Lauren pushed her towards the closet.

A few moments later Keegan waked out and did a spin. "What do you think?"

"Keegan! Where did you find that dress?"

"Modcloth.com. They have all kinds of cute, vintage-looking dresses."

"I love that color on you. It's almost the same color as your eyes."

Keegan stared at herself in the mirror, taking in the strapless sweetheart neckline, and she pulled up the rows of gathered silk. She smiled as she touched the bow that completed the dress. "It is pretty cute!"

"You are going to give poor Donald a heart attack."

"Your turn, Anna. Hurry up, we don't have much time."

Anna came out a few moments later, throwing her hands up in the air as she said "Ta da!"

"Wow, all I see is legs and sparkles. Speaking of giving people a heart attack. If Xavier doesn't notice you tonight, he must be blind." Lauren reached out and ran her hands over Anna's sparkles.

"You haven't said much about Josh lately." Keegan looked at her curiously.

"We're fine. I'm just thinking that I need to break up with him before I head off to college. He wants to stay in Tennessee, and I don't see that for myself."

"Well, that's too bad. At least you guys have had a couple of good years together," Anna remarked.

"Katrina should be here soon to pick us up. I asked her to drive in case we have a couple of drinks."

"Good thinking. I miss Kat. We haven't seen her in a while."

They ran downstairs when they heard Katrina yell, "Hello, is anyone home?"

"You are such a dork, Katrina, that's why we love you," Keegan greeted her aunt.

Kat looked young and hip in her tight blue jeans and fitted red sweater. She let out a long whistle. "You guys look HOT!"

The girls giggled while bundling up before they made the cold journey to the car.

Lauren wasn't kidding when she said the party was at a mansion. There was an indoor pool and guys were already jumping in it. Keegan noticed Donald over by the pool table. He looked up at the same time, a wide grin spreading across his face as he handed his pool stick to another guy and walked away from the game.

"You are gorgeous," he murmured, one arm curling around her to drag her body against his. "I can't believe you even give me the time of day."

"You are ridiculous. I'm the lucky one." Keegan put her arms around his waist as he leaned down to kiss her.

"Get a room!" someone yelled.

Donald laughed, and Keegan's face turned bright red.

"Let's go dance." Donald pulled her into the next room.

Keegan glanced around and couldn't get over the extravagance of the place. A huge chandler hung above them and tables lined the walls overflowing with food. A live band was playing, complete with light show and disco ball. Keegan barely knew the girl who was throwing the party, but she had gone all out.

She smirked at Donald, amused. "I see you learned some new moves."

"Yep, thanks to your Christmas present. Give me another week and I'm asking Lauren for a rematch."

Keegan glanced around trying to catch a glimpse of Anna or Lauren but there were too many people. "Where are the rest of the guys?"

"No idea, and I don't really care. I just want to be with you." He touched the side of her face and smiled down at her.

"Let's grab a drink before I get dehydrated from all this dancing." Keegan led him off the dance floor and to the food, where she grabbed a plate and filled it with snacks.

"Do you want soda or a drink?" Donald asked.

"Soda or punch is fine."

"Ok, I'll go get in line."

She watched as he walked off with his lazy gait and smiled to herself.

"There you are. I have been looking all over for you!" Lauren screamed over the music.

Keegan raised an eyebrow. "I can hear you fine. What's up and where is Josh?"

"I just broke up with him. He's so upset."

"I thought you were going to wait till the end of the school year?"

"I figured I might as well get it over with now. It's kind of cruel to lead him on."

"That's true. Are you ok?"

"Not really. I need a drink."

"Go tell Donald, he's in the line."

Lauren gave her a thumbs-up and glided away, scanning the drinks line for Donald.

Later, Keegan reflected that telling Lauren to get a drink was probably not the best idea she had ever had. She stood in the bathroom, the sounds of the party muffled by the closed door, and held Lauren's mass of dark curls back as her friend got sick in the toilet.

Supporting a very heavy Lauren on the side of her own body, Keegan escorted her out of the house. The cold air seemed to sober Lauren enough for Keegan to let her fall to the white wicker couch on the front porch while she texted Donald and Anna that they needed to leave.

"Too much?" Donald asked, tugging his big black coat on as he closed the front door behind him.

Keegan turned around to find Lauren had fallen over, her face planted in the cushions as she snored.

"At least she's breathing," Keegan sighed. "Can you take us home?"

"Of course."

Once Anna joined them, they all piled into Donald's mother's car. Keegan was exhausted by the time she got home and put Lauren in bed.

Chapter 21

Tommy and Rourk both made it through Airborne school. Rourk was surprised; he ended up having a lot of fun. Tommy struggled because he had a fear of heights. Somehow, with Rourk's encouragement, he managed to make it through unharmed.

Once again, Rourk found himself singled out as the Distinguished Honor Graduate. This time, however, neither Tommy nor Rourk had any family in the crowd.

They were given a weekend pass, before they had to head to Fort Bragg, North Carolina for the Special Forces selection process. The initial selection process was only three weeks long. If they made it through that, it would depend on which field they were placed in. The training would be anywhere from six months to over a year.

Tommy was really nervous that he wouldn't be selected. If Rourk had anything to say about it, he would make it through with flying colors. Having Tommy around made the days go by quicker. Keeping an eye on the kid gave Rourk something to do to keep his mind busy, to keep his thoughts off Keegan. He couldn't help but think that Keegan would really like Tommy. He hoped someday they would be able to meet.

"Come on, Tommy, let's get out of this place," Rourk said, grabbing the last of his things.

Tommy followed suit, checking around the room one last time before he closed the door. "Right behind you. If I never came back to Fort Benning it would be too soon."

"Let's get a hotel downtown. We can get some real food, and maybe catch a movie."

"We should try to get into a bar." Tommy laughed.

"I don't drink, Tommy."

"I'm not talking getting drunk, man. Maybe we could just get a couple of beers."

"My mother was killed by a drunk driver."

Tommy looked stricken. "Oh man, I'm sorry, I had no idea. You're not exactly an open book when it comes to your personal life."

"It's okay. It was a long time ago."

"Maybe we can find a mall and try to pick up some girls."

Rourk stared at Tommy for a moment. Rourk was not interested in girls, but it might do Tommy good to get his mind off his ex-girlfriend. "Sure, we could try that. I'm not very good around females though. So I'll sit back and take notes from you."

Tommy chuckled. "I'll give you some pointers. First one, you need to learn to relax."

Rourk and Tommy caught a taxi to a nearby hotel where they booked separate rooms. They had been bunk mates for so long; some solitude was just what Rourk needed. After they cleaned up, they went out for dinner, then grabbed a taxi to the mall.

It was small and run down. It was already getting dark outside, and shoppers were few and far between.

"I don't know if you are going to have any luck with girls in here, Tommy," Rourk remarked as they strolled down the aisle towards the main shopping area.

"Let's go to the bookstore. There are always hot chicks hanging out there."

Rourk thought of how many times he had seen Keegan getting her white chocolate mocha at bookstores. "Sure, sounds good. I could use a cup of coffee."

They spent a couple of hours at the mall, and Rourk stood back and watched as Tommy got turned down again and again. It was pretty funny, he had to admit.

"One more time, Rourk. Let's go talk to those two girls." He nodded towards a brunette and blond sitting in the food court. Rourk shook his head and followed.

Tommy walked up and put his hand on the table. "So ladies, how would you like to hang out with me and my buddy over there? We're going to be green berets."

The blond looked up at him and said, "Get lost."

Tommy turned towards Rourk and shrugged his shoulders. "Alright, let's go watch a movie."

Rourk had to give him credit for trying—most guys would have given up sooner. A few good movies had come out since they had entered basic training over three months ago, and the thought of relaxing in front of one was a nice one.

It was hard to believe it was already February. Just a few more months until Keegan's birthday.

Once the weekend was over, they were back in their bunks to pack for Ft. Bragg. They were traveling by a van since there weren't many of them left.

"Rourk, I'm scared."

"You should be scared, Tommy. This is the make or break point. If you make it through the next three weeks, more than likely in less than a year you will be wearing a green beret. If you don't make it, you'll be thrown back to the regular army."

"Thanks, that was encouraging."

"Well, you need to know how important this is. I know you can make it."

"You really think I'll make it?"

Rourk smiled over at Tommy. "I really do."

"Well, I can't let you down so I guess I'm going to have to get selected."

"I guess so." Rourk leaned back against the seat and closed his eyes.

"Well, at least we shouldn't have to clean floors once we get there."

"Let's hope not. I've cleaned enough floors and bathrooms to last me a lifetime."

"They didn't tell us that part at the recruiter's." Tommy laughed.

"Yeah, the recruiter seemed to leave out all the good parts."

Like all training, time seemed to fly. After a couple of weeks of "indoctrination" phase, where they did tons of physical exercise in preparation for the selection phase, they finally got a class date.

They shipped out to Camp MacKall, North Carolina, less than an hour away from Ft. Bragg. The selection class started with 345 "candidates" as they were called. Within the first week, they had lost 50 from the PT test, swim test, and those that chose to leave because they realized they had bitten off more than they could chew.

Rourk and Tommy were in different huts, which was what they called the large barracks buildings the candidates stayed in, but they saw each other several times throughout the day and spent any free time they had hanging out.

The second week was spent running through the woods doing land navigation from point to point. Rourk thought the course lanes were almost laughable in how short they were compared to what he was used to. Each night he checked on Tommy to see how he was doing and to make sure to keep his morale up.

"I don't know man. I only found two points today. I think there were four. They're gonna drop me for sure."

"Relax, Tommy. They don't expect you to do everything perfect. They don't even expect you to find all the points. If you do, it's a bonus. They just want to see that you have the ability to continue to drive on even when things suck. As long as you don't quit and show them you have the drive, you'll make it. You're doing good."

"Easy for you to say. You don't even look tired. I'm beat down. How many points did you find today?"

"Four. After four points, they had me sit over and start up a fire. And I may not seem like it, but I'm tired too. I just happen to be in a little better shape than you. Don't worry about it. Don't think about the negative, just keep thinking about the positive and your mantra. Say it for me."

"It's all mind games. Countless others have made it and so can I."

After the second week, almost half of the class was gone. They had a couple of days of rest where they weren't running around in the woods, but still didn't get any more sleep and instead had some grueling log and rifle PT sessions. Not as many were quitting as when they had first arrived, but each day, one or two more candidates would show up at the cadre's door, knock, and voluntarily withdraw, or VW, from the course.

By the start of the third week, what they were calling SR week, there were 170 candidates left. They were placed into 12 separate teams with 14 or 15 men each. Again, Rourk and Tommy were not together.

After the end of the first day, Rourk found Tommy sitting on his bed taking care of some of the blisters on his feet.

"How'd today go?" Rourk asked as he sat down on Tommy's bunk.

"Ugh, probably about the same as yours. How many guys from your team quit?"

"Three. We started with the ammo crate carry. Within the first two kilometers, the first two VW'd. After lunch and right before we started the second event, the third guy went up to the cadre and VW'd. Left us with an odd number, but gave us an extra rest man."

"My team lost five. What the hell? I can't say it didn't cross my mind a couple of times while as my grip was giving out that it would be easier to just call it than suffering through this, but I didn't want to let you down. What the hell does SR stand for anyway?"

"Situation, Reaction. Typical military, putting an acronym to everything. Don't think of it as letting me down, think of it as letting yourself down. Look how far we've come already." Rourk moved to the floor and started to stretch a bit. His legs were starting to get stiff sitting on the bunk.

"I know, it's pretty crazy."

At the end of the 24 days, both Rourk and Tommy were standing in formation waiting to hear if their roster number would be called.

"Listen up candidates," the Senior Assessor Cadre addressed them. "If I call your number off, fall out of formation and move into classroom number 2."

The tension and nervousness was in the air as numbers were called out in random order. "17, 64, 311, 224, 152…" In all, twenty-seven numbers of the 133 candidates left were called. Neither Rourk or Tommy's number was called.

After the last candidate that was called had entered into the classroom, the Senior Assessor Cadre looked over the ones that were left. "Congratulations men. You've been successfully selected for further training."

Over half of those standing let out a cheer. Rourk smiled and looked over at Tommy, who had a grin from ear to ear and was shaking the hands of those who stood around him. After they were dismissed, Tommy came over to Rourk and shook his hand.

"We did it!"

"Yes we did. I told you that you would make it."

"Of course, it's not over yet. We still need to find out what our MOS will be, and from there how much longer our training will be." Tommy ran his hand through his hair.

"Do you have a preference?" Rourk glanced over at Tommy.

"I'm hoping for Medic, but I'm not sure if my scores are high enough." Tommy said.

"That's another year of training. I'm hoping for anything, but medic." Rourk laughed. "Where do you want to be stationed?"

"It doesn't really matter to me. What about you?"

"I'm hoping for Washington State, 1st Group."

"Really? Why? It's cold and rainy there man."

"I like cold and rainy." *Not really.* However, for whatever reason Keegan's dream was to go to Alaska. Rourk would really prefer to stay near Tennessee and go to 5th group at Fort Campbell, Kentucky. He only planned on staying the initial four years, and then he would go back to the Army of the Light so it didn't really matter where he lived.

"Tonight, we pick up girls." Tommy slapped Rourk on the back.

"Sure, Tommy. We saw how good that went last time."

Tommy looked down at his bandaged feet. "Let's just grab something to eat and get some sleep. At least we get a couple of weeks of downtime to let our feet heal."

Chapter 22

Thaddeus took a sip of his hot chocolate and looked around the coffee shop before sending Anna a text. *Sorry I've been busy. Can you get away today?*

Her response was immediate, making him roll his eyes. Keegan and her friends were surgically attached to their phones. *Of course. Where do you want to meet?*

Pick me up at the Starbucks near Target.

Now?

In about twenty minutes.

Ok.

Thaddeus grinned. Anna was right, this cloak and dagger stuff was pretty fun.

Anna pulled up out front in her old, beat-up car and Thaddeus chugged the last of his hot chocolate as he walked out the door. He tossed it in the trash can out in front of the store.

It was a cool, sunny day with the kind of warm breeze that heralded spring. Thaddeus was glad it was finally April. Cold weather sucked.

"So where are we going?" Anna looked over at Thaddeus, both of her hands wrapped around the wheel.

Thaddeus eyed her bright blue highlights warily. She was such a weird chick. "To the vault."

"The vault. It sounds so mysterious." She put the car into drive and pulled away from the curb. "Thanks, for letting me in on this, Thad."

"No problem." He didn't want to tell her she was his only option. That might hurt her feelings. He pointed for her to take a left.

"So do you think this will work?"

"I hope so. But as I'm sure you know, there are no guarantees with magic."

At least we can say we tried."

"I have to admit. I feel slightly bad for Donald. He's innocent in all of this."

"He'll be ok." Thaddeus shrugged.

"How do you know he'll be ok? Did you have a vision?"

"Maybe."

"You're not going to tell me what it was are you?"

"Nope."

"I wouldn't want your gift, Thaddeus," Anna answered in a quiet voice, shooting a glance over at him.

"No, you wouldn't. It's not as cool as people think."

"Speaking of cool. I think it's pretty awesome you are helping out your sister."

Thaddeus cleared his throat and shifted uncomfortably. "I'm helping Rourk."

"Same thing."

Giving her one of his impish smiles, he said, "Anna, I'm going to have to wipe your memory once we get back. You're not supposed to know where the vault is."

"You can trust me. I would never tell anyone."

"I'm sorry, Anna, you have to agree to that or we can't go any further."

"Fine. But just take away the directions nothing else. I like my memories." She paused. "Most of them anyway." She stole a sideways glance at him, her eyes narrowed. "Can you make my crush on Xavier go away?"

"You wouldn't want that, Anna."

"Yeah, I guess you're right. I don't suppose you can tell me the formula to my prefect match could you?"

"Hmm, that is certainly against the rules," Thaddeus murmured, rubbing his chin in his best evil genius impression. He grinned. "If this plan works, I'll look into it."

"Ack! Are you serious? I was just joking. You could really do that?"

"Sure, it's not that hard."

"I wonder what he looks like, my soulmate?"

"Anna, focus. You are going to turn right up ahead. Drive ten miles and take a left on to a hidden driveway. We are going to have to walk about three miles in the woods." He leaned over, looking down at her feet on the pedals and nodded. "I'm glad you wore comfortable shoes."

Once they arrived, Thaddeus had her park the car just off the driveway and they started through the woods. "You didn't say it was going to be three miles uphill, and it's freezing."

"It's not all uphill and it's definitely not freezing. It's almost sixty degrees.

You sound like Keegan." Thaddeus rolled his eyes.

"Fine. Okay, so how is this going to work?"

"Well, you are going to read the Book of Shadows. Find a dream spell, and an enchantment spell. I'll memorize them and write them down once we get back to the coffee shop."

"You can do that?"

"Of course, I have a photographic memory."

"How could I forget? The Great Thaddeus."

"That's me." He came to an abrupt halt, one arm swinging out to stop Anna. "Ok, we're here."

"What do you mean we're here? There is nothing but woods."

Thaddeus just grinned. "Anna, take my hands and close your eyes."

Anna did as he said. Suddenly, she felt like the floor had dropped from under her and her stomach flipped. As quickly as it started, it was over.

"You can open your eyes now."

Anna did, and looked around the room in awe. "This is beautiful. Hey, I thought you were supposed to cloak me or something like that?"

"This was easier. No one will know you are here, and we'll just teleport out."

"So this is the famous vault?" Anna walked forward, Thaddeus at her back as she gazed around the room, taking in as many details as she could.

The walls were a shimmering gold color and home to intricately carved wooden bookcases that held what, by sight, seemed to be thousands upon thousands of books. In the center of the room under high ceilings, several heavy wood tables were spread, some of them already holding opened books beneath softly lit lamps. The vault had the dim, comforting feeling of being underground, and it literally hummed with an energy that tickled Anna's skin.

"Somehow I doubt it's famous. But yes, this is the vault. Pretty cool, huh?"

"I'd say." Anna ran her hands along the jewels that were embedded in the gold walls. There was a variety of colors, catching the lights from the tables so that they sparkled as she moved past them. They looked like a treasure.

"Okay, let's get started." Thaddeus moved to the center of the room and closed his eyes, his hands hanging loosely at his sides.

Anna had a moment where she thought she could see the man he would become one day. She always forgot he was only twelve because he was so much more mature due to his gifts. For just a moment, she saw past the twelve year old and to the person he would be. It was an odd sensation. She'd known him since he was little; the idea of him growing up had never occurred to her.

Opening his eyes, Thaddeus walked to a bookshelf in the left corner and grabbed purposefully for a leather bound book. It was the Book of Shadows.

"How did you do that? Magic?"

"Some would say it's magic, but I just used my photographic memory. So we didn't have to waste a lot of time trying to find the book."

"You're pretty cool, Thad."

"And you're weird." He handed her the thick black book.

"Thaddeus, it's charged with energy. It completely surrounds it."

"I would hope so." He grinned. "It was someone's magic book at one time."

Staring down at the book between her hands, Anna slowly shook her head. "I can't believe I am touching a real Book of Shadows. One from another witch. I have dreamed of this moment for a very long time. I'm afraid to open it."

Thaddeus reached over and opened the book, putting it on the table in front of them. "There. Now find the passages we need."

Anna rolled her eyes at him for ruining her moment, then closed them and placed both hands on the book. Thaddeus paced around her, his lips pursed as he waited.

"Page 333," Anna said excitedly after a few minutes. "The numbers 333 keep playing over in my head."

"Well, check it out."

Anna flipped ahead in the book, careful not to harm the aged, yellowed pages. "Oh my Goddess, Thaddeus. It is page 333. How cool is that? The enchantment spell." A note of reverence was in her voice. "Thaddeus, we could do so many things with this one spell."

"Anna, don't even think about it. We are here for one reason and one reason only. Do not make me regret bringing you here. You would not like the consequences."

"I'm sorry. You're right. Magic is just so powerful. Okay, so here is the spell. Do you want me to say it aloud or do you need to read it to memorize it?"

"I'll read it." He scanned the page quickly. "Ok, now we need to find the dream spell."

Once again, Anna closed her eyes and placed her hands lightly on the book. "I'm not getting it, Thad."

"Try again and relax your mind."

Anna thought about the way her mind cleared when she sat and watched the sunrise or sunset. Since Magdalena had asked her to do the seven day exercises, Anna had tried to keep up with doing it at least once a week. She found that same peace and stillness inside her, then her eyes popped open. "Page 213. Incredible."

"Hurry up, we can't stay in here too long." Thaddeus tapped his fingers on the long wooden table.

"Ok, here it is, 213. I can't wait to try these out."

"Well, if everything goes as planned you can start the dream spell tonight."

Anna jumped up and down.

"What is it with you guys and always jumping around like fools? You're not three years old."

"Did you memorize it? That's it, Thaddeus, I'm hugging you and you can't get out of it." She slipped her arms under his and picked him up, spinning him around the room. He was a lot heavier than she had expected.

"Put me down," Thaddeus growled.

"Fine. Can you show me the rest of the vault?"

"No. Close your eyes and grab my hands."

Anna had that same feeling as if she was dropping from the sky. When she opened her eyes they were back in her car. "Hey! Why did we have to hike that hill if we could have teleported from the car?"

He grinned. "I missed my workout this morning."

"Ugh. Thanks a lot. My legs are already sore." She smacked him on his shoulder.

"Ok, give me a piece of paper."

Anna grabbed her notebook and handed it to him. He started writing so fast Anna couldn't keep up.

"Ok, here are the spells. I'm not a witch so I don't know everything you are supposed to do. Do you have an altar?"

"Of course."

"Well, I'll just give you the spell and you get a hold of the things you need. If you need any help finding something, send me a text. Don't forget—no one is allowed to know we are doing this. Not even your mom."

"I know, you can trust me. Keegan is my best friend." Anna glanced sideways at him. "So are you going to erase my memory now?"

Thaddeus chuckled. "You are so gullible. I was just messing with you. You couldn't find your way back there if you tried."

Chapter 23

Anna emerged from her bath and blew out the candles. The scent of rosemary, lavender, basil, and mint filled the air. She inhaled deeply, taking in the relaxation of the room. Walking slowly to her altar, she lifted the quartz crystal pendent from where it lay across her wooden pentacle and clasped it around her neck. She reached for her white robe, pulling it on while trying to remain calm and not let her excitement take over.

Her hands were shaking as she grabbed the loose earth she had collected from outside and poured it into her antique crystal bowl. She lightly placed the bowl down so it was facing north, the place of power. She paused, kneeling before the small bowl, dipping the fingers of her power hand into the earth. Magdalena had taught her to take just a moment to attune herself with each element by reflecting on how it had touched her life recently. Earth was stability and knowledge, just as Magdalena had become Anna's stability and an endless source of magical knowledge.

Lifting the censer and a small cone of incense, she placed them to the east, letting the cone rest atop the pile of sand in the censor. She lit a match and the smell of sandalwood filled the room. Inhaling deeply, she let it fill her senses, thinking of the warm winds of spring slowly blowing in as winter faded.

Taking the silver candle from her altar, she lit the wick and placed it to the south next to a moonstone. She kneeled before it, staring into the flame. She thought of how fire was strong and determined, as she was determined to bring Keegan's bond back.

Anna picked up the last element—her small brass cup that was filled with water. Carefully, she carried it and placed it in the western quarter. She swirled a single finger in the liquid, watching the water ripple. Water was an emotional element. It made her think of love.

Seating herself in the center of the circle, Anna lit a single purple pillar candle on the floor in front of her. She lifted both of her arms to the ceiling and closed her eyes, her voice flowing smoothly into the dimness of her room.

> *God and Goddess I ask of thee*
> *Give me the ability to send forth this dream*
> *Across the Earth or water's bound*
> *Whether he be in the sky or on the ground*
> *By the powers of fire let it shine bright*
> *By the powers of the earth and air send it*
> *tonight*
> *By the powers of water to sweep within the*
> *dream's door*
> *And by the powers of 3 shall Rourk remember*
> *it evermore.*

Anna kept her eyes closed, focusing on the images she wanted to place in Rourk's mind.

Rourk sat on his bed and stared at the ring. The ruby and diamonds sparkled in the light as he twirled it around his finger. His mother whispered in his ear, "It belongs to Keegan now."

Rourk shot out of bed, his breathing ragged as he swiped his hand across the sweat on his forehead. *It was only a dream.*

It had seemed so real. He couldn't remember the last time he had heard his mother's voice. Rourk ran his hand through his hair. His heart was pounding. He glanced over at the clock to see it was barely past midnight. He hadn't been out very long. Closing his eyes, he tried to will himself to fall asleep.

His father was holding the ruby ring in his hand. Crystalline red prisms of light danced on the walls. "Your mother would want her to have it, son."

Rourk reached for the ring, taking it from his father's hand. "What if she says no?"

"You will never know unless you ask. The ring belongs to her."

Rourk tossed and turned, drifting in and out of consciousness. Each time he awoke, he wondered where the dreams were coming from. They were so lifelike, and he rarely recalled his dreams.

Keegan's face lit up, the ring on her hand glowing with a brilliant light. "I love it! I love it! Thank you, Rourk." She threw her arms around him and kissed him, sending electricity through his body.

Rourk angrily threw off his sheet and jumped out of bed. Wrapping his arms around his waist, he leaned forward, squeezing his eyes shut. He wasn't sure he could take the pain much longer. He missed her so much. The dreams were just another element of torture.

It was useless trying to go back to bed. Stepping into his running shorts, he headed out for a ten mile run.

As if he could run from her.

Anna smiled as she blew out the candle and wondered if it worked. She figured that would be enough for tonight. She planned on sending him dreams for the next three days, and after that once or twice a week. She couldn't believe it could be this simple.

Please, Goddess, let this work.

Chapter 24

He was avoiding sleep as much as possible because every time he closed his eyes, the dreams haunted him. He threw himself into his training and pushed himself as far as he could, trying to push the images out of his head. That damn ring was driving him crazy, and hearing his mother so often made him want to punch something.

There was one point during training they had to go four days without sleep or eating. He started hallucinating scenes with his mother and Keegan. They were spinning around and around with their hands clasped between them. The ruby ring was throwing light around like a disco ball. Rourk tried to get to them, but every time he got close, they disappeared. He was worried he was losing his mind. Although, he knew lack of sleep and food could make a mind do strange things.

He finally gave in and called his father.

"Father, I will need the ring for Keegan's birthday."

"I advised against this." His father's deep, gruff voice came crisply across the line.

"Yes, I know."

"Then, why?"

"I won't know unless I try. The worst she can say is no." Although, Rourk thought, that would be the most terrible thing to ever happen to him if she did.

"How do you know you'll be here for her birthday? What about training?"

"I got selected as weapons specialist so I will have plenty of weekends free. I will be able to make it for her birthday. I would be there even if I had to go AWOL."

"You're a grown man. I won't stand in your way."

"Thanks, Dad." Rourk hung up the phone. He was exhausted, but he still fought sleep as long as he could. Eventually, when he drifted off, his mother came to him again.

"You did the right thing son. You know the ring belongs to her."

Rourk woke up and he could have sworn he felt his mother brush his hair to the side. He was losing it.

Rourk wasn't sure what happened, but that was the last dream he had about the ring. He was relieved; his body needed the rest.

He couldn't wait to see Keegan again, even if she did turn him down. He knew he had to ask her. That is what chosens did. He had told her he was coming back for her on her birthday and he wasn't about to break that promise.

He didn't get to see Tommy as much, because he got picked up for the engineer program. Rourk got selected for the weapons slot which was fine by him. The training was much shorter, and they had a lot more freedom to do what they wanted. They had their own rooms, and were able to come and go as they pleased as long as they didn't miss training. The training was fun for Rourk. He loved guns and he got to shoot a lot. He figured Tommy was having a good time learning how to blow up things.

When they got their duty stations, Rourk was surprised that Tommy also got 1st Group in Washington State.

"That is pretty crazy. I'm sorry you didn't get 5th Group like you wanted."

"I actually requested 1st. I figured if you could put up with rain and cold, so could I."

Rourk gave his friend a big smile. "I'm glad, Tommy. Maybe we will even get on the same team."

"That's what I'm hoping." Tommy grinned.

"Mom, I'm going to get the girls. We're going to look for our prom dresses." Keegan reached over her mom and grabbed a chip from the bag on the table.

"I thought I was going to take you?" Keegan had never seen her mom pout before.

"Sorry, I'll text you the pics and you can help me decide."

"Ok, don't forget."

"I won't." Keegan kissed her mom and headed out the door.

Summer was quickly approaching. Keegan decided to take down the top to her Jeep before she went to get her friends. After two seconds trying, she realized what a pain it was to do it alone and ran back inside the house.

Her mother was still at the table. Keegan smiled sweetly. "Mom, can you help me take the top down?"

"Sure, give me a second." She slipped on her shoes and headed out.

With the two of them doing it, they got the top down in record time and Keegan slid in to the driver's seat, cranking the engine.

"Don't forget to send me the pictures," her mom yelled as Keegan pulled out of the driveway. Keegan waved an arm to show she had heard her.

She loved the breeze against her skin and the sun beating down on her bare shoulders. She cranked up the radio and sang along on the drive, navigating the roads with ease.

Keegan stopped at Lauren's first. Lauren ran out in a yellow tank top, cut-off jean shorts, and flip flops. She pouted as she hopped in the passenger seat and slammed the door behind her. "Ah Keegan, my hair is going to get messed up."

"Stop being a baby." Keegan reached over and popped open the glove box, pulling out a bandana. "Here, put this on till we get to the mall."

"Fine." Lauren pulled down the mirror while she pushed her mass of curls under the bandana. "I actually look pretty cute."

"You always look beautiful," Keegan answered, signaling as she turned off of Lauren's street. "Now, let's get Anna. I'm so excited she actually wanted to go shopping with us."

"I know. I think she's sad we are all going to be moving soon for college," Lauren said loudly over the sound of the wind in the car.

The thought of it subdued Keegan, as well. "It is sad! You'll be in California, I'll be in Alaska, and Anna will be in Seattle. At least we'll all be on the west coast. I'm sure we'll manage to get together often."

"I hope so. Although, don't plan on me visiting you too often in Alaska. I have no idea why you want to go to that frozen tundra."

"It has a great marine biology program."

"So does California, and you don't have to freeze to death."

They pulled into Anna's driveway and she came bouncing out. She was dressed pretty mild today with a black T-shirt and a black tutu skirt. She had black flats on her feet and streaks of red in her hair.

"You make us look so boring." Lauren turned in the seat to stick her tongue out at Anna.

"Can we stop at Starbucks on the way? I'm in need of caffeine," Anna said as she vaulted the side of the Jeep and plopped into the backseat.

"You won't get any arguments from us," Keegan told her, aiming for the nearest Starbucks.

Once they got to the mall with coffee cups in hand, they chose to check out the dresses at Macy's first.

"I know short dresses are in, but I really want to wear a long dress to prom. That's been my vision of prom since I was a little girl." Wrinkling her nose, Keegan put the short purple dress she was holding back on the rack.

"Good luck finding one." Anna spread her hands out at the sea of short dresses in front of them.

"Plus, you're so short you're going to have to get it tailored big time." Lauren fingered a shimmering blue dress. "Let's just try on some of the short ones first. If you still want a long dress we'll search the whole mall if we have to. What do you think of this one?" Lauren held up the short strapless dress with scrunching and fake gems she had been eyeing.

Keegan glanced over. "For you? I don't think so. You have that athletic straight figure, so you want to make it appear that you have curves. You know, an optical illusion."

"Shut up, Keegan. I'm not that straight. We can't all have a J-Lo booty like you." She pouted, putting the dress back.

Keegan grabbed a black strapless number that flared out at the waist, and had a purple ribbon around the waist, shoving it in Lauren's hands. "Here try this one on."

"It's so plain."

"Just try it on."

Lauren stepped out of the dressing room, and spun around. "Keegan, how do you know this stuff? It's perfect."

"That really does look good. What dress do you think would look good on me?" Anna asked.

Keegan looked Anna up and down. "You can really wear anything. It's gotta be funky to match your style. Oh, what about this?" She picked up an all black lacy dress with ruffles. "It's so vintage looking."

"That's cute, but I kinda like this one." Anna showed them an off-the-shoulder teal dress that had a flowing top and ruffles on the bottom.

"You do? That doesn't look like your style at all. Try them both on." Keegan pushed her in the dressing room.

A few minutes later she came out in the all black dress and the girls cooed about how great it looked. Lauren clapped her hands together and said, "Go try on the teal one. I can't wait to see it on you."

When she emerged a couple moments later, both Lauren and Keegan gasped.

"Wow, Anna, you look amazing. You're right. You have to go with that one." Keegan snapped a picture.

Keegan grabbed a few dresses and tried them on. She could try on clothes all day. She loved them all, but nothing felt like the one. So they moved on to the next store.

Three stores later, when they were about to give up, Keegan's phone chirped in her pocket. *Where are my pictures?*

"Ugh, guys I forgot to send my mom pictures. Let's go to the next shop we see and try some on and I'll go to another mall later with my mom."

"What about that store?" Anna pointed to a bridal shop.

"That's a wedding shop." Lauren looked at Anna like she was crazy.

"Yeah, but they have colorful gowns. Let's just go try some on, it might be fun."

"Sure, why not?" Keegan laced her arms between theirs and they headed to the store.

The sales lady must have been bored or in need of a sale, because she treated them like royalty. She ran around, grabbing gowns for them to try on and shoving them over the top of the dressing rooms.

The girls walked their self-made runway, twirling around and posing dramatically. The sales woman seemed to be having as much fun as they were. They snapped tons of pictures to send to Keegan's mother.

"Ok, Keegan, you were right. Long gowns are so much cooler. I vote we take back these short dresses and get long ones." Lauren spun around in a hot pink a-line gown with glitter all over.

"As long as you promise you are not going to buy that one!" Keegan was laughing so hard her eyes were watering.

"I didn't mean this one." Lauren rolled her eyes. "We need to start looking seriously instead of just playing around."

"I'm not taking back my dress. I'll find somewhere else to wear it. I will get a long gown, though. I hope we're the only ones with long gowns. We'll really stand out." Anna grinned.

Keegan flung the curtain open and came out in a strapless silver mermaid dress that clung to her curves and sashayed down the walkway.

"Oh my god! Keegan, that dress is stunning. It looks like it was made just for you." Lauren took a picture with her phone.

"She's right, this is the one you have been looking for. Do you love it?"

Keegan's face beamed. "It's perfect!"

"I love how it has the drop waist to show off your booty, and your tiny waist." Anna laughed. "Spin around again. Oooh, it even has the corset lace in the back. You have to get this one."

"Send a picture to my mom."

Anna laughed. "Your mom replied back 'wrap it up.'"

"Yay! Okay, let's find dresses for both of you now."

"Oh, I forgot we just got a shipment in," the clerk said quickly, snapping her fingers. "One minute. I think I might have the perfect dress for both of you." She hurried to the back of the store.

She came out holding a long black gown with polka dots, and a few others in various styles and colors.

Anna grabbed the polka dotted dress. "I call this one."

She disappeared into the dressing room. She popped out in the strapless gown, laughing as she spun in a circle. "I love this one! Take my picture and send it to my mom."

It was simple and beautiful at the same time. A small dark pink belt was wrapped around the waist, and the bottom of the dress flared out in the front shorter than it was in the back.

"Okay, now I have to find something," Lauren said. "What else do you have in that pile?"

Lauren tried on two that were okay, but not perfect.

Keegan eyed the substantial pile of dresses they'd built up. Digging one out from underneath, she handed it to Lauren. "Here try this one."

Lauren came out in the plum colored, one-shoulder taffeta gown. The color was striking against her alabaster skin and dark hair.

"Oh, this is the one," Keegan squealed. "You look so curvy in it."

"I look curvy? Well, if I look curvy, I'll take it!" Lauren declared, making her friends laugh.

Anna nodded, reaching out to touch the soft material. "It's very glamorous."

Lauren turned side to side, checking herself out in the mirror. "It's beautiful, isn't it?"

"Yes, it is. Strike a pose." Keegan waited for Lauren to turn then snapped a photo.

"Would you guys like me to take a picture of all three of you?" the clerk offered.

"Oh, that would be great." Keegan handed her the camera. *I wonder if I should add this picture to Rourk's scrapbook?*

Since Christmas, when her family had suggested she take pictures for Rourk, she had been gathering some in a small scrapbook. Eventually, she would send it to him. She just never felt the time was right.

"Should we look for accessories now?" Lauren asked as they left the store with their purchased dresses in hand.

"I'm too tired. We'll have to do that another day." Anna shifted the dress to her other arm and sighed. "Shopping is exhausting. I don't know how you guys love it so much."

"Whatever, you had fun and you know it," Keegan teased, poking her in the side.

"I did have fun. Can you believe we will be graduating soon? It's kinda scary. Soon our lives are going to be so different."

"I'm excited about the changes. I can't wait." Lauren hugged her dress closer and smiled.

"We have to promise to get together as often as possible. We also have to

Skype."

"Agreed."

After Keegan dropped them off at their houses, she turned towards home and thought of how much fun she and her friends had together over the years. She smiled wistfully, wishing it didn't have to change.

Chapter 25

"Mom my hair is a mess!" Keegan wailed, staring forlornly in the antique vanity mirror. She lifted her hands to her head, but Emerald swatted them away.

"It's not a mess. It looks beautiful. You look beautiful. You'll be the most gorgeous girl at prom." Her mother tugged at a curl and laughed as it sprang back up. "I love when you wear your hair curly. It looks natural and wild, just like you."

"Do you really think I look okay?" Keegan stared at her mother's reflection in the mirror. Her mother's smile was beautiful.

"More than okay, Keegan. You are a striking young woman. Stand up so I can see the dress." Emerald gestured with both hands for her daughter to move.

Keegan slowly rose from her chair, brushing her palms nervously down the front of her silver gown. It made her feel feminine.

"Spin around. You know you want to."

Keegan laughed and spun. "It is the perfect dress."

"I'm sure your father will say it's too perfect. It really accents your curves. You are definitely not a little girl anymore." Emerald sighed. "Makes me sad, in a way. However, I'm also looking forward to the next stage in your life. You're going to do great things, I know."

"Mom, I'm nervous to move so far away from you guys."

"I know, honey, I'm nervous too. Who is going to cook for you?" Her mother gave a sad laugh and looked away. "Thank goodness for the internet. We will stay in touch. I can always come see you in Alaska when I need my Keegan fix. Of course, you will come home for the holidays I would hope."

"Of course." Keegan dabbed at her eyes with an old t-shirt and sniffed. "Okay, let's change the subject before you ruin my makeup."

"Donald is picking you up right?"

"Yes. I'm sure he will look great all dressed up. He's already so cute."

Her daughter's dreamy eyes made Emerald nervous. She rubbed her face with one hand then looked into Keegan's eyes. "Keegan, I really hate to ask you this, but I know a lot of kids have sex on prom night. Do I need to be worried? Or get you some protection?"

"What? No, mom. I'm not ready for that. It hasn't even crossed my mind. I still have the 'wait for your chosen' mentality, I guess." Keegan looked down and moved her brush around the vanity, surprised she wasn't embarrassed by her mother's blunt question.

Keegan could see how relieved her mom was to hear her answer. "I'm glad to hear that. If you change your mind, please let me know. I know that your situation is different from most. If you feel you are ready, I'll take you to the doctor and get you on birth control. I don't want to be a grandmother just yet."

"I will, Mom." Keegan leaned over and gave her mom a quick hug. "Thanks for helping me get ready for prom."

"Let's go show the boys how fabulous you look." Emerald took her daughter's hand, tugging her towards the door.

"Wait, I almost forgot the mask." Keegan grabbed the mask from her bookshelf. It was a very dramatic looking mask. Meant only to rest over her eyes and cheekbones, it had cat-shaped eyes with spiraling lace that feathered from the corner of each. The base of the mask was burnished gold and covered in intricate black designs. A single small hoop rose from the top of the mask like the crown of a tiara.

As they walked down the stairs, Keegan holding her mother's arm for support, Emerald yelled, "Check out the princess!"

Her father looked up from his Macbook when they rounded the corner into the living room. "I think you need to go back up and change into something that doesn't make you look so…what is the word I'm looking for?" Keegan's face fell as he paused, but he rubbed his beard and grinned. "Just kidding. You look wonderful, Keegan. It's hard for me to see you so grown up."

"Dad, I'm almost eighteen. You need to let go of the little girl image you have of me."

"Never," he said with a smile.

"What do you think, Thaddeus?" Keegan glanced over at her brother.

He was sprawled across the love seat, his feet propped up on one arm and a book open across his chest. Raising an eyebrow, he answered, "You look ugly. However, I'm sure you already know that with your big ego."

"Funny." Keegan swatted him on the shoulder.

"Ouch. Did you see that mom?"

The doorbell rang and the four of them yelled in unison, "Come in."

"Hey!" Donald called as the front door clicked open. A second later, he appeared in the archway between the foyer and the living room. His tux was black and the vest peeking through the jacket was the exact silver of Keegan's dress.

When his bright blue eyes landed on Keegan standing in the middle of the room, he stared. "Wow." He paused, unable to find any more words, and blushed when the rest of the family laughed. "Sorry, that's all I can think to say."

"Thaddeus, go grab my camera," Emerald said. "Let's get some photos of these two together."

They spent the next twenty minutes taking photos, some nice and posed and a few goofy ones added at the end for good measure. Keegan smiled thinking about how someday she would look back at the photos and recall a wonderful moment in her life. Photography was the greatest invention.

"Ok, we really need to get out of here," Keegan said, waving at her family as she took her boyfriend's arm. "Come on, Donald. Bye guys, don't wait up."

Richard cleared his throat and stood, looming menacingly over the two of them. "Donald, just because it's prom night don't get any ideas in your head."

"Of course not. I respect your daughter. You have made it clear as long as she is living under your roof…"

"If I had my way, I'd lock her up until she was thirty," Richard said gruffly, scowling.

Keegan rolled her eyes. "Bye!"

Her mother yelled out the door as they left. "You forgot your mask."

Keegan let go of Donald and ran back inside to grab it. "Thank you. I'd be lost without you."

"Yes, you would." Emerald chuckled.

Donald held the door open to his mother's sedan. He gave her a lopsided grin. "I borrowed the good car."

After she was settled, he walked around and got in on the driver's side. In the silence before he started the car, he said softly, "Keegan, you are too stunning for words."

"Don't make me blush," she replied, her cheeks already heated. Giving him a sideways glance, she said, "You look pretty sexy yourself in that tux. I noticed you couldn't go without the Chucks. I like it."

"Thanks."

They stared at each other a moment longer before they met in the middle of the car for a deep kiss. He wrapped one of her curls around his finger as she slid her hands across the smooth fabric of his suit jacket. Keegan felt flushed when he finally pulled away, her lips warm. "Let's get to the hotel before we miss all the fun."

Keegan was impressed that they could turn a boring room into a beautiful space for a masquerade ball. Lauren, who had worked tirelessly on the prom committee, must have aimed to make sure everything was perfect.

As she and Donald walked through the door, confetti was thrown over them and Keegan laughed in delight. They entered beneath an arch of purple, gold, and black balloons with a large, hand painted sign that read "Masquerade" in swirly letters.

From the ceiling of the ballroom, purple and black sheer cloth draped elegantly, framing a beautiful chandelier of cut glass that was dimmed enough to only cast a little light on the dance floor. Tables of students spread around the area where other kids mingled or danced.

The band was playing a slow song so she pulled Donald straight to the dance floor.

"This is amazing." Keegan laid her head against his chest.

"Yes, it really is. This has been the best school year for me. I almost wish it didn't have to end."

"I know what you mean." Keegan pulled him a little tighter.

After the song was over, Keegan said, "I need to find the girls so I can see them in their dresses."

"Sure, I'll go find the guys and we can meet up in about half an hour."

Keegan gave him a quick kiss and hurried off in search of them. People kept stopping her to tell her how much they loved her dress, which made her glow with pride. She finally saw Lauren and Anna together near the punch table.

"Someone spiked the punch." Anna handed a cup to Keegan.

"Awesome. It was probably Spencer or Calvron." They laughed and downed their drinks. The fruity liquid had a strong taste of alcohol.

"Where are your dates?" Keegan asked. The two of them had accepted invitations from two guys from their class.

Anna giggled, grabbing the spoon and refilling Keegan's cup as she held it out. "We ditched them."

"You ditched them? Why?"

"Because they were lame."

Lauren nodded her agreement, her face hidden behind her cup.

"I guess that's a good reason. Give me another."

When they all had another drink in hand, Keegan raised her paper cup. "To us magical creatures."

The tapped their cups and downed the liquid.

"Whoa, this stuff is strong." Anna giggled.

"You're cut off." Lauren took her cup.

Keegan put an arm around both of their shoulders. "You guys are great. So are you having fun? You both look gorgeous."

"Sure, if you call standing by yourself in the corner drinking spiked punch fun," Lauren mumbled.

"Well let's get out there and dance." Keegan grabbed them and started pulling them along.

"Hey, I wanted another drink," Anna complained.

"Lauren cut you off. Come on."

They spent the evening dancing, laughing, and having a great time. Eventually, the guys joined them. Everyone cleared a spot for Lauren and Donald to have a dance off. It was a riot.

After the prom, they all congregated outside in the parking lot.

"Calvron, I think you should make a magical land for us to hang out in for the evening," Keegan said, looking over at him expectantly.

Only Calvron could pull off the blindingly white tuxedo with a baby blue shirt. His shoes had pointy toes that made Keegan giggle. He tapped his chin thoughtfully. "That's a great idea. It will take me a little while. Let's all head over to the location and I can get started."

"Yay!" Keegan gazed up into Donald's eyes, smiling. "This will be a prom to remember, that's for sure."

"It's ready!" Calvron yelled an hour later, his voice drifting over from the darkness beyond the light of the headlights.

Keegan and Donald had been sitting on the tailgate of Calvron's truck, chatting with the others. It was the kind of humid Tennessee night that made Keegan want to stay outside forever and the companionship of her friends made her nostalgic for it to never end.

She squealed when she saw the glass double-doors. Calvron had outdone himself, as usual. He had made three distinct setups. One was an old fashioned diner: cooks, waiters and all surrounded by red pleather booths and checkered tablecloths. Another section was a disco center with flashing lights and music that could only be heard when you crossed into the area. The third was a relaxing coffee shop; it even smelled like one.

Keegan skipped over to give Calvron a hug. "This is perfect!"

"I'm starving, let's eat first," Anna said, heading for the diner.

The rest of them followed after her. Keegan marveled at the stainless steel area. She ran her hand across the vinyl table and sat down on the red seat. She laughed when it squeaked under her weight.

The waitress sidled up to the table, dressed in a gray, cotton dress with her name—Pattie—stitched at the breast. Her hair was bright blonde and wrapped up in a high bun. She had on inches of makeup and bright red lipstick.

"I'll take the works!" Keegan told her. "Eggs, bacon, toast, potatoes with cheese, and some coffee."

"Sure thing, sweetie. What about the rest of you?" Her voice was deep and hoarse. She cracked her gum, staring at them.

"What she said," Anna answered, handing her menu over to the woman. There was unanimous agreement as everyone ordered the same thing.

"So, it's almost time to graduate," Lauren said with a sigh, adding cream from the pitcher to her coffee.

"It's about time," Sam joked, nudging Spencer, who nodded.

"I think it's sad." Keegan stirred her coffee, watching the sweetener dissolve instead of letting her friends see the tears in her eyes.

"We'll stay in touch," Calvron told her, reaching over to lay a hand on her arm.

Donald slipped his own arm around her shoulders, squeezing her to the side of his body. "Of course we will."

The food was delicious. Keegan ended up having another plate, as did the boys.

After eating, they decided to go hang out in the disco room. When they walked through the door, their outfits changed. Keegan cracked up laughing. Calvron had a huge afro and the guys had on bell bottoms and long sleeved, collared shirts with the buttons undone. The girls, of course, looked hot in their mini skirts and platform shoes.

They danced beneath the disco lights for what seemed like hours, even though they'd already danced most of the night away at prom. When they were sweaty and tired, they made their way to the coffee shop to rest and relax.

Dinner had been great, and the disco crazy, but the most enjoyable thing for Keegan was the time they spent over their coffee, reminiscing about the past.

Chapter 26

Keegan's stomach was in knots. She didn't expect to be this nervous; it was only a high school graduation after all. All she had to do was walk across the stage and smile while she shook the principal's hand. She smoothed down her gown and reached up to make sure the cap was in place, waiting for her name to be called.

"Keegan Clarke," was announced over the loud speaker and her heart skyrocketed.

Taking a deep breath, she walked forward and prayed she didn't fall and make a fool of herself. She had worn ballet flats under the gown to reduce the risk.

She made it across the stage, smiling all the while, and shook the principal's hand. There was a slight awkward moment when she tried to shake with the wrong hand. She always messed that up because she was left handed. Everyone in the crowd laughed. The rest of the ceremony passed in a blur.

Once off the stage, she ran over to Anna and Lauren. "Eeek! I can't believe we graduated." They wrapped their arms around each other, face to face in a big group hug, and bounced up and down.

"I know it's so crazy. We're going to be at college, out on our own in just a couple of months." Lauren sighed and smiled.

"I'm sad high school is over. I don't think I'm ready to move on to college." Anna crossed her arms across her chest.

"You'll be fine. You are going to an awesome art school and you'll meet all kinds of cool people."

"I know, but I'm going to miss you guys." Anna wiped a tear away.

"Don't even start crying. This is supposed to be a happy time. If you cry, we'll all cry," Keegan said.

"That's right, no crying until we board our planes to the new adventures that await us." Lauren looked at Anna and smiled slightly as she wiped away a tear herself.

"Let's go find the boys. That will keep us from being all sappy and emotional." Lauren encircled her arms with theirs as they headed over to find the guys.

Donald, Spencer, and Sam were chasing each other around the gymnasium—big surprise there. Keegan smiled as she saw Donald sneak up behind Spencer. Those guys were clowns. She knew it was going to be hard for them to be separated. She didn't even know where they had decided to go to school. She would have to ask once they finished playing.

"Okay, well they are occupied. Want to go see if there is anything to eat?" Keegan asked.

"I did see some cake when we walked in." Anna grinned.

On their way to find the food, their parents caught up with them. "You didn't think you could sneak off without us taking some photos did you?" Anna's mother shooed them together.

The girls made funny faces and threw up the peace sign.

"You guys will miss this," Lauren's mother said wistfully.

"We're done with the mushy talk, Mom."

"Alright, well go have fun with your friends," Emerald sighed, packing her own camera away. "Don't forget we have to go to the family dinner tonight."

"Thanks for the reminder." Keegan waved as they walked away.

They found the cake and waited in line. There wasn't much in the manner of food other than cake, chips, and soda.

Keegan had her cake up to her mouth when Donald came around and ate it right out of her hand. "Hey! You know, now you have to get in line and get me another piece of cake."

"I'll get you two." He gave her a big grin, the corners of his eyes crinkling. Keegan leaned forward, giving him a peck on the lips.

"You guys are sickening." Lauren rolled her eyes at them.

"Where are you guys going to college?" Keegan asked Calvron and Spencer after Donald had left for the cake table.

"We're going to UCLA. Donald was supposed to go as well, but I hear he might be going to Alaska instead." Calvron stared intently at her.

"What, you guys were supposed to go to college together? He never told me that." Keegan's mind was racing. Donald was going to give up going to college with his best friends to be closer to her. She really didn't like that idea at all. She knew she wouldn't give up her plans for him.

"I'll talk to him about it later. I really had no idea." Keegan pulled at the sleeve of her gown.

"I didn't know you guys were going to UCLA. That's where I'm going, as well. To study law." Lauren smiled sweetly at them. "We'll have to hang out sometimes."

"Well, that sucks. You guys are going to be together, and Keegan and I are going to be off on our own." Anna shot Lauren a dirty look.

"Hey, you guys picked your schools, I had nothing to do with it."

"We should make plans to meet up once a month," Keegan cut in. "Maybe Calvron can set up a magical world there.

Calvron stroked his chin. "I'm sure I could work something out."

Donald strolled back up to group and handed Keegan her cake. "What did I miss?"

"We were just talking about getting together once a month after we leave for college," Anna told him, stealing a bite from Keegan's plate.

"That would be cool." Donald put his arm around Keegan.

"Ok guys, this graduation is lame. Any idea of what we can do?" Keegan looked around at the gang.

"Let's go play laser tag." Sam grinned.

The girls looked at each other and shrugged their shoulders. "Sure, why not."

They had a blast. The guys were surprised the girls were able to hold their own. Keegan was going to miss days like this.

Chapter 27

Donald and Keegan had just walked outside to go swimming in the natural swimming pool at her house. The day was bright and hot, the sun sparkling off the water as they dropped their towels on one of the tables surrounding the pool.

Keegan turned to stare up into his startling blue eyes. "Donald, why didn't you tell me that you were supposed to go to college in California with the guys?"

"Keegan, I want to be with you. If you're going to Alaska, that's where I want to be." He looked down at her sincerely as he took her hands.

"I think you should go to UCLA. It's not good to change your plans like that. We can take turns visiting each other once or twice a month. Plus, I'm going to be so busy with school, I wouldn't have much time for you anyway."

"Are you saying you don't want me to go?" Donald pulled his hands away from her, his lips pressing into a thin line.

"It's not that I don't want you around, you know I do. It's just, I think you should be with your friends. We can make it work. Besides, what if I hate Alaska and you are stuck there finishing up your program?"

"I could always switch, same as you."

"I'm asking you to do this for me, Donald. Please, just go to UCLA. I promise I will visit you a lot. I feel horrible taking you away from your plans."

"But, it's what I want. I want to be with you. I don't care where it is. I love you."

Keegan was starting to get mad. She wrapped her arms around herself and rubbed her arms, taking a few deep breaths.

Donald noticed and said. "Ok, Keegan if that is really what you want. But, I want to see you every weekend not just two times a month."

"We can try." She smiled and threw her arms around him. "Thank you. I feel so much better now. It has been eating away at me."

"Let's spend as much time as we can together for the rest of the summer."

Keegan laid her head against his chest, relieved. She wasn't sure why it bothered her so much that he was willing to give everything up for her.

Later that day, Anna showed up. "Hey, is Thaddeus around? I have to ask him something about the Xbox."

"You want to see my brother?" Keegan looked at her in disbelief. "I thought you came to hang out with me."

"Don't be ridiculous, of course I did. I just have to see him for a second."

"Well, he's in his room."

Anna walked up the stairs with a smile on her face, still tickled by the cloak and dagger stuff. She knocked on the door and Thaddeus yelled, "Come in, Anna."

"Hey, how did you know? Oh right never mind." She gave him a sheepish grin. "Well, part one is over. I've been feeding him dreams and if he's going to give her the ring, he would have decided by now. But, we didn't think of the tricky part."

"What's that?" Thad looked up from his game, pausing it.

"We need to get a hold of the ring."

"Ah, yes that is tricky. Well, we can ask his father for it," Thaddeus said.

"Wouldn't that be a little strange? Hey, do you happen to have a ruby ring we could spell?" Anna put her hand on her hip and raised an eyebrow.

"Just leave it to me. I'll get you the ring. When do you need it by?"

"Well, summer is almost over. I need it before I leave for college, because I'm not sure I'll be back here again before her birthday."

"Okay, I'll get it to you by this weekend. I'll figure something out. Where there is magic, there is always a way." He gave her one of his impish grins.

"If Keegan asks, I was asking you about a zombie game."

"Okay, get out of here. Don't forget to shut the door."

Once the door was closed, Thaddeus sat back in his chair to think. How could he get the ring? He could use magic, of course, but maybe he didn't have to. He picked up his phone and called Rourk's dad. He didn't have to say much to get him to agree to help out. He wanted Rourk to be happy and didn't care how that happened.

Anna and Keegan were watching sappy chick flicks and eating popcorn.

Keegan told Anna about talking Donald into going to school in California.

"I think that's a good idea. It's a little strange he wanted to follow you to Alaska. Even as much as I love you, I have no desire to follow you to Alaska." They both laughed.

Summer passed by in a blur. They all spent as much time together as possible, but it was rapidly coming to an end.

They decided to have one big party before they all went their separate ways. Calvron held it at his house since his family had so much room.

The girls came through the door and were shocked at how many people were there. There had to be over two hundred kids dancing and yelling. They made their way over to the guys.

"Calvron, did you use magic to pull this together?" Keegan wondered aloud.

"Nope, my parents don't let me use magic at home."

"Well, it looks amazing." Anna said as she glanced around the large open room.

"We have a pool out back and some pool tables if you guys want to go back there."

"Sure sounds fun. We didn't bring swim suits though." Lauren shrugged.

"Who said you needed suits." Calvron winked.

"Gross, you wish." Lauren swatted at him.

"There are actually a bunch of suits out there. My parents keep lots on hands for guest."

They had a great time. No one mentioned it was the last time they would hang out like that for a while, even though Keegan figured it was on everyone's mind.

The ring shimmered on Anna's altar under the glow of the circle of candles surrounding her. Her heartbeat was a quick pulse in her throat as she touched a single fingertip to it, closing her eyes and searching for the power inside it. It made her skin tingle.

Taking a deep breath, she released it, imagining a brilliant white light surrounding her body as she rested her hands back in her lap. She let everything else fade away—everything that had bugged her during the day melted under the positive energy. She took a couple of breaths to center herself before she began.

The picture she had of Keegan was a great one. Anna had captured it while she wasn't looking. It was her profile, with her auburn hair tucked behind one ear and dangling on the other side. The sun was behind her, making her hair a halo of fire. A small smirk was on her lips. Anna couldn't remember what she was looking at in the photo, but it had amused her.

Anna put the photo on top of her stone pentacle on the altar, face up. She lifted the ring, eyeing it once more in the candlelight before sitting it on the picture.

She began folding the corners of the picture in one by one, taking her time to make them meet in the center, while she chanted,

In the name of my lady and her consort,
And by the law of three times three,
Let this ring draw Keegan to wear it,
So from darkness she shall be free.

She repeated the chant three times, securing the picture-made envelope that held the ring with a black ribbon. When it was ready, she placed it purposefully back on top of her pentacle.

The candle holder was an antique Anna had pulled from the attic. It was gold but had lost its shine a long time before. Its greatest aspect was the hollow base, which allowed her to position the holder over her pentacle and the talisman.

The pale pink pillar candle she had already anointed with cinnamon oil. The smell was divine and made her want cookies. She fit it in the shallow dish of the holder and lit the candle.

Lighting her sage bundle, she blew gently on it to make it smolder and smoke, then wafted it around her altar in the shape of a heart three times. She put it in the censor dish on her altar to burn out. Clapping her hands once to signal the end of the ritual, she declared, "Blessed be."

She would burn the candle for 13 minutes every night after sunset for 13 days to push the spell. Raising an eyebrow at her handiwork, she smiled. "Now, to see if it works."

Keegan's mother wanted them to get to Alaska a few days early so they could set up her new room. She had decided to get an apartment right outside of the college instead of staying in the dorms. For some reason, her father was very relieved by this. She might get a roommate just so she didn't have to be alone. At the very least she was getting a dog. She still couldn't believe she was going to be so far from home.

"Keegan, are you ready to go?" her mother yelled up the stairs.

"No, I'm not ready."

"Well, we have to leave in a few minutes or we will miss the plane."

Keegan glanced around her childhood room and wanted to crawl back in the bed and stay there. She was actually scared to be going to a strange place all by herself. She didn't want to tell her parents that, though. Taking a deep breath, she picked up her bags and headed out the door.

"Hurry up!"

"I'm coming, stop rushing me!" Keegan ran down the stairs.

Her father and Thaddeus, who were going to drop them off at the airport, were waiting at the door. Thaddeus grabbed her bags from her, which surprised her.

Once they got to the airport, her father hugged her for a long time. Keegan wiped tears from her eyes.

"Stop crying, Keegan, you will be back next month for your birthday. After that, for Thanksgiving and Christmas." Thaddeus looked down at his feet.

"You know you're going to miss me, little brother."

"Maybe a little bit." He gave her a slight smile.

"Ok, let's go Keegan," her mother said. "I'm excited to get there and get your apartment set up. We have a lot of shopping to do."

Keegan smiled—shopping was the magic word. "I really want my place to be cool. I was thinking to go for the retro look. I hope they have good stores there."

"Well, I wouldn't count on that but we'll make do." Her mother put her arm around her as they walked towards the gate.

"Thanks for coming with me mom."

"I wouldn't miss it."

Keegan had settled into a routine. Thankfully, her earliest class was at 9:00 am so she got to sleep in. She had started volunteering at the fish and wildlife service where she made a few friends, but nothing that came close to her friends from Tennessee. Donald had already come to visit twice. She loved showing him around. They had fun going hiking, fishing, and whale watching. She couldn't believe how cold it got so quickly there.

She kept in constant contact with Anna and Lauren by text and Skype. They seemed to be adjusting well to their new schools, but they were all looking forward to returning to Tennessee for Keegan's birthday party.

Chapter 28

Rourk boarded the plane, nervous anticipation racing through his body. Soon, he would see Keegan again. It had been almost a year since he had laid eyes on her. He had no idea what her reaction would be when she saw him.

Leaning his head against the seat, he closed his eyes and thought of her. Of course, all he could see was darkness. He longed for the days when he could close his eyes and see her face clearly. That seemed like a lifetime ago.

He was trying to mentally brace himself for her rejection. He hoped he would be able to hold himself together. Noticing that he was gripping the seat tightly, he released his fingers. Thankfully, it was a short flight home.

When he got off the plane, his father was there to meet him. It was nice to see a familiar face in the sea of strangers.

"Rourk, you look great," his father said, shaking his hand.

"Thanks, Dad. How have you been?"

"I've been well. Let's get you home so you can cook me something to eat. I'm surprised I haven't wasted away without your cooking skills."

Rourk laughed. "That sounds good. I'm so sick of the mess hall food."

He tossed his bag in the back of his father's truck and settled into the passenger seat for the drive home. The familiar highway felt good. To Rourk, Tennessee would always be home, no matter where he lived.

"So you still want to give Keegan the ring?" his father asked, never taking his eyes off the road.

"Yes, I am going to give it to her." Rourk paused, then gave a wry grin. "Well, I'm going to try to give it to her. She might turn me down."

"I've been thinking about it, and I'm glad you are going to try. You are right. You are an elf and that is what chosens do."

Rourk was slightly surprised by his father's change in opinion, but he let it slide.

"I will know soon enough." Rourk relaxed his posture and leaned his head back on the seat.

"How is training going?"

"It's going good. There are some good guys there. I've noticed a few other creatures of the light. The training is actually fun now that it's mostly just weapons and less of the mind games."

"How's Tommy?"

Rourk smiled. "He is doing good. He has really taken to the engineer program. He's actually a very intelligent man. We're both going to 1st Group."

"That is great. Some of my best friends I met as a team guy. I should probably look some of them up now that I think of it," his father mused, his eyes far away.

At home, Rourk cooked steaks and potatoes. It was nice to navigate his kitchen again, and he couldn't wait to sleep in his own bed.

It took all of his self control not to go over to Keegan's house. He knew he had to wait till tomorrow. His pulse quickened at the thought.

Rourk went for a run in his woods and enjoyed the crisp fall air against his skin. Once he got home, he jumped in the shower let the hot water wash away the tension. He wondered if he should call Thaddeus and find out what Keegan's plans were so he knew when the best time to visit would be.

Wrapping a towel around his waist, Rourk walked down the hall to the kitchen and pulled out a soda from the fridge.

Greg had the newspaper open on the table in front of him. "Thaddeus called while you were in the shower. He wanted to let you know you were invited to Keegan's party tomorrow at three."

Rourk grinned and shook his head. Why was he not surprised? Thaddeus was something else.

Rourk woke up tense knowing that today, he would find out, for good or worse. He walked into the kitchen, where his father was sitting down with a cup of coffee.

"Dad, can I see the ring?"

"Of course, let me go grab it. It's in my room."

"Your room? I thought you always kept it in the safe."

Greg paused, then smoothly said, "Oh, well I got it out when I knew you were coming home."

Rourk poured himself a glass of orange juice while he waited, and then sat down at the table, stealing his dad's newspaper. His father came back in, holding a small green velvet box.

"Your mom would be happy to know you were passing it on."

"Hopefully passing it on. You are more positive than I am, Father."

Rourk took the box and slowly opened it. It had been years since he had looked at the ring. It was beautiful; it had been in their family for generations. He picked it up and inspected it in the light. The ruby was large and oval, set flush within the antique etchings and diamonds. It almost seemed to be glowing.

He wondered if Keegan would like it. "It is beautiful."

Greg nodded. "Yes, it is. Your mother loved that ring. I don't think she ever took it off."

Rourk glanced over and noticed his father was still wearing his simple gold wedding band. Rourk placed the ruby ring back in the box and snapped it closed. "I'm going to go for a long hike. I need to clear my mind."

Rourk looked at his watch for the hundredth time. It was now 2:30; he needed to head over to Keegan's. Taking a deep breath, he put the ring in his pocket and yelled out to his father, "I'm leaving."

"I hope it works, Rourk." His dad came to the door. "I'm proud of you, son. I know this is not easy."

Rourk grimaced and walked out the door. He climbed into his old truck and closed his eyes as he turned the key. *Please, let this work.*

He entered the long driveway at Richard's house. There were several cars parked out in front of the house. *Great.* He hadn't thought about having an audience. *Pull yourself together.*

One last deep breath and he opened the door. Stepping out of the truck, he felt his pocket to make sure the ring was still there. Head held high, he marched up to the door. He didn't even have to ring the doorbell. Thaddeus opened the door as he approached.

"So good to see you, Rourk." Thaddeus grasped his hand and smacked him on the shoulder.

"Thanks." Rourk stepped into the house and glanced around looking for Keegan, but she was not there.

"Everyone is down in the den."

Rourk's stomach was in knots as Thad led him to the den. There were a few of Keegan's friend's sitting around watching TV. The shapeshifter had his arm around Keegan and she was smiling.

Rourk wanted to rip his throat out.

"Keegan!" Thaddeus yelled.

She turned, startled, and jumped to her feet, staring wide-eyed at Rourk. "Oh."

The tiger had slithered to his feet beside her, his body tense.

Everyone's eyes were on Rourk. He was so full of conflicting emotions about seeing Keegan that he was letting their stares get to him. The faces in the room no longer looked happy. Rourk must have crashed the party.

"Hello, Keegan. I told you I would be back for you on your birthday. Here I am."

Donald stood taller and moved closer to Keegan, his arm around her shoulders. You could cut the tension in the room with a knife. The movie was playing in the background but it might as well have been complete silence.

"Rourk, I don't know what to say." Keegan shifted uncomfortably. "I thought you were still in training."

"I am. I took a weekend pass. I don't break my word." He pulled the ring out of his pocket and opened the box.

Keegan's hand flew over her mouth. She shrugged away Donald's arm and walked towards Rourk as if she was in a trance, her eyes on the ring. Once she reached him, she reached out for it, quickly pulling her hand back as if it were on fire. It was the most amazing thing she had ever seen.

"It's beautiful, just like I've always imagined it would be," she said wistfully.

Rourk's heart was in his throat. "It's yours, Keegan."

"It's so pretty. The lights are dancing all around it. Why are there sparkles coming off it?" Keegan reached up above the ring and pinched at the air, giggling.

No one in the room said a word as they watched the exchange.

"Maybe I could just try it on?"

"Of course you can." Rourk pulled it from the box, and Keegan started giggling like a little kid, bouncing on her toes.

"It's calling me. It's telling me to just put it on. How can a ring talk?" Keegan laughed. She sounded as if she were drunk.

Rourk took her hand in his and slid the ring on her finger.

Keegan gasped, jerking her hand away from Rourk and staring wide-eyed at the ring.

"How could you? You tricked me!" Keegan yelled at Rourk, glancing back at Donald before she wrinkled her nose at the ring as if it were diseased.

Rourk stared at her confused. "Tricked you? What do you mean?"

Keegan reached up and grabbed the back of Rourk's head, pulling him to her and kissing him greedily. Almost as quickly, she shoved him away. "What did you do?"

Rourk started at her, and touched his lips.

"How could you do this to me? You didn't even give me a choice?" Keegan was freezing, goose bumps racing across her skin. She looked around the room and everyone was frozen in place except her and Rourk.

Rourk looked around the room. "Keegan, are you okay? I didn't trick you. I am your chosen. I am supposed to give you this ring on your birthday. It's tradition, you know that. I'm pretty confused myself. Why is everyone frozen?"

"A side effect of the black magic. When I get angry, I freeze things. They will be okay once I calm down." She stared down at the ring and whispered, "It's back."

"What is back?" Rourk's heart was racing.

She lifted her eyes to his. "The bond. I'm so angry at you I can't see straight. But, I want to wrap myself in you and never let you go. I've never felt so conflicted before." She glanced back at Donald, frozen in place. "I care about him."

"I can see that." Rourk glared over at Donald, his jaw clenched. He pulled her close, staring down into her blue-green eyes. "Keegan, I love you. I am your chosen. We are meant to be." He slowly traced his finger down the side of her face and outlined her full lips with his finger before he bent down to kiss her.

Keegan didn't resist. She heard the cracking, but she didn't care. She continued to kiss him as if no one else were there. She gently pulled away and whispered his name. He groaned and tangled his hands in her hair. Their eyes met for an instant, and she leaned in to kiss him again when she heard Thaddeus clear his throat.

Keegan pulled away, her cheeks flaming. Donald was standing closer than he had been, his shoulders slumped and his eyes wounded. Keegan lifted her hand towards him, then let it drop. "I'm so sorry. It's just too strong, I can't fight it."

"Can't or won't?" he said, his voice dangerously soft.

Keegan opened her mouth to reply, but noticed her brother giving Anna a high five. She jerked towards them with a glare, momentarily forgetting Donald. "You did this, didn't you?"

Anna smiled. Thaddeus just stared.

"You didn't even think of Donald's feelings." Keegan motioned to her boyfriend where he still stood, his hands limp at his sides as he glared at Thaddeus and Anna. "Or bother asking me if this is what I wanted."

"It's what was meant to be, Keegan," Thaddeus said, leaning against the wall.

"Who are you to say what is meant to be and what is not?"

"Keegan, chill out. We didn't do anything. The rings have always cemented the bond. All we did was make you want to try on the ring." Thaddeus glanced over at Anna. She was still smiling.

"Were you in on this?" Keegan crossed her arms and looked up at Rourk.

"No, I had no idea. However, if they had asked me I would have willingly been involved. I would have done anything to get our bond back." Rourk met her eyes.

Keegan reached for him without even thinking, her hand cupping his cheek.

Donald hung his head, taking a deep breath and letting it out. He bolted from the room, morphing into a tiger before them, knocking over furniture as he took off at full speed.

Startled, Keegan stared after him into the dim evening beyond the door. She looked back at Rourk, her heart aching.

"I'm going after Donald."

Consumed

Book Three

For my daughter

Chapter 1

Keegan rushed for the door. Stopping briefly in the doorway, she turned to stare at Rourk with slight smile playing across her face. Her chosen was beautiful. The sun gleaming through the open windows reflected off his soft, rust colored hair. His cool grey eyes met hers and her heart raced. It took every ounce of her self-control not to return to his arms.

Donald deserved more than that. She had to find him.

"Keegan, don't." Rourk's voice was filled with pain. He took a single step forward, his khaki pants rustling in the dead silence of the room. Keegan gazed a moment longer, taking in his messy hair, his plain black t-shirt—everything that made him Rourk.

"I'll be back. I promise." She tore her eyes from him and she was gone.

It was cool outside. Fall had arrived early for Tennessee; it was usually still hot for Keegan's birthday. She pulled the long sleeves of her sweater over her hands, shivering. It was still warmer than Alaska.

Keegan glanced around in the hope of seeing Donald, but he was in his tiger form so he was probably long gone. Her family's property was huge—he had so many places to hide. The woods spread around her, dim and thick even under the bright afternoon sunshine. He could be anywhere.

Frustration and confusion rushed through her body. She wanted to talk to Donald, but she also longed to be inside with Rourk.

She had never expected her bond with Rourk to come back or to hurt Donald, the shy and sweet shape shifter she'd had started to fall for over the past year. The Great Battle —being killed and brought back to life with black magic— severed her bond to Rourk. Afterwards, she couldn't even remember meeting Rourk, let alone their time together. She'd broken one good man's heart, and now, with the bond restored, she was about to break the heart of another.

Suddenly, everything had changed again. She groaned, ran her hands through her tangled mess of auburn hair, and headed towards the woods.

After an hour of walking, she knew it was useless. She couldn't really blame Donald for disappearing; if she had been in his position, she probably would too. Sitting down on the enormous trunk of a fallen tree, she sighed and looked around, rubbing at the goosebumps on her skin. The leaves were turning vibrant shades of red, orange, and yellow, and were just starting to fall off the trees. She grabbed a leaf from the ground at her feet and spun it around between her fingers.

It was hard for her to believe a year ago today on her seventeenth birthday her life path had changed so dramatically.

Suddenly, she felt fur rub up against her arm. *How had he snuck up on her?* She turned and rubbed his head with both hands, giving him a sad smile.

"Turn back into your human form so we can talk," Keegan pleaded.

The tiger shook its head, his feet shuffling among the leaves as he circled her.

"Fine." She closed her eyes, letting her hands rest in her lap. "I'm so sorry. I really never dreamed this would happen. You know an elf's bond to their chosen is too strong to fight. I've never heard of an elf that was able to resist their chosen. My aunt Brigid tried for a while, but even she gave in."

The tiger lay down at her feet, warming them. She opened her eyes. His big blue eyes were sparkling and a tear ran down his face. She moved to wipe it away, but he jerked his head back.

"I could lie to you and tell you that we can try," she told him quietly. "I think we both know it would not work. It would just be prolonging the inevitable. Donald, you are very special to me and always will be. This last year that I spent with you gave me some of the happiest times of my life." Keegan leaned to run her hand through the soft fur of the tiger's back. "I will never forget the time we've had together. I just don't think it's fair of me to lead you on. I think we need to accept that our time is over."

The tiger laid his head between his paws and moaned as if he were in pain, avoiding her eyes.

"Please, talk to me."

The tiger rose up to his full form and walked around her body, nudging her as he went. His fur felt so soft and warm against her skin. Keegan wrapped her arms around the big cat's neck and pulled him close to her. It sounded as if he were purring.

"I'm sorry." Keegan wiped her tears with one hand, still clinging to him.

The tiger pulled away. He let out a loud roar that echoed through the trees and sprinted off, his powerful body moving so fast he was gone before she knew it. Keegan's heart ached at the thought of causing such pain to someone she cared for. She hoped someday he would be able to forgive her.

Once he was out of sight, she slowly made her way back to the house. She wasn't sure she was ready to face Rourk. Although, just thinking of him made her pulse race and her face flush. As much as she cared about Donald, he had never had this affect on her. As she reached the door, her stomach was in knots. She took a deep breath before she pushed the heavy wooden door open.

Thaddeus and Rourk were sitting in the living room when she walked in. Rourk's brow was furrowed, his hands gripped his thighs. She met his gaze, and saw his concern melt into relief. He let out a deep sigh, and his body visibly relaxed.

Thaddeus stood up, tugged his hooded sweatshirt down over his blue jeans from where it had bunched against the couch. "I'm going to play Xbox. I'll see you later, Rourk."

"Not so fast." Keegan glared at him, her hands planted on her hips. She wanted to scream at him for keeping his secrets so well, but she tried to calm herself instead. It wouldn't be nice to freeze him accidentally. "Why didn't you tell me about all of this? You could have at least given me a warning, or heaven forbid, a choice."

"You *could* tell me thank you." Thaddeus raised an eyebrow and gave her one of his famous impish grins.

"You crushed Donald." Keegan wrapped her arms around herself and looked down at her feet, trying to erase the memory of the tiger's sad eyes.

"Donald will be fine." His tone was matter-of-fact.

"How can you be so sure? Did you have a vision?" Keegan looked up, her eyes wide.

"Let's just say there's a white tiger in his future. I know it's hard for you to believe Keegan, but he will get over you," Thaddeus said sarcastically, and with that, he turned and headed up the stairs.

Keegan was surprised to feel both relief and a pang of jealousy at the thought of Donald loving someone else. She glanced over at Rourk, who had been staring at her silently during the exchange.

"I still don't think this is fair." Keegan pouted, folding her arms across her chest. *And I want to know what you're thinking, Rourk. Can you still love me?*

As if hearing her unspoken question, Rourk stood up and crossed the room until he was in front of her. He was bigger than she recalled, and the softness of youth in his features had been replaced by the harsher angles of manhood. It had been almost a year since the last time she saw him. She stared up at his rugged face, thrilled and apprehensive to realize he was there to claim her. Everything about him was intense; his gaze, his muscular body, the tension and energy between them. She looked up into his eyes and knew she would follow him anywhere. The moment he touched her, she allowed her body to melt into his.

He really is mine, this time, forever.

"I've waited so long for this day." His voice sounded rough. He rested his chin on her head and pulled her closer, his strong arms cradling her waist in a way that made her feel special, cherished. It was futile to resist their connection, and she wondered how strong black magic was to counter what she felt in her mate's arms. She'd been an oblivious fool, but no more.

As of now, their fates were sealed. They belonged to each other.

Chapter 2

Keegan's mother came through the door with her hands filled with groceries. Her pale cheeks were flushed from the chill outside and her ginger, pixie-style hair was windblown. She stopped mid-step and grinned, balancing the largest of the bags on her hip. "Well, hello Rourk. I hope you are staying for dinner?"

"If it's ok with Keegan. I would love to stay for dinner. Here let me help you." He stood from the couch in one smooth movement and crossed the living room. Taking the bags from her mom, he headed towards the kitchen.

Keegan's mom waited until he was out of earshot, her eyes lit with excitement, and then said, "Keegan! Does this mean what I think it means?"

Face serious, Keegan met her mother's blue eyes. "Yes, the bond is back. I'm sure you're happy."

"You are not happy about this?"

"I don't know, Mom. It's all so sudden. I just broke Donald's heart. I barely know Rourk, but I'm so drawn to him I can't do anything *but* be with him."

Keegan turned to watch Rourk with a small smile. Beyond the counter that separated living room from kitchen, he was bustling around as if he had been doing it forever. He was putting her mother's groceries away. Keegan sighed. "I guess I am a little happy. He's perfect isn't he?"

"Yes, he is your perfect match." Her mother nodded, and a big grin broke across her face. "This is so exciting. We need to start making plans."

Startled, Keegan asked, "Plans for what?"

"Your wedding, of course. There is so much to do. I haven't given it any thought since you lost the bond. Do you want the hand fasting to take place on the property or somewhere else? Ohh...we could have the wedding in Ireland.

Keegan, we are going to have so much fun shopping for a dress." Her mother's enthusiasm was infectious, but the whole idea was crazy.

"My wedding? I barely know him. I just started college. There is no way I am getting married right now." Planting her hand on her hip, she glared at her mother.

Emerald rolled her eyes. "Keegan, you know that is the elfin tradition. You meet your mate at eighteen and you get married. Tradition is the foundation of our society. I married your father a month after we met. It's the way it is. This is not news to you, so stop overreacting."

Shaking her head vehemently, Keegan stood firm. "You can forget it. It's not happening. At least not until I finish college. I'm sure Rourk will understand."

"Understand what?" Rourk appeared at Keegan's side and looked back and forth between the two women, his brow furrowed.

Turning her glare from her mother to her chosen, Keegan said, "My mom wants to start planning our wedding. I told her I'm not getting married until I graduate college."

Rourk grinned, shoving his hands in his pockets. "You are so cute when you are angry."

"Are you ok with waiting?" Keegan asked, exasperated.

"I think this is something we can talk about later. I don't see the need to rush into anything." Rourk put his arm around Keegan and looked down at her with a big smile. "I'm just happy our bond has been returned."

Keegan shot her mother a satisfied look and said, "I told you so."

Her mother rolled her eyes and headed for the kitchen. "Well, we'll see what your father says about this."

Keegan smiled at Rourk after her mother was gone. "Thank you, for understanding. We have our whole lives ahead of us. I don't think we need to rush into getting married."

Rourk reached over and touched the side of her face, his eyes searching. "Whatever you want is fine with me. As far as I am concerned, we are bonded and that is enough."

"Are you sure?" Keegan touched the side of his arm and electricity shot through her. She jumped. "Did you feel that?"

Rourk laughed. "Yes, Keegan, it always feels like that when we touch."

She grinned. "That is pretty cool. I still don't recall our time before the bond broke. I wish I did."

He wrapped his arms around her and gave her a brief but tight hug. "We will start fresh today. So how is school going? I have no idea what you have been doing this last year. It was torture for me not to be able to see you through my mind's eye."

"Can you see me now?"

Rourk closed his eyes and thought of Keegan. She materialized as clear as if he was looking at her in front of him. He opened his eyes and grinned. "I can see you again. Every night I would close my eyes and think of you and all I could see was darkness."

"I'm sorry." Keegan stared down at her hands.

"It's not your fault. You have nothing to be sorry about. Tell me about school."

Shrugging, Keegan sighed. "It's ok. It's actually a lot harder than I expected. I've always been used to not having to study. Now I actually have to pay attention and take notes. I've made a couple of friends. Really the only thing I enjoy is volunteering at the wildlife station, and taking photos. It's so beautiful there. You have to come see it."

"I would love to come see you. I get weekends off most of the time now that we are in the advanced training. They don't treat us like children any longer."

"What about you? How's your training going? My father told me you were making quite the impression." Keegan tugged him to the couch and pulled him down beside her.

"It's going well. I'm going to be stationed in Washington. It was the closest I could get to Alaska."

Keegan's hand covered her mouth. She stared at him wide-eyed. "You were trying to get stationed closer to me? Even though our bond was gone?"

"The bond was gone for you," he said quietly, gently squeezing her hands between his. "For me it was as strong as ever. I've always wanted to be close to you."

"Why did you leave then? You could have tried harder." She couldn't help the tiny bit of irritation in her voice.

"Keegan, leaving you was the hardest thing I've ever had to do in my life. I left because it wasn't fair for me to stay here. You were too young and besides I saw you with the shapeshifter in the woods." Rourk clenched his jaw.

Keegan froze, her heart pounding. "You saw us? Why didn't you say anything?"

"I was too hurt. I had to get away before I did something stupid. I knew you weren't doing anything wrong. You had not yet turned eighteen. You were *supposed* to be dating until you met me. Things just got messed up with the black magic." Rourk paused briefly. "Hell, I couldn't even blame the shapeshifter. Why wouldn't he be attracted to you?"

"I'm glad you came back for me." Keegan reached over with both hands and pulled his head towards hers. She wrapped her arms around his neck, and pressed her lips against his. The electricity raced through her body.

Rourk pulled away and looked into her eyes. "I love you."

Keegan sighed and snuggled closer, resting her head on his shoulder. "I love you too. I don't think I can ever recall feeling this content."

The front door opened and her father appeared. A huge grin spread across his face as he caught sight of his daughter. Closing the door firmly, he said, "I see you got quite the birthday present Keegan."

Keegan laughed. "I guess you could say that."

Rourk stood up and shook Richard's hand. They didn't have to say anything, they just exchanged knowing grins.

Emerald came out from the kitchen grinning like a fool. "Isn't this great? I knew it would all work out. Although, your daughter is refusing to get married. She wants to wait until after she graduates college."

Richard shook his head. "Why is it every time Keegan does or says something you don't agree with she is my daughter?" He winked at his wife. "Let's worry about this another day and just enjoy having Rourk back into our family. What's for dinner? I'm starving."

Keegan interrupted whatever her mother was going to say by jumping up and thrusting her hand out for them to see. The ruby was hard to miss with the lights reflecting off it. "I almost forgot to show you my ring." Keegan looked down at her hand, smiling. "I used to dream of this exact ring when I was younger."

"Yes, I recall all the times you asked me what would happen if your chosen didn't give you a ruby ring." Emerald chuckled. "It's beautiful. I love the antique setting and how the ruby is set flush." Emerald glanced over at Rourk. "How long has this been in your family?"

Rourk shrugged his shoulders. "I don't know the exact timeframe. My mother passed away when I was too young to understand all of this. I just know it has been many generations."

"Fate is a wonderful thing." Emerald looked over at her husband and they shared a smile.

"Keegan, can't we talk you into a wedding? We're long overdue for a party, and I'm sure the men would love to see Rourk." Her father rubbed his beard, looking at her from thoughtful, hazel eyes.

Keegan shot him a dirty look, then sighed. "Dad, forget it. It's not happening. You'll get your wedding. Just not right away."

Richard looked at Emerald and shrugged. "Don't say I didn't try."

Rourk put his arm around Keegan. "Richard, how is the camp? Have you still been working closely with Creed?"

"Things are going as well as can be expected. Creed has turned out to be a great ally. We're making progress, but as you know it's often one step forward and two back. I don't think we'll be out of a job anytime soon."

Rourk nodded in agreement. "I'm looking forward to getting back to the Army of the Light. I have to admit I have been enjoying the training, and working with the humans. I can understand why it is tradition for elves to join the human army. It's a great experience."

"We look forward to having you back. Did you sign up for four or six years?"

"Just four. I figured Keegan would be done with college and ready to move back by then. If not, we'll figure something out."

Keegan shivered, leaning into Rourk's side. "I think I'll be ready. Alaska is already freezing and it's only September."

Thaddeus came down the stairs, his heavy footsteps pounding the hardwood. "Rourk, how long are you going to be here?"

Keegan's heart dropped. She hadn't thought he would be leaving soon. They would be separated again. She clung tighter to his waist, peering up at him with her eyes wide.

"I only have a couple of days off. I have to be back by Monday," Rourk told Thaddeus, glancing down at Keegan apologetically.

Keegan pouted, pulling away from his arms. "That's so soon. I have to go back to school on Monday, too. I can't believe we just found each other again and we're already going to be separated."

"You might as well get used to it, Keegan. Rourk is a warrior. He will often be gone," Emerald said matter-of-factly, leaning on the kitchen counter.

"It still doesn't make me happy." Keegan crossed her arms and kicked the floor, her lower lip jutting out even more.

Thaddeus shook his head at Rourk. "I feel bad for you."

They all laughed before going their separate ways to wait on dinner. Her mother ended up making steak for fajitas.

When dinner was ready, they gathered around the table and chatted. Keegan reached for her second tortilla, and said, "This is good mom. Have you been working on your cooking skills?"

"Keegan, you should know better than to ask that. It's a frozen mix I just had to throw it in the pan and let heat up. Just because elves can't use modern technology in battle doesn't mean we can't use it in the kitchen. Speaking of cooking, I'm surprised you haven't wasted away on your own. Have you been cooking or eating out every meal?"

"A little of both. I've found I actually enjoy cooking but it just kinda sucks cooking for myself."

"You can cook for me next weekend." Rourk grinned at her across the table.

"Really? You will come see me next weekend?" Keegan's face flushed with excitement.

"I will come to see you every chance I get."

Richard pointed his fork and spoke through a mouthful of food. "Don't forget to sign up for frequent flyer programs. You'll have free tickets before you know it."

Emerald rolled her eyes at her husband. "He is obsessed with frequent flyer programs."

Thaddeus took a bite, then asked Rourk, "How's Tommy?"

Rourk grinned. "Tommy is doing great. It's like he's a new man."

"Who's Tommy?" Keegan asked.

"A friend I made during training. He's also going to be stationed in Washington. I can't wait for you to meet him."

"There is so much I don't know about you. For some reason I never pictured you having friends. You sort of come across as a loner." Keegan grabbed her glass and took a sip.

Thaddeus laughed. "I think Tommy is Rourk's first friend."

Keegan frowned, looking intently at her boyfriend. "Is that true?"

"I guess he is. I never really thought about it."

After they finished dinner, Rourk asked, "Would you like to go for a walk?"

She smiled. "Of course!"

Grabbing her phone on the way out the door, she saw she had several texts from her friends asking what had happened after they left.

She slid the phone in her pocket; she would fill them in later.

Chapter 3

Keegan grabbed a sweater before they left the house. She looked at Rourk while she slipped her arms into the green wool. "I get cold easily since I came back from the dead."

"Well, you picked the wrong place to move. You must be freezing in Alaska." Rourk laced his fingers through hers, leading her down the path.

Keegan laughed. "Yeah, it wasn't a very well thought-out plan. I just always wanted to go to Alaska. Their marine biology program is one of the best." She ran her fingers over his hand and giggled. "That is the weirdest thing. I can feel the vibrations from your skin."

He stopped, pulling her near. His hands spanned across her back as he smiled down at her. "I've missed hearing your laugh. Hell, I've missed everything about you."

"Well, looks like you are stuck with me now." Keegan wrapped her arms around his waist, leaning her head against his chest.

"You have always been the only one for me, Keegan." Rourk turned and lightly ran his thumb across her bottom lip before he leaned down to kiss her—softly at first and then with more urgency. He eventually pulled away, his grey eyes searching hers. "I can't lose you again."

"Wow. You keep kissing me like that and you won't have anything to worry about." She nudged him with her hip. Taking hold of Rourk's arm, she pulled him over to a group of large rocks, where she sat down and tugged at him to join her.

"What happened with the shapeshifter?" Rourk leaned down and picked up a small stone, not looking her in the eyes.

"He wouldn't talk to me. I really hurt him, but he's always known this was a possibility." Keegan moved her shoe around on the grass, searching for words. "I told him it was over because I couldn't resist the bond."

"Do you love him?" His eyes met hers and his face was expressionless.

"What?" Keegan looked over at him, surprised by his question. She had asked herself the same thing over and over while she was with Donald.

"I said, do you love him?" Rourk's expression was calm but the edge in his voice gave her no doubt as to how he felt.

Keegan put her hand on his knee and shook her head. "No, I didn't love Donald. I could never bring myself to say the words. I'm not going to lie—I cared about him a lot, and I still do."

"Did you two—you know?" Rourk looked away, staring into the distance. His face was hard.

"Huh? Did we what? Oh... Did we have sex?" She smiled, touching his face gently. "We didn't have sex. Never even came close to it."

Rourk's entire body relaxed and he let out a barely noticeable sigh.

Keegan wanted to kick the ground. All the pain she had caused Rourk... Curious, she couldn't help but ask. "Would it have mattered if I had been with him in that way?"

"It would tear me apart, but it would not change how I feel about you. I'm glad you were not." Rourk lowered his eyes, one of his hands coming to rest atop hers on his leg.

Keegan gave him a shy smile, scooting closer. "I guess I have been saving myself for you."

"Keegan, I want you to be with me because it's what you want. I don't want you to feel obligated because of the bond." He sounded worried, his statement coming faster than usual.

It broke Keegan's heart that she had hurt him for so long. Now the man she was meant to love—the man she loved—seemed to not think her feelings were real. *What do I say to make this right?*

"We're elves, Rourk. This is what we do. I've dreamed of meeting my chosen since I was a little girl. We got sidetracked, that's all. I believe we are exactly where we are meant to be." Keegan looked up at the sky and spread her arms wide. "Someone up there believes we are meant to be. Who am I to argue with fate? I'm not going anywhere. I want to learn everything about you, and spend as much time with you as I can." Hoping she had said the right thing to prove her love, she rested her head back on his shoulder.

"I'm so glad you said that, Keegan." Rourk closed his eyes briefly, one arm slipping around her shoulders so he could hold her tight. "I have been worried you were angry the bond was back. I thought maybe you were wishing it could be changed."

Laughing, Keegan said, "If I were angry the ground would be frozen. I'm not angry. I was just caught by surprise."

He pushed her away so he could look at her, one hand brushing her hair back. "Thaddeus told me about the frozen issue. He also said that Donald was able to help you control it. What if I don't have that same affect on you?"

Keegan thought it was cute that he had focused on *that* part of the freezing. "I've gotten better at controlling my temper. I've been using my father's breathing exercises and my mom gives me distant healings, which help keep me calmer." She paused. "It's too bad that issue didn't go away when the bond came back. I guess that would be asking for too much."

"It could be a good tool to have."

"Always thinking like a soldier..." Keegan teased.

"It's what I am."

Keegan jumped up, putting both her hands on his shoulders. He was so gorgeous when he looked surprised. "I just realized something. You are going to be in Washington and that's where Anna goes to school— in Seattle. Maybe I can transfer there next semester." Excitement lit up her face and her cheeks flushed. "I'm going to have to start researching the schools."

"You would do that?"

"Of course. Don't tell my parents, but I really don't care for Alaska. I mean it's beautiful and all, but the malls close early, and I don't have any real friends."

Rourk's grin was wry. "Your secret is safe with me."

Keegan plopped back down on the rock. "Ouch." She rubbed the side of her leg. "I can't believe we have to be separated soon. When will you move to Washington?"

Rourk pulled her towards him. "It depends. Two to four months. Definitely by the beginning of the new year. I will come see you every weekend unless training prohibits it. Plus, I'll have time off for the holidays."

That made her remember her Christmas present. "Speaking of holidays, I never told you thank you for the lens. I've been keeping a scrap book for you of photos I've taken."

"Really? I can't wait to see it."

"Well, you will have to wait. It's at my apartment in Alaska."

"How do you like having your own place?"

"I hate it. It's so quiet. I need to get a dog." Keegan grinned. "I always pictured us having an English bulldog named Santa."

Rourk laughed loudly. "That's pretty funny. I say next weekend we go in search of a bulldog."

Keegan threw her arms around him and squeezed him. "We're going to have so much fun together."

Rourk stood up and pulled her with him. "It's getting late. I should probably head home."

Keegan pouted. "I don't want you to leave. Maybe you can stay the night."

He lifted an eyebrow. "I don't think that would be appropriate."

"Well, then let's just stay up all night out here."

"Are you sure? Your parents might get upset."

"Are you kidding me? They are so excited our bond is back, I don't think they would care what we did. Plus, I'm eighteen now." She smiled sweetly.

"Ok, let me call my father and let him know I won't be home tonight." Rourk pulled his phone out of his pocket and flipped it open, walking away as he made his call.

Keegan watched him, thinking it was adorable he still had an old school phone. He probably didn't even have a laptop. She would have to bring him into the technology world.

Rourk strode back towards her. She loved his confident walk. "You were right. He was thrilled to hear the bond was back and happy to hear we are staying together tonight."

"I told ya. So, what do you want to do?" Keegan rocked back and forth on her heels.

"I don't care as long as I am with you. We can sit here all night, or go for a drive. What time is it anyway?"

Keegan looked down at her phone. "It's almost midnight. We could always go to an all-night diner and have some coffee."

"That sounds great. Should you run in and tell your parents?"

"Nah, they are probably asleep. I'll send my mom a text though, just in case."

They walked back down the path to the house and towards Rourk's truck. When Keegan saw the tiger sitting in the middle of the driveway, her heart ached for Donald. Rourk must have felt her tense, because he turned and saw the shapeshifter, too.

Rourk kept his eyes on the feline while he opened the door, and Keegan slid into the truck. The tiger walked closer and Keegan's heart raced as she thought, *Is he going to attack Rourk?* She watched as the two of them stared at each other. Finally, the tiger turned and slowly stalked away.

Once Rourk was in the truck, Keegan turned towards him. "I'm sorry I've made such a mess of things."

"I told you, it's not your fault. Hopefully, the shapeshifter is smart enough to realize there is nothing he can do to change things. As much as I hate the thought of him being around you, I know what it feels like to lose you, and I feel somewhat bad for him."

Keegan sighed, letting her head fall back to the headrest. "Thank you for being so understanding. I'm sure this has all been hard for you."

Rourk glanced over at her, and then back to the road as he put the car into gear and aimed for the road. "You have no idea. I'm just glad it's behind us and we can move forward."

Keegan slid over in the middle so she could be closer to him. She placed her hand on his thigh and laid her head against him. "Did it feel this natural when we met the first time?"

"Yes." His lips brushed her hair. "It felt as if we had known each other our whole lives in an instant. The memories of the time we spent together were the only things that kept me going."

"You will have to tell me all about our time together. I have the photographs, I just don't have the story behind them." Keegan wanted to remember more than *anything*, but no matter how hard she tried, it was impossible. It made her want to cry that she had lost those memories of him.

"Another day," Rourk answered quietly. "Today, I want to enjoy the present and not worry about the past."

"Ok. Why don't you tell me about your training?" Keegan sat up so she could watch him in the dim cabin. Every so often a car would pass and the headlights would illuminate his face.

"There's not much to tell. It's not that much different from the elfin military training. It gets frustrating sometimes because I know better ways to do things, but I can't let on. I'm in the weapons training. It's pretty amazing how advanced some of the weapons are."

Keegan laughed. "I was just thinking when I saw you with your old school flip phone that you weren't very technologically inclined. Do you even have a laptop?"

"Should I?

"Ah yeah, how else am I going to talk to you when we are separated? Put that on our list of things to do when you come visit. Actually, we'll do that tomorrow. So you can have it for Monday. Do you have your own room?"

"Yeah, we have our own rooms now. They are pretty small but they work. It's nice to have the privacy."

"I probably can't come visit you, can I?"

Rourk thought about it for a minute. "I think it's best if you wait until I get to Fort Lewis, in Washington. I don't like the idea of you coming into the barracks. I should be able to get my own place there. I'll probably have Tommy as a roommate."

Keegan shrugged. "Ok, as long as you come visit me."

"Every chance I get. You will probably get sick of me."

"Somehow I doubt that."

Rourk pulled into the diner and parked. They strolled inside, their arms wrapped around each other.

After they were settled with menus and drinks, Keegan stared at Rourk across the table. "How did this happen so quickly? I went from not knowing anything about you to feeling like we have been together forever."

"I think we can thank your brother." Rourk's half-smile made her heart skip a beat.

"Yeah, I was probably a little too harsh with him." Keegan looked down at her ring and back up at Rourk with a look of pure adoration. "A magical ring."

They stayed up for hours talking and driving before ending up in the woods, where they watched the sun rise. Rourk dropped her off as the sun had finally crested over the horizon and the birds were singing their morning songs.

Keegan stood in the front doorway, watching his truck pull away and felt a deep sadness wash over her. She felt like chasing after the truck and jumping in.

Chapter 4

When Keegan walked through the door, she found her mother at the kitchen table reading a book.

Her mom laid the book face down and looked up. "I take it you had a good night?" she said, then took a sip of tea.

Keegan sat down across from her mom and rested her chin in her hands with a sigh. "It was wonderful. Do you always feel like this around Dad?"

Her mother smiled. "Of course. It's the way it works."

"Do you guys feel electricity when you touch?" Keegan slumped back in the chair, a wistful smile on her face.

"Yes. Not that your father doesn't drive me crazy at times, but overall I feel happiest when he is around."

"So the electricity thing doesn't go away with time?" Keegan raised an eyebrow.

"No, but you do get used to it though. Once it becomes normal, you don't notice it till you're separated and he returns."

Keegan stood up and rubbed her stomach, grimacing. "I'm going to grab something to eat. My stomach feels a little funny."

Walking over to the bread box, Keegan opened it and pulled out the loaf. She dropped a couple of slices into the toaster. When it was ready, Keegan buttered it and topped it with some cinnamon.

"Where's Thad?" she asked.

"In his room, as usual," her mother answered, flipping her book over and turning the page.

"Ok, I'm going to go talk to him." Keegan chomped on the toast as she mounted the stairs. She couldn't stop smiling, thinking about her time with Rourk.

Just before her hand hit the door to knock, her brother yelled, "Come in."

"Even after all these years it's still freaky when you do that." Keegan opened the door and glanced around at his nearly empty room.

It always looked strange to her that Thaddeus only had a bed and a dresser. It was never really messy in his room, either. Between the stark white walls and the blah carpet, it looked like a hotel room instead of that of a teenage boy.

Everybody likes different stuff, I guess, Keegan told herself. She walked over and sat on Thaddeus's bed to watch as he killed zombies on the Xbox.

She let him blow some stuff up first before she finally spoke. "Thanks for bringing back the bond. I'm sorry I acted like a jerk earlier."

"It wasn't really me. Anna did most of the work." He didn't bother to turn around. His fingers were flying over the controller buttons.

"Really?" Keegan said, surprised. She stared at his head full of short, auburn hair. "Well, I guess I need to thank her."

"Probably a good idea." Thaddeus paused. Keegan wasn't sure if it was for effect or because he couldn't speak for too long of a period and play at the same time. He went on. "She thinks you are mad at her."

"Ugh. I forgot to text her back." Keegan searched for her phone in her pockets, but it wasn't there. *Must have left it downstairs.* "I lost track of time with Rourk. I still can't believe he is my chosen. He's everything and more of what I used to dream as a little girl."

"He's a good guy. You better not mess up your chance with him." Gunshots rang from the television and more zombies fell.

"I won't." She stood up to leave, and swayed. She reached out with one hand to grab the bed post and steady herself. Her head felt so light. "I'm going to go lay down for a bit. I'm not feeling so hot."

Thaddeus took one hand off the controller and waved it in her direction. His eyes were still glued to the TV. "Shut the door on your way out."

"Yeah, yeah. We all know you like your privacy. You really should get out more."

For the first time since she came in the room, Thaddeus actually looked up at her. Granted, it was a glare and it lasted two seconds before he went back to his game, but it was acknowledgment.

Keegan giggled. Some things never changed. She had to admit, she did miss having her little brother around.

Speaking of little brothers... Keegan thought, frowning. She had barely seen Warrick since she had been home. After her nap, she'd have to go find him.

She closed Thaddeus's bedroom door and walked down the hall to her own room. Her head was pounding. *I'm probably just tired from staying up all night*. And there was the time difference from Alaska, too.

Keegan walked in her bedroom and looked around. She smiled. Her sweater was still on the back of the chair, and her brush was on the floor. Her mother had left everything exactly as it was the day she left.

She missed being home. College was cool and all, but she was lonely in Alaska. At least Rourk would be coming to see her; that brought a smile to her face.

She was exhausted from staying up all night. She peeled off her clothes and crawled into bed, dozing off quickly.

Next thing she knew she woke up to a sharp pain in her chest and a horrible pain in her stomach. She felt like she was having a panic attack—or what she imagined must be what a panic attack.

Keegan picked up her phone and texted her mom. *Can you come here?*

She curled into a ball beneath the covers and took a few deep breaths, trying to get past the pain. A couple minutes later there was a light knock at the door before it opened.

Her mom came through—a shadow in the pale hall light as it spilled into the dark room. "Keegan? What's wrong?"

Keegan felt a little better having her mom near. "I think I need a healing. My chest and stomach hurts. Maybe I ate something bad."

Her mother walked up to her bed and sat down, the bed springs squeaking. She touched her hand lightly to Keegan's head. "It wasn't something you ate. It's the bond."

Her mother's hand was cool and comforting. Keegan's eyes widened and she clutched the pillow beneath her cheek. "What do you mean 'the bond'?"

Her mom gave her a wry smile, barely visible in the dim room. "Like everything in life, there are consequences to having a magical bond. It cannot be perfect. Rarely can you get pleasure without pain." She shifted on the bed. "When you are separated from your chosen, you are going to experience physical pain until you are reunited."

"What? Why didn't anyone ever tell me this?" Keegan pulled the blankets up to her chin with a grimace. *I'll have to deal with this often?*

"And ruin the excitement of meeting your chosen?" Emerald ran a hand through her short hair. She stared at Keegan, her brow furrowed. "There usually has to be great distance between you to cause this much discomfort. Rourk doesn't live that far away."

"You're telling me that if Rourk came back the pain would go away?" Keegan eyed at her mother skeptically.

"Yes. The closer he gets, the more the pain lessens." She brushed Keegan's hair back, her eyes shiny in the dark. "I always know your father is on his way home long before he arrives."

"Dad is gone so much! I've never noticed you to be in pain."

"I am a healer, Keegan. My body heals itself, although it cannot heal the heart. So, my heart aches—much like yours is now—until your father comes back."

"Well, that's just lovely," Keegan said sarcastically. She pulled the covers higher with a *humph*. "Is Rourk in pain now?"

"Yes, Keegan." She pursed her lips. "You may not have realized, but Rourk was in pain the whole time you were separated."

Keegan's heart skipped a beat and a flood of anger filled her. She hated that she had caused him physical pain. "Why didn't I feel pain before?"

"He was always close by before your bond broke. If you recall, you went into that slump once you couldn't see him again."

"I can't believe he's been in physical pain since he left to join the military."

"Your father is glad for the pain. He says it makes him never forget me. Rourk probably feels the same way." Her mother's eyes softened. "He loves you, Keegan."

Keegan was silent as she processed all the information her mother had given her.

Her mom put a gentle hand to Keegan's face. "Do you want me to give you a healing?"

"No. I'm going to call him. To see if he will come back. I want him to tell me that what you say is true. "

Her mother laughed. "You always have to see things to believe them. Call him."

Keegan made the call and within minutes, the pain had subsided. She waited impatiently in the kitchen with her mother, pretending to drink hot chocolate. Her heart fluttered when she heard the knock from the front hall.

Keegan hurried to let him in. She flung the door open and wrapped her arms around him. "I'm so glad you came. Were you in pain?"

Rourk pulled back and looked down at her. "You were in pain?"

"You weren't?"

Rourk's hair was tousled as if he'd just rolled out of bed. He was wearing the same pair of pants and shirt as he'd worn the night before.

Keegan thought he looked beautiful. But then she felt guilty for pulling him out of bed and all the way to her house in the country after neither one of them had gotten much sleep. *I'm so selfish*, she thought.

"Not really pain," Rourk answered, cupping her face in his hands. "There was a slight discomfort, but nothing like when I am far away from you." Rourk glanced over at Emerald.

She met his eyes but said nothing.

"How much pain on a level from 1-10?" Rourk demanded, his eyes on Keegan's.

"I don't know. Maybe a 6? I'm not good at measuring pain."

Rourk wrapped his arms around Keegan and pulled her to him before saying, "Emerald, is that normal?"

Her mother shrugged. "No, Rourk. Not as far as I know. However, since my healing energies heal me, I never feel the full affect. Maybe we should call Katrina or Brigid. They would know better."

Rourk nodded. "Please."

Emerald grabbed her phone from the table and dialed. She smiled at Rourk when Katrina answered. "Hey sis, I have a question for you. When Drew is gone, how far away does he have to be in order for you to feel the pain of his absence?"

Her sister was silent for a moment on the other end of the line. "Well, that's an odd question. Hmm, I would say at least four hours away."

"Four hours!?" Emerald closed her eyes. "Ok, thanks, was just wondering. I'll explain more later, but suffice it to say that Keegan and Rourk got their bond back."

Emerald pulled the phone from her ear and they could all hear Kat's "Woohoo."

"I swear Kat, you are just as bad as a teenager. I'll call you later." Emerald hung up the phone and turned to face them.

"So, this is not typical. Keegan you always have to be the exception don't you?" Her mother took a deep breath and looked at Rourk.

Keegan pulled away from Rourk's embrace and crossed her arms. "Hey, I didn't even know *anything* about any of this till I woke up tonight with the worst pain ever."

"We're not blaming you, Keegan," her mother said. "I'm worried this might have something to do with the black magic."

"Maybe our bond is just stronger than most." Keegan smiled at Rourk.

Emerald shook her head. "I've never heard of anyone's bond being stronger than others. Elfin bonds should be equal across the board. You have been around enough elfin families to know that."

"Well, you did say I was exceptional." Keegan smirked.

"I would have to agree with that statement." Rourk rubbed the back of her neck. His calloused fingers sent chills down her spine.

"Focus you two. This is serious. Soon you will be separated several thousand miles. What if the pain gets worse with distance?" Emerald paced back and forth deep in thought.

Rourk dropped his hand and sat down in one of the chairs. With his elbows on the table, he let his head drop into his hands. "I can't stand the thought of Keegan being in pain because of me."

Keegan walked over and put her hand on his shoulder. "I'm sure it won't be that bad. It's worth it to be with you."

Rourk looked up surprised. "Do you mean that?"

"Of course I do." She turned her back to him and plopped down on his lap, wrapping her arms around his neck.

Rourk buried his head in her shoulder. "I'm so sorry, Keegan. The last thing I wanted to do was cause you pain."

"We won't even know how bad it is until I get to Alaska. Where are you stationed right now anyway? I guess I should have asked that earlier." *I can really be an airhead*, she thought with an inward chuckle.

"Fort Bragg, North Carolina. A long way away from where you are."

"Well, soon you will be in Washington, and that is much closer. I need to start looking into transferring schools."

Her mother glanced up, eyes wide. "I think that is a great idea! Why don't I come back to Alaska with you so I can be there if you need a healing. I can do the distance healings, but they are not as effective. Maybe your brother can figure something out with magic to help lessen the pain."

"That sounds great, Mom." Keegan didn't want to admit it to herself, but the thought of having her mom in Alaska made her happy. She'd been so lonely and bored living so far away.

"I need to go work on some healing remedies. I'll see you guys later, ok?"

"Thank you," Rourk told her with a grin.

Emerald just smiled and disappeared through the doorway.

Chapter 5

Keegan turned her attention back to Rourk. "What do you want to do today? I know one thing for sure. I am not leaving your side until I have to board the plane." Rourk squeezed her hand and looked away.

But Keegan saw the distress on his face. It was obvious that it *killed* him he was causing her pain. And they both knew there would be more to come.

"I don't really care. We could just hang out together. If you want, we can go on an actual date." Keegan ran her hand up the side of his arm, unable to resist touching him. "I think that would be fun. We have so much to learn about each other."

His face lit up. "I would love to go on a date with you. Do you have anything special in mind?"

Keegan thought for a moment. "There's a new movie out I've been wanting to see. We could do a repeat of our first date." She gave him a sly smile. "I think it will end much better this time."

"Pizza and a movie sounds good." He gently kissed her forehead.

Keegan yawned. "I didn't get much sleep. I'm still tired. Let's go in the living room so I can lie down."

Rourk sat in the corner of the couch so that Keegan could stretch out with her head on his thigh. He ran his hands through her hair, staring at her face as her eyes fluttered shut. She was sleeping in a matter of minutes.

Rourk thought about how lucky he was. He leaned his head back against the couch and worried about being separated from her again. A sharp pain pierced his heart. He almost wished he hadn't signed up for the human military. But, he made a commitment, so he brushed the thought aside. He and Keegan would figure something out. They had to…

Keegan stirred. Her cheek was numb from Rourk's leg. *How long was I asleep?*

She rolled over and looked up at him. He was rubbing his eyes. "Did you fall asleep too?" she asked, giving him a sleepy smile.

Rourk nodded. "How are you feeling?"

"Much better after a nap." She stretched out her legs and wiggled her toes. "I'm hungry."

"Aren't you always?"

"Hey!" She swatted his arm. "Yeah, I guess I am always hungry. I like to eat. What can I say?"

Keegan rolled to a sitting position and stretched. She stood and offered her hands to Rourk, pulling him to his feet. They moved into the kitchen.

"I can make you something to eat if you want." Rourk stood behind the grey granite counter. She noticed it matched his eyes.

"Are you sure? You know how to cook?" She was skeptical.

"Yes." He laughed. "I know how to cook. I cooked for you at the cabin. I know you don't recall—I made you vegetarian meals."

"Umm, Ok, sure. You really seem too good to be true." Keegan smiled at him and waved towards the kitchen. "It's all yours."

"Your mom won't mind?"

"My mom spends as little time as possible in the kitchen. She won't care, I promise."

Rourk walked over and peered into the fridge. "Your mom keeps the fridge stocked."

"Well, we are a house full of elves with big appetites."

Keegan watched as he took out some vegetables. He washed and chopped the celery and carrots expertly, then grabbed the ranch dressing out of the fridge and placed it before her. "Here. Snack on this while I cook something up."

She picked up a piece of celery and dipped it, then smiled. "I guess I'll keep you around."

Rourk walked around the counter to where she sat on the stool. "I sure hope so because I can't lose you again."

Keegan bit her lip and looked up, her eyes sparkling. "I'm not going anywhere."

Rourk leaned down and kissed her. One of the amazing slow and passionate kisses she'd come to expect from him.

"You must have driven the girls crazy," she murmured as he pulled away.

Rourk shook his head. "It's so odd you don't recall our time together. Keegan, you are my first and only girlfriend."

"What? Are you serious? You're so hot. I don't believe it." Though, if she was going to be honest, she loved the thought of being the only one for him. The thought of anyone else having ever kissed him made her the tiniest bit jealous.

"I've never been interested in anyone but you. Although, if Tommy had his way I would be dating half the state." Rourk chuckled and went back to cooking.

"Oh really—I can't wait to meet this Tommy character." She narrowed her eyes, pointing her half-eaten celery stick at Rourk as menacingly as she could.

"Character is a good word for him. You'll like him."

Rourk pulled out chicken and cut it into strips as the pan was heating up. Keegan found that she loved watching him cook. He looked so at ease in the kitchen, which was odd because he screamed soldier when you saw him in public. She really couldn't wait to find out more about him.

She smiled to herself. *We have a lifetime ahead of us to do so.*

"What time is your plane leaving?" Keegan asked, crunching into another celery stick.

He didn't turn to look at her, but his voice was subdued. "Tomorrow at 9 pm. It was the latest flight out I could get."

Keegan shifted uncomfortably on the stool. "I'm leaving at 6pm. I have a long flight. And classes Monday morning."

He was silent a moment. "This is going to be hard."

"I know," Keegan said. She sighed. "I've never felt this way before. I feel panicked at the thought of being separated from you."

Rourk looked down at the pan and moved the chicken around. "I know. I'm not looking forward to leaving you. I just got you back. It's going to kill me to see you get on the plane."

Keegan realized she was choked up, and didn't answer. Instead, she covered a carrot in dressing and ate it.

Rourk scooped up the chicken and placed it on a bed of lettuce and tomatoes then sprinkled some shredded cheese on top. He placed it in front of her along with the dressing. "I hope this is good enough."

Keegan gave him a look of adoration. "It's perfect. Go get yours so we can eat."

They ate in silence, neither wanting to talk about the fact that they would be saying goodbye soon. Keegan felt anxious anytime she thought about him leaving her. *Please let it not be as bad as I think it will*, she thought.

After they ate, Keegan said, "I'm going to jump in the shower, then we can go shopping for your laptop."

Rourk grabbed her hand and pulled her towards him. "I'll be right here when you get back." His kiss sent fire through her body.

She smiled, then turned on her heel and ran up the stairs. Her cell phone was laying on her desk. She grabbed it and sent Anna a text. *Thank you!*

You're welcome. Everything is good?

Perfect other than we have to be separated tomorrow.

Yeah, that sucks.

Guess who is moving to Washington next semester.

NO WAY! We should be roommates.

That would be crazy!

Ok I have to jump in the shower. I'll talk to you once I get back in Alaska. Bye.

Keegan held the phone tight to her chest with a huge grin across her face. She jumped in the shower and got dressed in record time. *I'm glad I left so many of my clothes here instead of taking them all to Alaska*, she thought as she shimmied into a pair of faded jeans. She pulled on a pale blue sweater, and then quickly applied some mascara and blush. One last look in the mirror, and she ran back downstairs to Rourk.

He was sitting on the couch with her father. He jumped to his feet when she appeared. "You look great."

Keegan felt her cheeks flush. "Thank you. Are you ready to get out of here? Do you want to go to your house and get changed?"

Rourk looked down at his day-old clothing and shrugged. "I guess I should."

Keegan looked over at her father. "Tell mom, we are going out and we'll be back later tonight. I doubt we'll be home for dinner. We have a date tonight." Keegan wrapped her arms around Rourk's waist and squeezed him tightly.

"Have fun." Her father turned back towards the TV.

Keegan grabbed a coat from the closet. "We'll drive to Nashville to get the computer. The stores are better, and they have better restaurants."

"Whatever you want is fine with me."

When they walked into Rourk's house, Keegan was surprised how comfortable and homey it felt. "Have I been here before?"

"Yes, when you picked me up to go away for the weekend. To the cabin. I'll be right back."

Keegan was amazed at how quickly Rourk showered and changed. *Must be nice to be a guy*, she thought. *They don't have to worry about make-up or what to wear.* He was even sexier than normal fresh out of the shower, with his hair still damp and his shirt sticking to his chest. She couldn't keep her eyes off of him.

Rourk ran his hand through his hair subconsciously. "Is something wrong?"

Keegan waved a hand in front of her face. The room felt hot. "No, I just can't believe you're mine."

Rourk laughed. "I can't believe you feel that way." Rourk strode toward her and wrapped his arms around her. He pulled her tightly against him and bent down to inhale the scent of her hair. She had a woodsy sent about her that he found very sexy.

"We better get going. We have a long day of shopping ahead of us." Keegan grinned, squeezing him tight around the waist.

"Then we should go." With a smile, Rourk took her hand and led her out the door.

They merged onto the highway and passed beneath a large green sign for Nashville. Keegan was glad to see traffic wasn't bad at all, so it would be a quick drive. She loved going shopping.

"What kind of music do you like to listen to?" Keegan asked as she changed the stations.

Rourk shrugged. "I don't really have a favorite. Whatever you like is fine. I don't normally listen to music."

Keegan was aghast. "We are really going to have to lighten you up. Ok, well, what do you like to do with your free time?"

Rourk chuckled, then said, "I enjoy hiking, reading, running, shooting, training. You now the usual things."

Keegan crinkled her nose. "You sound like my brother. He's so boring."

Rourk laughed loudly. "I'm sure I'll have more excitement in my life now that you are part of it."

Keegan grabbed his hand and lightly traced her finger in circles on his skin. "I sure hope so."

They talked during the hour drive. Though, looking back, Keegan realized she did most of the talking, which seemed to be fine by Rourk.

When they got to the mall and found a parking spot, Keegan hopped out of the truck and said, "Ok. We have to go to the Apple store. My father will never let me live it down if you don't get a Mac."

"I'm clueless about computers," Rourk said honestly. "You can pick it out and I'll pay for it. I trust your advice."

"Sounds good to me." Keegan hurried forward, excited to get to the mall. She realized Rourk wasn't beside her, and twirled around. He was lagging behind, with his hands shoved in his pockets.

"Hurry up, slowpoke!" Keegan called, laughing.

Rourk shook his head, amused, and lengthen his stride to catch up with her.

For hours, Keegan dragged him into countless stores. Rourk spent at least a month of his military pay. He didn't mind at all.

Chapter 6

Today was their last day together at least for a few days.

Keegan felt sick to her stomach at the thought of leaving him. It didn't seem fair; they had just found each other.

As if he could read her mind, Rourk reached over and ran his hand through her hair. "It will only be a few days. I'll be coming to see you Friday night and we'll have all weekend together."

Keegan pouted. "That's so far away."

Rourk laughed. "It's not that far away. It's nothing compared to the year we spent apart."

Keegan's face fell and guilt flooded her. "I feel horrible that you were miserable for a year while I was out having fun with my friends."

"There is nothing to feel sorry for, Keegan. You didn't know. We can't change what the black magic did, we can only move forward." He kissed her gently on the lips. "It's the way of the elf. We weren't supposed to meet until we turned eighteen, anyway."

Keegan laid her head against him. "I guess you're right. It still sucks though."

Warrick ran into the room giggling and breaking their sorrowful silence. Keegan smiled and scooped him up. "You're going with me tonight. You better not throw a fit on the plane."

Her little brother stuck his tongue out.

Keegan laughed and put him back down. "Go play with your blocks or something."

As Warrick ran away, headed for the toys, Rourk stared after him with a smile. "It must be pretty neat to have siblings," he said.

Keegan heard the wistfulness in his voice. It had never occurred to her that Rourk was an only child and that it could be a lonely thing. To lighten the mood, she rolled her eyes. "That's one way to put it. Although, I have to admit it would be odd to be an only child. You must have been lonely growing up."

"I didn't know any better. Being alone was normal to me."

"Keegan, Rourk, come have some breakfast." Her mother peeked out of the kitchen. There was a streak of flour on her cheek that made Keegan laugh.

They walked to the table hand-in-hand.

"Are you packed? We have to leave by 3:00." Her mother stood at the stove, scooping the last remnants of scrambled eggs from the skillet. She looked at Keegan.

Keegan reached over and pushed some eggs on her plate. "No, but I'm only bringing my backpack so I don't really have much to pack. It will just take a few minutes."

"Do you mind if I drive you guys to the airport?" Rourk asked before taking a sip of his juice. "I'd like to spend as much time as possible with Keegan."

Emerald' eyes twinkled as she glanced over at him. "That would be nice of you. I'm sure Keegan won't object."

Keegan felt her face turning red. "Are you sure you need to come with me mom?"

"It's better to be safe than sorry. We're not sure how the distance will affect you. I have to run to the store today and get a rose quartz necklace for you. I'm going to charge it with healing energies and hopefully that will ease some of the discomfort."

Rourk finished chewing his toast, then said, "Having a healer in the family comes in handy."

"Yeah, especially when Keegan was little. She was quite the daredevil. I lost count of how many times I had to fix her up after one of her stunts." Her mother had a faraway look—a slight smile on her face as if she was visualizing a memory.

"I can picture that." Rourk squeezed her hand across the table.

"Come on Mom, I wasn't *that* bad."

"Whatever, Keegan." Emerald turned to lean against the counter and crossed her arms. "Then where did all the scars on your legs come from?"

Keegan looked down at her plate and shrugged. "Ok, maybe I was that bad."

"Where did you get that scar?" Rourk touched a long gash on her shin. His finger made her shiver.

"We were at a camp in Maine, and I thought the water was deeper than it was when I jumped off the dock. Turned out it wasn't very deep at all, and I landed on a huge rock."

Thaddeus walked in as she was speaking. When she finished, he said, "A dare devil klutz—quite the combination."

Keegan threw a biscuit at him, but Thaddeus just caught it and took a bite.

Rourk had stayed quiet during the exchange, watching them interact. "You guys have a great family. My house is always so quiet."

"Well, get used to it. You're part of the family now. Lucky you." Thaddeus smirked.

Rourk looked over at Thad with a serious expression on his face. "Thanks to you. I will forever be in your debt for bringing back our bond."

Thaddeus gave him an impish grin. "You might take that back after dealing with the drama queen for a while."

Rourk grinned and shook his head. "Somehow I doubt that." He paused, his eyes on Thaddeus's. "Seriously, thank you."

Thaddeus shrugged. "No problem."

Emerald set her mug down on the table. "What are you guys going to do today?"

Keegan looked over at Rourk. "Not sure. I guess just hang out around the house. Maybe we'll go for a hike. I also want to look online at the schools." Keegan turned towards Rourk. "Speaking of online, we need to set up your computer and make sure you know how to use it for our chatting. Come on, let's go to my room."

Emerald raised an eyebrow, but didn't say anything.

Rourk glanced around her room, taking it all in. He noticed a picture of Keegan with the shapeshifter on her nightstand. Keegan caught his gaze. "Sorry." She leaned over and took the photo down.

Rourk took it from her hands and stared at. "You looked happy."

Keegan shrugged. "He's very funny, and we had been friends for years."

"That's what worries me. I'm not exactly fun, Keegan. I'm not known for my sense of humor. What if you grow bored of me?"

Keegan smiled and met his eyes. "I think you are the sexiest, most exciting man I have ever met. Just the thought of getting bored of you is laughable. You are an elfin warrior. How could you possibly be boring?"

Keegan loved the way his eyes crinkled when he smiled.

"I love you Rourk. I've never loved anyone else," she said softly.

Rourk needed to hear her say that. "Every day for the rest of my life, I am going to try to show you how much you mean to me."

Keegan walked over to where he was sitting on the edge of her bed. She bit her lip, reached over, and put her hand behind his head. Electricity shot through her when their lips met. She closed her eyes and enjoyed the sensations that rushed through her body. When they finally pulled apart. Keegan grinned. "Yeah, I don't think you have anything to worry about. Definitely not boring."

Rourk shook his head and laughed. "Let's get this computer set up."

Keegan pulled the new laptop out of the bag and plugged it into the wall.

It didn't take too long to get the account set up, and Keegan showed him the basics of Skype. He didn't even have an email account, so she set that up as well. Who didn't have an email account these days? He did have a military account, but that didn't really count since they couldn't correspond that way.

"All done. We still have some time. What do you want to do?"

"We could go for a walk? We've been inside all day."

"Sure, want to go to my favorite spot? I'll bring my camera."

"I'd love to. Although I have been there many times already."

Keegan looked surprised. "Oh really?"

"Yes, when you used to think of me it would mentally beckon me. Many times I watched you taking photos or sitting on the rocks, thinking."

Keegan gave him a funny look. "You know that's pretty creepy."

"I know." His smile was chagrined. "I couldn't help it. I tried, I really did. I just couldn't stay away from you."

"Anyone else I would call the cops on." She held her hand out for him to grab. "However, since it's my fault for always thinking about you, I guess it's ok. I hope I didn't do anything embarrassing."

"Just make a few spills once in a while, which only made me crazier about you. You would always grin when you tripped."

"I've actually gotten much better with my balance since I started training with Thaddeus and my mother."

"Well, now you can train with me."

"I can impress you with my ninja skills." Keegan gave him a sly smile.

"Everything about you impresses me."

"See, that's why I love you so much." Keegan led him out of the room and down the stairs.

"Do you think we should pack a lunch?"

Rourk involuntarily flinched and tensed up as he recalled the memory of Keegan eating lunch in the woods with the shapeshifter. He needed to push all of that behind him and just look forward. The was no sense holding onto all of the jealousy he felt. "Sure, lunch sounds great. Do you need some help?"

"I got it." Keegan packed up their lunch and they went out for a couple of hours. Already the sadness was starting to set in at the thought of leaving Rourk so soon.

Keegan stopped to pick up a rock and Rourk continued on ahead. She tossed the rock back and forth between her hands as she watched him walk. His shoulders were so strong and broad... Grinning, she dropped the rock and ran up behind him and jumped on his back, latching on to him. Rourk laughed and spun her around.

Keegan kicked her legs. "Put me down."

"Nope, I'm carrying you the rest of the way. You don't weigh much more than a ruck-sack."

Keegan laughed. "Ok, but don't blame me when your back hurts."

They reached the creek and Rourk let her down.

The woods stretched around them and the creek twisted before them. Some of the trees were already bare, but many were still crowned by red and orange that lit like fire in the sunshine.

They walked to the edge of the crystal clear water, their shoes crunching on dried leaves. Keegan looked around, closed her eyes, and took a deep breath. "This is my favorite spot on earth." She grasped Rourk's hand, smiling. "Now I get to share it with you."

"Thank you. That means a lot to me."

"Do you have a favorite spot?" Keegan asked.

Rourk shrugged. "No, I just love being outdoors; it really doesn't matter where it is. I don't have a particular spot. Although, there is something about the Tennessee woods that makes me feel at home."

"Do you want to move back here when you are out of the Army?"

Rourk tilted his head and looked at her closely. "I figured we would move back here since your family is here. Is that what you want?"

Keegan thought about it for a minute. "Yes, I would like to come back here. As long as we can still travel."

Rourk turned to face her, cupping her face in his warm hands. "I would love to see the world with you."

Keegan just smiled, a flush covered her cheeks. She took the blanket from him and spread it over the ground, before pulling out the sandwiches and drinks.

"Sit down so we can eat." She gestured for him to sit next to her.

Rourk complied. He popped open a can of soda and leaned back on his hand. "Keegan, I have not felt this at peace in a very long time. It's almost too good to be true."

"Don't jinx us. This is wonderful, but I will be leaving in a couple of hours." She stared at him intently, memorizing the expression on his face. "I don't want to be away from you, Rourk."

Rourk leaned forward "I know. Just remember—I will be thinking of you every minute and counting them down until I can visit you."

They spent two hours relaxing by the creek and learning more about each other. Finally, it was time to pack up and head out to the airport.

Keegan felt a lump in her throat thinking about it.

Chapter 7

Keegan took a last look around her room, saddened to leave it again. It hadn't been that long since graduation, really. Not very long since she'd moved to Alaska. But it *felt* like ages. She hurt to leave her room behind. So many things had changed...

"Come on, Keegan, we can't miss the flight." Her mother yelled from downstairs.

"I'm coming!" she yelled back, exasperated. She grabbed her bag from the bed and hurried back down the stairs.

Rourk took the bag from her hand and threw it over his shoulder. Keegan smiled as she stared after him—she loved how broad his back was. He turned slightly and reached his hand out for her. She grabbed it and squeezed, feeling the connection from his body to hers.

Keegan jumped in his truck and scooted into the middle so she could be as close to him as possible. Her mother and Warrick were settled in the backseat. Warrick was already screaming because he didn't want to be buckled into the car seat.

Keegan laid her head on Rourk's shoulder and didn't speak for most of the ride. She was afraid if she talked about it, she would cry. There was no sense in making it harder on Rourk than it already was.

Keegan peeked up at Rourk and noticed his jaw was tense. She reached up and ran her finger along his jaw and smiled when he relaxed. They exchanged a quick glance, but neither of them spoke.

When they arrived at the airport, Rourk pulled into the garage and found a spot. While her mother wrestled with Warrick, Keegan and Rourk got their bags out of the truck.

The walk inside was just as silent as the drive. Keegan held Rourk's hand, her own palm sweaty and her heart aching at the thought of leaving him. Her mother was subdued as well.

Outside the security line, Rourk turned to Keegan with sad eyes. Emerald stepped away from them, making a show of fussing over Warrick so that they could say goodbye.

"I'll stay here till the plane leaves," Rourk said, touching his forehead to hers. "I wish I could go back and wait with you."

"Me too. I don't want to say goodbye." Keegan closed the space between them and flung her arms around his neck. She couldn't hold back the tears any longer.

"I will be there in a few days. It will go quickly." Rourk tilted her chin up so she could meet his eyes. His grey eyes looked pained.

Keegan rubbed her face with the sleeve of her jacket and tried to give him a smile. "I'm sorry. I promised myself I wouldn't cry. I'm such a baby sometimes."

Rourk gave her a sad smile. "Just a few days."

Keegan turned and walked towards the security line. She glanced back to find Rourk staring intently at her. He was breathtaking to look at. He stood as still as a statue, his eyes only on her.

She grabbed her phone from her coat pocket. *Miss you already xoxos*

She grinned when she saw him reach into his jeans and pull out his flip phone. A wide smile broke across his face. He looked so cute pecking away at the keyboard.

Miss you more. I love you Keegan don't forget that

Never. I love you 2 I'll text you when we land.

Thank you. I guess texting isn't so bad after all. Rourk replied.

They finally boarded the plane. Keegan felt a strong urge to run off the plane and back into Rourk's arms. Instead, she plopped into the seat and folded her arms across her chest. "This sucks."

"I know, honey. Here put this on before we take off." Her mother pulled a gaudy pink crystal necklace from her bag and held it out.

"Couldn't you have picked a better color? You know I don't look good in pink. And it's so clunky." Keegan grabbed it from her mom and smiled when she felt the energy radiating of it. "Wow, Mom, that's powerful."

"I had to use rose quartz. It's the love stone. I'm hoping that on top of the healing energies, it will keep the pain at bay. Here let me put it on you."

Emerald reached over to clasp the necklace around Keegan's neck. Warrick kept trying to pull it off. *This is going to be a long flight*, Keegan thought with a sigh. At least they were in first class so they had plenty of room.

She grabbed a magazine and started flipping through it. When she realized she wasn't even looking at the pages, she shoved it back in the pocket of the seat. She wondered if Rourk had left yet. Probably not. He would wait until the plane was in the air.

About thirty minutes later, they finally took off. Her mother kept glancing over at her, worry lines on her brow.

Keegan rolled her eyes. "I'm fine, Mom. I'll let you know if I feel any pain."

Her mother nodded and started quietly reading a book to Warrick. After a couple moments, he grabbed it from her hands and threw it across the seat. Her mom sighed and pushed a strand of hair behind her ear.

Warrick started crying and pulling on his ears. Keegan watched as her mom placed her hands over his ears and the crying stopped instantly. Keegan secretly wished she had been born a healer. Her power of invisibility was cool and all, but she rarely got to use it.

The further they got in the air, the tighter Keegan's chest felt. She grabbed her mom's hand and squeezed it, gasping.

"How bad is it?" Her mom reached over, placing a hand on Keegan's forehead.

"It's just in my chest. Feels funny, like a tightening."

"Not in your stomach?"

"No, just my chest." Keegan put her hand over her heart and grimaced. It felt like her heart was in a vise as it slowly cranked shut.

"Great, the necklace is working." Her mother smiled and sat back in the seat.

"What do you mean *great*? It hurts."

"I know it hurts," her mom whispered. "But I cannot heal the heart, you know that. This pain you just have to learn to live with."

"Wonderful." Keegan threw her head back against the seat.

"Just take some deep breaths and try to relax. Hopefully you can fall asleep. This is a long flight."

"Thanks for the reminder." Keegan stretched out her legs and turned her head to the side. "Let me see Warrick."

Her mother handed the baby over.

Keegan stuck out her tongue and made funny faces. Warrick giggled loudly when she acted like she was going to gobble up his hands. He eventually got tired and fell asleep, so Keegan handed him back to her mother, thankful he had been a distraction at least for a little while.

The pain in her chest hurt, but it was bearable. She closed her eyes and thought of Rourk. She was surprised that she could actually see him. He was walking around in his house packing his stuff. Keegan watched as he sat down on his bed and buried his head in his hands. Keegan's heart ached for him. She watched as he stood up and walked to the kitchen and grabbed a drink.

Keegan opened her eyes and shook her mom's arm. "Mom, I can see Rourk when I close my eyes."

Her mom smiled sleepily. "Of course you can. He is your chosen."

"But we're so far away. I thought that only worked when we were close by like at the house."

"No, you can see him anytime you close your eyes and think of him. Unless he decides to block you."

"Well, that's better than the webcam."

"Eventually your bond will grow stronger as time passes, and you can speak to each other with your mind."

"Seriously?" Keegan's eyes were wide.

"Yes, but it takes a lot of energy. Your father and I rarely do it unless something important is happening. It's just easier to pick up the phone and text." Her mom turned her head where it was against the headrest and eyed her. "Don't overuse the gift to see your chosen. Make sure you give him privacy. "

"I'll try, but it's so fun." Keegan closed her eyes again.

Rourk was now in the living room talking to his father. Keegan wished she could hear what they were saying. Rourk had his forearms resting on his knees and was leaning forward while his father talked. She watched as he stood up and walked into his room. He grabbed his backpack and headed towards the door. He walked out without turning to his father one last time. They must have already said their good byes.

Her mom shook her arm. "Keegan, I told you not to invade his privacy."

"What? I was just trying to sleep." Keegan said innocently.

"Sure you were," her mother said, shaking her head. "That's why you have a goofy grin across your face."

Keegan laughed. "He's just so cute!"

Chapter 8

Rourk was waiting to board the plane and he couldn't stop smiling. He leaned back in the hard plastic chair, not seeing anything around him.

All he could see was Keegan.

The bond had returned. He had really believed she was lost to him forever. Now, she was his once more and all they had to do was make it through this separation period. That would be easy compared to what they'd already been through.

Rourk hated to admit it, but he was upset that Keegan wanted to postpone their handfasting. It was tradition after all. When elf mates turned eighteen, they were wed—it was how it had always been and always would be.

However, at this point, he was willing to wait if that was what Keegan wanted. He just hoped nothing came between them again. He didn't think he could handle losing her a second time.

How did his father make it through the day without his mother? The very thought of Keegan dying... Rourk couldn't even think about it.

His phone dinged in his pocket, and his heart dropped. Multiple scenarios of Keegan in pain flashed through his mind as Rourk fumbled to get his phone out of his pants. When he flipped it open, relief flooded his body.

Landed. I'm fine. The necklace worked.

The thudding in his chest calmed to a dull ache. Rourk took a deep breath and let it slowly before tapping out an answer. *That's great. I was worried.*

If I close my eyes I can see you :)

Rourk chuckled. *I know. You forget I feel a pull when you think of me.*

Ack! You knew I was watching you?

Well, I knew you were thinking of me.

Sorry, my mom says I should give you privacy.

He didn't think he could ever text as fast as she could. He typed his reply. *I don't mind. I love knowing I crossed your mind.*

A crackly voice over the loudspeaker announced it was boarding time for his flight. Rourk didn't want to say goodbye, even if it was only for a couple hours.

Gotta board plane. I'll text you when I land.
Ok. Love You xoxoxos
I love you.

Rourk took a deep breath and acknowledged the pain that tore through his chest. A reminder of their bond. A pain he would gladly bear.

Flipping his phone closed, Rourk stood and shoved it into his pocket. He walked to the counter, where he handed off his ticket to a slender brunette with an honest smile.

He had a long flight ahead of him, and he had to switch planes in Chicago. Thankfully, the first flight passed uneventfully and actually landed on time. He wasn't so lucky with the second flight, which was on a two hour delay—and almost stretched to three hours.

He sent Keegan a text. *Landed in Chicago.*
YAY! It's late here so going to head to bed soon. Text me when you get home so I know you made it safely.

Warmth flooded his body. It was something simple—just a girlfriend who wanted to know her boyfriend returned home safely. But it made him feel alive.

Ok.
Night xoxo
Goodnight.

Keegan held the phone to her chest and sighed.

She was propped against the headboard on her bed, sitting in the semi-darkness of her bedroom. A triangle of light spilled across the floor from the open bathroom door, illuminating the fluffy purple rug that covered the hardwood.

Her mom and Warrick were already fast asleep on the fold-out couch in the living room; she couldn't hear a peep from them. Her room felt quiet and empty. Something was always happening back home, with her parents constantly in and out and her brothers yelling and stomping around. Even knowing her mother was in the other room, Keegan still felt homesick.

Since she had been in the air all day, she felt kinda gross. She pulled off her sweater and stepped out of her jeans, throwing both on the floor. Keegan walked into her little bathroom and stood in front of the mirror beneath the harsh globe lights. She lightly touched the necklace and smiled. With her fingers still on the chain, she closed her eyes and searched for Rourk.

He was nodding off in a chair at Chicago O'Hare. Keegan recognized the airport from all the times her family had flown through it—it was one of the major international airports that had flights all over the world. Rourk was slouched so that his head rested on the back of the black chair, and his hands were clasped tightly over his chest. His military backpack rested between his feet.

Keegan felt a rush of pride. He was hers.

She opened her eyes with a sigh, and reached back to unhook the necklace. As soon as the chain fell from her fingers to the bathroom counter, searing pain rushed through her body. Keegan dropped to her knees with a cry, hanging on to the edge of the sink. She tried to reach for the necklace but the pain intensified. She curled into a ball on the cold tile floor and clutched her stomach.

"MOM!" Keegan screamed.

Her mother was by her side in an instant. Emerald immediately noticed the necklace on the bathroom counter and snatched it up. She dropped to her knees to clasp it around Keegan's neck. "Oh Keegan, I'm sorry. I should have warned you not to take off the necklace."

While Keegan cried silent tears and the pain subsided, her mom pulled a towel from the rack and covered her. Emerald wrapped her arms around Keegan and asked softly, "Are you ok?"

Keegan wiped her eyes and nodded.

"Are you still in pain?"

Keegan nodded again and wrapped her arms around her stomach, letting her weight rest against her mother. They sat silently for a moment, Emerald slowly rocking Keegan until she calmed down.

Emerald brushed Keegan's auburn hair from her face, then cupped her daughter's cheek as she said, "Put on some clothes and go lay on your bed. I will give you a full healing."

Keegan used her mother's hands as support so she could stand. She slowly made her way into the darkened bedroom and fumbled through her dresser for some pajamas. Each movement was painful. She stepped into her clothes as another tear left a cold trail down her cheek.

Keegan couldn't believe something as beautiful as their bond could cause this much pain. The pain had eased slightly once her mom put the necklace back on, but there was still a deep throbbing throughout her body.

Emerald put her arms around Keegan and guided her to the bed. "Close your eyes. It will be over shortly."

Keegan laid back on the soft bed and closed her eyes. She pictured Rourk as she took several deep cleansing breaths. Her mother's hands felt like they were on fire when she placed them over Keegan's stomach.

Despite the uncomfortable heat, it was as if her mother's hands were drawing all the pain out of her body. Keegan could feel it coursing beneath her skin and into her abdomen, where it disappeared into her mom.

Within minutes the pain was gone.

Keegan pushed to her elbows, trying to sit up.

"Shhh, stay still, Keegan," her mom chastised. "I want to give you a full healing. It will take another twenty minutes. Just lay there and relax."

Keegan must have fallen asleep, because the next thing she knew she awoke and her clock said it was 7:00 am.

Ugh, I do not want to get up and get ready for school, she thought irritably. The damn necklace was making her neck itch. It wasn't very comfortable to have a giant rocks hanging on her chest—especially sleeping with said giant rocks.

She stretched beneath her covers, putting off leaving the warmth of her bed for the cold of her room. Sounds from the kitchen indicated her mother was up and around, so Keegan finally headed for the bathroom.

After brushing her teeth and hair, she grabbed her black and white polka dotted robe and went out to the kitchen.

Her mother was sitting at the table, her fingers tapping gently on her steaming mug of tea. She was still in the sweats she'd slept in, her short hair sticking up wildly on her head. Emerald looked up, her brow furrowed in concern. "Feeling ok?"

Keegan shrugged, tugging her robe tighter. She slid into a seat at the small table. "Yeah, I feel fine. Just the throbbing pain in my heart. I guess I'll get used to it. That's nothing compared to the pain last night. I'm glad you were here."

"I'm sure you won't forget to leave the necklace on now." Her mom gave her a wry grin.

Keegan looked down at her chest and picked up the crystal necklace, angling it to catch the early morning sunshine. She let it drop. "Mom, it's so ugly. Couldn't you have found something better looking? "

"No, I told you it had to be rose quartz. You are lucky I was able to find those stones and have the necklace made in such a short amount of time."

Keegan recalled the pain that ripped through her body. She looked over at her mom and quietly said, "Thank you."

"You're welcome. Do you want me to make you some breakfast before you go to class?"

"Sure. How long are you staying?"

"I was thinking I'll stay 'till Thursday since Rourk is visiting on Friday. I don't want to be in the way."

"That sounds good, Mom." Keegan smiled. She was really pleased to have her. "I'll show you around town when I get back from classes."

Emerald eyed her daughter. She cleared her throat and shifted in her seat. "Keegan, are you sure you don't want to tie the knot?"

Keegan fought the urge to roll her eyes. She really did understand why her family was so set on it—and Rourk too—but she had to be true to herself. "I'm sure. Not right now. Just give me some time. It's not like we are going anywhere."

"I'm going to start planning anyway," her mother said as she stood. She wandered to the fridge and pulled the eggs from it. "It will be fun. We can look at dresses if you want."

"What part of I'm not getting married anytime soon don't you get?" Keegan grumbled.

Her mother ignored her. "It takes forever to find the perfect dress, and it's never to early to start. Plus, you know you love trying on dresses."

Keegan watched as her mom cracked several eggs into a large bowl and began whisking them. *How does she do it?* Keegan wondered, shaking her head. *I'm actually excited at the thought of trying on wedding dresses.*

She didn't want to admit defeat, but pretty dresses won *every* time. "Well, I guess it couldn't hurt to try on a few."

Her mother grinned. "It's settled, then. We'll look while I'm here."

"Shopping is pretty lame here, Mom. Trust me on this. Let's just wait 'til my next visit." Keegan jumped up to pour herself a glass of orange juice.

"Fine." Her mom sighed and poured the eggs into the pan.

Keegan took her glass of OJ and went back to her room to get her phone. She texted Rourk, but when five minutes passed and he didn't reply she figured he was busy training. She had to stop herself from closing her eyes and checking on him. This newfound gift was going to be hard to resist.

She refilled her juice back in the kitchen as her mom set the table for breakfast. Keegan had to admit it was nice to have her mother there to cook for her again. It was good to have the company.

"This is great, Mom." Keegan filled her plate with food and took a seat across from her mother.

"Glad you approve. Your brother doesn't seem to agree."

Keegan smiled warmly at Warrick as he tossed his eggs on the floor. "He doesn't know what he's missing."

There was no sound but for the clink of their silverware and Warrick's occasional laugh as he tossed more food beneath the table.

"Thanks for making breakfast," Keegan said when she was finished. She dumped her plate in the sink and kissed her mom on the forehead. "I need to go see if I can find something to wear that matches this necklace."

"It's not that ugly, Keegan. I think it's quite pretty."

Keegan raised an eyebrow and smirked at her mom. "Uh huh. Whatever you say, Mom."

In her bedroom, she stared into her closet and thought, *I need to go shopping*. Since she hadn't brought a lot of her wardrobe with her to Alaska, she was seriously lacking.

She decided on a white off-the-shoulder sweater. If she had to wear the necklace she might as well put it on display. She pulled out a pair of loose-fit jeans and slipped into them. What was she going to wear for shoes? She had to walk around campus so she decided on her frayed white Converse sneakers.

Keegan put on some light makeup. She liked the neutral look—a bit of pale, pink blush and shimmery eyeshadow with some clear lipgloss. Her mother always told her natural was best. She curled her hair in front of the bathroom mirror, leaving it to hang down in big waves.

Good enough, Keegan thought, unplugging her curling iron.

The dolphin earrings that Donald had given her for Christmas were resting on a corner of the sink. When she saw them, her heart felt heavy. She wondered how he was doing and if he would ever talk to her again. It pained her that she had hurt him so deeply.

Thaddeus *did* say Donald would find someone else. That was one small ray of hope. Keegan was glad to know he would find happiness. He deserved to be happy.

Keegan enjoyed the time she spent with her mother and Warrick. The apartment was usually so quiet. Being able to come home from school and see them was wonderful.

They did some of the touristy things around town that Keegan had always wanted to do. Warrick loved the train ride up the mountain, where the snow was thick on the evergreen trees. Keegan took them to the wildlife sanctuary she had been volunteering for, where she introduced them to the staff and animals.

Her mother didn't care to have pictures taken, but Keegan made them humor her. She got some amazing shots of her mom and her brother. Alaska was a beautiful place for photography enthusiasts. She filled an entire memory card—it would keep her busy editing after they were gone.

When the time came for them to fly home, Keegan felt stronger with the underlying pain that came from the bond. Her mother's constant help and healing had prepared Keegan for her absence.

She was sad to see them go, but also excited.

Rourk would be there soon.

Chapter 9

Keegan woke up elated on the morning of Rourk's arrival. As she stood before the bathroom sink brushing her teeth, she was stricken by the thought that for the first time, she and Rourk would *really* be alone. The idea made her shiver in expectation…and in nervousness.

Is today the day I lose my virginity? She thought as she tossed her toothbrush into the holder. Goodness! She certainly hoped so!

She wondered if she should go to the drug store and get some protection. Although, Rourk did seem like the kind of guy that would take care of something like that. Plus, it would be so embarrassing for her if she had to. She decided to leave that up to him.

Keegan tore through her underwear drawer trying to find something sexy. She laughed as she picked up her *Hello Kitty* underwear. That would not work. Maybe she should go shopping. It would give her something to do while she waited for him to arrive.

Yes, she thought, nodding to herself. She threw on pair of sweatpants and a *Save the Dolphins* t-shirt and drove to the mall.

If you could call it a mall. As she parked the Jeep in the nearly empty lot, she thought it looked more like a dingy strip shopping center. It was a large, yellow brick square with dirty glass doors and cracked sidewalks. Unfortunately, it would have to do. She had no other option.

There was a big department store, so she went there first. All the underwear seemed so adult. Either too sexy or too old looking. She picked up a pair of granny pants and stared at them in disgust. Finally, she decided on a pair of black boy shorts with matching bra. At least she would match. She couldn't wait to get home and try them on.

On second thought, she was already at the mall, so she might as well stop at Starbucks and get a white chocolate mocha. Keegan smiled and strolled down the hall looking in the windows but not really seeing anything. Only three more hours and Rourk would be there. She had butterflies in her stomach and couldn't seem to wipe the goofy grin off her face. People probably thought she was crazy, but she didn't care.

When she got home, she decided to take a quick shower. By the time she finished getting ready, it would be time to pick up Rourk from the airport. She grabbed her phone and texted Anna. *Ack Rourk will be here soon!*

YAY!

Have you heard from Lauren? She never returns my texts anymore.

She hasn't been talking to me either, Anna replied.

Keegan stared at Anna's text, worried. *I hope she is okay.*

Maybe we can go visit her next week.

That would be cool. I can afford to miss a couple of days of classes. Actually, she would be happy to miss school.

Have fun with Rourk and I want DETAILS!

Of course. Xoxos. Keegan smiled when she hit send.

She turned the shower on as hot as she could stand it and stepped into the tub. The water felt great as it pelted her skin. She used her special scented soap: sandalwood and vanilla. She wanted to be perfect for Rourk.

The necklace felt so heavy and annoying in the shower. She had to remind herself to be grateful for it. Keegan lathered up her legs to shave while she was singing at the top of her lungs to one of her favorite Adele songs. She wished she had a voice like that girl—Adele sang like an angel.

She nicked herself as she was dancing. *Damn it! That's what I get for not paying attention.*

Keegan toweled herself off and pulled on her new underwear set. The bra had a bit of lace to it and the bottoms were just plain black. She twirled around in front of the mirror, checking herself at all angles. She shivered at the thought of Rourk's hands on her body. *How did I get so lucky?*

In her room, Keegan pulled out a dress she had found shopping with her mom. She had fallen in love with it when she saw it on the hanger. It was a v-neck dress with small ruffles down the buttons. Halfway down the fabric, there were cute ties on the side. She wanted the blue, but went with the gray, because it would match the necklace better. She pulled it over her head and brushed down the front to smooth it out. Keegan grinned and touched the little cap sleeves.

She looked over at the clock: one hour to fix her hair and makeup. She had put her hair in a bun in the shower so she didn't have to wait for it to dry. She sat down on her vanity desk and let her tangled mess of hair fall free from the bun. She smiled; she wouldn't have to do too much to her hair. It was nice and wavy from being wrapped up.

Keegan decided she didn't want to go overboard with the make-up. It seemed guys didn't like make up as much as girls did. Who would have guessed it? At least, that's what Donald and crew said. Keegan felt a pang of guilt when she thought of Donald. He always said she looked best without a trace of make up and her hair wild. He had always made her feel beautiful.

Keegan shook off thoughts of Donald, and went back to her make-up. When she was done, she had about twenty minutes left. She couldn't stand waiting in the silence of the apartment, so she grabbed her cardigan and went to the airport.

She couldn't wait to see his face; she was so tempted to try to visualize him in her mind. Her mother was right—it wasn't fair for her to check up on him all the time. Besides, she was going to have him there in the flesh in a few moments.

She parked the Jeep, jumped out, and shuffled inside. She was lost in thoughts of Rourk, and slammed into an older guy who was walking out of the building.

"I'm sorry," Keegan told him with a slight smile.

He smiled back and said, "No problem."

She walked up to the board just inside the doors to see Rourk's arrival gate. His flight was advertised as Gate B6—and was on time—so Keegan took a deep breath and tried not to run in that direction.

In just a few moments, my chosen will be walking through the entrance, she thought. The airport was busy since it was a Friday evening, but Keegan found a bench and sat down, watching people greet each other. She realized she had forgotten her camera. She smiled. *Oh well, we will have a lifetime of photos ahead of us.*

Keegan felt the pain in her chest subsiding. He was closer. She stood up when she saw people coming through the gate. Her heart was pounding so fast. She scanned the crowd, searching for his face and her heart skipped a beat as his intense grey eyes met hers. He walked confidently towards her with his back pack slung across one shoulder. She loved the plaid shirt he had on over his plain blue t-shirt. He was wearing cargo pants and looked like a model out of an outdoor magazine.

She rushed forward as he approached and flung her arms around his neck.

Rourk laughed when she caused him to lose his balance. "I take it you are happy to see me?"

She pulled his head towards hers and kissed him lightly. "You have no idea. This week seemed to drag on. I couldn't get you out of my mind."

Rourk laced his fingers with hers and they walked outside. "Well, I'm here now. All yours for the weekend."

Keegan narrowed her eyes. "You better be all mine forever."

Rourk grinned and shook his head. "You know I am."

"Are you hungry? Do you want to go out to eat or just head to the apartment?" Keegan asked, her heart fluttering at the thought of taking him home.

"Let's just head to your place. It was a long flight. I can always cook us something to eat."

When they got to her Jeep, she handed Rourk the keys. "You can drive. You need to learn your way around since you will be visiting me so often."

Rourk grabbed the keys and threw his bag in the back seat. He had to push the seat back quit a bit. "You are tiny."

Keegan blushed. "Well, female elves aren't known for being huge."

"I think you are perfect." Rourk leaned over and kissed her softly. She loved how she felt when their bodies connected. She couldn't wait to get him back to the apartment.

Keegan caught him up on her visit with her mom. She pretty much chattered non-stop until they reached her apartment. Once they pulled in, Keegan suddenly felt shy and nervous.

Her hands shook a little as she unlocked the front door. She flung the door open and dramatically announced. "This is it! My first home of my own."

Rourk stepped through the doorway and looked around. The living room was brightly decorated, showing off Keegan's personality—which was a stark contrast to his plain room. He took in the black couch with purple and pink throw pillows in front of a big flat screen TV. The floors were hardwood with strategically placed throw rugs in bright colors. There was a lime green ball hanging down from the ceiling as the light. He really hoped she didn't plan to decorate their place like this.

"So what do think?" Keegan's face lit up and her eyes sparkled.

"It's interesting. It certainly looks like it belongs to you," he answered honestly.

Keegan clapped her hands together. "I love it. My mom and I had so much fun decorating."

"Where do you want me to put my bag?" Rourk asked.

"You can just leave it by the door or put it in my room down the hall."

Rourk tried to hide his surprise. He set the bag down by the door. He hadn't even thought of their sleeping arrangements.

"Do you want to eat first?"

"Sure, I'm hungry."

"Me too." Keegan opened the fridge. "How does a frozen pizza sound? We can watch TV and eat."

"That works. Do you need me to help with anything?"

"Nope. Do you want a soda?"

Rourk walked into the kitchen and took the can of soda from her hand and set it down on the counter. "I just want to look at you for a moment."

Keegan felt her face flush. "Umm, ok. That's kinda weird."

"I missed you so much." Rourk took his finger and lightly traced the side of her face, sending shivers through her body.

"Me too." Keegan's voice was barely over a whisper.

Rourk wrapped his arms around her and pulled her close. He laid his chin on her head and inhaled. "I love the way you smell."

Keegan wiggled to get her head out from under his chin and looked up at him. "I love you."

Rourk smiled, "You better get that pizza in the oven. I know you get cranky when you are hungry."

She swatted him on the arm. "Well, if someone hadn't come in and interrupted me." She pushed him out of the kitchen. "I'll be out in a minute."

Keegan watched him through the doorway while she unwrapped the pizza. She was afraid she was dreaming and someone was going to pinch her and she would wake up. It was all too good to be true. She threw the pizza in the oven and hurried out to join him on the couch. She didn't want to be apart from him, even momentarily.

She sat down and felt the electricity race through her body when her thigh touched his. She wanted to drag him into the bedroom, but figured she would let him make the first move. Instead, she reached down and grabbed the remote off the glass coffee table. "Do you want to watch anything in particular?"

Rourk shook his head no. "I don't really watch TV."

"Well, you are in luck. How does a show about vampires sound?" Keegan laid her head on his thigh and kicked her feet up on the couch.

"Sure. Sounds good."

After they ate the pizza, and the show was over. Keegan felt butterflies in her stomach. It was time. She looked up at Rourk. "Are you ready to go to bed?"

Rourk glanced around. "The couch will be fine."

"The couch? You came all this way. I finally have a place to myself, and you want to sleep on the couch? No way! You are sleeping in my room."

Keegan pulled him up and lead him towards her room.

"Keegan, I don't think this is a good idea. I don't know if I can control myself around you."

"Who said you had to control yourself?" Keegan gave him a sly grin that she hoped looked sexier than it felt.

Chapter 10

Rourk tensed as Keegan lead him into her bedroom. *Why hadn't he thought of this? He had been so thrilled to spend time with her he hadn't even thought of sleeping arrangements. Maybe he should have stayed in a hotel.* He really didn't know if he had the self control to resist her. She was so incredibly sexy.

Keegan turned and grabbed his hands pulling him the rest of the way into her bedroom. Rourk glanced over at the huge bed that took up most of the room. She slid her arms around his waist and smiled sweetly up at him. The electricity coursed through his body. Keegan took a couple steps backwards, pulling him with her, and then fell back on the bed giggling.

Rourk stared down at her. She was biting her lip and looking up at him expectantly. He closed his eyes and let the tension release from his body as he leaned down and got lost in her kiss. Keegan ran her hands through his hair and the kiss intensified. Rourk broke away and Keegan pulled him back for more. His mind screamed stop, but his body wouldn't listen.

She lifted up his shirt and ran her fingers up his chest. Rourk couldn't breathe.

"Keegan, don't." He pushed her hand back down.

She looked surprised. "What did I do wrong?"

Rourk rolled over to the side. "You didn't do anything wrong. I just don't trust myself."

"What do you mean you don't trust yourself?"

"Keegan, I want you so badly. I don't think I can stand being alone with you like this." He ran his hand through his hair, his brow knitted together. He couldn't meet her eyes.

"I want you too, so there *is* no problem." She reached for him again and he pulled away. Keegan sat up as Rourk stood beside the bed.

"It's against tradition. I know it's old fashioned, but I strongly believe in tradition." His voice was absolute.

Keegan's eyes widened. "You are my chosen. We're bonded, so it's ok. I want this, Rourk." She reached out for him. "I want you."

"We're not married. Why do you think elves get married so soon after they are bonded?"

"I don't know. I never really thought about it." Keegan flopped back onto the bed and rested her head on her hand.

"Keegan, I'm sorry. I can't. I know you want to hold off on the handfasting and I can accept that. However, you have to accept that we will not have sex until we are married. This is really important to me."

She sucked in her breath. "Are you serious? I bought matching underwear today. I can't believe you are turning me down."

"I'm not turning you down. Don't be ridiculous. I want you more than I've ever wanted anything in my life. I would marry you right now, and spend all weekend in bed with you."

Keegan sat up and pulled her knees to her chest, wrapping her arms around them. "I don't want to get married just to have sex. I'm still not ready to get married."

"You know I will wait forever for you." Rourk reached over and tucked a strand of hair behind her ear. "You just tell me the date and time and I will be there."

Keegan wiped a tear from her cheek.

"Why are you crying?" His voice sounded panicked. "I don't want you to cry."

"I don't know. It's stupid. I was excited and nervous thinking I was going to lose my virginity today, and now I feel like an idiot. My own chosen doesn't want me." Keegan threw a pillow across the room, her anger obvious.

Rourk was worried she would turn the room into a block of ice. "Keegan, look at me."

She slowly raised her head to meet his eyes, a sullen look on her face.

"I'm sorry you don't agree, but this is who I am. You say that you love me right?' Rourk asked gently.

Keegan nodded.

"Well, you need to love this part about me as well." Rourk reached out to take her hand. "We have a lifetime to spend together, and I'm sure plenty of it will be spent in bed. Let's just spend this time getting to know each other more. Ok?"

Keegan wiped her nose with the back of her hand and nodded. "Will you still sleep in my bed with me?"

Rourk hung his head. "I can't. I'm sorry."

"I promise I won't attack you in the middle of the night."

Rourk took a deep breath. "I hope I don't regret this. Yes, I'll stay in here."

"Thank you. I'm going to change into my PJ's I'll be right back." Keegan rummaged through her drawer looking for the least sexiest thing to wear and then headed to her bathroom. She came out a few minutes later wearing Power Puff Girls pajamas. "How's this?"

"You look adorable." Rourk noticed she still had the necklace on. "Come here."

Keegan walked over and Rourk stood up. He put his hands around her neck to unlatch the necklace. Keegan jerked away. "No, don't take it off. It hurts too much."

"Keegan, I am here you don't need it anymore."

She looked skeptical. "Are you sure?"

"Trust me." He unlatched the necklace and set it on her nightstand.

Keegan grinned. "No pain." She reached up and kissed him. Rourk hesitantly returned the kiss.

"Don't worry, Rourk. I promised, so you need to trust me." She kissed him again.

"It's not you I don't trust, it's me. This is much harder than you can imagine. I've lain awake many nights dreaming of being alone with you."

"You have? Seriously?" She crossed her arms across her chest. "You're not just saying that to make me feel better?"

"Of course not, Keegan, you are beautiful and you are mine. I want to explore everything about you. I just want to wait until you are my wife."

"That's really sweet." Keegan pulled his hand to her lips and kissed it.

"I know you're tired after that long flight. Why don't you get changed and we'll try to get some sleep." She crawled under the covers.

Rourk left to grab his backpack from the living room. He changed into a pair of shorts and T-shirt. He wished she would just agree to marry him so they wouldn't have to deal with this. It was almost funny—Keegan had been torturing him since he first laid eyes on her. He should be used to it by now. He would endure anything she threw his way.

He got under the covers and she snuggled up against him. She fit perfectly in his arms.

Rourk ran a hand through her hair, his other arm tucked tightly around her small frame. She was asleep in no time. He lie awake awhile, listening to her breathe. His last thought before he dozed off was *I am the luckiest man on the planet.*

Chapter 11

Keegan woke up and flung her arm across the bed to find it empty. *Was her night with him a dream?*

She rubbed her eyes and sat up, the blankets falling away from her. She looked around for any proof that he had been there, but saw nothing but the faint indentation in her purple satin sheets. She flopped back on the bed and grabbed the pillow next to her. Bringing it to her face, she pressed its softness to her face and breathed deep. *Yep, he's real.* She loved the smell of him—he smelled like the woods.

But where is he? She jumped out of bed and tugged her favorite robe from the hook over her door. It was a fluffy lavender robe from Target that had been worn so many times the elbows were going thin, but she loved it. She stepped into some slippers and went to search for him.

Love swelled in her chest as she stopped at the doorway of the kitchen. The early morning sunshine slanted through the window and illuminated him. His hair was mussed from sleep, sticking haphazardly up, and he was in a pair of sweatpants and a t-shirt. Keegan had never known him in such an intimate aspect.

Rourk was hovering over the coffee pot. He jabbed at a button; then, he frowned and punched another. When nothing happened, he swore under his breath and jerked the coffee pot out, glaring at it.

Keegan smirked and shook her head at his troubles with the coffeemaker. She closed her eyes and called on the power inside her. The tingling sensation that accompanied her main power of invisibility rushed through her body: starting from her head and claiming her body all the way to her toes. She loved to sneak up on people.

She tiptoed forward until she was right behind him.

"Need some help?" she asked and was disappointed when he didn't jump.

"I didn't hear you." Rourk turned wide eyes in her general direction. His brow furrowed as he searched the room for her.

Keegan let go of her power, and her body shimmered back into view. "I would hope not. What would be the fun in being invisible if you could be heard?"

His smile was huge. "I've never seen you use your power. Do it again."

She closed her eyes, relishing the familiar sensation as it ran through her body, and she was gone.

Rourk laughed. "Ok, you can come back now. I'm impressed."

When she appeared beside him, Rourk turned and grabbed her around the waist. "I wasn't sure you were ever going to wake up. It's almost 9:00."

Their lips touched lightly, and Keegan felt hot and restricted beneath her robe. She stepped away. "What time did you wake up?"

"Five-thirty. Same time I usually wake up."

Keegan crinkled up her nose. "Yuck. I can't believe you willingly get up that early on a weekend. What have you been doing?"

"Not much. I stayed in bed for awhile. Then I figured I'd come see what you had to make for breakfast. However, I can't seem to figure out this thing." He gestured to the coffeemaker where it sat innocently on the counter.

She reached over and flipped a switch on the side, and it started making noise. "That's because it's set to automatically go off at 9:30 on the weekends. I like to wake up to the smell of coffee."

"That is a great smell to wake up to," Rourk agreed, pulling her close once more. This kiss was tender and slow, and he tangled his hands in Keegan's long hair, drawing it out. When he finally pulled away, he murmured, "How does french toast sound?"

"Yummy, that's one of my favorites." Keegan rubbed her hands together.

As he opened the fridge to pull out the eggs and milk, Keegan took a seat at the table, tucking her legs underneath her as she watched him. He turned on the stove and cracked a couple eggs in a bowl, then said, "Do you have any plans for us today?"

"Yes, we're going to pick out our puppy. I found a local breeder."

Rourk chuckled, whisking the egg mixture with a fork. "I almost forgot about the bulldog."

"I can't believe you already forgot about a member of our family." Keegan placed her hand to her chest in mock surprise. "We aren't going there till three so I thought I could show you around town, and where I go to school."

"I'd love to see where you have been spending your days." Rourk dipped a piece of bread in the mixture and slapped it in the pan. It started sizzling on contact.

"We might even get lucky and see the northern lights while you're here." Keegan's eyes lit up. "It's the most amazing thing I have ever seen in my life. Wait until you see the pictures." She paused. "Actually, you should see them in person. If we don't see them this weekend, I'll show you the pictures."

"That is something I would like to see," Rourk replied. He flipped the three pieces of toast cooking in the skillet and glanced at her.

Keegan stood and held up a finger as she walked backwards for the door. "I do have something to show you though. I'll be right back." She banged into the door frame and made a face, rubbing her elbow.

Rourk laughed.

"Not funny." She stuck her tongue out. She found the brown leather album on the desk in her living room. It was thick—much thicker than Keegan had meant for it to be.

She brought it back to the kitchen and placed it on the table. "These are the photos I've been saving for you. I took them with the lens you gave me."

Rourk brought her a plate of french toast and a mug of warm syrup. He sat down across from her and reached for the album. Slowly, he turned the pages and took in parts of Keegan's life he had missed.

Keegan reached over him and pointed at a photo. It was a close-up of dark gray rocks; the power of the lens allowed the droplets of water on the surface to stand out. Speaking through a mouthful of toast, Keegan said, "Those were taken at my favorite spot with the fisheye lens."

"They're beautiful, Keegan. You are really talented." He turned the page.

Keegan pointed with her fork at the page he was on. "That's a bunch of graduation and prom pictures. I had my mom take some for you."

Rourk looked over at her, one of his hands splayed across a picture of Keegan in her slinky gray prom dress. "So you took all of these photos especially for me?"

"Yeah, it was my father's idea."

"Keegan, this is an amazing gift." Rourk's voice was soft and full of emotion. "It means so much to me, knowing you were thinking of me as these photos were snapped."

He turned his smoky eyes to hers, and she thought he had the most intense eyes of anyone she had ever met. Keegan knew he meant everything he said one hundred percent. "I'm glad you like it. Why don't you finish making your breakfast and then we can see the rest?"

After Rourk had his own plate, Keegan paged through the album and told him about each photo as he ate his food. When she closed the last page, both of their plates were empty.

Rourk cleared his throat. "Thank you."

Just those simple words coming from him made her feel so happy. She reached across the space between them and ran her fingers through his hair. "You're welcome."

"I'm surprised you are not going to school for photography. Those shots are amazing."

Keegan sighed, dropping her hand to her lap and fiddling with the drawstring on her robe. "I've been seriously considering changing my major and going to an art school for photography."

"Why don't you?"

"Well, I've dreamed of being a marine biologist since I was old enough to know what one was," she said simply and shrugged. "I feel like I'll let my parents down if I don't go through with it. I really do love science and marine life. It's just not as much fun as I expected."

Rourk took her hands into his. "You should do what makes you happy. Your parents would not be disappointed as long as you were doing what you wanted to do."

"I've actually been looking into art schools in Seattle. I'm just not sure. I think I'll feel like a failure if I don't finish my biology degree." His hands were so much larger than hers; they were so much more creased and calloused.

"That's silly, Keegan. You can always do both if it's that important to you."

Keegan let go of his hands and pulled at her sleeves. "What I would really like to do is photograph animals. I would love to get some underwater photos of dolphins and other marine life." She shrugged. "That's probably silly."

Rourk reached over and pulled her into his lap. He swiped one hand through her hair, his skin warm as he rested his palm against her cheek. "It's not even slightly silly. I think that is an amazing idea. You could get the best of both worlds."

"You really don't think it's crazy?" She bit her lip, one hand playing with the hem of his T-shirt. Her heart thudded as she waited for his answer. His opinion meant so much to her.

"I really don't. But, it's your choice, so you need to decide what is best for you."

Keegan grinned. "Well, the photography program is much shorter. Which means we could get married sooner."

"I'm not going to lie. I like the sound of that." Rourk kissed her, a slow, lingering touch of his lips. When he pulled away, he caught her eye and said, "Whatever you decide, I'm beside you."

Wrapping her arms around his neck, Keegan squeezed. She was embarrassed to find she was a little teary-eyed. She took a deep breath, drawing in Rourk's earthy smell. His hair was like satin on her cheek.

I'm so lucky to have him.

Keegan took a deep breath and pulled back with a smile. "I'm going to get ready. I'll be back in a little while."

"How long are you going to be?" Rourk asked.

"Total? About an hour. It takes girls a little longer to get ready," she teased, and then winked at him.

"Ok, I'm going to throw on some clothes and go for a run. I'll be back in about 45 minutes." Rourk kissed her one last time before she stood up.

Keegan rocked back and forth on her feet, her hands clasped in front of her, as she watched him walk away. She felt so at peace with him around. Once he walked out the door, she headed for the shower.

Keegan pulled the Jeep into the driveway of a large, red-brick home with a huge fenced-in yard. The shutters on every window were black, and the front door was framed by tall bushes shaped into spirals. She jumped out and pocketed her keys, then met Rourk at the front of the vehicle.

"I'm a little nervous. This is our first big purchase as a couple." She grasped his hand and squeezed it. "The house looks nice. I'm sure they take good care of the puppies."

"I've always wanted a dog. Not sure I would have picked a bulldog though." He laughed, tucking Keegan's hand into the crook of his arm as they began walking up the driveway. "Aren't they supposed to be lazy?"

"Hey, don't talk about Santa like that. Lazy is good! I just want someone to keep me company when I'm alone. We can always get a more active dog later, if you want. I'm sure he'll want a friend."

They mounted the three steps to the porch and came to a stop on a generic black and brown "Welcome" mat. Keegan reached over and rang the doorbell.

A woman who looked to be in her mid-forties open the door and greeted them with a warm smile that reached her pale blue eyes. "You must be Keegan and Rourk. Come in."

They stepped inside, and the woman closed the door behind them. Keegan glanced around in awe—the house was beautiful. The foyer ceiling soared above their heads, where a large, crystal chandelier hung down past the white railing of the upstairs balcony. To either side, arched doorways opened into equally large and open rooms: One filled with over-stuffed couches and chairs in warm, neutral tones and the other with a long dining table covered in fine China. It felt warm and inviting.

"The puppies are in the back room," their hostess said with another eye-crinkling smile. "And I'm Marjorie, in case you didn't remember."

"It's a pleasure to meet you, Marjorie. I'm Rourk,"—he put an arm around Keegan—"and this is Keegan."

The house was decorated in an understated, simple way. Lots of browns, reds, and gold made it look like a page out of a magazine. They passed through a huge kitchen filled with all stainless-steel appliances. It smelled like cinnamon which made Keegan hungry.

Marjorie came to a stop in front of a gated doorway. She unlatched the small wooden gate to let them pass through.

It was a small spare bedroom with hardwood floors and a single twin-sized bed covered in a plain white blanket. Six bulldog puppies, shaped like sausages and in a variety of colors, were wrestling on the floor.

"Oh my goodness!" Keegan clapped her hands together. She got on her knees and picked up an all-white bulldog, then kissed its face. His fur was so soft, and he had that adorable puppy smell—a sharp tang. She glanced at Rourk. "How are we ever going to choose?"

Rourk was still standing in the doorway. He chuckled and shrugged.

"Get over here!" Keegan teased him. She picked up a second wiggling bulldog—white and covered in black spots—and squeezed both puppies to her chest. "Which one do you like best?"

Rourk sat down beside her on the floor and gently took one from her. It squirmed in his grasp, trying to get it's little head around so it could nibble on Rourk's fingers. "They are all pretty cute. Do you like the ones with colors or the all-white ones?"

"Well, I always wanted one with different colors…" Keegan trailed off, eyeing the spotted one in Rourk's lap. The one she still held licked her face, its tongue wet and scratchy. Keegan giggled. "But the white one is super-cute, and he seems to like me. Is it a boy?" She held the puppy up and looked at its belly. "Oh shoot, it's a girl. Do you think we could name a girl Santa?"

"I think you can name a dog anything you want to name it." Rourk reached over to scratch behind the little dog's ear. She kicked her arms and legs as if she were trying to get to him. "Although, I don't think the name matches the dog. She should have a cool name like Athena."

"Hmm, Athena. I actually love that! I think she likes you," Keegan said as she handed the dog to him.

"I think we should take this one home," Rourk declared and looked the puppy in the face, inspecting it. She had dark eyes that were nearly hidden in the rolls of her face, and her nose was pale pink. Rourk laughed when she put a paw on his nose and licked him. "It's so fat and wrinkly."

Keegan stood up and brushed off the seat of her pants. She turned to Marjorie, who was watching from the doorway. "We would like to take this one. I wish we could take them all."

The woman smiled as she leaned to take Athena from Rourk's hands. "I understand. It's heartbreaking for me when they leave us, but the people who get them give the puppies the love they need. You picked a good one. This one has a great personality."

"She had her 9 weeks shots just last week, so you'll need to take her for the 12 weeks soon." Marjorie passed Keegan a computer print-out. "Here's the vet information, as well as what kind of food she's been eating."

They thanked her and paid for the little dog, then left.

Keegan held Athena snugly against her chest as they walked for the car. In the cold air, her cheeks were rosy and her eyes were twinkling.

"I love seeing you so happy," Rourk murmured, snaking an arm around her shoulders.

"I am happy. I'm not sure I have ever been this happy in my life." Keegan glanced up at Rourk's thoughtful face. "I know it sounds corny, but I've always felt something was missing until you."

"I feel the same way." Rourk kissed the top of her head.

As Rourk made to get in on the passenger side of the car, Keegan stopped him. She grinned sweetly. "I really want to hold Athena. Will you drive?"

"Of course." He shook his head, amused, and switched sides.

They made a quick stop at Petsmart to pick up all the necessities, plus a few extra toys. While they shopped, people kept stopping to stare at Athena, and asking if they could pet her. You would have thought she was a super model with all the attention she received.

"This puppy is going to be spoiled," Keegan said wryly as Rourk piled their bags into the back of the Jeep. "We might have gone a little overboard."

Rourk scratched Athena's head, earning a kiss in return—from the puppy and from Keegan. "She's worth it."

They walked into Keegan's apartment with the new addition to the family, and Keegan put her down on the floor as Rourk locked the door behind them. Athena ran around sniffing and checking out the place. Keegan followed her into the kitchen, where she checked out the stove, then slipped under the table. A second later, she shot from beneath the table and into the living room, her toenails scrabbling for purchase on the hardwood. Athena did three quick circles and went to the bathroom. On the rug. Rourk laughed, and Keegan rushed around trying to clean it up.

Soon after, the puppy fell asleep in front of the fireplace.

Keegan wrapped her arms around Rourk's waist, and they watched the little dog snore away.

"I'll make us some hot chocolate. It's so cold here," Keegan said with a shiver, and then shuffled off to the kitchen. She smiled when she pulled out the Godiva hot chocolate—it always made her think of her mother. Her mom loved to make the hot chocolate on cold days.

"Marshmallows?" she asked as Rourk came in the room.

"Of course." He grinned. He took a seat at the table.

Keegan put the saucepan on the stove and poured a generous portion of milk into it. She turned up the heat and left it to boil as she measured out the cocoa powder into two mugs. She could feel Rourk's eyes on her the entire time.

What a perfect day. She got to spend it with Rourk, and now they had a pet to make it even more complete.

"Do you think she'll like it here? With us?" Keegan asked, leaning her hip on the counter next to the stove. The milk was just beginning to bubble.

Rourk cocked his head. "Athena?"

"Yeah. What if she doesn't like us?"

"Athena will love you," he answered, his voice heavy with emotion. "And she already likes it here—she fell asleep."

Wrinkling her nose, Keegan said, "So? What does that have to do with it?"

"When an animal feels comfortable enough to fall asleep somewhere, it means they're happy." Rourk smiled. "It's the same as humans. Don't you sleep best at your parents' house?"

Keegan turned off the heat, thinking about his words. She poured milk into both mugs and stirred. "I suppose you're right."

"It's true."

Keegan dropped in some marshmallows and carried the mugs to the table, sitting down across from him. She wrapped her hands around her hot chocolate and felt the warmth radiate through her body. "Tonight, we'll take her out to look for the northern lights. Maybe she will bring us good luck."

They both smiled at Athena, who was still snoring away in the living room.

Later that evening, they drove out about an hour into the woods to a spot in the wildlife sanctuary where Keegan volunteered. It was the best spot to see the northern lights, according to all of the people Keegan worked with at the sanctuary. She'd checked online, and chances were good the lights would make an appearance that night.

When they pulled up to the park ranger's checkpoint, an older man with dark gray hair popped out of the booth and strolled up to the Jeep. Keegan rolled down her window, and Athena went crazy in Rourk's lap. "Hey, Roger. How'd the tours go today?"

The man gave her a crooked smile that deepened the age lines in his face. "Wasn't the same without you. You have a way with the kids."

"Giving tours is my favorite part," Keegan told Rourk. "I love interacting with the guests."

"And she's the best we've got, too," Roger said brightly, tipping his wide-brimmed hat up and squinting into the dim car.

"I'll be in on Tuesday." Keegan turned in her seat and gestured to Rourk and the puppy. "I want you to meet Rourk, and our newest addition, Athena."

"Pleasure to meet you, sir," Rourk answered politely.

Roger reached through the window to shake Rourk's hand. "Nice to meet you. Keegan talks about you all the time. It's nice to put a face to the name." He dropped a quick pat to Athena's head; her stubby tail wagged so fast it moved her whole body. Roger chuckled, then reached up and took off his hat. "You're a lucky man, Rourk. Keegan's a great kid. She never complains, no matter what chore we throw at her."

Rourk nodded his head in agreement. He was well aware of how lucky he was.

"We're hoping to catch a glimpse of the lights," Keegan told Roger excitedly.

"It's a good night for it. Have fun." The ranger turned and walked towards his four-wheeler, parked next to the checkpoint booth. He gave them a hearty wave, then revved the engine and wheeled away.

Keegan drove down a winding dirt road for several minutes before she finally pulled into a clearing in the woods. As she put the car in park, Rourk snapped Athena's tiny leash onto her new purple collar.

"I really hope the lights decide to show themselves tonight," Keegan said quietly. It truly was a breathtaking sight, and she wanted to share it with Rourk.

"Even if they don't, it's been a great day with you anyway," Rourk answered as they climbed from the car. He put Athena down and she promptly did her business in the grass.

"You're right," Keegan said with a sad smile. She stopped to praise Athena, handing the puppy a small treat from her pocket.

They held hands as they walked towards the picnic tables barely visible at the tree-line.

"You really enjoy working here, don't you?" Rourk glanced over at Keegan's face in the darkness.

"I love it. Not all of it is fun, but I know it's all worthwhile to preserve the land and help the animals."

"It's admirable." He held her hand as Keegan climbed onto the top of the table, then placed Athena in her lap before sitting beside her.

A burst of green lights lit up the sky, followed by splashes of pink and purple. Keegan gasped—she never got sick of it. Rourk's strong hand wrapped around her own, and they watched as random ribbons of color danced in the sky.

"It's beautiful. I've never seen anything like it." Rourk's eyes were locked on the skyline.

"I know. It's incredible. What an amazing world we live in," she said wistfully, as she laid her head on his shoulder and pulled the little wrinkled bulldog closer on her lap.

The weekend passed in a blur. Keegan wanted to cry when Rourk placed the necklace around her neck. "I'm not ready for you to leave."

"I know. I'll be back in a few days." Rourk leaned down and kissed the top of her head.

"How are we going to make it through this? It seems cruel."

He gave her a sad smile. "We'll just take it one day at a time. We have the computers; that helps."

"It's not the same." She threw her arms around him and laid her head on his chest. His heartbeat was loud and steady.

"It's time to go." His voice sounded hoarse.

The drive to the airport was long and rough. Keegan tried to not let him see her cry—she didn't want it to be any harder for him than it already was.

After they said their good-byes, Keegan sat in a chair at the security checkpoint for over an hour. When the pain started in her chest, she knew he was gone.

Chapter 12

Rourk woke up before his alarm went off. His first thought was *Keegan*—the same thing he thought every morning. There was a four hour time difference, so she was most likely fast asleep.

He closed his eyes and thought of her, then smiled. She was curled up in her bed with the covers tucked under her chin. Her hair was a mess, tangled and spread across her pillow. She looked so peaceful with Athena curled into a little white ball at her side.

They were together again; he had to remind himself everyday. It was unbelievable—all those months of pain without her were suddenly history. Rourk gazed longingly at her for just a moment longer, then snapped opened his eyes.

He could watch her all day, but he knew it was wrong to invade her privacy like that. Gathering some clothes, he went to take a shower.

When Rourk finally sauntered from his room, Tommy was waiting outside.

"Hey, man," Rourk said, clapping his friend on the shoulder. "Good to see you."

Tommy raised an eyebrow and leaned away. "What has you so chipper? I've never seen you this happy."

"I met a girl." Rourk grinned. *That's the understatement of the day*, he thought wryly.

"Seriously? What's she like? When can I meet her, and most importantly—does she have a sister?"

Rourk laughed. "She is perfect. You'll be able to meet her soon enough. No, she doesn't have a sister, just two brothers."

"Figures." Tommy sighed. "What about friends?"

Rourk knew his friend was obsessed with meeting a new girl. He'd never known anyone to have such bad luck as Tommy. It wasn't that he was a bad-looking guy—average, really. He was tall and lanky with pale blond hair, blue eyes, and freckles across the bridge of his nose. But, what did Rourk know about girls and their tastes?

"I'm sure she has some friends."

"How did you meet her?" Tommy narrowed his eyes. "You're not exactly smooth with the ladies."

"She's from the town where I grew up. I've liked her for a long time, and she finally noticed me."

Tommy slapped him on the back. "That's great man. I'm happy for you."

"Thank you. I know you two will get along great. She'll be going to school in Washington."

"Really? So she probably does have some cute college friends." Tommy stroked his chin as if he were deep in thought.

It was time to change the subject. If he didn't, Tommy would go on about his lack of a girlfriend all morning.

"I'm looking forward to getting out of here and onto a team," Rourk said, shifting his rucksack on his back. The days of training had started to drag, and he was ready for a new start.

"Me too. The training is cool and all but…" Tommy shrugged. "I'm ready to move on. Plus, there aren't that many hot chicks around here. At least, any that aren't already married."

So much for changing the subject.

"We don't have much longer. We'll get a lot of time off for the holidays, so it will pass quickly. I'm hoping we're there by the New Year. Are we still going to get a place together?" Rourk glanced over at Tommy as they finally headed down the hallway.

"Of course! I've been looking online. We can get a sweet place between both of our housing allowances. I'm talking a pool, Jacuzzi, gym, bike trails, you name it."

Rourk shook his head. "I'll leave that up to you."

"I won't let you down. See you at lunch." Tommy headed off in the opposite direction.

Rourk was thinking of Keegan as he strolled towards the compound. He missed her so much. He missed her smell, her smile, her kiss… Thoughts of her consumed his mind—he needed to compartmentalize so he could focus at work.

He frowned when his phone vibrated in his pocket. He flipped it open and read *TOMMY.*

It was from Thaddeus.

Thaddeus, his future brother-in-law, was a psychic and rarely tried to step in and change fate. It was forbidden for those with the gift of sight. So if Thad was warning him, Tommy must have been in terrible danger.

Shit. Rourk clicked number three on his speed dial and pressed the phone to his ear. It just rang and rang. His heart thudded in his chest. He couldn't stand the thought of something happening to Tommy.

Rourk took off in a sprint towards the engineer department. He tried Tommy's number again. Still no answer. Soldiers stared at Rourk as he sprinted past, but he barely noticed. He skidded to a stop and glanced around; he was on Tommy's usual path to work. *Where was he?* Rourk dialed again and listened to the ringing. *Come on, pick up.*

The screech of brakes sounded like a gunshot in the morning, followed by a sickeningly loud *thump.*

"No!" Rourk screamed. He raced forward as fast as he could, and ran around the large brick building that separated him from the street.

Tommy was lying on the ground. A large white truck was stopped in front of him. Not a dent on the truck, but Tommy was crumpled on the asphalt. Two guys were kneeling next to him. Someone yelled "Call 911! Get a medic out here now!"

Rourk felt like he was walking through water as he made his way forward. Tommy was his only friend—he couldn't bear it if something happened to him. Something he could have prevented. He hadn't reacted quickly enough—he had failed. Thaddeus had trusted him and he had failed. Rourk pushed his way through the spectators that had crowded around his best friend.

"Is he alive?" Rourk asked in a stiff voice. Blood was pooling around Tommy's head and dripping from his open mouth.

"He's still breathing, but he won't open his eyes or respond in any way. I saw it all. His head bounced pretty high off the ground." The man winced and looked back down at Tommy.

The driver paced nearby, his entire body shaking. He looked like he was just a kid. "He came out of nowhere."

Rourk glared at him, but didn't say anything.

"Where the hell is the ambulance?" Rourk snapped.

Just then, a dark-haired man in uniform ran forward, a medical bag in hand. "Out of the way, I'm a medic."

Rourk felt a spark of hope. Special Forces medics were highly trained. He would know what to do. Tommy was in better hands with him then an ambulance attendant. Rourk watched as he tore off Tommy's shirt. He cringed when he saw the blood.

Rourk's phone buzzed in his pocket. He closed his eyes and pulled it out. He really didn't want to talk to anyone. It was Thaddeus, so he snapped his phone open and walked away. "I was too late. It's bad."

"My mother is coming." Thaddeus's voice was subdued.

Rourk cleared his throat, pain in his chest. "Will he be ok?"

"I honestly don't know. It's not your fault, Rourk. We don't have control over certain aspects of life."

"I should have been faster. Or talked to him longer this morning. He's like a brother to me."

"If he's still breathing when my mother gets there, he has a fighting chance."

"I have to go. I hear the sirens. Thank you for trying." Rourk clicked off the phone and shoved it in his pocket.

The ambulance pulled up and loaded Tommy onto the long flat board to immobilize his spine. *What if he was paralyzed?* Rourk thought, eyes widening. *Focus, Rourk…this is not helping anyone.*

Rourk strode up to the medic after the ambulance had pulled away. "What do you think?"

The man turned wary eyes to Rourk. He was a lean, fit man; his uniform was stained with Tommy's blood. He peeled off his blood-stained latex gloves as he said, "A friend of yours?"

"Yes."

The man took a deep breath, closing his eyes momentarily before answering. "I think it will be a miracle if he pulls through. The chance of internal injuries is too high. Who knows what that head injury did, or the state of his spinal cord. I'm sure it will be touch and go for awhile. I guess it depends on if it's his day to go or not."

Rourk grimaced. He knew the man spoke the truth. "Can you drop me off at the hospital?" he asked.

"Sure. My truck is over there." He pointed across the street to a large parking lot.

"Thank you." Rourk shifted his rucksack to the other shoulder and walked off with the man. He wondered if Tommy could hold out until Emerald arrived.

They drove in silence. The medic pulled up to the emergency entrance to drop him off. "Sometimes it's better if they don't make it. I know that sounds harsh, but the things I've seen…"

Rourk nodded his head in agreement. He had also seen men walk away with injuries that made them wish they had died in battle. A car accident wasn't quite a battle, but brain injuries usually didn't end well. "Thanks for the ride." Rourk slammed the door shut.

The man waved and pulled out. Rourk took a deep breath and walked to the entrance.

"Rourk." The woman's urgent voice came from his right. He whirled to find Emerald striding towards him. "Do they have him?"

"Yeah. The ambulance left us behind, so they got here pretty quick."

She nodded. Her hair wasn't brushed; her short ginger locks were sticking up as if she'd just rolled from bed. Rourk figured she had—Thaddeus had likely woken her up and told her what was happening. Emerald probably took just long enough to get dressed before she teleported.

"I won't be able to get to him," she murmured, watching as an older couple shuffled by on their way into the building. She turned her bright blue eyes back to Rourk. "I'll have to find a quiet place. Go. Go in and check on him."

Rourk turned and she followed behind. The doors opened, admitting them into the cool interior. The smell of hospitals always bothered him a little. There was just something unnatural about it.

He stood impatiently in line to ask where they had sent Tommy. He stood rigid as he heard the people in front of them ask ridiculous questions: Where was the bathroom? How much longer do they have to wait? Can they make an appointment to come back later? Rourk tried to calm himself. Finally it was his turn. "My brother was hit by a vehicle and has been admitted. Can you tell me where he is?"

The woman behind the counter looked tired. Her mousey-brown hair was pulled into a bun that was falling apart, and there was a large coffee stain on her blue scrub shirt. She glanced at Rourk with non-sympathetic eyes. "Last name?"

"Sanders."

She tapped on her keyboard, the computer screen reflecting off her glasses. "He's in surgery."

Rourk's heart thudded. "Already?"

"Yes."

"Can you tell me what's wrong with him?"

She shook her head. "Confidential."

Rourk wanted to scream. Instead, he shoved his hand through his hair and took a calming breath. "What floor is he on?"

"Ninth floor."

"Thank you." Rourk and Emerald headed for the elevator. He wished Keegan was with him. He felt like he was about to unravel. He'd check on Tommy's status and then give her a call.

"I'm going to the restroom so I won't be disturbed. I'll find you when I'm done."

Rourk nodded and walked to the front desk. The nurse behind the counter smiled as he walked up. He leaned on his elbows atop the desk and said, "Can I have an update on my brother? Tommy Sanders?"

The woman stared at him for a moment. "That's funny. Your name-tag says Kavanagh."

Without missing a beat, Rourk said, "He's my stepbrother."

She nodded and pecked away at the keyboard. "He'll probably be in surgery a couple of hours. You're welcome to wait in the waiting area." She pointed to a small glass room to the left.

"Thanks. Can you let me know when they bring him out?"

"Yes, I'll have the doctor give you an update when they are done. Have you informed your parents?"

"Not yet. I was hoping to have some news before I freaked them out."

"Standard procedure. If he has them in his file, they will be notified."

Rourk nodded and moved to the waiting room. It was small and dimly lit. There was an old lady knitting in one corner as she watched the news; a stressed-looking young woman and a baby in another corner; and a middle-aged man who looked in serious need of sleep. Rourk couldn't help but notice how far they'd each sat away from each other, as if they were worried the other's bad luck would rub off.

Rourk slouched in a seat, dropped his head in his hands, and closed his eyes. He visualized Keegan. She was sitting in a classroom, her pen writing furiously on a notebook as she bit her tongue in concentration. He didn't want to bother her in class—he'd call her when he knew more.

It was only an hour before his phone buzzed. It was Tommy's mother. "Have you heard anything?" she asked anxiously.

"No, ma'am." Rourk looked around the room. The sun was high in the sky outside the one small window. The baby had finally gone to sleep.

"We're on our way. Our flight leaves at noon. Will you call me if you hear anything?" Her voice cracked over the sound of a loudspeaker in the background. They must have already been at the airport.

"Of course. Safe flight."

Two hours and thirteen minutes later, a man in scrubs walked into the room. Everyone stood wide-eyed as he entered. "Sanders?"

Rourk stood up and walked into the hall with the doctor, his palms clammy.

"I'm Doctor Wilson," the man said, offering his hand to Rourk. They shook.

"Your brother made it through the surgery," the doctor said. He was a tall man with large hands and creases on his face from the mask that hung around his neck. He rubbed his thumbs on his forehead. "Something odd happened. We went in to stop the internal bleeding, but once we got inside, we couldn't find anything. It just…vanished." The doctor shook his head. "I've never seen anything like it."

Rourk thought, *That's because you've never seen an elfin healer.* "Does that mean Tommy will be ok?"

"He's not out of the woods yet. We still have to worry about his brain. There's swelling. We need to wait and see if the swelling goes down on its own or if we have to make a hole to reduce the pressure." He paused and gestured for Rourk to have a seat in the uncomfortable metal chair outside the waiting room door. Doctor Wilson sat beside him, placing a hand on Rourk's arm. "There's also the matter of him regaining consciousness. In some cases, people never wake from comas."

"Thank you for being honest with me. When can I see him?"

"We're going to move him to ICU for observation. I'll have a nurse come get you when he can have visitors. Are his parents on the way?"

"Yes. They're coming from across the country, so they will be delayed."

The doctor clapped him on the shoulder one last time, and then left.

Rourk went back to the waiting area. He called Keegan—he needed to hear her voice. He filled her in on what had happened.

"Do you want me to come?" she asked softly, her voice soothing as it came over the line.

"No. We'll wait and see what happens. Your mom is here."

"Oh. Good." She was silent a moment. "I'd really rather come, Rourk."

"Stay in school, Keegan. I'll call you when I know more."

They talked for a few more minutes and said their goodbyes. Rourk stared at his phone and realized he felt much more centered after talking to his chosen.

Emerald breezed through the door into the waiting room and wrapped Rourk in a hug. When she pulled away, she held tightly to his shoulders and asked, "How's he doing?"

Rourk gave a half smile. "The doctors are baffled. They went into operate, and the internal bleeding had ceased on its own…"

"That's great news!" She stepped closer, looking around the room. She pushed both hands back through her hair, then smoothed it, before she said quietly, "I don't have as much control when I can't touch the person."

"They're worried about the brain swelling, and the fact that he hasn't responded."

Emerald sat heavily in a chair, leaning forward with her elbows on her knees. She looked tired. "I need to get in to see him."

"He's in the ICU so only immediate family members are allowed in. I'm still waiting for them to give me the go ahead to see him."

Emerald smiled. "Brother?"

"Yes."

"Alright, when they call you back just go along with what I say."

They waited and waited, flipping channels idly on the small, staticky television until a nurse finally came in and called Rourk back. Emerald stood up and followed him.

The nurse held up a hand to Emerald and shook her head. "Family members only."

"I'm a reiki master and also Tommy's godmother. His parents contacted me and wanted me to get in a soon as I could to give him a healing. It will only take 15-30 minutes. I know many hospitals now use reiki before and after surgeries." Emerald's tone was no-nonsense and held just a hint of command. Rourk was impressed.

The nurse thought about it for a moment. Rourk could almost see the wheels turning: It was still against policy, but her eyes held belief in the new age side of medicine. She shrugged and motioned for them to follow. "This way."

She led them to a service elevator at the end of the hallway, and pushed the button to go up. "When we get upstairs, you'll need to scrub your hands with sanitizer and we're going to give you face masks. We don't want anything brought into the room that could harm Tommy."

Rourk and Emerald both nodded, and Rourk answered, "Yes, ma'am. Absolutely."

The elevator was dimly lit by a single bulb. After the fluorescent lights of the waiting room and hallway, it was a welcome break on Rourk's eyes. They reached the 11th floor and the elevator dinged open.

After preparing to enter his room, Rourk and Emerald followed the nurse to an open, sliding-glass door marked by a number *10* and a clipboard with *T. Sanders* across the top.

"Twenty minutes," the nurse said softly.

"Thank you," Rourk and Emerald said in unison.

Tommy looked small and broken in the hospital bed. His body was stretched flat on his back and the bed was slightly raised so his head was higher than the rest. Several beeping machines were attached to him: one monitoring his heart rate which was slow and steady. There was a tube was coming out of his throat, and his eyes were closed.

Rourk took his hand, a lump in his throat. "You have to pull through Tommy. We're in this together."

Emerald moved to the other side of the bed and closed her eyes as she placed her hands lightly above the white gauze that covered Tommy's head.

Rourk watched Emerald curiously. A healer's magic was an incredible gift; they could heal almost anything, especially someone with the power of his chosen's mother. He knew if anyone could help Tommy it was her.

Emerald moved her hands around different areas of Tommy's head, her eyes closed. Her breathing was steady. She moved her hands down his chest—she would rest her hands in an area for a couple of minutes, then she would move to the next spot and repeat. She went over the rest of his body down to his feet, and then back to his head again.

The door opened and the nurse came in. "It's been twenty minutes. You can come back once they transfer him to the seventh floor."

Rourk was worried. He'd expected Tommy to wake up and be fine after the healing, but his eyes were still closed. Maybe it was his time.

As they walked towards the elevator, Emerald pulled Rourk into a half-hug. "I've done all I can, Rourk. I believe he will be fine, but we have to wait until he wakes up to be sure."

"I know." Rourk pushed the down button, then turned to face her. "I can't thank you enough."

The sound of the nurse's voice broke the silence of ICU as she called out the door of Tommy's room. "He's awake! Get the doctor."

Emerald smiled knowingly and patted Rourk's arm. "I'm going to head back now. I left Warrick with Thaddeus. You know what a handful that little man is."

Rourk smiled. "Thank you, though I feel like that's not enough."

"It's more than enough. I'm glad I could help. That boy has a clear soul. The earth would be darker without people like him."

Rourk watched as Emerald stepped into the elevator. She waved, and the doors closed. Rourk knew she'd be gone before the elevator opened on the next floor. *So much power in such a little body.*

He called Keegan and gave her the good news. Rourk didn't need to hear from the doctors; he knew Tommy would be fine.

Thankfully, Tommy *was* fine. A week later, he was released from the hospital with nothing more than a few bumps and bruises, and the OK to return to work. There was no apparent brain damage, and his memories were still intact, as well as has reasoning skills. The doctors were shocked at his quick recovery.

Tommy kept telling everyone that a redheaded angel had saved him. Of course, the doctors wrote it off as a side-effect of his head injury. Rourk kept the truth to himself.

Chapter 13

Keegan's phone kept buzzing on her night stand. She was so tired that she could barely keep her eyes open, but she rolled over and answered. "Hello."

"Keegan?"

She rubbed her eyes and looked at the clock: 3:33 in the morning. "Lauren, what's wrong?"

"I'm sorry to call so late. It's Donald. He's out of control."

Keegan's heart dropped, and she sat up in bed. Athena rolled over on her back and growled in her sleep. "What do you mean? Is he ok?"

"Ok, is a relative term. He's drinking all the time. I think he's even doing drugs. Plus, he's sleeping around with every girl he meets. And tonight he shifted into his tiger form on campus."

Keegan's hand flew to her cover her mouth. "Oh my god. Did anyone see him?"

"A couple of guys said they saw a tiger running around the campus. But everyone blew it off as they were drunk and didn't believe them. Thankfully, the campus is surrounded by woods so he wasn't visible for too long. The guys are at their wit's end with him. They don't know what to do. Calvron thought maybe if you came to talk to him it would help."

"He won't talk to me. I've sent him several texts and tried to call him, but he never responds."

"Do you think you could come here and try to talk to him in person? Keegan, this is bad. He can't be shifting in public."

Keegan sighed and rubbed a hand over her eyes. *First, Tommy, now Donald...* She pulled Athena close. "I don't know Lauren. I really don't think it would help, but I guess I can try. Anna was talking about coming to visit you soon. I will talk to her in the morning and find out when we can get a flight out."

"Thank you. I'm going to tell Calvron. I'll talk to you tomorrow."

"K. Bye." Keegan ended the call and sat back in her bed. She couldn't believe Donald was losing it like that. It wasn't like him. She knew he was upset, but she never knew him to lose control. He had always been the one to calm her when she was losing her temper. She really hoped she could do the same for him. But, she seriously doubted there was anything she could do. He couldn't stand her. She wrapped herself in the blankets and tried to fall back to sleep but spent the next three hours thinking about Donald.

When she saw it was a decent time, she picked up the phone and called Anna.

"Hey, do you want to go see Lauren in the next day or so? She called me last night and told me Donald was out of control. He shifted on campus!"

"Are you serious? Yeah, I wanted to go see her soon anyway. I don't have classes tomorrow, and I can skip today. Want to see if we can get a flight out today?"

"Sure, I'll get online and see if I can get us tickets and call you back. Talk to you in a few minutes." Keegan ended the call and went straight to her computer. First, she got a flight to Seattle and then purchased tickets for both of them to California. Good thing for her dad's American Express, she thought wryly.

Keegan shrugged into a robe, then walked into the kitchen and turned on the coffee pot. She needed to let Rourk know, and she was worried he would be upset. She couldn't hide things from her chosen. Keegan closed her eyes to check on him. He was sitting in a small room surrounded by guys in uniforms. *Goodness, he looks hot in uniform.* Keegan grinned to herself. She watched as he looked up and tried to hide the smile forming on his lips. He knew she was thinking of him. She sent him a text that they needed to talk. She watched as he stood up and walked out of the room. A minute later, her phone rang.

"Rourk I have to tell you something that might not make you happy." Keegan paused as she sat on the couch and cradled a mug of coffee against her chest. Athena danced about on the rug in front of her, pulling a trail of toilet paper across the floor.

"You can tell me anything. Nothing will change the way I feel about you." Rourk tensed he had no idea what she was going to say and wasn't sure he wanted to hear it.

"I'm going to California today. Lauren called me and told me that Donald needs help. He has gotten out of control—he even shifted on campus. I'm not sure there is anything I can do to help him, but I need to try. He helped me so many times when I was about to lose my temper." Keegan paused briefly and hurried on. "You have nothing to worry about. I don't have feelings for him in that way anymore. I just want to try to help him as a friend. You are the only one for me."

She heard Rourk take a deep breath. "I trust you, Keegan. If you feel you need to do this, then I understand."

"You do?" She could hear the shock in her own voice.

"Yes, it's who you are. Your friends are important to you. I'm not going to say I am thrilled about the idea, but I will not try to stop you. How long do you think you will be there?"

"I'm not sure. Just a couple of days I think. I will be back before you come to visit. If anything keeps me there longer, you can meet me in California."

"Ok, keep me updated. Thank you for letting me know. I love you."

"I love you, too. You're the best! I'll text you and keep you in the loop. I can't wait to see you this weekend." Keegan smiled, hoping he could hear it in her voice.

"Me either. When are you leaving?"

"I'm flying out in three hours, and then I'll get a connecting plane with Anna this evening."

"What about Athena?" Rourk asked.

Keegan glanced down at the ball of white rubbing its back on the fluffy purple rug. The puppy jerked to a stop and panted, her dark eyes staring up at Keegan. "Oh. I don't know. I guess I could find a pet-sitter."

"Check the phone book for kennels. You can put her up for a few days."

Keegan nodded to herself. "Great idea."

"Ok, I have to get back into work," Rourk said. "I'll talk to you soon."

"Oh, one last thing." Keegan lowered her voice. "You are the sexiest man in that room."

Rourk laughed loudly. "Bye, Keegan."

Keegan disconnected and smiled as she refilled her coffee in the kitchen. She called Lauren and Anna to fill them in on plans before pulling out the phonebook to find a kennel. After the puppy situation was sorted, she packed her bags for the trip. She didn't bring much since she didn't plan to be there for long.

It was so good to see Anna. She had chopped her hair off: it was completely pink. Keegan hugged her tightly and didn't want to let go. "You look great. I love the hair. It looks so retro."

Anna fluffed up the side of her hair. "Thanks, I bleached it and it was driving me crazy so I went with pink. It was supposed to be red, but this is how it turned out." She shrugged.

"Well, it looks amazing. You look like a hip art student."

Anna was wearing skinny jeans and a long teal t-shirt with a belt cinched at her waist. Keegan definitely thought she looked like an art student; it was a look not many people could pull off, but Anna was stunning.

"You look fantastic too," Anna said, leaning over to hug Keegan again. Keegan had just thrown on a pair of holey jeans and a peasant top, going for comfort over style for the plane ride.

"Thanks."

"Let's go grab something to eat. There is an awesome bagel shop near by, and we can catch up." Anna laced her arm through Keegan's and led her to the parking lot.

They chatted about school on the drive to the bagel shop. Anna had made a lot of friends, and even gone on a few dates—which made Keegan feel like a failure. She still wasn't sure why she wasn't making a lot of friends in Alaska.

They walked into the bagel shop, and Keegan glanced around. It was a great atmosphere for hanging out: College students with laptops and books spread across their tables were sipping coffee and eating bagels. The walls were brown and hung with local art sporting reasonable price tags, and the large, dark mahogany counter was scarred by time. Keegan could see why Anna enjoyed hanging out there.

The girl at the cash register smiled. "Are you getting your regular today, Anna?"

Anna seemed to have found a place she fit in. Keegan was happy for her.

"Yep, that'd be great, Erica."

"What about your friend?" Erica turned her pale green eyes to Keegan.

"Um, do you have white chocolate mocha?"

"We sure do! What size?"

"Some things never change." Anna nudged Keegan with her elbow and smirked.

After they received their drinks, and Anna's bagel, they found a small table in the corner.

"We really need to get a place together. Living in a dorm sucks." Anna flung her bag over the back of her chair and fell into it. "My roommate is so annoying. Half the time, she shows up at three a.m. drunk or with some guy. Believe me, that is not something you want to wake up to."

Keegan shuddered. "Ugh. I would say not. Well, start looking for a place for us. I plan on moving here in January." She glanced around and motioned with her coffee cup. "This place looks much more happening than Alaska."

Anna's face lit up. "I'm so excited! I've really missed having you around."

"So, what has been going on with you? Are you dating anyone?" Keegan raised an eyebrow and took a sip of her coffee.

"Keegan, there are so many hot guys here it is insane! I just want to gobble them all up." She tilted her head towards a guy across the room.

Keegan glanced over, trying to be surreptitious. He was indeed nice eye candy. "Can't you cast a spell on him or something?"

"Why yes, actually I can. However, I want someone to like me for *me*, not for a spell. I'm not opposed to using one if I get too desperate though." Anna winked.

Keegan laughed. "I've really missed this."

Anna leaned forward and lowered her voice. Her sparkly blue eye shadow glinted in the low light hanging over their table. "So Donald really shifted in public? You must have done a number on that poor boy."

"I feel horrible. Hopefully, we can talk some sense into him."

They sat and chatted for a couple of hours before they went to Anna's dorm room and picked up her bag; they had a flight to catch and a tiger to save.

Lauren, Spencer, Sam, and Calvron greeted them at the airport. They all looked older and more mature; it made Keegan kinda sad. She missed the days of them chasing each other around school like children, getting yelled at by teachers to slow down and grow up.

Calvron's style had changed significantly. He was at one point as outrageous as Anna had been, but was more subdued now. He was wearing a pair of dark jeans and a plain red t-shirt. His messy blonde hair hadn't changed.

Lauren pulled the girls into a hug. She hadn't really changed: her dark hair was still long and curly and pulled back into a low ponytail. The pink sundress she wore showed off her toned arms and legs. Lauren was one of the most beautiful girls Keegan knew.

It hadn't been that long since they had seen each other, but it felt like a lifetime. They were growing apart, and they all knew it. It was hard to let go of childhood.

Calvron cleared his throat. "We have a serious problem and even I am at a loss of what to do."

Keegan was flooded by guilt. She knew she was the cause of the whole mess.

"Can't you use magic to rein him in?" Keegan asked.

"I've been trying, and it has been helping somewhat, but not nearly enough. I think he has to hit rock bottom before we can help him. I thought maybe if we staged a sort of intervention, we might be able to get through to him." Calvron met Keegan's eyes. "I hope you can get through to him."

Keegan shook her head. "I can try. Just don't be surprised if he wants nothing to do with me."

"Where is he now?" Anna wondered aloud.

"We have no idea," Sam answered with a shrug. "He's been gone for days, and we can't find him anywhere."

Anna spoke up. "I can find him. I'll put a tracking spell on him."

They all looked at Anna in surprise.

"Obviously you've been working on your skills." Calvron sounded pleased. Keegan noticed the way he appraised Anna, as if he were seeing her in a new light.

"Yes," Anna answered, blushing. "I've found a couple of solitary witches in Seattle. We meet up once a week for ritual and discussion. I've learned so much."

"Let's get out of here." Spencer grabbed Keegan's bag and carried it for her as they headed for the door. He was tall, with black hair and vivid green eyes. He bumped gently against Keegan and whispered, "It's not your fault."

She sighed. "I feel like it is. It makes me so sad."

Blond-haired, blue-eyed Sam overheard and butted in. "You should feel bad. You shattered the poor guy's heart."

Calvron stopped walking and turned towards them, eyeing Sam sternly. "No one is to blame. It is what it is. We live in a world of magic. We have to accept that we don't always have control of our life path. That's something Donald needs to learn."

This declaration quieted them all as they got Anna's and Keegan's luggage and walked out the door.

Lauren spoke up as they reached her car in the parking garage. "We'll go to my place. It's big, and I don't have a roommate. Anna, do we need to stop and get anything for the spell?"

Anna shook her head no. "I have everything I need."

Lauren's apartment was in an old converted warehouse in an artsy district of the city. It didn't look like much on the outside—just a big, concrete square—but inside, it was lofty and spacious.

"It's mostly students," she told Keegan as she locked the door behind them. "My neighbors are all really cool. There are parties almost every weekend somewhere in the building."

"This is gorgeous," Keegan said, and sighed as she thought of her tiny apartment in Alaska. The ceilings were high, with exposed ductwork and track lighting. One wall was nothing but windows that looked out over a busy street. The floor plan was open—the kitchen counter overlooked a centrally placed living room with a matching black leather couch set and television.

"You guys can stay in here," Lauren said, opening a closed door down a small hallway. "It's my only spare room, just the one bed but it's king-sized. Do you mind?"

"Nope," Anna said and flopped on the black comforter.

Keegan laughed, dropping her bags against the dresser. "I can't believe how nice this place is."

"Yeah. My parents are paying for it, just as long as I keep my grades up." Lauren touched the doorframe. "I really didn't want to live in a dorm."

"No, you really don't!" Anna called, her voice muffled from the blanket.

"Her roommate is a drunk," Keegan clarified, and Lauren nodded sagely.

"My bedroom is across the hall, and the bathroom is right next door. Do you guys need anything right now?"

"Something to drink would be great," Keegan answered as she realized she was thirsty.

Lauren nodded. "I got juice and stuff." She glanced over at Anna. "Are you going to get ready to do the ritual?"

"Yeah. I'll meet you guys out there in two minutes."

Anna hadn't brought her robe from home, so she felt a little naked as she set the living room for the ritual. She made do with a pair of sweatpants and a t-shirt made of cotton—natural materials that wouldn't stunt the use of her magic.

"Lauren, can you turn the lights down?" she asked when she was done arranging her tools.

Lauren nodded and killed the lights. The wall of windows let in just enough of the slowly disappearing daylight.

Anna took a deep breath, standing before the coffee table—her impromptu altar. "I need complete silence for this to work."

She walked around with her pocket compass to locate North, where she placed a bowl of salt. To the East, a burning stick of Sandlewood incense. At the South, Anna set a white votive candle, and to the West, a small cup of water. She took out a photo of Donald and placed it on the altar, along with a black onyx crystal. She knelt down before the table, closed her eyes, and began to chant.

Keeper of Donald, hear me now…open your ears.
Find for me where we need to be
By moon, sun, earth, air, fire and sea.
Someone I lost I need to find,
By the power of three this spell I bind.

Anna said the chant three times. When she was done, she focused on the energy that surrounded her and concentrated on Donald with her eyes tightly shut. At first, she saw nothing but the darkness of her eyelids and was worried the spell wouldn't work.

Take deep breaths, she heard the voice of her old teacher, Magdalena, echo in her mind. Anna relaxed and pictured Donald's face: his bright blue eyes and crooked smile. The haze started to fade away. A tiger formed in her mind's eye; he was laying on a patch of pillowy grass in a forest. He looked around, as if he knew someone was there. The tiger yawned and stretched to a standing position, and then took off in a sprint.

Anna followed him through the woods, her astral body easily keeping up. When he shifted to his human form, Anna had to suppress a laugh—he was naked. She could see why Keegan had been attracted to him. She watched his muscular frame as he walked behind a tree and grabbed a bag he had obviously placed there earlier. He walked back out in jeans and a flannel shirt. With his hands shoved deep in his pockets and his orange hair reflecting the evening sun, Donald walked over a hill and down into a clearing with Anna on his tail.

Before long, Anna saw a sign that said Arcata.

The room was eerily silent as Anna's eyes opened. She sat stoically, watching the candle melt till nothing was left. She felt Lauren and Keegan's eyes on her. Finally, she rose to her feet. "I know where he is."

"Where?" Keegan asked.

Anna looked over her shoulder. Her friends were nearly invisible—it had gotten dark since she started the ritual. "Arcata. It's beautiful there."

Lauren looked puzzled. "That's over four hours away by car."

Anna shrugged. "All I know is that's where he is, and he's walking through town now."

"I'll call Calvron and tell him," Lauren said, pulling out her cell phone.

Keegan pushed herself from the floor and dusted off her hands. "I hope this works."

The girls climbed into Lauren's silver Prius and started the four-hour journey in search of Donald. Calvron and the guys would be meeting them in Arcata.

Keegan turned sideways to look at Lauren. "So, tell us. Are you seeing anyone?"

Lauren grinned slyly. "Actually, I recently met a guy. He is the hottest guy I've ever laid eyes on." She paused dramatically. "And he's a dark fairy."

Keegan and Anna's eyes widened in surprise. Anna gasped, "A dark fairy?

Is that even allowed?"

Lauren shrugged. "I've never heard of it before. I Googled it, but you know what info on the internet is like."

"Yeah. Elves live at the North Pole with Santa," Keegan said wryly.

"Exactly." Lauren shrugged. "From what I can tell, it's kinda like the dark and light elves, Keegan. Not so much an 'evil' thing, just... *different*."

"I know what you mean," Keegan responded, touching Lauren's arm. "My dad is friends with the leader of the dark elves now. It's still weird."

Lauren nodded. "Yeah, that is weird. Anyway, I just can't resist him. Grab my phone and open the pictures, you'll see him."

Anna reached forward and grabbed Lauren's phone from the center console. She pecked at the screen, opening up the images, and said, "Wow! He is hot! I guess I can't blame you."

Keegan turned towards the back and reached for the phone. "Hotter than Rourk?"

Anna looked back down at the photo. "Much hotter."

"Let me see that." Keegan grabbed the phone from Anna. She stared down into the face of a striking young man. He had olive skin, high cheek bones, a perfect nose, and the palest green eyes she had ever seen on a person. He was beautiful. "He doesn't look evil."

Lauren grabbed the phone from her and glanced down quickly to smile at the picture. She turned her eyes back to the road. "He isn't evil," she said indignantly. "Tristen is the most thoughtful, intelligent man I have ever met. You'll see when you meet him."

Chapter 14

They reached Arcata before night fell completely.

The town was not a large one, so they drove around in hopes of spotting Donald—with no luck. Old-fashioned mom-and-pop stores lined the streets. There was a good crowd on the sidewalks: couples out for evening strolls and smiling shoppers walking in and out of the stores.

Calvron called Keegan's cell after about an hour. "Anything?"

"No, nothing," Keegan said, dejected.

"Figures." He sighed through the phone line. "Alright, well, we're hungry. You want to take a break for dinner?"

"Sounds good."

"There's a great place called Bertha's—Lauren knows it. We'll meet you there."

"The guys wanna eat. Bertha's?"

"Yeah, it's their favorite," Lauren answered, making a U-turn and heading back in the other direction.

A loud bell chimed as they walked through the door at the diner, startling Keegan. She was on edge because of Donald, but she hadn't realized how famished she was. It had been a long time since she and Anna had eaten lunch at the airport. The smell of pot roast made her stomach growl.

Calvron asked the employees if anyone had seen an orange-haired guy lately. One of the waitress said she saw him earlier that day, walking down the street.

"I stopped and asked if he wanted a ride and he refused." She shrugged her shoulders and went on to the next table.

After dinner, they ended up getting a couple of rooms at a small hotel, deciding they would start the search fresh in the morning. The room smelled clean, and the bed looked soft and inviting. The girls dropped their bags on the ground. Keegan threw herself on the bed, Anna went to the bathroom, and Lauren pulled out her phone to text her boyfriend.

Her legs crossed at the ankles and her hands behind her head, Keegan stared at the ceiling and thought of Donald. She hoped they found him soon; in two days Rourk was supposed to be visiting her in Alaska.

Keegan ran her fingers over the stones on her necklace and smiled. She had grown attached to the ugly necklace because it reminded her of her bond with Rourk. She loved knowing that he knew when she was thinking of him. They had texted back and forth a few times while she was searching earlier, and she was anxious to see him on Friday. She also checked on him throughout the day with her mind's eye; she couldn't seem to stop herself. She was addicted to him.

Keegan woke up to the sound of Lauren and Anna laughing. They were already up and dressed. Sometimes, she really wished she were a morning person.

"I need coffee," Keegan groaned from the bed.

Her friends turned and looked at her.

"It's about time," Anna teased with one eyebrow raised.

"We've been waiting for hours for you to wake up," Lauren said.

Keegan threw the blankets to the side and swung her feet to the ground. Rubbing her eyes, she walked to the bathroom. "I'll be ready soon. Can someone get me some coffee?"

The girls glanced at each other and Lauren said, "Sure. There's a coffee shop down the street. We'll be back in a bit."

When Lauren and Anna walked through the door of the coffee shop, they found Donald sitting at a table in the corner. His bright orange hair would stand out anywhere. He looked up when he heard the bell chime; his body stiffened when he saw them.

Lauren slid into the booth and Anna followed. They stared across at him, not sure what to say.

"What are you doing here?" Donald said gruffly.

"We're here to help you." Lauren reached over to grab his hand.

"I don't need any help." He pulled his hand back.

"Keegan is here." Anna said softly.

Pain flashed across his face. He turned away, his eyes studying the people hurrying past outside the window "Why?"

"She said you haven't returned her calls or texts, so she was worried about you," Lauren said quietly.

"Where is she?"

"She's back at the hotel. She slept in so she sent us for coffee."

The corner of his mouth quirked up as if he were going to smile and stopped himself. "Tell her to go home. I don't want to see her, and I don't need your help." He stood up, threw a $20 bill on the table, and walked out.

"Well that went well." Anna reached over and grabbed a slice of toast from his plate while Lauren rolled her eyes.

They ordered their coffees and went back to the hotel. The guys were already waiting in the lobby, so they filled them in on the exchange.

Calvron narrowed his eyes and tapped a finger on his chin. "I could probably track him if he changed into his tiger form."

Spencer and Sam exchanged looks, and the three guys bolted out of the hotel, hoping to catch Donald before he got too far.

Anna handed Keegan her coffee as she came out of the bathroom still wrapped in a towel.

"We saw Donald at the coffee shop," she said with a frown.

Keegan stopped, clutching the towel at her chest. "What?"

"Yeah. He was sitting inside. We talked to him."

"I'm sorry Keegan, but I really think he doesn't want to see you," Lauren cut in as she sat on the bed.

"I didn't think he would." Proof that he didn't filled her with sadness. She hated that she had caused his unhappiness. "But, Calvron asked me to try, so I have to."

Calvron, Spencer, and Sam showed up a couple of hours later and knocked on the girls' door.

"Hey," Keegan said when she opened it. "Did you find him?"

Spencer shook his head. "No. He's gone."

"Again," Calvron said disgustedly.

Anna grabbed her bag and started setting up her altar. "If you guys can step out really quick, I'll track him."

Keegan watched in awe as Anna's movements were sure and quick. She had turned into a completely different person. Gone was the quirky, awkward girl Keegan had grown up with. She had been replaced by a beautiful, confident—and powerful—witch.

Anna eventually turned towards them and motioned for Keegan to let the guys back in. "Maybe we should just leave him alone. He really doesn't want to be found, and I don't think he's ready for our help."

Calvron stepped towards her. "What did you see? Where is he?'

"He's not far from here. He's in the woods. Watching us." Anna sighed and began to put away her crystals.

Keegan looked up from the bed. "He's close?"

"Yes. He's behind the hotel in the woods." Anna started picking up her things. She held onto her crystal for a few minutes and closed her eyes, smiling.

"I think I should go talk to him by myself." Keegan walked over and grabbed her coat. She needed to at least *try* to speak to him. Alone.

Sam spoke up. "I don't think that is a great idea. We should all go together. He's made it obvious he doesn't want to see you. You'll probably make him run."

Keegan zipped her jacket. "I'm going. Don't follow me." She walked out the door and didn't look back.

The woods weren't that far away. She thought about Donald as she walked, and all the good times they had shared together. He was her rock when she was dealing with her emotions of coming back to life from the black magic. She wasn't sure what would have happened to her had it not been for him. Every time the darkness came to her, he had been there to push it back. She owed him.

She walked into the woods and looked around at the huge trees. She knew he would know she was there if he was in his tiger form. She walked deeper into the woods and tried to be as loud as possible, stomping on fallen branches so that they cracked under her feet. "Donald, please come talk to me. I know you're here."

Rocks fell from above, startling Keegan; she looked up and saw it was Donald. He was standing on the edge of an embankment not too far from her, watching her. He looked different. He was scruffy with a few days' growth on his face, and his hair was crazier than usual. She smiled when she noticed his shirt was buttoned wrong.

The hill wasn't that high so she started to climb up. Donald didn't move; he just watched her. She'd almost made it to the top when she slipped on the loose rocks and started sliding back down. He ran towards her and offered his hand.

Keegan grasped his hand. Donald grabbed her forearm and pulled her up. His hand was so warm against her skin. She stared into his startling blue eyes. "Thank you."

Donald returned her stare, but didn't say anything. He dropped her hand and shoved his own hands in his pockets.

Keegan thought carefully before she spoke. She didn't want to make it any worse.

He looked so much older than the last time she saw him. She knew she would only have one shot at getting through to him. "It seems the tables have turned. What's going on with you Donald? I'm not worth this. You deserve so much more."

"You're worth it to me." Donald kicked at the ground, refusing to meet her eyes.

"I'm sorry I hurt you. You have to know that was never my intention."

"I'm not mad at you, Keegan. I know it's not your fault." He looked off in the distance. "I just can't seem to accept that you're gone. You're everything to me."

Keegan didn't know what to say to that. Her heart ached for him.

"Are you happy?" Donald asked. Keegan could hear the pain in his voice.

"Yes." She took a step towards him. "But I'm not happy that you're going through this."

"Can't you try to fight the bond Keegan? We were great together."

"I couldn't if I wanted to," she said softly.

"Why are you even here? Why don't you go back to your chosen?" Donald glared at her.

"Magic is beyond us, Donald. We just have to accept it. You *will* find someone new and forget all about me."

"I don't want anyone else."

Donald reached for her, both of his hands grasping her arms. He pulled her against him and tried to kiss her.

"Donald!" Keegan pushed him roughly away. "I can't."

"You had no problem kissing him when we were together," Donald spat, his hands balling into fists at his sides.

Keegan stared at him, wondering if the Donald she knew was still inside him.

"I want you to see something. I want you to see the strength of an elf's bond." Keegan reached up and unclasped her necklace, letting it drop to the ground.

Pain flashed in her eyes as she clutched her stomach and doubled over. The pain hit her with an intensity she hadn't expected; she couldn't breathe.

"What's wrong?" Donald bent down and tried to hold her up, but she fell to the ground and curled up as the pain coursed through her body.

Donald was frantic. "Keegan, please, what's going on? Tell me how to fix it."

"Necklace." She managed to get out between clenched teeth.

Donald looked around in a panic and found the necklace of pink stones laying on the ground. He grabbed it with shaking hands and tried to clasp it around Keegan's neck.

Slowly, the pain dissipated from her body, allowing her body to relax. She stayed on the ground, waiting for it to disappear entirely.

Donald was on his knees beside her, his breath coming fast. He wrapped his arms around her, holding her tightly. "Keegan, what just happened? Are you ok?"

Keegan pulled herself up to sitting position and tried not to think about the lingering pain. "When I'm separated from Rourk, that is what happens to my body. My mom made a necklace to keep the worst of it at bay."

Donald stared at her, the disbelief clear on his face. "He did that to you? I'll kill him."

She had never heard the edge in his voice before. "He didn't do it. The bond did. I told you—we can't fight the bond. Would you want me to be in constant pain?"

Donald looked away, his jaw clenched. "Are you only with him to avoid pain?"

Keegan smiled sadly. "No, my heart needs him Donald. I can't be with anyone except him. We are made for each other, and I love him."

"If you came here to make me feel better, you didn't do a very good job. You need to leave." He stood up and put distance between them.

"Please, don't shut me out. I still want to be your friend."

Donald laughed. "Not going to happen." He shifted and took off into the woods.

Keegan reached down and picked up his clothing. Her heart ached—she really thought she would be able to get through to him. It seemed she might have made things worse.

Back at the hotel, she told everyone what happened, then called Rourk and filled him in.

"So am I coming to Alaska or California tomorrow? I need to get my ticket," Rourk said calmly.

"I don't know what to do. I don't think I can help him. I don't think anyone can help him until he is ready. They want to stay the weekend and see if the guys can get through to him. I don't know if I should stay or just go home. Anna and Lauren are staying."

"I'll make my ticket to California. I know you want to be there. I really don't care where I go as long as I'm with you."

"Thank you. I can't wait to see you."

"Keegan, please don't take off your necklace again until I'm around. I really hate knowing you were in pain."

"I won't. I promise. I really thought it would help."

Chapter 15

During the flight, Rourk thought about the shifter, and tried to see things from his point of view. Rourk knew what it felt like to lose Keegan, and it wasn't a good feeling.

However, the boy should simply have more self control than he'd been showing. Rourk was slightly disgusted with the fact that he shifted in public; it was really inexcusable.

Because of the time difference, his flight touched down in California fairly early. His pulse quickened as he walked off the plane. Just the thought of seeing Keegan drove him crazy. He had to consciously tell himself not to push people out of the way to get to her. Through the sea of people, all he saw was her beautiful smile. He loved the way her eyes lit up when she saw him. He lengthened his stride and pulled her into his arms, inhaling the scent of sandalwood and vanilla. "I've missed you."

"You better." Keegan grinned. "I'm so glad you're here. I felt lost without you."

Rourk ran his hands through her hair and she tilted her head to meet his lips. It was as if all the people in the airport disappeared and it was only them. He loved the way she made him feel.

Rourk took a step back to take her in. He smiled when he saw the blush creep up her face. "How are you doing?"

"I'm fine, much better now that you're here. Thank you for coming." She gave him a slight smile. "I'm sure it's not easy for you."

Rourk laughed. "It's fine Keegan. As long as I am with you I really don't care where we are." He laced his fingers between hers and walked out towards the exit. "I get to properly meet your friends."

Keegan squeezed his hand. "Don't expect a warm welcome from the guys, but Anna and Lauren will be excited to meet you. I got you a room next to ours. I hope that is ok?"

"Thank you. So, no luck talking sense into Donald?"

"He wouldn't listen to me. I think he hates me."

Rourk shook his head. "He doesn't hate you. If he hated you, he wouldn't be taking things so hard. I'm sure he wishes he could hate you. It would make his life easier."

Keegan tilted her head to the side and looked up at him, her blue-green eyes looked serious. "Did you wish you could hate me?"

"No, I didn't bother to try to fight my feelings for you. I knew it would be useless." Rourk wrapped his arm around her and pulled her closer. "We're together now. I don't like to dwell on the past."

Keegan knocked on the door and Lauren flung it open. "It's about time. Rourk, it's so good to finally meet you. I don't think we got introduced at Keegan's birthday party." Lauren winked and nudged his arm.

"Keegan talks about you two constantly. She is lucky to have such great friends." Rourk smiled over at Anna, and she waved back.

"Are you starving? There's a little diner down the street. Actually, my stomach just growled. We're going to eat." Anna stood up and moved towards the door.

Keegan looked over at Rourk and he shrugged. "That works for me. Let me just throw my bag in my room and I'll be right back."

Keegan grinned at the girls after he left the room. "Isn't he amazing?"

Lauren gave a mischievous grin. "Spill the beans. How's the elven sex? I imagine with his intensity it's incredible."

Keegan looked down at the tan worn carpet and focused on a spot on the floor. "I wouldn't know. He wants to wait till we get married."

"Get out of here!" Anna pushed her and almost made her fall to the ground. "That boy is too good to be true."

Anna sighed. "How is it possible that the three of us are still virgins? We're hot right?"

Keegan laughed, and Lauren was strangely quiet.

"Lauren!" The both said at the same time.

Anna screamed, "You lost your virginity and didn't tell us?"

Lauren had a far away look on her face with a secret smile. "I told you about Tristen."

"We want details. Is it wonderful?" Anna asked.

"You have no idea. I can't even begin to describe it. It's like we're brought to another dimension. I know that sounds ridiculous, and I'm sure it's because we are both fairies, although I have nothing to compare it to." Her face flushed red.

A knock on the door startled them out of their thoughts.

Keegan opened the door. Rourk stood on the other side, running his hands through his hair. "Am I interrupting something?"

"Nope, just girl talk. Let's go eat." Keegan put her arm through his and they left for dinner.

Lauren had invited the guys, but Keegan guessed they decided not to show up. Which was understandable, but the girls found it slightly annoying. It wasn't as if Rourk had any control over being Keegan's chosen.

Keegan enjoyed seeing her friends get to know Rourk better, although he seemed uncomfortable being grilled by them.

"When are you moving to Washington?" Anna asked.

"If everything goes as planned we should be moving next month."

Keegan's eyes lit up. "Really?"

Rourk put his hand on hers. "Really. Tommy has already been looking for a place for us."

"Ohhh…who is Tommy? Is he hot like you?" Ann grinned wickedly and rubbed her hands together.

Rourk's face flushed, and he looked at Keegan for help. "He's a friend I made at basic training, and we'll be roommates. He's a great guy."

Anna slumped in her seat. "Great guy is codeword for not a sexy beast."

They all laughed.

"Keegan, you'll be moving soon too, right?" Lauren reached over and grabbed a napkin.

"Yep. I'm going to move in with Anna—well, we're going to get a place together."

"I'm so jealous." Lauren sighed. "Tristen and I will have to come visit once you guys get settled in."

"Sounds pretty serious." Keegan raised an eyebrow.

Lauren smiled. "I hope it is. We haven't been together long, but I know he's the one."

"I don't think I'll ever find anyone." Anna frowned.

Keegan decided to change the subject. "So what are we going to do about Donald? I have to leave by Sunday."

"I don't know, maybe we should just leave him alone. I wouldn't want someone chasing after me if I wanted to be alone," Lauren said.

"Does anyone know if he has shifted in public again or if it was a one-time occurrence? That's the main issue. Can you imagine if the humans realized shifters were real? That would be trouble for all of us." Rourk glanced around at the girls seriously before he took a bite out of his sandwich.

"I've only heard of the one incidence, but who knows? There could have been more. He gets drunk all the time and loses control. I don't think he has been to a class in weeks," Lauren said.

Keegan lowered her head. "It's all my fault. I should have handled things differently."

"It's not your fault, Keegan. You have no control of how someone reacts." Rourk squeezed her hand under the table.

They spent the day driving around and looking for Donald. Occasionally, they stopped to ask passers-by if anyone had spotted him, but no one had. He was probably hiding in the woods, or he had moved on. After a day of no luck, they all went to their rooms for the night and agreed to try again tomorrow. If they didn't have any luck, Anna would use a spell to track his location again.

Rourk had an idea of his own, but he didn't want to let the girls in on the plan. Tracking was what he did best. He knew as long as Donald was in the area, he could find him. Usually, Rourk would take the hard route and search for him without using his powers, but they were running short on time. He wanted to get this wrapped up so he could spend more time with Keegan.

He shook his head at the simplicity of it all, closed his eyes, and thought of nothing else but Donald. Rourk saw the dimly lit room with a tacky neon sign the said "Beer Here." He tried to look around for clues, but his gift only allowed him to see the person he was thinking of and whatever was directly behind that person. Donald was sitting at a bar drinking and looking pissed off. Rourk snapped his eyes open.

He grabbed his laptop; he was surprised how much it had come in handy. Rourk searched for local bars: there were five. He would check them systematically. He wasn't sure what he would say to the shifter, but he was hoping he could talk some sense into him. Rourk grabbed his jacket and headed out on foot.

The town was quiet as he walked the streets one by one, going into the bars, and not seeing Donald. When he made it to the third rundown bar, he heard raised voices and thought his luck had changed. No one noticed Rourk when he walked in. They were too focused on the commotion in the corner.

The bar was dark and smelled of cigarettes and cheap perfume. Three guys had Donald backed into a corner. His eyes were wild, liked a caged animal, and Rourk knew his instinct was to shift. Rourk couldn't allow that to happen.

A hush fell over the patrons as Rourk walked confidently up to the three men. A man with a goatee had a beer bottle with broken, jagged edges and was holding it by the stem.

"Leave him alone," Rourk called out evenly.

"Oh yeah? And what are you going to do about it?" A bald guy with bulging muscles glanced over at Rourk with a laugh.

"Let's just say it won't be pretty. Let him go now and you guys can all walk away unharmed."

"Get out of here, Rourk. I don't need your help," Donald spat.

"I told you to keep your mouth shut, punk." The guy holding Donald against the wall punched him in the face.

Donald wiped the blood from his mouth and glared at Rourk.

Rourk said nothing. He watched the largest man with tribal tattoos walk towards him.

"Oh so you think you're a tough guy, huh?"

He must have been at least 6'2" and over 200 pounds. He had on a worn leather jacket. He looked like he had been in his share of fights in his day. His nose was crooked from being broken too many times. As soon as he was in striking distance, Rourk sprung. He knew better than to hesitate. The large man threw a punch, which Rourk blocked easily. Rourk slammed his head into the guy's nose and blood poured out. The man seemed dazed and started to fall forward. Rourk swiftly turned the man to face his buddies. Rourk had the guy's elbow pressed against his own back. He groaned.

"Let my friend go," Rourk said calmly.

"I'm not your friend." Donald glared at Rourk.

The two men that had Donald looked at each other and the one with the broken bottle dropped his grip on Donald and moved forward. Rourk kneed the bald one hard in the back and as he dropped to his knees, Rourk slammed his elbow into the guy's temple. The man dropped to the ground. Rourk then went after the other man, who was still advancing towards him.

He had a crazed look in his eyes as he rushed forward, ready to strike. Rourk sidestepped and raised his arm to block the glass and rammed his other hand into the man's throat, crushing his windpipe. The guy's brown eyes widened as he dropped the glass, and his hands flew to his throat.

The last man standing fidgeted nervously. He was much smaller than the others. He pushed Donald towards Rourk. "You can have him. Just make sure he never comes back to this bar again."

Rourk nodded at the man and grabbed Donald's arm to lead him out.

Donald yanked his arm away. "Don't touch me."

"You're welcome."

"I didn't ask for your help. Why are you even here?" His words slurred slightly from too much drink.

"I know what you are going through. Trust me. It's not too long ago that you took Keegan from me. Not that I blame you, I would have done the same thing."

Donald stopped walking and stared at Rourk. "You have no idea what I am going through. I feel empty. I just want to feel again. When I was with Keegan…"

"Let her go. She is not coming back and you know it."

"What do you think I have been trying to do?" Donald hung his head.

"Shifting in public is trying to let go? You are putting everyone in danger with your recklessness. I would expect more from someone who had earned Keegan's affection. You can't fight magic, shifter. If Keegan had chosen you over me, I would have walked away and let her be happy. If you cared for her half as much as you claim, you will do the same." Rourk turned and walked away.

Chapter 16

Keegan woke up to the ding of her phone. She wiped the sleep from her eyes and was surprised to see it was from Donald.

I'm sorry for being such an ass. I need to go away for awhile and get myself straight. Tell the guys I'll be back next semester. You deserve to be happy. Rourk is a lucky man.

Keegan fumbled to reply. *Are you ok? Do you want to meet?*

I'm long gone. Don't worry about me, I'll be fine. Someone talked some sense into me.

I'm glad you are ok. I'm sorry I hurt you.

Not your fault. Take care, and thank you for the time we had together.

Keegan wiped a tear from her cheek. *We had fun. You'll always be special to me.*

But I'll never be your chosen.

No, I'm sorry he was picked for me long before we met.

I know. Bye Keegan.

Stay safe. Keegan sat up in bed and stared at the phone. She truly hoped he was ok. She wished she could tell him what Thaddeus had told her about the white tiger, but she knew that would be crossing the line. He had to find her on his own. Let life take the course it was meant to take.

Anna and Lauren were stirring. Once they were awake, Keegan filled them in on the texts.

"I wonder what changed his mind?" Anna murmured, stretching under the covers.

"I don't know. He didn't say."

"There's nothing else we can do," Lauren said. She was lying on her stomach, hugging her pillow with both arms.

Anna smiled. "I guess it's time to go home, then. Our job is done."

Keegan decided she would just stay there with Rourk since he only had one more day. There was no sense in having him pay for another plane ticket. Anna and Lauren packed their things and said their goodbyes, followed by Spencer, Sam and Calvron, who were angry Donald hadn't contacted them.

Keegan got dressed and knocked on Rourk's door. He opened it with a welcoming smile.

"Wasn't sure you were ever going to show up." He wrapped his arms around her waist and pulled her in.

"Just had to say goodbye to everyone. It's just me and you left." She bit her lip and smiled up at him.

"You have no idea how happy that makes me." Rourk's grey eyes twinkled in the sunlight.

"Donald texted me that he had to get away to get himself right again."

"That's good." Rourk's expression didn't change.

"He said someone talked some sense into him. Do you happen to know who that was?"

"We might have had words." Rourk stared down at her, his face stoic.

"Whatever you said seems to have helped. He said you were lucky."

"I am lucky." Rourk tucked a finger under her chin and tilted her head up for a kiss.

Keegan loved the feel of his lips on hers. He tangled his hands in her hair, intensifying the kiss until she was breathless. She always got so caught up in their kisses.

Grudgingly, she pulled back, and stared into his grey eyes that she loved so much. "So, what do you want to do today? And please don't say hiking."

Rourk laughed loudly. "Ok, well, that was my first thought. There are tons of trails around here. What would you like to do? Shop, play tourist, or just hang out in the room?"

"As much as hanging out in the room sounds appealing, I think I would want to attack you. We should probably play tourist. I've never been to California before. This town looks pretty neat; we can go explore. If there is nothing of interest, we can always take a long drive to the next city." Keegan ran her fingers up his arm. It made her fingertips tingle.

"Rourk, I want to get married," Keegan blurted, and then blushed.

He took a step back, his hands on the side of her arms as he looked at her closely. "Where is this coming from?"

"I want to be with you always. It's killing me being separated from you."

"You will always be with me, and we would be separated regardless because of the military. I will soon be in Washington with you."

"I know but I want to wake up with you every morning, and greet you when you get home from work."

"Does this have anything to do with Donald? I don't get the sudden change. You know I would marry you today, but I need to be sure this is what you really want and not some whim."

"Well, it does kinda have something to do with Donald." She felt Rourk's body tense up.

"Not in a bad way. You're the only one for me. We're meant to be together. I've just been stubborn. I don't even know why I tried to go against tradition. It was just sprung on me so quickly." She gazed into his eyes. "I want to be your wife. I want to grow old with you and someday have little elf babies running around."

Rourk grinned widely. "You have made me the happiest man in the world."

"That's a little dramatic. But I like the sound of it." Keegan leaned up and Rourk kissed her.

"So how soon are you thinking? We could fly out to Vegas tonight." Rourk raised an eyebrow and grinned.

"It's fall and I've always wanted a fall wedding. I really want to get married on the property at my favorite spot. My mom is going to freak out." Keegan was starting to get excited about planning the handfasting. Her mind raced with all the things they would have to do. Elves tended to have large weddings. Any excuse to throw a party was a good one.

"I love the idea of getting married there—it seems right." Rourk couldn't believe she had changed her mind. He had been prepared to wait years.

"We'll all have time off for Thanksgiving. Is that too soon? I don't know if I'll be able to find a dress that quickly since it's only a little over a month away." Keegan felt a sudden urge to call her mother. She wished Anna and Lauren hadn't left they could go in search of a dress. Her mind was running a mile a minute.

"It's not soon enough as far as I'm concerned."

Keegan laid her head down on his chest and could hear his heart beating loudly. "I love you," she whispered.

Rourk pulled her tight. "Go call your mom. You know you want to."

"You read my mind." She reached in her pocket and pulled out her phone.

Rourk smiled as she paced back and forth, chattering away to her mother. She finally ended the call. "She's over the moon, and she started ticking off a list of things we had to take care of. I didn't realize so much went into planning a wedding. As far as I'm concerned it could just be us and my family. I'd be happy. I don't need anything elaborate."

"I'm sure it will be perfect. I guess I'll have to ask Tommy to be my best man."

"Oh goodness. I wonder if I can have two maids of honor? I can't pick between Anna and Lauren!" Keegan could feel the panic rising in her chest.

"You'll figure something out. They'll understand no matter what you decide."

"You're right. I'll deal with that later. For now, I want to enjoy spending the day with you before we have to be separated again." She reached for his hand and they headed for the exit together.

"I wonder how Athena is doing? I hate that I had to leave her for so long."

"I'm sure she is doing fine. It was just a few days. You can always call and check up on her if you're worried."

"That's a great idea."

Keegan scrolled to find the kennel's number and dialed. She talked on the phone for a couple of minutes before thanking the person on the other end and hanging up. "She's fine. All the kennel workers love her. The little runt probably doesn't even miss us."

Rourk laughed.

"Let's walk instead of taking the car. I saw they had a bike rental shop; we can really be tourists," Keegan said.

"That sounds like fun."

Keegan wrapped her arm around Rourk's waist as they walked, their feet in perfect rhythm. She shivered at the chill in the air, but it was nothing compared to Alaska. The cool air felt refreshing. She randomly pulled Rourk into some of the little stores and picked up some knick-knacks. Keegan found a beautiful green amber necklace for her mother. She pulled out her phone and looked up the meaning on Google. She smiled when she saw it was rare and often a favorite for healers to help with chronic ailments.

Pushing the door open to the bike shop, they were met with a loud bell as they entered. Keegan laughed when she saw the bikes were all bright orange, old-school cruisers. She asked for one with a basket in case they found more shops. She wouldn't let Rourk take off without getting a photo of him on the bike. He looked so out of place riding it.

He led the way to a bike trail that meandered along the coast. The view was stunning—rugged cliffs that lined the coast so that the ocean crashed against them. Keegan skidded the bike to a stop over and over to take photos. She couldn't wait to add them to her travel collection. There was just something about seaside towns that she found so relaxing, and being with Rourk made it perfect. They spent hours riding around and enjoying each other's company. As usual, the day went too quickly.

Saying goodbye was not getting any easier.

Keegan's heart felt like it was tearing in shreds when they separated at the airport. She glanced at her watch—she still had an hour and twenty minutes before her plane would leave. Of course, she and Rourk were on different concourses. She was hungry, so she slowly trudged to a little shop to grab a snack. She noticed a wedding magazine on the rack and flipped through it. Unable to resist, she added it to her purchases. She still couldn't believe she was going to get married in a little over a month. What she *really* couldn't believe was the idea didn't freak her out at all. She was young, but so what? So were all the other elves that got married. They seemed to be doing fine. She couldn't imagine her life without Rourk in it.

Keegan picked up her phone and called Anna to fill her in on the news.

"Guess what?"

"No idea. You saw the yeti?"

"Close. Rourk and I are going to get married next month!"

"Seriously? That's awesome, Keegan. I'm envious of you guys. I guess that means we won't be roommates."

Keegan hadn't even thought of that. "I'm sorry. I didn't even think of that. I was really looking forward living with you."

"It's ok. You're a slob anyway and that would have driven me crazy."

"I've gotten better." Keegan laughed.

"I'll just find a studio for myself. I have to get out of these dorms. At least we'll be in the same city. So, what's the big plan?"

Keegan told her how she wanted to get married on Thanksgiving break at her parents' property.

"The timing is great since we all planned on going home for the holidays. Don't make me wear a horrendous bridesmaid dress. I'm serious, no bright yellow or big ruffles."

Keegan paced around the seating area. There was so much planning she hadn't thought about. "I promise your dress won't be ugly."

"Make sure Rourk brings some of his hot military friends."

"You're too much, Anna. Ok—I'm at the airport. I'll call you soon. I can't wait to see you again."

Keegan still had time to kill, so she opened her magazine. Most of the dresses were way too fancy for her taste. She pictured herself wearing a flowing, simple ivory gown in chiffon. She could feel the stress rising when she wondered if she would have time to find the perfect dress. Her body temperature was quickly dropping. Taking a few deep breaths, she tried to center herself; she closed her eyes and thought of Rourk. Her body relaxed when she pictured him walking onto the plane. He stopped mid-step and smiled.

She knew he realized she was thinking about him. Crisis averted—she didn't freeze the airport. That would not be good, especially with all the cameras and security. *Imagine explaining* that *to Mom.*

Chapter 17

Keegan wasn't sure how she made it through the week without Rourk. It felt like the longest week of her life. Her classes dragged on. The only thing that made time speed up was when she volunteered at the wildlife shelter. Having the computers certainly helped, but it just wasn't the same.

This weekend, they were meeting in Washington, and Rourk was bringing his friend Tommy so they could check out the area and the apartments Tommy had seen online. Keegan was excited to meet a friend of Rourk's. She still couldn't get over his close call with the accident and was very grateful that her mother was a healer. She was also a little nervous—she felt like she needed Tommy's approval.

Anna was waiting outside the gate when Keegan came out of the security checkpoint. Anna had once again morphed her looks. Today, she had an ultra short pixie cut and her hair was almost black. Her crazy green eyes stood out even more with her dark hair and light skin.

Keegan squeezed her tightly. "Your hair looks amazing. I have no idea how you can pull off so many looks. You're like a chameleon."

"Please tell me this isn't your attempt to hook me up on a blind date with Rourk's buddy."

"You wish!" Keegan laughed. The thought had crossed her mind, but she wanted to meet Tommy before she pawned him off on one of her best friends. She wanted to make sure he was good enough for her.

"You're right, I was hoping." Anna bumped Keegan with her hip. They laughed and headed to a nearby cafe.

They caught up and talked about the wedding plans. "I think we'll just let Lauren pick out the dress, if that's ok with you?" Keegan raised an eyebrow.

"Let me think about this. I could spend hours trying on dresses or let

Lauren pick. I think I'll go with Lauren."

Keegan nodded. "As much as I hate to admit it, she does have the best taste out of the three of us."

"You won't hear me complaining." Anna bit into a peanut butter cookie, and then filled Keegan in on the apartment she had just rented. Keegan couldn't recall the last time Anna had been so exited about something. She was curious to see if the place lived up to Anna's descriptions. One of her new witch friends had recommended it, and Keegan was certain magic had been involved in securing the apartment and moving in so fast.

Keegan was getting anxious to see Rourk. As much as she enjoyed seeing one of her best friends, time seemed to stop when she was waiting for her chosen. She kept glancing around and checking the clock on her phone. When she wasn't with Rourk, it was as if the clocks stopped, and sadly, time sped up when he was around.

"He'll be here soon. Calm down," Anna chastised, reaching across the table and snagging Keegan's phone.

Keegan touched the necklace she had grown to love. "I know. I just miss him so much."

Rourk was impatient to see Keegan. Tommy was talking his ear off, but he only heard half of what he was saying. He tried to nod at the appropriate times. He realized he was tapping his foot and immediately planted his foot firmly on the ground. Keegan was the only person that had been able to get under his skin. He didn't feel in control when it came to her. Not that he minded. When was this plane going to land? He looked at his watch yet again.

Finally, he heard the landing gears and a wave of relief washed over him. It wouldn't be long now. The excitement was building in his chest as they walked towards the greeting area.

Keegan raced to him as soon as he passed security. He loved that she was as excited as he was to be back with her. "I missed you," he whispered in her ear.

"It felt like it took you forever to get here." She pressed her body to his.

"I know." He buried his head in her hair inhaling her scent.

Tommy cleared his throat. "Are you going to introduce me or what?"

Rourk jerked away from Keegan and cleared his throat. "I'm sorry. I forgot you were here."

"Thanks…"

"Keegan, this is Tommy—my friend I've told you about."

Keegan took in the tall, slender blond boy with kind blue eyes and freckles scattered across his face. There was nothing remarkable about him, but he had an infectious smile. She found herself liking him immediately. Keegan turned to introduce Anna, but she wasn't there.

Where did she go? Keegan glanced around and didn't see her anywhere. Great. She grabbed her phone out of her pocket to find out where she went and noticed she had a text from her.

Went to get the car meet you out front.

"Anna's waiting out front." Keegan wrapped her arm around Rourk's waist and smiled up at him. "Let's go. Where is your hotel?"

"We got a place close to Anna's to try to limit the inconvenience."

"That was a great idea."

Keegan steered them towards Anna's old beat-up brown Buick. She had no idea how that thing was still running, or how it had made the cross-country trip. Anna jumped out and ran around to open the trunk. She looked up and nearly bumped into Tommy. "Oh."

Tommy inhaled sharply. "You're Anna?"

She nodded slowly. "You're Tommy?"

They reached for the trunk at the same time and pulled back their hands quickly as they touched.

"You shocked me!" Anna laughed.

"You shocked me. You're, like, electric." Tommy gave her a crooked grin.

Rourk and Keegan watched the exchange. There was obviously a mutual attraction going on. *Maybe I'm not so bad at match making after all*, Keegan thought with a smirk.

As if Rourk knew what she was thinking, he grinned and shook his head while he opened the front door for her. "Stay out of it." He reached down and kissed her, and she wished they were alone. It was going to be hard to share him this weekend. She wanted him all to herself.

Anna took off down the road. She kept glancing in the mirror at Tommy and smiling. Keegan couldn't believe it—she had never seen Anna take to someone so quickly. It was good to see that she had moved on from her long time obsession with Xavier.

Keegan turned in her seat. "Do you guys want to be dropped off at the hotel or go to Anna's for a bit?"

"I'm not in a rush to get to the hotel. I'd like to see where Anna lives." Tommy looked at Rourk. "If that's ok with you."

"Apartment sounds good." Rourk had just got Keegan; he wasn't ready to part ways.

Keegan turned back and gave him a grateful smile.

Tommy leaned forward in his seat and draped his arm over the front seat. "So, do you like living in Washington?"

Anna glanced over her shoulder and flashed him a dazzling smile. "I love it here. It's so beautiful, even with all the rain. There's so much to do outdoors and tons of cool coffee shops."

"Eyes on the road before you get us killed," Keegan said, poking Anna in the arm.

Anna gripped the steering wheel tightly, her eyes back on the road. "You're right. I just get so excited about this place. It's home now."

"How far is your apartment from here?" Tommy asked.

"It's not too far. About another twenty-five minutes." Anna turned up the radio and tapped her fingers along with the music. She kept glancing at the guy in the backseat. She had joked about meeting Rourk's friend, but she had no idea he would be so incredible sexy. He probably thought she was a weirdo. She never had any luck with guys.

Anna eased the car into her parking lot. She couldn't remember if she had picked up around her place before she left or not. She had been too excited to see Keegan. Oh, well. Too late to do anything about it now.

The guys grabbed their backpacks and followed Anna and Keegan up the cobblestone walkway. Keegan was surprised by the flowers that paved the way. There were daisies and peonies in a variety of colors, flanked by bushy spider plants and tall, yellow black-eyed Susans. The lawn was emerald green.

"Anna, how do you keep your flowers alive?" Keegan asked. "I can't even keep a houseplant for more than a couple of weeks."

"Magic," Anna replied casually.

Keegan sucked in a breath and looked at Tommy to see his reaction. He was unfazed. It must have gone over his head—or he thought she was joking.

"Good one." Keegan laughed.

Anna fumbled with her keys and unlocked the small, bright blue door. She pushed it open, switching on the light as they walked though.

Keegan gasped—it was beautiful. Anna's new home was a tiny studio apartment that felt like a hidden oasis. Pots of herbs perched on all the windowsills and crystals were scattered around every available surface. A small altar occupied a corner of the living area; Celtic music played softly in the background. The whole apartment smelled of patchouli. She still had a few unpacked boxes in the corner.

The place seemed like it was made especially for Anna. It was obvious that she loved the place from the way she cared for it—from the pressed pagan tapestries on the walls to the shiny, clean hardwood floors. Keegan could see why Anna had fallen in love with it.

"Do you guys want coffee?" Anna threw her keys on the counter and walked into the kitchen.

"Sure. I could use a cup." Tommy dropped his bag at the doorway and followed her to the kitchen.

Keegan and Rourk looked at each other and shared a smile. Keegan pulled him towards the black suede futon. "I'm so glad you're here."

"Me too." He buried his head in her hair. "I missed your smell."

Keegan laughed. His voice sent chills down her spine.

"Just think—next month, I will be Mrs. Kavanagh. Keegan Kavanagh. I like the sound of it."

"We'll have to start calling you K-squared." Tommy laughed as he walked back into the room.

"K-squared has a nice ring to it." Anna trailed behind him, holding a mug in her hand. "Do you guys want a cup? If so, help yourselves."

Rourk glanced at Keegan. "Want me to make you one?"

"Sure. Milk and two sugars. And no one is calling me K-squared."

Rourk stood up, and Tommy went with him, staying silent until they were in the kitchen. "Holy shit, Rourk. Why didn't you tell me that Anna was a goddess? I don't think I've ever met anyone so incredible in my life."

"I never noticed." Rourk shrugged. He opened several cabinets searching for Anna's coffee mugs before Tommy indicated the right one.

"Never noticed? It's blinding," Tommy said in a hushed tone.

"I feel the same way about Keegan. She's the only thing I notice when she is around." Rourk looked over the counter at Keegan who was sitting on the couch with her feet tucked beneath her while she talked to an animated Anna.

"I'm sure she's way out of my league." Tommy's face fell as his eyes drifted to Anna.

Rourk stirred Keegan's coffee and poured himself a cup—he drank it black. In the military, you didn't always have the luxury of milk and sugar.

"You never know until you try. Stranger things have happened," Rourk finally answered, thinking of Tommy's miraculous recovery. He narrowed his eyes as he tapped the spoon on Keegan's mug. "She's Keegan's best friend. Don't even think of hurting her."

"Duly noted. I doubt she'd even give me the time of day."

Rourk put the spoon in the sink and went back to the sitting area. It wasn't exactly new territory, the fact that Tommy was always going on about girls. Rourk just wanted to be with Keegan. Tommy could take care of himself.

He handed the cup to Keegan and their hands brushed; she smiled when the tingling sensation shot through her from the contact. Her smile was luminous.

The four of them sat and talked for an hour, catching up. Keegan found it amusing to watch the attraction between Anna and Tommy. She caught them stealing glances at each other several times. Who would have guessed it?

Chapter 18

When his third mug was empty, Rourk patted Keegan's leg and smiled. "Are you ready to check out some apartments? If we don't get started soon, we'll have to push it off till tomorrow."

"I thought you would never ask."

Anna sighed. "I guess that means I have to get up. It's so nice having company."

Tommy pulled a notebook from his backpack. "Do you know where this apartment is?"

She took the paper and stared at it. "Not really. But we can plug it into the GPS and it will show us the way."

Tommy laughed. "Well, I have a few different ones I'd like to check out, if you don't mind?"

"I'm at your service. You ask, and you shall receive."

"Anna, watch what you say around this one," Rourk warned with a grin.

"He's right. A beautiful girl like you…" Tommy winked. "Shouldn't say things like that. I might take it literally."

Anna's face flushed red. "Let's go before I say something I might regret."

As everyone gathered their belongings, Anna grabbed her car keys from the table by the door. They were lying next to a huge amethyst geode.

"Nice rock," Tommy said as he hefted his bag on his shoulder.

Anna narrowed her eyes. "It's not just a rock. It's a crystal."

"Sorry." He held his hands up in mock surrender. "It's pretty, that's all I'm saying."

Anna rolled her eyes and pushed him towards the door.

Tommy had made several appointments before Keegan had decided it was time to get married. So, even though he and Rourk weren't looking to live together anymore, they figured browsing together would accomplish just as much as if they did it separately.

The first place they checked out did not live up to the brochures. The smell of fried foods and cigarettes hit them as they walked through the main entrance. An older lady with graying hair sat behind the counter. Her eyes were wide-set and her nose was crooked—like it had been broken but never reset. Tommy told her he had made an appointment online to check out an apartment. She reached under the counter and pulled out a key.

Rourk thought there was no way in hell he was going to live in this dump with Keegan. The elevator shook as they headed to the sixth floor.

"It looked so nice on the website," Tommy mumbled under his breath.

"We're here. We might as well check it out. Maybe it will surprise us," Keegan said.

Tommy fiddled with the key a couple minutes and finally pushed the door open. They walked into the empty foyer. There was wallpaper peeling off the wall and brown spots on the ceiling. The carpet was so old and dirty that the color was indistinguishable.

"Who uses wallpaper anymore?" Keegan asked as she ran her hand down the wall. It felt sticky.

The rest of the apartment was more of the same. They just did a quick walk through and crossed it off the list. The woman didn't seem too surprised when they handed the key back and said they were going to check out some other places first.

The next place they went to was much better. The price was quite a bit higher, and the apartments were pretty small, but at least they were clean. They peeked into the gym first, and then went in the back to see the pool before they looked upstairs.

Tommy glanced around the living room. "I like it. It's much bigger than our barracks, and the gym is top notch. Really all I need is a clean place and somewhere to workout. There are lots of hiking trails, too. Plus, it's not too big for just me."

Rourk walked into the kitchen and turned on the faucet. The water ran clear, and it heated up quickly.

Anna looked at Keegan. "What do you think?"

"It's ok. I'd still like to see the other two places."

Rourk nodded his head in agreement.

The next place they didn't even bother to go in. There were bars on all the windows. Never a good sign. Anna turned the car around without a word, and they plugged on to the next location.

As soon as they pulled up, Keegan knew it would be her home with Rourk. A private gate opened to a landscape that was breathtaking: lush plants and colorful flowers placed strategically around meandering paths. But, that wasn't what caught Keegan's eye: it was the waterfall she could hear in the distance. It made her feel like she was home. "This is it Rourk."

He laughed. "We haven't even been inside."

"I don't care. I can feel it. This is where we are meant to be."

He draped his arm around her shoulder. "We'll at least look at it before we sign the papers. Ok?"

"I guess I can agree to that." She grinned up at him and threw her arm around his waist. "This will be our first home as a married couple."

Rourk leaned down and kissed the top of her head. "We need to make sure they accept pets."

"Oh, they better!" Keegan marched up to the counter. She narrowed her eyes at the young man behind it. "Do you allow pets?"

He pushed his glasses back further on his nose. "Yes. But you have to put down a pet deposit. Which is one month's rent."

"That's pretty steep." Keegan said.

He shrugged his shoulder and looked back down at his paperwork.

"We'd like to check out a two-bedroom."

"Do you want to see a villa or an apartment?"

Keegan looked up at Rourk questioningly.

"Whatever you want."

"We'd like to see a villa." The man made a phone call, and a tall blond woman wearing too much make-up came out to meet them. She towered over Keegan. "My name is Lisa, and I'll be your tour guide today." It was obviously a well-rehearsed line, and it looked awkward on her face. She had probably gone overboard on the Botox. "Right this way. You're in luck—we do have a villa open. They usually go quickly."

Keegan rolled her eyes. They probably said that to everyone.

They walked through the apartment building and out the back door. Keegan sucked in her breath. A sense of calmness came over her as she stepped foot on the stone pathway. Off in the distance, she could see little wooden bungalows. That was the only way she could think to describe them. They had small porches, each with two wooden chairs and a matching table that appeared to be made of branches. She squeezed Rourk's hand, and he squeezed back. There was enough distance between each bungalow to give a sense of privacy.

"1303 is open. It's at the back of the property, so I'm afraid you will have a walk in the morning to get to your vehicles. Would that be a problem?"

"Not at all," Rourk replied.

Keegan looked back at Anna with a big grin. Anna gave her the thumbs-up.

The woman wasn't kidding that it was a walk. About ten minutes later, they reached 1303 tucked in the back of the complex. Keegan felt the excitement rise in her chest. The closer they got to the bungalow, the louder the rushing water from the waterfall. She didn't dare ask the woman about it. Besides, it would be much more exciting for Rourk and her to find it on their own.

Once they reached the doorway, the woman turned the key and pushed the door open. Keegan could have squealed with delight. It was small, but cozy. The first thing she noticed was the skylight. The walls were light mocha, and the kitchen was modern with matching stainless-steel appliances. The woman led them into the master bedroom—it was bigger than her room in Alaska. What really took Keegan by surprise was the bathroom. Smooth stones covered the walls, and it had a deep sunken tub. She ran her hand over the antique-looking faucet.

It really was perfect. Keegan smiled. "We'll take it."

Rourk laughed. The realtor turned and looked at him.

"What's the monthly rate?" he asked.

Lisa told him a figure and he grimaced. It was over his monthly housing allowance. He looked over at Keegan; her face was flushed with excitement. He had been saving a lot of money since he joined the military. "Where do we sign? We won't be moving here until December, will that be a problem?"

"Only if you mind paying for it until you move in. I can't hold it. If you want to take the villa, your rent starts on the day you sign on the dotted line."

"So we could stay the night here if we wanted?" Keegan's eyes widened.

"As long as you fill out the paperwork and pay the deposits, you will get the keys today."

Keegan clapped her hands together. She turned and looked up at Rourk, her blue-green eyes dancing with excitement. "Can we?"

Rourk knew he wouldn't be able to say no. He just nodded. "Of course. Let's get it today."

"I'm sure it's going to take a while for you guys to do the paperwork," Tommy cut in. "Is it ok if Anna takes me back to the other apartment so I can see about securing one for December? If that's ok with Anna."

Anna smiled at him. "I'd love to. We can grab something to eat too."

After they arrived back at the complex's main building, they said their goodbyes and parted ways. Rourk and Keegan were led down a hallway to Lisa's office to sign papers. Keegan was beyond thrilled. Soon, they would be married and living together. Her childhood dream was coming true. She glanced over at Rourk—he was so much more than any fantasy she had made up as a little girl. She stared at his rugged profile and had to consciously stop herself from running her fingers down his strong jaw line.

He caught her eyes on him, and his lips curved into the slightest smile.

He knew she was thinking about him. After several faxes back and forth between the bank—and many signatures later—Lisa handed them the keys. "It's all yours. At least until your lease runs out."

"Thank you!" Keegan snatched the dangling keys and looked down at them in her hand. They really did it; the place was theirs. She held the keys up and shook them at Rourk. "We need to go shopping to furnish our home."

Rourk pictured Keegan's brightly colored apartment with its strange, globe lanterns and fluffy rugs. "What do you say we go with a look that matches the villa? Keep it earth tones and natural looking?"

"That's a great idea!" As they walked back out into the sunlight, Keegan rambled on about simplistic looks she had seen in magazines and stores that used only recycled materials.

Rourk tried to hide his relief and smile. He wasn't sure he could handle a living room with fuzzy pink pillows.

"Let's go home." Keegan grabbed Rourk's hand and tugged him towards the path that led to their new home. "We have to find that waterfall."

"I knew you were thinking that." Rourk looked up at the sky. "The sun is setting. Why don't we save it for tomorrow? I don't think it's very far from our place."

"Do you want to stay here tonight?" Keegan asked.

Rourk hesitated. "We don't have anywhere to sleep. Maybe we should wait till tomorrow or the next visit."

"We could go shopping tonight and buy a mattress and sheets."

Rourk grabbed both of her hands; they always felt so warm. He didn't know if it was just her body heat or the connection between them. "Keegan, I know you are used to having everything you want. Believe me, I want to be able to give you anything you desire. But, I don't think you've seen a soldier's pay check. You are going to have to get used to having less. The rent alone is going to eat up a huge chunk."

Keegan was surprised. "Rourk, money is something we will never have to worry about. My uncle has set up funds for all the children. You know he is wise with numbers."

Rourk pulled his hands back. "Keegan, I don't want us to live off your family's money. I want to support you on my own."

"It's not their money. It's mine. As soon as I turned eighteen, I got access to my trust fund. Having this money allows us to travel. For you to be a solider and not have to worry about how we are going to pay the electric bill. My father has no problem with it. My uncle uses his mental gift to help his family. There is no shame in that."

Rourk considered Keegan's words. It still didn't set right with him. However, he knew as a soldier he would never be able to provide Keegan with the lifestyle she was used to. "You can use your money to buy extras and travels, but I insist on paying the bills and providing food for the table."

Keegan chuckled. "You're so old-fashioned. I love it. And it's our money."

They spent the next hour or so talking about where they would put the furniture. Rourk paced off the measurements, and Keegan entered them into her notes on her phone. She kept track of how many curtains they would need and tried to compile a list for kitchen and bathroom supplies—although she was sure she was forgetting things. There were big purchases to be made, too, like a washer and dryer. So many things to do.

Keegan's phone went off in her hand—Anna was on her way to pick them up. She hated to leave, but agreed that it made more sense to start shopping tomorrow in the daylight. It wouldn't be easy getting the furniture down the stone pathway in the dark, after all.

Chapter 19

Keegan ended up staying the night at Anna's. She would have rather stayed with Rourk, but he got a hotel room with Tommy.

"So what do you think of Tommy?" Keegan grinned and crossed her legs on the couch. The television was playing softly in the background. She sipped her mug of hot cocoa; she hadn't felt so relaxed in a long time.

"Keegan, I don't know what to think. I've never been so attracted to anyone before. Even with Xavier. That obsession grew out of knowing him since I was young. This was instant, and it took me by surprise. He's hot, isn't he?"

Keegan pictured Tommy in her mind, and hot was not one of the words that came to mind. Maybe because he was Rourk's best friend, she couldn't think of him that way. "He seems nice, and Rourk thinks he's great. That says a lot about him."

"I wonder what he thinks of me?" Anna reached for a handful of popcorn.

"That's a ridiculous question. The attraction was obviously mutual."

"Seriously? Are you just saying that? I didn't get that vibe from him."

"Then you're blind." Keegan flipped through the channels. After a few moments of staring blankly at a sitcom, she glanced over at Anna. "This is nice. I miss our girl time."

"Me too. Childhood friends are impossible to replace. Even the witches I meet here, they're cool, but it's just not the same. I miss Lauren, too."

Rourk and Tommy showed up bright and early. Keegan jumped out of bed as soon as the knock sounded—seeing Rourk was well worth getting up early. She threw her hair in a ponytail and hurried out to join her friends.

He met her with a big smile and a kiss. The smell of coffee filled the room. Anna had a huge spread of fruit on the table and was standing at the counter cracking eggs. It was hard to believe they were all growing up and living on their own.

"Do you need any help?" Rourk asked.

"Don't tell me you cook too? Keegan, why haven't you married this man yet?"

"Soon. Speaking of, Anna and I are going to have to go off on our own today in search of *the dress*."

Anna turned to Tommy and mouthed. *Help me!*

"I saw that." Keegan stuck her tongue out at Anna. "It won't be that bad. We'll set a cap of two hours. I don't want to be apart from Rourk any longer than needed."

"I guess I can live with two hours." Anna carried the plate of scrambled eggs to the table.

"Rourk, we gotta hit those trails while we have the chance," Tommy begged.

"You read my mind." Rourk reached over and scooped some fruit onto his plate.

"Hiking doesn't get much better. I feel at one with nature when I'm outside." Anna said wistfully. "Take a poncho. You can pretty much count on it raining as soon as you step foot in the woods."

Keegan was frustrated when she climbed into Anna's car. "Two hours and nothing!"

"I think you're being too picky. There were some very pretty dresses. You looked beautiful in them all."

Keegan sighed and threw her head back on the seat. "They were ok, but they weren't *the dress*. You know when you're little you always dream of finding the perfect dress. When you slip it on, you just know it's the one."

"Not all little girls dream of their wedding day. I'll probably get married in jeans."

"You wouldn't dare!" Keegan laughed, but cut it short as she reconsidered. "Never mind, I wouldn't be surprised."

"What are you and Rourk going to do for the rest of the day?"

"I know we're going to search for that waterfall at the apartment complex, and maybe do some furniture shopping. Do you mind keeping Tommy busy? I feel bad since you just met him."

"That's fine. I'll show him around, and we'll grab something to eat." She grinned over at Keegan. "I'd like to get to know more about him anyway."

Keegan texted Rourk and let him know they were on the way. He replied that they were going to meet them at Anna's.

When they pulled in, Rourk and Tommy were waiting at the door. Keegan's face lit up at the sight of him, and her heart rate accelerated.

"Any luck?" Rourk asked.

"Nope. Maybe next time." Keegan tried to keep the frustration out of her voice, but didn't think she succeeded.

"You'll find something." Rourk reached for her hand. "What do you want to do first?"

Keegan looked up at the sky it was a beautiful crisp morning and not a rain cloud in sight. "We should probably go in search of the waterfall first."

"I was hoping you would say that." Rourk turned towards Anna. "Do you mind dropping us off at the apartment? We could call a cab."

"Don't be ridiculous. Of course I don't mind. I wanted to show Tommy around that area anyway."

Rourk held open the back door for her. She slid in and scooted to the middle to be closer to him.

"I wonder how far away it is?" Keegan asked as she listened to the soothing sound of the falls.

"I don't think it's too far away." Rourk led her into the woods. He walked soundlessly, but Keegan's footsteps were loud and cumbersome.

Keegan glanced around and took in the beautiful wilderness that surrounded her. She loved the feeling of peace that washed over her when she was closest to nature. She heard animals scurry as they approached. The sun shone brightly through the forest. Keegan tilted her face up and felt the warmth on her skin. Even though the air was chilly, she pictured the warmth of the sun and it radiated throughout her body. She loved being an elf.

They were well off the beaten path. She trusted Rourk's instincts. The sound of rushing water grew near and excitement filled her chest. She squeezed Rourk's hand, smiling at him.

"I love how excited you get. You're like a little kid; it's cute."

Keegan giggled and looked around wistfully. "I can't explain it…"

"You don't have to—I feel the same way. I'm just better at masking my emotions than you are."

Keegan's thoughts drifted to their handfasting. "Are you nervous about getting married?"

Rourk stopped in his tracks and turned towards her. "Why would I be nervous?"

"I don't know, I thought it was common to get cold feet. At least that's what they always show on the movies. The guy freaking out about being tied down to the same person for the rest of his life."

Rourk chuckled. "Not one fiber of my being is nervous about marrying you. In my eyes, we are already married. This is a formality to tell the world and to honor our ancestors with the tradition. I've never wanted anything more than to be united with you, Keegan. You are my chosen, the only woman I will ever love."

Keegan stared up at his rugged face and into his intense grey eyes and knew he spoke the truth. She reached up and lightly traced his lips. Rourk pulled her close, pressing his body firmly to hers as their lips met. Keegan's body felt weak with desire. She couldn't wait until she could experience him fully.

Rourk pulled away and smiled down at her. "Soon," he whispered as he lightly brushed her hair off her shoulder.

She wondered if he had read her thoughts or if it was just that obvious. She felt the heat rising in her cheeks. She smiled recklessly and took off in a run, dodging the fallen trees and feeling the wind through her hair. She felt alive. Rourk laughed, a sharp burst of sound in the stillness of the forest, and gave chase behind her. She wasn't sure where she was going, but she ran till her legs ached. It was as if something was guiding her and she was along for the ride.

Her breathing labored, she finally came to an abrupt stop. "It's here." She pointed into a thick patch of trees and shrubs that were not meant to be walked through.

Rourk walked ahead of her and pushed through the thick undergrowth, holding branches back for her as he advanced. The sounds of the falls grew stronger. Finally, they broke through to a clearing. Keegan gasped—they were standing on the edge of a ledge, and below them was a wild, rushing water fall at least 50 feet tall. Mother Nature never ceased to amaze her. She was at a loss for words as she and Rourk stood, hands clasped, taking in the beauty.

"Can we get closer?" Keegan asked eagerly.

"We could, but I think we'll leave that for another day. We don't have the proper gear. Now we know where it is, so we can come back often."

"Our spot." Her eyes shone with excitement.

"Yes. Our spot," Rourk repeated as he draped his arm around her shoulder and pulled her closer.

They stood for a long time in silence, staring at the magnificent waterfall as the sun began to sink.

Rourk looked up as a drop of rain hit his cheek. "The rain comes so unexpectedly here. We need to head back."

Keegan closed her eyes and inhaled deeply, wanting to take the peace and tranquility back with her. Opening her eyes, she looked up at her chosen and nodded. Rourk quickened his step as the rain started to pelt down on them. He was upset with himself for not bringing rain gear. He worried about Keegan getting sick. Rourk glanced back at her and grinned. Even with her hair plastered to her head, she was still the most beautiful creature he had ever laid eyes on. He gave her hand a soft squeeze and continued forward. When he looked at her he didn't see the young girl that she was now, he saw the woman she would become: strong, loving, loyal, and full of adventure. He didn't know what he did to deserve to spend the rest of his life with her, but he was thankful.

It took them about an hour to make their way back to their villa. Rourk fumbled with the key, anxious to get Keegan inside so she could warm up. He pushed the door open and let her go first. "I'm sorry I wasn't prepared for the rain. I should have known better." Rourk shook his head in disgust.

"It was fun." Keegan peeled off her jacket and rubbed her hands together to generate warmth. "Thanks for catching me. If it weren't for you, I would have fallen at least twice."

"I doubt that. You underestimate yourself at times, Keegan. The way you found the falls was impressive. I think it would have taken me longer."

"You're just saying that." She kicked off her shoes. "It was pretty strange. As if the falls were calling to me."

"They probably were." Rourk glanced around the living room. He smiled ruefully. "This is not good. We have no dry clothes or towels. Maybe we should have gone shopping first."

"At least there's heat. I'm going to take a hot shower. I'm chilled to my bones."

"Throw your clothes out here, and I'll put them in front of the fire place."

Keegan got undressed and tossed her clothes outside the door. They didn't even have a shower curtain so she turned on the bath instead. She ran the water as hot as she could stand it and sunk into the tub, letting her head relax on the rim. *It should be illegal to be this content*, she thought, as the warmth radiated throughout her body. She eased herself lower in the tub until her head was completely submerged. *That feels much better.* Her scalp was no longer tingling from the cold. After soaking for about twenty minuets, the water was starting to cool so she pulled herself out of the sunken tub.

She looked around and realized it was not a well thought-out plan. She was dripping wet and not a towel in sight. She tiptoed to the door and cracked it open. "Rourk, we have no towels."

She watched as he ran his hand through his hair and looked around trying to figure out what to do. He pulled off his undershirt and handed it to her through the crack. "That's the best I have until our clothes dry or Anna gets here. Sorry."

"That's fine." Keegan grabbed the white shirt from his hands and closed the door quickly before she pulled him inside.

Keegan put the T-shirt to her face and inhaled his scent. She grinned to herself and thought, *It smells like rain.*

She used the shirt to blot the water off her body and stood there in the bathroom, starting to shiver. *Now what?*

She pulled his shirt over her head. It was wet, but it was the only option and at least it wasn't freezing like her other clothes. Slowly, she opened in the door and walked out to the living room.

Rourk looked up and inhaled deeply, unable to look away. For a long moment, his gaze held hers. He stayed rooted in his spot, and she advanced. By the look in his eyes, Keegan knew he was teetering on losing self-control. She was so tempted to take advantage of the situation. But she knew how important waiting till they said their vows was to him, so she broke the silence. "You go ahead and jump in the shower, and I'll call Anna." She busied herself moving the clothes around in front of the fire.

She heard his footsteps and then the door shutting. This was not a good predicament to be in. There had to be something she could do. Suddenly, she had an idea. She pulled on her wet jeans and jacket and ran over to the nearest neighbors.

The door was answered right away. An older woman with grey hair and sad brown eyes opened the door.

"I'm sorry to bother you. We just moved in next door and we got caught in the storm. We haven't bought any goods for the house yet so we don't even have towels. Is it possible I could borrow a towel?"

The woman checked Keegan over, as if to make sure she was a trustworthy person, then smiled. "Come in. Of course you can borrow a towel. I'll be right back." The woman hurried to the back of the villa and came out holding two fluffy pink towels.

Keegan reached for them and gave her a grateful smile. "Thank you so much. I promise I'll return them."

The woman waved her hand. "Don't worry about it dear. I have a closet full of towels and it's just me. You can keep them."

"Oh, well, again—thank you. We're only just now setting up the house, but once we move in next month, maybe you can come over for lunch?" Keegan said.

The woman smiled warmly, and it reached her eyes making her look beautiful. "That would be wonderful."

"I hate to take your towels and run…"

"Nonsense. You hurry along before you catch a cold."

"Thanks." Keegan waved and ran back to their place.

The water was still running when she walked in so she tapped lightly on the door. "I got you a towel. I'm going to throw it in ok?"

He must not have heard her because there was no reply. She opened the door just a crack and threw the towel in.

Standing in front of the fire place, Keegan shimmied out of her jeans and set them back down to dry off. She wrapped the towel around her and waited for Rourk to come out.

She laughed when he entered the room in the pink towel wrapped at his waist. She tried not to stare too long at his broad shoulders—she was fearful of caving in herself.

"Where did you get the towels?"

"Neighbor. She seems nice. I also called Anna. They should be here in a few moments. They were at her apartment so I told them to bring our backpacks."

Rourk breathed out a sigh of relief. Seeing Keegan almost naked nearly made him come undone. He appreciated the fact that she had defused a situation that could have easily gone a different way. "Thank you."

"I don't want you to have any regrets about our first time together."

"I'm glad you understand."

"I might not agree, but I understand."

"We really need to do some shopping."

"Yes, a kettle is first on our list. I would kill for a cup of tea or cocoa right now."

Rourk smiled gratefully at her. The change of subjects was most welcome.

"I wonder how long before Anna gets here?"

As if on queue, there was a knock at the door. Keegan ran to open it. Anna looked back and forth between them standing in their towels. "Are we interrupting something?"

"Be quiet and get in here." Keegan pulled her by the arm into the house. Tommy was right behind her with the two backpacks slung across his shoulders.

Rourk grabbed Keegan's "You go first."

"Nice towel." Tommy smirked.

Rourk looked at him indifferently as he pulled his dry clothes out of bag.

They spent the rest of the afternoon shopping for their place. When they were done, Anna had them all over for dinner. She made sweet and sour chicken and rice, and it was wonderful. After the boys left to go to their apartment, Anna turned on Keegan. "So? Did you do it?"

Keegan laughed. "Do it? How old are you?"

"I could feel the tension when we walked in. It's been killing me not knowing."

"No, we didn't have sex. I'm going to honor his wishes and wait till we're married."

Anna sighed. "That is pretty romantic."

"What about you and Tommy? Anything?"

Anna's shoulders slumped and she fell into the chair. "Nothing. I was hoping he would try something, but he was a perfect gentlemen. I don't think he's into me."

"Maybe you have to make the first move."

They stayed up, chatting like the old days, and Keegan was sad that they would be leaving the next day. There was so much to do before they moved to Washington.

Chapter 20

Keegan was really starting to stress out.
She had decided to take a few days off classes and go home to Tennessee with Athena in hopes of finding a dress. Rourk was going to meet her there for the weekend. The wedding was only two weeks away, and she hadn't found a gown she loved. She really didn't want to settle with an *ok* dress. It had to be perfect. She was probably driving her mom and the girls crazy, but she couldn't help it.

Her grandmother was sitting at the table with her in her mother's kitchen. "You know, Keegan, in my day we wore blue wedding dresses."

Keegan crinkled up her nose. "Blue?"

"Yes, it was an Irish tradition."

"Really? What did your dress look like?" Keegan was so curious about this. Maybe that's what was wrong in her search for a dress. She was so stuck on finding a white gown that she hadn't bothered to look at anything else. She knew Rourk loved tradition. Maybe she could surprise him with a blue wedding dress.

"Oh, it was beautiful. Long and flowing. I don't think I ever felt more beautiful than on my wedding day," her grandmother said wistfully. "I still have it stored away."

"You do?" Keegan's eyes were wide with surprise. "You have to let me see it."

"We can go see it now if you'd like."

Keegan jumped up and grabbed the keys to her grandmother's car. "What are you waiting for?"

Her grandmother chuckled. "You always were so impatient."

They walked through her grandmother's door and she automatically turned on the hot water for tea. Her mother did the same thing; it made Keegan smile. Keegan followed her down the narrow hall to her bedroom. "It's in the closet."

Keegan waited while her grandmother sorted through the hangers. "Here it is." She pulled out a long white garment bag.

"May I?" Keegan asked.

"Of course, dear. I'm sure it's out dated now. It's been so many years." Her grandmother looked off in the distance, lost in her memories.

Keegan slowly unzipped the bag. She felt like she had found a buried treasure. Energy coursed through her body. She gasped as she lightly took it out of the bag. "Oh, Nanny. It's gorgeous." Keegan held it up to her body and stared at herself in the mirror. "Can I try it on?"

Her grandmother looked her up and down, her eyes scrutinizing her granddaughter. "Sure, I was about your size when I got married. Although I had a little more in the chest department, and you have a little more in the booty department."

Keegan giggled. "Funny. I'll be right back. I can't wait to try this on."

The kettle whistled, and her grandmother hurried away.

Keegan's hands shook when she stepped into the gown. She loved that there was history to the dress. When she couldn't reach to finish zipping the dress, she poked her head from the bedroom and yelled, "Nanny, can you try to zip me up?"

A couple of minutes later, her grandmother walked in to the bathroom. She stopped in her tracks and covered her mouth. "Keegan, you look…magical." She walked behind her and zipped up the dress. "It's a bit lose in the top, but nothing I couldn't fix with thread and a little time."

Keegan looked at her reflection. The dress was a pale blue, the color of robins' eggs. *Ice blue* crossed her mind. The strapless top was flattering to her figure. It was all chiffon, which flowed out on the bottom in soft drapes. A ribbon with a white flower was wrapped twice around her waist.

"Oh Nanny, please let me wear this dress. Nothing else will ever live up to this dress. It's too perfect for words," she begged.

Her grandmother smiled sadly. "I had always hoped one of my daughters would ask to wear it. But you know how they are. They are all so strong-minded they wouldn't think of doing something that wasn't their idea. I would be honored if you would wear this dress at your wedding." She wiped a tear away.

Keegan wrapped her arms around her grandmother and gave her a squeeze. "Thank you. I knew there was a reason I wasn't having any luck finding a dress. There was one waiting for me all along."

Suddenly, the wedding felt real. She had *the dress*. In two weeks, she would be a married woman. She couldn't wait to start her married life with Rourk. When she came back out to the kitchen, her grandmother was gathering knitting supplies.

Keegan reached for the red yarn.

"Of course you would be drawn to the passion cord." Her grandmother chuckled.

"What are you doing?" Keegan pulled out a chair and sat down.

"Making the handfasting cord."

Keegan's eyes widened. "You are making them?"

"Of course who else is going to make it? Your mother? She couldn't knit to save her soul."

"I don't know. I guess I just thought they were bought or made in bulk."

"That's silly! Each one is made specifically for the couple. Once I complete my part, I'll pass it on to your brother, and he will have it charged with magic for good luck."

"What does the blue stand for?"

"Loyalty, honor, and patience. All very important in a marriage."

Elves loved tradition, and handfastings were one of the ways they kept the ancient traditions alive. "What about the broom and sword?"

"We will use a sword of your father's, of course. And the broom will be the one Rourk's parents used at their handfasting."

"Wow." She was deeply touched that they would be using the same broom that Rourk's parents had used. Of course, she also loved the idea of using her father's sword. It would be a beautiful ceremony, and she was genuinely getting anxious for it to arrive.

"What other traditions are there?"

"Oh goodness. Too many to mention. Most of them are small details you wouldn't even notice if not pointed out."

"Such as?" Keegan promoted her to continue.

"Lavender in your bouquet for devotion, the veil to ward off evil spirits, coin in the shoe for wealth, tilt your face to the sun after your vows to have beautiful children, bagpipes, braided hair, bells for gifts... I could go on and on."

Keegan placed her chin in her hands and sighed. "It's going to be a beautiful day, isn't it?"

"Of course. Why don't you get back to your mother's so I can finish up the cords? You can bring the car back tomorrow."

"I can take a hint." Keegan smiled at her grandmother. "Thank you. I can't wait to tell mom about the dress."

"Well, get out of here. I'll see you tomorrow." Her grandmother went back to her knitting, a smile playing across her face.

Keegan rushed into the house. "Mom!"

"Just a minute." Her mother yelled down the stairs. "I have Warrick in the bathtub."

She didn't feel like waiting so she took the stairs two at a time. "I found the dress!"

"Oh Keegan, that's wonderful I was starting to get concerned. Where is it?" Emerald was perched on the edge of the tub, pouring water over Warrick's head to rinse out the suds.

"It's at Nanny's. She needs to take in the top a little. Well, a lot."

"Where did you find it? I thought we hit all the local stores?"

"You'll never believe it. It's Nanny's wedding dress. It's perfect."

"Oh."

"Oh? That's all you have to say?" Keegan raised an eyebrow.

"I guess I'm just a little sad you didn't ask to try on my dress."

Keegan laughed. "Nanny said the same thing about you and your sisters."

"She did?"

"Yep, it hurt her feelings."

Emerald pulled Warrick out of the tub and toweled him off. He wasn't very happy about it. "I guess I never thought to ask her either. I was so focused on finding a new dress the thought never crossed my mind. I'm glad you asked her. I'm sure it made her happy, and I know you'll look stunning."

Keegan reached for her brother. "I was hoping I could wear your veil. Nanny told me it was to ward off evil sprits. I can't think of two stronger people than you and dad."

Her mother's eyes misted and she leaned forward, wrapping her arms around Keegan and Warrick. "I would be honored if you wore my veil. Let's have some tea and go over the plans. Did you decide what to do about your maid of honor?

"Actually, I did. I'm going to have both of them since Rourk is having Tommy and Thaddeus. I don't think they need to be labeled. They will be my two best friends standing by my side on one of the most important days of my life."

"That's sweet. Surely they have their dresses by now?"

"Yeah, Lauren picked them out in California. She sent me some pictures they are perfect." Keegan flipped through the photos on her phone, and then handed it to her mother.

"Oh, that is perfect for a fall wedding. Lauren always has the best taste."

Keegan took the phone back and looked down at the silk taffeta, dark brown dress that fell just above the knee. The ruffled crossover collar was what really made the dress. She looked at Lauren for a moment longer; she was positively glowing in the dress. Keegan was curious to meet her boyfriend—

Tristen, the dark fairy.

"I have everything taken care of as far as the food, music, and flowers. It's going to be a magical day." Her mother gave a sad smile as she set a cup of tea in front of Keegan. "It's hard to believe my little girl will be tying the knot soon. Seems like just yesterday you were running around in pigtails and getting into mischief."

"I don't think that has changed much—other than the pigtails." Keegan grinned.

"Oh, that's not true. You've grown up a lot. You will continue to blossom." Her mother reached out and put her small, warm hand on top of hers. "Rourk brings out the best in you."

"I definitely feel more centered since the bond has returned."

Thaddeus strolled into the room and sat down next to Keegan, then nonchalantly asked, "How's Anna?"

"Fine. Why?" Keegan looked at him curiously. She could never tell what her brother was thinking. She knew he worked with Anna to get his bond back so maybe he was just making small talk. But, she always had to wonder if he had seen a vision.

"Just wondering. I know you met up with her last weekend. Didn't Rourk bring Tommy?"

Keegan narrowed her eyes. "Yes, is there something I should know about Tommy? Anna was quite taken with him, and I don't want her to get hurt."

She watched his face intently to see if he would give anything away. His lip twitched as if he wanted to smile, but was fighting the urge.

"Nothing you should know. I haven't had any visions of Tommy causing any trouble for Anna."

Keegan crossed her arms and sat back in the chair. She knew her brother was keeping something from her, but she also knew it was useless to bug him. He never gave away anything he didn't want to.

"I'm just curious how she's doing learning the craft. She's a very powerful witch."

"Oh, well she's found a couple of witches to practice with. She has gotten stronger."

Thaddeus stood up and walked to the counter to grab an apple. "Mom, want me to take Warrick out with me?"

"Where are you going?" Emerald asked.

"Just out in the woods for a walk. I think it's time I start taking him. Quality time."

"That's fine, just be careful. Make sure you have your phone on you."

Thaddeus rolled his eyes at her and scooped up his brother from floor. "Come on, little guy." He hoisted him on his shoulders causing him to giggle.

"Have fun," Keegan yelled after them.

Keegan and her mother shared a smile.

Athena sat at the door and whimpered when the door shut behind them.

Chapter 21

Rourk showed up on Friday, and Keegan was ecstatic to see him. She longed for the day that they would be together every night. Although, she knew that would never be reality. Even after they were married, he would still have to leave for stretches of time because of his work. Once they were both in Washington, it would get easier. They pulled into her parent's driveway, and Keegan turned towards Rourk.

"Guess what?" She grinned from ear to ear and grabbed him by the arms.

"You found out you have a new power?" Rourk teased.

"Close. I got accepted to the art school in Seattle. I'm changing my major to photography. I'm still going to keep up with my science courses in case I change my mind and want to go back to Biology."

"Keegan, that's great news. I'm proud of you." Rourk leaned over the center console and wrapped his arms around her. "Have you told your parents?"

"Not yet. I keep putting it off. I guess I'll tell them this weekend." Truth be told, she was nervous to tell them. She had no idea how they would react.

"I'm sure they will be happy for you."

"We'll see…"

"Speaking of parents, my father has been giving me a hard time about not seeing us enough. Do you mind coming to his place tonight for dinner?"

"Of course not. I'm sorry I'm so greedy with my time with you. I didn't even think about your dad missing you. We should make something to bring over for desert. What's his favorite?" She loved the idea of cooking something for his father. She was sure he had to be lonely with the house all to himself.

Rourk thought about it for a moment. "I've never seen him turn away homemade chocolate chip cookies."

"Great, that will be easy to make." Keegan pushed open the door and jumped out of her mom's Land Rover. She shivered when the cool air hit her face. She was glad they had a weather manipulator on hand. They would be able to turn up the heat a notch for their outdoor wedding.

"What are you smiling at?" Rourk asked.

"Our wedding. I can't believe we will be married next weekend. It seems too good to be true." Keegan pushed open the front door and let the warmth of the house seep into her body. Athena ran up, wagging her little stub of a tail. Rourk reached down and picked up the puppy.

"Hot chocolate?" Her mother peeked out of the kitchen.

"Definitely. It got cold early this year." Keegan hung her jacket on the rack, and Rourk handed off the dog and did the same. She pulled off her winter cap, and her curls bounced out.

"I didn't notice you cut your hair with it all up in the hat." Rourk reached up and touched a curl. "It looks cute."

"I was inspired by Anna's latest transformation. I'm not quite as daring as her; just went a little shorter."

"You would look great bald."

Keegan laughed. "I wouldn't go that far."

"What are your plans for the day?" Emerald asked.

Keegan glanced over at Rourk. "Not sure. Tonight, we are going over to Rourk's house to have dinner with his father. Speaking of fathers, is dad home? I feel like I haven't seen him in forever."

"He's home. He took the boys out to give me some quiet time."

"Which we are interrupting," Keegan said apologetically.

"Nonsense. I barely get to see you anymore. Sit down, you two, and tell me what's going on in your lives. Rourk, how's work going?" She set a mug of cocoa in front of him, and then took a seat across from Keegan.

"It's a lot of fun. I can see why Richard stayed in so long. The human military is a great community." He picked up the mug to take a sip but when the steam hit his face, he decided to let it cool down. "I'm certainly looking forward to getting to Washington and being placed on a team."

"It's too bad you guys weren't going to be stationed closer." Emerald sighed.

"We'll be back here before you know it. Rourk doesn't plan on staying past his contract. Right?" Keegan raised an eyebrow. Of course, she would go anywhere with him, but she missed her home. A few years away wouldn't be too bad.

"As far as I know, I just serve my term and then come back here to the Army of The Light. Of course, that could change." Rourk lightly squeezed Keegan's leg under the table.

"Speaking of changes. I've decided to change my major to photography."

She might as well spit it out while it was just her mother, and Rourk was there to back her up.

"Really?" Her mother took a sip of her cocoa and set the mug down. "You've always wanted to be a marine biologist. Are you sure you want to make that big switch? You haven't really given it a try. I could tell how much you loved working at the sanctuary."

"I've been thinking about it for the last couple of months. Photography makes me happy. I can always go back to school later for biology." Keegan's shoulders slumped in anticipation of her mother's criticism over her choice.

"Well, I think it's a wonderful idea. You are clearly talented, and life is too short to be unhappy."

"Really?" Keegan's mouth hung open. "I thought you would tell me it was a ridiculous idea and be upset that I wasted money on school."

Emerald laughed. "Not at all. It's your life, you have the right to change your mind if you want to. When I was growing up I wanted to be so many different things. The only reason why I was surprised is because you never wavered on your path until now. Ever since you were old enough to talk, you told me how you wanted to work with dolphins."

"Well, now she can take photographs of dolphins." Rourk smiled over at Keegan.

"I guess you better start working on your scuba license." Emerald sat back in her seat with the mug between her hands.

Keegan had thought for sure her mother would disapprove of her choice. But once again, she had surprised her. She hoped someday she would be as understanding of a mother.

"Oh, that's a great idea. Rourk, we should do that once we get to Washington. I've always wanted to scuba."

Richard and the boys walked through the door. Warrick came running up to his mother and held his arms up.

"What's this I hear about scuba? Did you already get picked up for a scuba team Rourk?" Richard took off his coat and tossed it over the chair. Emerald gave him a disapproving look so he picked it up and put it on the coat rack.

Keegan's dad was a big, burly man with flame-colored hair and a bushy beard. He looked dangerous because of all his visible scars, but in reality, he was just a teddy bear to those he loved. Keegan gave him a big smile.

"No, Keegan was just saying we should take classes together."

"That's a great idea. I'm quite certain you will be picked up for a scuba team. They usually take the most physically fit. Never hurts to get a leg up."

"I'll find out soon what team I'm on."

Emerald moved to the stove and put on some more milk to make cocoa for the rest of them. Keegan loved being at home with her family.

Thaddeus sat down and filled them in on the day. They had been out teaching Warrick about tracking. He already knew the difference between a deer's print and a dog's—not too bad for a three-year-old. Richard grabbed a piece of paper and pencil off the counter and drew several different prints. He held it up to show Warrick. The baby walked over, staring at the paper silently for a moment.

"Deer." He pointed at the correct hoof.

"Dog." Warrick clapped.

"Bear?" Warrick asked.

Richard picked him up. "You got it. That's a bear. I think we have another warrior in the family, Emerald."

"I would hope so." She handed Warrick a marshmallow, and he struggled to get out of his father's arms. They all watched as he ran out of the room. It was amazing to see a young elf start to show signs of their powers.

"Emerald, did you tell them about their wedding gift yet?" Richard asked.

"No, I was waiting for you."

"We were trying to decide on a suitable gift, and your mother came up with a great idea. If you are interested, we'd like to give you the twenty acres around Keegan's spot. The place where you will be wed."

Keegan jumped up and ran around the table, throwing her arms around her father. "That's the best gift ever. Isn't it, Rourk?"

Rourk smiled. "Thank you. I agree, it's the perfect gift. We can build Keegan's dream house there."

Richard squeezed his daughter back. "Don't forget—I said it was your mother's idea."

Keegan reached over and hugged her mother. "I love you guys."

"Great. I thought we were rid of her." Thaddeus smirked.

"Oh hush, you will be out of the house by the time they move back. Take your brother into the play room." Emerald handed the youngest off to Thaddeus. Thaddeus mumbled under his breath but grabbed his brother and left. The little dog ran behind them.

Rourk opened the truck door for Keegan and the cold air hit her face. She pulled the plate of warm chocolate cookies closer to her body as they hurried up the walkway to Rourk's father's house.

Greg opened the door before they got there. "Come in. Get out of the cold."

Keegan handed him the plate of cookies. Greg peeked under the wrapping and grabbed a cookie. "Mmm, these are great. I have a soft spot for homemade cookies. Rourk's mother used to make them all the time."

"Rourk told me they were your favorite. Is that roast I smell? It smells delicious." Keegan shrugged off her coat and placed it on the coat hanger.

"Yes, it's pot roast. Rourk had to give me a crash course in cooking before he left for the military. Whoever invented the crock-pot was a genius." Rourk's father led them into the living room. Rourk and Keegan sat on the couch while Greg took the seat across from them.

"So, this time next week, you will be my daughter-in-law. I wish Rourk's mother had been here to see it." Silence filled the room.

"I would love to have known her. I'm sure she was an amazing woman." Keegan looked over at Rourk. "My grandmother told me we would use the broom from your wedding."

Greg stood up. "That's right. I almost forgot about that tradition. I'll be right back." He hurried out of the room.

"Does it bother you to talk about your mother?" Keegan asked quietly.

Rourk shook his head. "It makes me miss her more, but I don't think that is a bad thing. I wish my father would talk about her more. I was so young when she died."

Greg walked in the room carrying a large box and set it down on the coffee table. He gingerly opened the wooden box; the hinge creaked. It obviously hadn't been opened in a while. Rourk and Keegan leaned forward in their seats to get a closer look.

Keegan's hand flew to her mouth. "Oh, thank you for sharing this with us."

Greg smiled sadly. "I've never been able to talk myself into opening this until now." He pulled out her long, off-white dress and brought it to his nose. "There's still the slight scent of lilacs. Your mother's favorite scent. That was the best day of my life."

He handed the dress to Keegan and pulled out a photo album. Rourk walked over and stood behind his father to look at the photographs. His parents made a striking couple: his father with his chiseled good looks and his mother with her natural beauty.

Keegan stood beside Rourk. "Your mother was breathtaking."

"That she was," Greg said softly. He shut the book and handed it to Rourk. "You two can look through the rest of this stuff. I need to check on dinner. This is harder than I expected." Moisture glistened in his eyes as he stood and walked to the kitchen.

Keegan placed her hand on Rourk's shoulder, not sure what to say.

"Why don't you look at what else is in there?" Rourk's voice sounded strained.

"Ok." Keegan knelt in front of the box and pulled out the most beautiful broom she had ever seen. It was handmade from dark brown twigs and wrapped in white ribbon that had shamrocks embroidered on it. Ivy climbed up the handle. Keegan ran her hands over the broom, her palms tingling, and she wondered how many generations it had been passed down. She closed her eyes and pictured Rourk's parents on their day and with smiles on their face as they jumped the broom.

"This is amazing." Keegan handed the broom to Rourk and looked back in the box. A green velvet box lay on the bottom. Keegan reached down and pulled the box out; she was curious to see what was inside.

She snapped the box open. A pair of blue sapphire and diamond antique earrings sparkled back at her.

Greg walked in the room and noticed the box. He gingerly took it from Keegan's hand, stared silently at them for a moment, and then handed the box back to Keegan. "These are yours. They were my mother's, and her mother's before that. I'm not sure how many daughters these have been passed down to. Hopefully, someday you will give me a granddaughter, and you can pass them on to her."

Keegan jumped up and threw her arms around Greg. "I'll be honored to wear them. Thank you."

Greg smiled. "You're welcome. Let's eat before it gets cold."

Rourk draped his arm over Keegan's shoulder as they walked to the dining room. She laid her head against him.

"Do you need any help?" Rourk asked.

"Sure. You can grab the drinks." Greg set the plate of roast in the center of the table, and went back for the rolls.

Keegan's stomach growled as Greg walked back into the room. He laughed. "Dig in! We don't want you wasting away on us."

She piled her plate with roast, potatoes, and vegetables. Rourk set a glass of water in front of her and then passed her a roll and the butter.

"Thank you." She smiled sweetly as she buttered the roll and took a bite.

"Dad, thanks for bringing out your wedding box to share with us. I know that wasn't easy for you," Rourk said quietly after some time had passed.

"It's what she would have wanted. Let's talk about your wedding. Where are you going for your honeymoon?"

Keegan looked up sharply at Rourk. "He won't tell me. He says it's a surprise."

"Surprises are good. Did you have any trouble taking time off?" Greg asked.

"No, I was due for time off. With the holidays, it worked out well." Rourk could tell his father wanted to change the subject, so he went into details about his training and upcoming schedule. Keegan told him about switching schools and their new home.

After they ate, Rourk made coffee and they sat around the fireplace chatting. It was a nice evening, and Keegan was glad she got to know Rourk's father a little better. The rest of the weekend flew by and once again it was time to say goodbye.

They next time they would meet, it would be their wedding day.

Chapter 22

Keegan took a deep breath and tried to steady her nerves. Her heart was beating at such an accelerated pace she could feel it in her throat. She couldn't believe today was the day she had been waiting for since she was little girl.

The household had woken to the sound of pouring rain. In her pre-wedding panic attack, Keegan got hysterical over the weather, and her mother had to remind her that the weather manipulators in the family would take care of it.

"Besides," Emerald had said, brushing Keegan's hair behind her ears. She cupped her face in one hand. "Rain on your wedding day is good luck."

But the weather manipulators didn't need to do anything. Within an hour, the rain had let up and the sun was shining brightly.

Keegan really hoped she didn't trip or do something completely embarrassing. She was so nervous that she didn't know how she was going to make it to the ceremony spot. Thankfully, with elfin weddings she didn't have to walk there by herself. Rourk would be waiting downstairs for her and they would walk together. She loved that they stuck so close to their ancestors' traditions.

Her mother was expertly braiding white ribbon into a section of Keegan's auburn hair with her petite fingers. She glanced up in the mirror, catching her daughter's eye. "You look stunning."

Keegan flushed as there was a knock at the door.

"Is everyone decent?" Thaddeus called out.

"Yes," they said in unison.

Thaddeus walked through the door looking dashing in his military dress uniform. His hair had been slicked down so that it didn't stick up like usual, and his uniform was perfectly pressed. He looked like a young man instead of a boy, and it brought tears to Keegan's eyes.

"I can't believe you are making me dress up," Thaddeus complained. He had a small white box in his hands with a green bow tied around it.

"It's tradition." Emerald said simply.

Thaddeus walked across the room and offered Keegan the box. "Dad said I had to give this to you before you left. For luck."

Curious, Keegan reached for the box. She shook it—whatever was inside shifted with a thump. Tentatively, she unwrapped the bow and slowly lifted the lid. A huge grin spread across her full lips. She pulled out the horseshoe and stared at it. Her brother had obviously put a lot of time into it. It was painted green and had three shamrocks on each side with Keegan and Rourk written in calligraphy. "You did this?"

Thaddeus shrugged. "I came across it on one of my runs. I figured it was meant for you guys. Rourk could use all the luck he can get marrying you."

Keegan stood up, straightening her dress around her legs before she flung her arms around her brother. "I love it! Thank you so much. I can't wait to put it up in our house."

"Don't ever let it tip upside down or your luck will run out." Emerald's eyes twinkled. "You know you have to carry that with your bouquet."

"Really? Let me guess—tradition? Well, I will proudly carry it."

"Now, get out of here so Keegan can finish getting ready." Her mother shooed Thaddeus out the door.

Her mother pulled her hair into a loose bun, leaving a braid coiled on each side. She slipped some baby's breath in the back. Emerald grabbed the blush and swiped it across Keegan's cheekbones.

Keegan watched wide-eyed as her mother pulled the veil out of a box. It was beautiful—long and flowing with Celtic symbols embroidered on the bottom. She secured it on Keegan's bun and then pulled a layer over her face. "Perfect. Stand up so I can get some pictures. Remember don't remove the veil until the kiss."

Keegan set the horseshoe on her vanity table careful to make sure it didn't fall down. She stood up and stared at herself in the full-length mirror. She lightly touched Rourk's mother's earrings and hoped she was watching. Today, she would become Mrs. Kavanagh. She felt like a different person. She could feel the magic flowing through her veins. "Thank you, Mom."

"Give us a ten minute head start before you go downstairs to meet Rourk." Emerald cupped Keegan's cheeks and smiled, tears in her eyes. "I love you. You are simply radiant." Her mother hurried out of the room.

Keegan looked at the clock—ten minutes was going to feel like a lifetime. She sat on her chair and took deep, cleansing breaths. *You can do this.* Next thing she knew, she looked at the clock and exactly ten minutes had passed.

She stood up and slipped into her heels. She made it to the door before she realized her feet felt too constricted and kicked the shoes off. Barefoot felt right. Her hands shook as she reached for the doorknob. One last deep breath, and she pushed the door open.

Holding her dress at the sides so it wouldn't drag, she headed for the stairs, feeling like she was floating. She looked down the stairwell and met Rourk's eyes—the intensity of his stare was overpowering. She could feel his quiet confidence from where she stood, frozen to the spot. He looked so striking in his military uniform.

"You take my breath away. I've never seen a creature look more lovely," he said softly, holding out a hand for her.

Keegan slowly descended the stairs, clutching the flowers and the horseshoe. Each step brought her closer to her new life with her chosen. When she reached the final step, she grasped his hand and could have sworn sparks flew when their skin met.

"Are you ready?"

"Definitely." Keegan nodded her head and laced her arm through her chosen's.

She wondered if Rourk could hear her heart pounding. It seemed to vibrate in her ears.

They stepped outside and the warmth of the sun greeted them. Birds were chirping all around, and there wasn't a single cloud in the sky. It wasn't cold, but just right—she knew that was a gift from the weather manipulators. Celtic music could be heard in the distance. Keegan squeezed Rourk's arm, and he smiled down at her.

Once they reached the clearing, Keegan inhaled sharply. She felt like she was in a fairy-tale. How had they managed to pull this together in such a short amount of time? Magic, of course. She smiled to herself. Her special oasis had turned into a botanical garden. Brightly colored flowers and lush greens replaced the bare winter grounds. Rows of white chairs flanked the spot where they would be wed; each chair was hung with purple lilacs.

As they approached, the Wedding March flowed through the air and everyone turned in their seats. Rows and rows of elfin families smiled back at them. Her heart felt full with love.

Anna gave her a small wave, and Lauren grinned. Thaddeus and Tommy were standing to the left and the girls to the right. The priestess, Sarah, stood in the middle with the cords draped on her arm. She had married Keegan's parents and most of the elves there.

Keegan felt like everything was moving in slow motion. She could feel the magic flowing through the air and the joy radiating off everyone around them. It smelled like a beautiful spring day with flowers in bloom. The stream trickled soothingly. Keegan tried to take it all in, to save the memory.

Sarah smiled warmly when they reached her. She was a lovely woman with a tall, willowy body and clear, pale skin. Her face was long, her eyes clear green, and her hair was crisp white and in a braid down the side of her chest. She cleared her throat.

"Today, Rourk and Keegan will be joined in a handfasting. Their hands will be tied together with a knot that binds them in such a way that they choose to be bound. This ritual symbolizes their oneness not only with each other but with all creation and thus their union is blessed, it's sacredness recognized by all creation.

"The soul shares characteristics with all things divine. It is this belief which assigned virtues to the cardinal directions: East, South, West and North. It is in this tradition that a blessing is offered in support of this ceremony." She paused.

Keegan felt the crowd behind them hold their breath

Raising both hands to the air, Sarah went on. "Blessed be this union with the gifts of the East. Communication of the heart, mind, and body. Fresh beginnings with the rising of each sun. The knowledge of the growth found in the sharing of silences.

"Blessed be this union with the gifts of the South. Warmth of hearth and home. The heat of the heart's passion. The light created by both for the lightest, the darkest of times.

"Blessed be this union with the gifts of the West. The deep commitments of the lake. The swift excitement of the river. The refreshing cleansing of the rain. The all encompassing passion of the sea.

"Blessed be this union with the gifts of the North. Firm foundation on which to build. Fertility of the fields to enrich your lives. A stable home to which you may always return."

Sarah smiled on Keegan and Rourk as she lowered her arms. "Each of these blessings from the four cardinal directions emphasizes those things which will help you build a happy and successful union. Yet, they are only tools. Tools which you must use together to create what you seek in this union.

"Know that before you go further, since your spirits have crossed in this life, you have formed ties between each other. As you seek to enter into this state of matrimony, you should strive to make real the ideals which give meaning to both this ceremony and the institution of marriage.

"With full awareness, know that you are declaring your intent to be handfasted before your friends and family, present, absent, and departed. The promises made today, and the ties that are bound here, will greatly strengthen your union; they will cross the years and lives of each soul's growth."

Smiling, Sarah asked them, "Do you still seek to enter into this ceremony?"

Together, Rourk and Keegan spoke. "We do."

"Rourk and Keegan, I bid you look into each other's eyes." Sarah waited while they turned their eyes to one another, and then went on. "Will you honor and respect one another, and seek to never break that honor?"

Keegan smiled at Rourk as they answered, "We will."

Sarah draped the blue cord over their hands.

"And so the first binding is made," she said. "Will you share each other's pain and seek to ease it?"

"We will."

She wrapped the yellow cord around them. "And so the binding is made. Will you share the burdens of each so that your spirits may grow in this union?"

"We will."

Sarah draped the white cord and smiled. "And so the binding is made. Will you share each other's laughter, and look for the brightness in life and the positive in each other?"

"We will."

She draped the red cord around their hands. "And so the binding is made." She swiftly tied the cords into three knots. "Rourk and Keegan, as your hands are bound together now, so your lives and spirits are joined in a union of love and trust. The knots of this binding are not formed by these cords but, rather, by the vows you have made. For always, you hold in your own hands the fate of this union. Above you are the stars and below you is the earth. Like the stars, your love should be a constant source of light, and like the earth, a firm foundation from which to grow. Have patience with one another. For storms will come, but they will go quickly. Be free in the giving of affection and warmth.

Sarah produced the two wedding rings, holding out her palm where they sparkled in the sunlight. "A circle is the symbol of the sun and the earth and the universe. It is a symbol of holiness and of perfection and of peace. In these rings, it is the symbol of unity, in which your lives are now joined in one unbroken circle, in which, wherever you go, you will always return to your shared life together.

"As you have stated your desire to be united, one with the other, take now these rings and place them upon each other's finger, as pledge and testimony to your love and commitment to each other."

Rourk reached forward and his hand shook slightly as he placed the braided white-gold ring on Keegan's finger. A magical hum raced through her body.

Keegan smiled and placed a larger version of the ring on Rourk's finger.

"I now proclaim you are husband and wife, thus are your hands fasted, two are now made one." Sarah opened her hands and grinned. "You may seal your union to your chosen with a kiss."

Rourk gathered the veil in his hands and pushed it over Keegan's head so that it fell down her back. He leaned forward, lightly pressed his lips to hers, and then intensified the kiss. Keegan got lost in the kiss, forgetting her surroundings. When Rourk finally pulled away, loud cheers went up from the crowd.

"Settle down. It's not over yet." Sarah laughed. She looked back to Rourk and Keegan. "This will be your first act of working together as a couple.

"Brooms are used for cleaning and sweeping. Therefore, that they are used to symbolize the sweeping away the remnants of the past which no longer serve us is appropriate. The sword symbolizes the wielding of power and personal responsibility. As the bride and groom jump they are reminded that remaining vigilant over these aspects of the day to day shall help them to achieve the quality of life that they aspire to. Anna, Lauren, and Thaddeus—will you now lay down the Sword and Broom?"

Anna and Lauren walked forward and laid down the broom.

Thaddeus came forward and crossed the broom with the sword.

"Now putting the past behind you, and remembering that you have the power to create a strong future. Jump together into your new lives."

Keegan grabbed Rourk's hand and gave him a reckless smile. He shook his head, smiling in return. Together, they jumped and landed safely on the other side. Keegan laughed and Rourk pulled her in for another kiss. As they broke apart, Keegan looked up at her guests and was surprised to see two tigers in the distance. One was obviously Donald—she would have known his form anywhere. And by his side was the white tiger.

Relief filled Keegan, and she was content knowing Donald was going to be alright. As usual, her brother was right.

Bagpipes began to play. Rourk wrapped his arms around Keegan, swinging her around and around. As other guests stood to join in, Keegan felt on top of the world.

"Are you ready?" Rourk asked with a smile on his handsomely rugged face.

Keegan nodded and grasped his warm hand in hers. With the other, she reached for the teleporter's hand. Keegan closed her eyes as her stomach dropped.

A moment later, Rourk squeezed her hand. "Open your eyes."

Keegan did and found she was staring up at a huge castle. She dropped Rourk's hand, rushing forward to grip the stone wall that surrounded it. The lawns around it stretched emerald green, while the mountains cradled it on three sides. It was gray stone and several stories high with more turrets than she could count. From a flag pole near the long drive, an orange, white, and green flag waved.

Her eyes danced with excitement as she turned and clapped her hands, her eyes on her husband. "Ireland?"

"Of course. Where else would I take you?"

Rourk turned to the elf that had transported them. "Thanks, Pete."

The silent man nodded and disappeared.

Keegan took a deep breath. "So. This is it. Are you nervous?"

Rourk's eyes met hers and he smiled deviously. "I can't wait. Let's get inside."

Keegan looked at the ground. "We don't have any bags?"

"Already in the room." He took her hand, and they hurried up the massive stone steps.

As Rourk reached for the large black handle, Keegan ran her hand down the intricately carved designs in the wooden door.

"It's beautiful," she whispered.

Rourk agreed and pushed on the door.

It opened to a large lobby, warmly lit by huge, iron chandeliers. The stone floors were covered in elegant Persian rugs and littered with antique furniture. They walked to the counter against the right wall.

A plump woman with red hair piled loosely in a bun on top of her head broke into a warm smile. "Dia dui."

"Dia is Muire duit," Rourk replied. "Reservation is under Kavanagh."

She glanced down at her ledger. "Ah yes, the newlyweds. I won't keep you. Here's your keys, room 303." She winked at Keegan as she handed the keys to Rourk.

Keegan felt her face flush.

They took the stairs to their room, stealing glances at each other and laughing. Once they got to the third floor, Rourk stopped and abruptly turned towards Keegan. Her heart skipped a beat when she looked up into his grey eyes.

He gently traced the side of her face causing her whole body to tingle. "Keegan, I am honored to be your chosen. I will spend the rest of my life trying to be the best husband possible."

"I hope someday I am worthy of your love——." Her words were cut off as his lips met hers, and he scooped her up in his arms.

Keegan laughed as he carried her through the door and down the hall to their room. She barely noticed the beauty of the hotel—the wooden walls and the pretty carpeted floors, all illuminated by lights shaped like torches on the walls. Her eyes were strictly for Rourk.

He fumbled with the key and pushed the door to their room open, then slowly lowered her to the ground. She glanced around at the beautiful room, and her eyes stopped at the huge wooden bed waiting for them.

Rourk came up behind her. He pressed his lips to her neck as he unzipped her dress. It fell to the floor, and shivers ran down her spine. She had been waiting for this moment for a long time. Slowly, she turned to face him.

"You're incredible." His voice sounded rougher than usual.

Keegan's hands shook as she tried to unbutton his shirt. His body felt so warm under her touch. She ran her hands up his muscular chest and sighed, her heart pounding. All of her senses were heightened, and her skin was on fire.

Rourk gently led her to the bed.

Hours later, she rolled to her side and rested her head in her hand, staring at Rourk. "Wow," was all she could manage to say.

He was resting against his pillow, both of his hands behind his head. There was still the faint glistening of sweat on his beautiful chest. Rourk grinned. "Well worth the wait."

"You can say that again." Keegan scooted closer and laid her head on his chest. His heart beat steadily beneath her ear. "I'm so excited to spend the rest of my life with you."

Rourk's arms wrapped around her again, pulling her close beneath the covers. In the dim light of the room, Keegan closed her eyes and fell asleep to the sound of her husband's heartbeat.

Acknowledgments

I would like to thank Claire Teeter, Rosanne Catalano, and Heather Adkins, my editors. They have both helped me grow as a writer. My children for their understanding. My husband for his encouragement. My youngest sister, Katrina, for being my biggest fan. Stephanie Mooney for the wonderful cover.

About the Author

Julia Crane is the author of the Keegan's Chronicles series. She has a bachelor's degree in criminal justice. Julia has believed in magical creatures since the day her grandmother first told her an Irish tale. Growing up her mother greatly encouraged reading and using your imagination. Although she's spent most of her life on the US east coast, she currently lives in Dubai with her husband and three children.

Find Julia online at juliacraneauthor.com

CPSIA information can be obtained
at www.ICGtesting.com
Printed in the USA
FSHW020945181118
53878FS